Sufficient Sacrifice

ENDORSEMENTS

In a trilogy of novels, Annette Valentine takes her readers on a deeply researched journey of a couple growing up in the 20s on rural Kentucky farmland to transient adjustments amid multiple moves. As the Industrial Revolution moves into the very stationary southern culture of the 40s and 50s, Simon Hagen joins this adventure in a search to secure a comfortable living and opportunity for his children that was not afforded him. Annette's vivid recall of childhood events chronicled through life's journey is amazing as detail after detail is remembered. *Sufficient Sacrifice* is an artistic portrayal of family dynamics revealing the reality of how relationships evolve and blossom into God's sovereign will.

JOSEPH L. HADDEN, D.D.S
Retired country dentist

Sufficient Sacrifice is a sensitive and satisfying conclusion in a trilogy salted with tears and sometimes peppered with stubborn defiance. Throw in a bit of Annette Valentine's quirky and unexpected humor with freshly turned phrases and you have a perfect blend for an interesting journey into a complicated family. It can be read as a stand-alone book, but it entices the reader to want to know more about the rich and memorable characters that Annette weaves into her story of ambition and expectations which affect future generations. A compelling story of redemption and grace and the peace that follows when we release ourselves to the One True Father.

MICA BAYNE COPELAND
Pharmaceutical Sales Representative, Hoffman La-Roche
Pharmaceuticals, Retired Vocal Artist, Volunteer

Excellent!! An absolute treasure that recounts the warm and sometimes harsh realities of a family striving to maintain a high standard of living amidst currents of mediocrity. Western Kentucky and Middle Tennessee are the landscape of an only daughter, after three boys, coming of age during the late 50s whose feelings of inadequacy under her parents' expectations work to widen a breach of separation. Accusations and miscommunications undermine sincere acts of provision and feeble attempts to keep mistakes from past generations from being repeated. However, humble submission to a greater provider cannot help but quietly restore through gestures as simple as a cone of cream.

BECKY HADDEN WISE
Educator, Carver Middle School
Spartanburg, South Carolina

This is the third novel in the trilogy entitled My Father Series. Throughout the three books, we are taken on the journey of three people: Simon Hagan, the patriarch; Gracie Maxwell, wife of Simon; and Alexandria Hagan, daughter of Simon and Gracie. Annette draws from her exposure in real life and has written these three stories with passion and love of family. Their stories are true to life and compelling, packed with challenges that many of us experience.

BARRY BINGHAM
Monsanto, 32-year career Human Resources,
Senior Management, Retired
St. Louis, Missouri

Annette has captured with beautifully nuanced, descriptive writing, the moods and loves and losses and yearnings that resonate in the human heart. This story is a landscape of redemption--from a child's view all the way through mature adulthood.

VIRGINIA G. STEWART, Ph.D.
Biblical Counseling
Hope House Ministries

Ms. Valentine's latest novel has filled me with memories of growing up in the foothills of the southern mountain ranges. This is a story of strife and struggle, sprinkled with abundant hope, love, and faith. A saga of a family's journey, never easy but always striving for a better life for their loved ones. I have truly enjoyed the third novel of this exceptional trilogy.

ROBERT GILBERTSON
Bob's Liquor & Wine, Founder, 1970
Knoxville, Tennessee

Annette Valentine is a remarkable writer. This book, along with her two previous books, are great reads for young and old alike. The events of her stories flow in such a seamless manner. I love the variety and choice of words that she uses to describe events in her books. I grew up on a farm, and I found many childhood memories I thought were long forgotten were suddenly aroused by certain phrases, or in some cases, even a single word that the author uses in her chapters. Her writing displays a beautiful description of the past.

DR. GARY L. CROMWELL, Ph.D.
Professor Emeritus in the Department of Animal Sciences
University of Kentucky

Sufficient Sacrifice

A Novel

Annette Valentine

NEW YORK

LONDON • NASHVILLE • MELBOURNE • VANCOUVER

Sufficient Sacrifice

A Novel

Published in New York, New York, by Morgan James Publishing. Morgan James is a trademark of Morgan James, LLC. www.MorganJamesPublishing.com

ISBN 9781631954368 paperback
ISBN 9781631954375 eBook
Library of Congress Control Number: 2020950836

Cover and Interior Design by:
Chris Treccani
www.3dogcreative.net

Morgan James is a proud partner of Habitat for Humanity Peninsula and Greater Williamsburg. Partners in building since 2006.

Get involved today! Visit
MorganJamesPublishing.com/giving-back

—————— • ——————

My mother and my daughter are the hearty, robust bookend-slices of my life, as much like whole-wheat end pieces could be, because soft, white bread would have been far too inert for the task of deliciously sandwiching the gooey stuff of my personality. Without Georgia Morris and Jenifer Hofmann, I would have been a mere cake of cream cheese.

—————— • ——————

Acknowledgments

I began the *My Father* trilogy over two decades ago when writing was a creative path for me, only a sideline. It was a fantastic, joyful sideline, but envisioning a novel or two novels (let alone this third one) was far outside my wildest dreams. But then (and don't we love the "But thens" in our lives?) . . . Maxine Bivins offered her condo at the beach for a getaway, and in that secluded spot, my writing discovered its foundation. I am grateful to Maxine for her offering. Neither of us could have expected it would be immensely valuable in shaping my vision or that it might cause me to get serious about writing.

People are not always aware their words have a significant influence on others or that persuasion can dramatically shape outcomes. Affirmation often takes a person from unbelief to belief, and when I began to believe in my writing, the confidence to take the next steps was rooted in reactions, advice, and encouragement from persons who were willing to read my work. It's a fearsome moment when a fledgling writer turns over her manuscript to a critic.

I had the privilege of having several people read my initial efforts and forever establish themselves as those to whom I am indebted for giving me poetic wings. I distinctly remember the call from my oldest brother after he read my first draft. Because I was driving, I pulled into a parking lot, holding my breath. (He's my brother, I thought—this had better be good.) His words went deeper than a big-brother pat on the head. He melted my heart, anointing me with the oil of sincere encouragement and the effervescence of his awe. Thank you, Joe Hadden.

Taking a chance on my friends when baking them a cake is very different from asking them to read my writing, and numerous friends who've enjoyed my cooking were less interested in consuming a 300-page novel. Cake is much less risky, and I have no idea who ate my earliest baking attempt, but I definitely recall the friend who read my first book. Charlotte Wood will always hold the position that firsts in any unique situation hold. Your first bicycle, your first date—they are stuck in a memory warp. She was the first to take particular delight in reading, then wrapping me in a security blanket of warm, fuzzy validation I could not shake. Why would I want to? Thank you, Charlotte.

From the first to the most recent and all those in between, I am grateful and thankful for each one of you. The most recent, bringing full circle to my complete gratitude for her support and infusion of selflessness into my life is Carolyn Wells. Her wealth of knowledge and experience, her rich display of intent, her readiness to give whenever her time and talents are needed—for these qualities of genuineness, I am honored to have her as a friend, an editor, a mentor, a researcher-extraordinaire, and an amazing link to my family's roots in Todd County, Kentucky. I am a better person, writer, and believer because of you, Carolyn. So, thank you, Lord, for bringing Carolyn Wells into my life.

My daughter, Jenifer, has spent countless hours reading and providing feedback. Tears and laughter, challenges, criticisms, and completely over-the-moon admiration from Jenifer has caused me to know my precious child in ways I would have never experienced without the awesome exchanges we've shared over my writing. Thank you, Jenifer, for your courage, your character, and most of all your special place in my heart.

My husband, Walt, has never flagged in his support. It is a simple-sounding acknowledgment, but from the beginning days of my writing when I did not type, he did. With his two index fingers, he typed my illegible scribbles, and with his kind, manly-manly way, time and again, he lifted me out of the heap where I might have trashed hours of efforts. Thank you, Walt, for reading aloud my manuscript—from Tennessee to Oklahoma and back—and not once complaining. To be married to the best friend God could have created, I acknowledge I have been blessed with the best, the one who has loved my worst writing and triumphed when together we discovered all worthwhile journeys improve with time.

Characters

Simon Newton Hagan—Kentucky-born adventurer, protagonist, and father

Gracie Maxwell Hagan—heroine; Simon's undaunted wife; Alexandra's mother

Alexandra (Alex) Elizabeth Hagan—daughter of Simon and Gracie Maxwell Hagan

Jeff Lee, Maxwell, Hickman (Hux)—sons of Simon and Gracie Hagan

Geoffrey Newton Hagan (Papa Jeff)—Simon's father

Beulah Jones—Alexandra's "second mother"

Jeremy Foster—early playmate of Alexandra's; Pricilla, his bullying sister

Moe Lee—significant friend from Gracie's past

(Miss) Francine—Gracie's stepmother

Mrs. Nightingale—friend of Alexandra's; lived in the trailer park next door

Suzette Mullins—Alexandra's childhood friend (Mrs. Mullins: her mother)

Bert Dillingham—grocery store owner

Pastor Owen—the Hagans' pastor in Gallatin, Tennessee

Mr. William Ramsey—Tennessee Valley Authority (TVA) interviewer

Uncle Henry (and Aunt Rose, Richard, Sonny)—Gracie's brother, wife, and sons

(Baby) Madeleine Maxwell—Henry and Rose's only daughter

Bertha Clark—Gracie Hagan's helper

Alan Geoffrey Hagan—Simon's deceased brother

Laddie-dog—hairy, beloved family member

Ted (Turk) Torrens—Alex's consequential high school boyfriend

Kathryn (Kit) Gorham—Alex's special friend

Lannie Sutherland, Westley (Wes) Turner, Stephanie Dukes, Sara Stokes, Brian Fessler, Howard (Weird Howard) Murdock—high school influences

Kit's parents—Mr. Gorham; Jackie

Melody Elaine (Gorham)—Kit's younger sister

Dr. Farley—Kit's analyst

Doc Begbie and Mrs. B—boarding house associates from Simon's past

Maureen—the Begbie's caretaker

Charlie Mallory—pastor in Highland Park, Michigan; Virginia, his wife

Lieutenant Dugan—Detroit policeman from Simon Hagan's past

Frat-bro Ben Campbell; the stunning Deanna Cunningham—Maxwell's friends

Lois Swank—drug store employee, Alex's accomplice

Mr. Bundy—drug store owner

Steve Lovelace—lineman from Bundy's Drug Store

Jackson (Jack) Edward Ridley—Alex's mature relationship

Emily and Ralph Hendricks—Alex's Indiana neighbors

Emma and Rodney, Millicent and Jim—Gracie's sisters and their husbands

Kent and Ginger—children of Jack Ridley

Matthew Jones—Beulah's husband

Annie—Maxwell's wife

Melissa—Jeff Lee's wife

Laura—Hux's wife

Marcus—boyfriend of Gracie's mentioned in her diary

Edna Brown—new owner of home in Murray, Kentucky

Mrs. Margie Carnahan—Meyer's Furniture Store saleslady

The Fugates, old Mrs. Phillips—neighbors in Murray, Kentucky

The Buxtons, Mrs. Merkel—neighbors in Gallatin, Tennessee

Miss Freeman—Alex's high school English teacher

PART ONE

Chapter 1

ALEXANDRA

My daddy was a tall man and carried himself like a dignitary in a royal parade, a grand figure with classic features, high forehead, and wavy dark hair. How could he have known the parade he took me to see when I was a child would create a picture in my mind that would last a lifetime? There in my memory, I can relive the excitement of the uniformed figures as they marched past us, their loud instruments jabbing and jerking in unison, their plumed helmets bobbing the air with a magnificent flurry.

Daddy stood poised and erect. His outstretched hand shielded me from getting too close to the traffic or into the path of the synchronized mass that rolled flawlessly by like a fast-moving convoy of military tanks. I can still see him reaching down to pick me up, lifting me high above the crowd so I would not miss the spectacle of the drum major strutting down the center of the street with his chin strap almost covering his face and his huge baton darting left and right. Somehow I knew if Daddy could have jumped from the curb, taken and spun that baton, and mimicked the awesome stride of exaggerated steps, he would have.

It was in the opening minutes as the national anthem was played and a soft breeze rippled the American flag that he set me on the edge of the street and moved his hand to cover his heart. His chest swelled as music filled the air. Pride for country struck a chord, and I could feel it tugging at the countenances of everyone around us. Daddy blinked hard to hold back the tears.

I have loved that picture of my daddy, spellbound and humbled, for it is surely where he first distinguished himself as the model for my admiration. Those fledgling beginnings of respect, before I ever knew what respect was, awakened in moments like these. In them, I saw something even bigger than he, something more powerful guiding him.

He was a charmer, and in all the years I knew him an aura surrounded his manner, even went so far as to orchestrate the graceful way he moved his hands. He could captivate me with his humor and tickle me with unexpected smiles that hid behind a serious exterior and waited for the right time to light up his face. Sometimes, though, a sternness punctuated his voice. It boomed like a big bass drum and shook me down to my toes. Simon Newton Hagan's presence convinced me as a youngster of the authority he held. He was how I might imagine God, and wanting to please him was natural—the way I might think of pleasing God (if I had ever given that a thought, which I had not). They both felt like giants, indistinguishable and easily confused.

Overnight my daddy became Father, and that's when expectations were understood. Rising to his perfection was impossible; stopping myself from toppling off the pedestal he designed for me was also impossible, and an ugly instinct to keep him at bay inched in as I began to grow up.

Oddly enough, I've found myself weighing such behavior against the attitude of a young opossum whose path I once crossed. The little creature huddled itself beside the tire of my car, attempting to bluff me with baby-sized, impassioned spit-hissing, hoping to stave off my approach. With fortitude unshaken, it stayed put, but as admirable as the defensive effort was, it was no more adequate for a confrontation with me than my multiple ones were with my father. He was neither amused nor threatened. By the time I stood up to him, he had experienced dozens of life's hissing opossums and had learned to shift directions when he saw them coming.

As a realist, my father was intent on dodging unwanted outcomes, perhaps too close to the path as a young man to know where it would lead. Because he was a dreamer, he wouldn't give up. In that sense, he had faith—the kind that moved him forward.

Then he met my mother.

If I had to compare her to another person, I could not. She was like a rare bird that perched itself for a time on the windowsill of my existence, then flew away, leaving behind a space invisible and sacred. People were her passion, as if they were precious gems to behold or prisms to be turned in the light. She detected in them a beautiful color that had been missed by the rest of us, and her genuine interest in them made her probe and question and cross-examine until she uncovered their sparkle.

I have no doubt my mother, Gracie Maxwell Hagan, saw in her children limitless possibilities, the same way she tended to see them in most folks. Constantly, she interjected encouragement and provided inspiration for everyone near her to be all they could be, prodding us to try just a little bit harder, be just a little bit more, climb just a little bit higher, and hang on just a little bit longer.

Unspoken events (ones she neatly locked into the past and ones I would not know until later) had struck my mother in the years before she met my father, and the cornerstone of her youth was altered. The resulting foundation and its strength were cast differently than his, not quietly, and not subdued. That he ever attempted to tame her is applaudable.

In time, their children were born, the first being my three brothers whom Daddy loved. But with my arrival, his devotion intensified and assumed a personhood all its own. It sprouted arms that wanted to reach around me and hands that wanted to dig a secure hollow, for he longed to keep me safe. His devotion became the cradle that rocked me and later the basket that carried me. It guarded the path in front of me and checked the road ahead for ambush, as if I were a long-awaited gift.

The indelible mark my father left on me has taken nearly a lifetime to uncover, and as an adult, I find myself returning to the magnificent remnant within that bears Simon Hagan's imprint, examining its faint lines, hoping it has not slipped into obscurity.

I still recognize him there, residing beneath layers of untold stories, eager to surface as an enduring legacy for my soul and upon the threshold of my beginning, prepared to sacrifice.

Chapter 2

SIMON

A rare Friday afternoon away from my supervisory job at the Tappan Stove Company had me in high gear on this November day in 1945.

"I have an errand, Gracie. It may take forty-five minutes or an hour," I said, making my way through the kitchen, "but I'll be back in time to take Beulah home. Do you need anything while I'm out?"

"I'm fine. So, no, Simon. Just check on the baby before you leave," Gracie said, fidgeting with a dark curl that lopped over her right ear.

She had a way of looking up at me that bespoke an agenda hiding behind eyes bluer than the sky itself. "It's nice you have a few hours off," she said. "The older boys might like it if you threw the ball with them before dinner . . . ran off some of that energy. I don't know how much daylight there'll be when you get back."

"It's mighty chilly for that, hon. We'll see." I began to unroll my shirtsleeves. "Tomorrow morning might be better."

So far, running off their energy had not been possible. I was well-advised to plan on playing ball with my sons no matter what the weather. The ball was, after all, the revered symbol of boldness and manhood,

and recognizing that fact was important even for three-and-a-half-, six-
and eight-year-old boys, but Alexandra was in the next room, sleeping.
After months of refusing to imagine a daughter, predicting another boy,
getting used to the name Richard Newton Hagan, it was Alexandra who
had arrived in our lives.

I slipped into the bedroom Gracie and I shared with the baby,
walked to the corner where Alexandra was snuggled beneath her
blanket and picked her up. With every breath she took, I was aware
of her uniqueness, an unexpected bundle of joy, an assignment all her
own. She was nothing short of a miracle. I could see that.

I carried her to the window in my arms, allowing sunlight to spill
across her tiny features, and admired the perfection of her fingers. I
uncurled them across my palm, touching their soft pinkness and the
intricacies of the minuscule fingernails. Lost in thought, I stroked her
face with the back of my hand as though she were a delicate flower.
Holding her close, I knelt beside her crib and bowed my head.

It wasn't the responsibility that I found daunting but the opposite:
all too often everything seemed so uphill. Accountability came with
the territory. Having grown up the eldest of twelve, I was accustomed
to feeling the weight of it, especially for my brother's rebellion and his
unnecessary death. Alan's life and his fate were his own undoing, but
for me, regret lingered, and time wasn't going to undo the past. Nothing
good could have resulted from such events—a story that did not have a
happy ending. But I knew better than to contend with God. If it meant
taking another long look at the Almighty—fearfully, humbly—then
that's what I would do. I'd cover her with my life if need be. I'd do
whatever it took to ensure Alexandra was guarded and protected. Her
story would have a happy ending.

My own father's memory began to percolate with the rich aroma
of long overdue respect: the strong hand Geoffrey Hagan laid on my
shoulder when lessons were to be learned and the abundance he shaped
for his own children; the resolve it took to be a strong father. It was my
highest calling. I wanted to reach out as if my father's presence were

somehow here to steady me as I got up from my knees, ready to take the same positive steps that characterized his.

After a moment I laid Alexandra in her crib. With my target set, I was out the door, buttoned up in my overcoat. Barely clearing the door frame with the top of my hat, I got in my '41 Buick and backed down the driveway.

Several blocks from home and into the heart of town, I parked the car and jumped out. Even my stride was energetic. The crisp November air blanched my face before I could step inside the bank.

Friday afternoons were always busy at the Bank of Murray, but today more so than usual. I waited in line for my turn at the window, trying not to appear eager. When my turn came, I tipped my hat and approached the teller.

"I'll be opening an account today. A savings account, please, in the name of Miss Alexandra Elizabeth Hagan. She's four months old today."

It was hard for me to believe her innocent demands had filled so many days and interrupted every night's sleep. I'd thought about this pivotal moment during many of them, planning on this trip to this bank.

Two one-dollar bills practically leaped from my wallet. I laid them on the counter, unable to stand still or make myself be silent. "I think it's good to get her started off right. Don't you?"

My comment hung somewhere above the marble surface that stretched between me and the teller, and it took several minutes before she handed me a small book. In it was Alexandra's name and the two-dollar deposit written in blue ink. Stamped in red was the date: November 2, 1945.

"Yes, sir, that's for sure, Mr. Hagan. Good to get her started off right," the woman said as if she'd been pondering my question all the while. Peeling off her glasses, she looked me straight in the eye. "She'll thank you one day. You have a good morning now, ya hear?"

I tucked the book in my breast pocket and turned to leave. Outside, I paused to let the irony of my father's similar intent soak in. Yet another morsel from the past resurfaced in my mind, back to the day so many years before when Dad rummaged in his pocket for two silver dollars while he led us by horse-drawn carriage to the train station in Russellville, Kentucky. He had taken and placed the coins in the palm of my hand and had spoken a few solemn words: "There's this," he'd said, transferring a portion of what he possessed, "and some beef jerky, wrapped." The gesture felt hallowed at the time, as if it were evidence of his investment in a new beginning for me.

There was no denying my departure on that frigid afternoon in 1920 had been prompted by Mother's needless death. Her passing a few months earlier had made no sense—not when it happened and not in this moment. As far as I could tell, it never would. I'd taken off at eighteen-years-old and gone my own way and left rural Kentucky. If adversity hadn't matured me in my youth, embracing my ambitions in Detroit during the Roaring Twenties had. Tolerating the disquietude against a backdrop of those nine years spent in the city of nearly a million people was one challenge, but the diagnosis of tuberculosis had spelled death for me, and at twenty-seven I simply refused to die. Having stood at a crossroads, I'd chosen the narrow road and taken it to the Southwest in hopes of recuperating.

The thought of how far I'd come held a gentle reminder of Mother's voice telling me to go about my days "as unto the Lord." Even now I felt the ache of losing her.

I glanced in both directions, then stepped from the curb, inwardly acknowledging my ever-deepening desire to be the father mine had been to me. I opened the car door with a purposeful tug on the chrome handle, then positioned my body behind the steering wheel.

The blue sky oozed through puffed gray layers of non-threatening clouds, and a lingering sun shone through the windshield with more than enough brilliance to reflect on my resolve: Alexandra would have my all—my protection, my provision. I told myself the bankbook in my pocket was proof of my intention to provide for Alexandra, and those three sons of mine would have the same security Dad's farm in rural Kentucky afforded me before my calloused, youthful resistance caused me to relinquish it.

Despite the cool, I cranked the window down on my Buick and was whistling a tune as I steered past the Bank of Murray. I turned on Elm Street, then rolled to a stop near the end of the driveway on the far-right side of our home. The two oversized wooden garage doors were shut. Shutting them was my doing. Gracie would never have let me leave them hanging open, not even for the short length of time it took me to go to the bank. I got out of the car, walked over, and opened them. Experience had taught me the necessary distance for opening them in front of my automobile.

Similarly, experience had taught me to gauge sufficient space to allow Gracie on various matters. Before our paths ever crossed, pieces of my life had taken shape in distant cities while I lay stranded in a sanatorium on the outer limits of civilization, battling tuberculosis. I'd not planned to meet twenty-three-year-old Gracie Maxwell upon my return to the South, but I did. Neither had I planned to fall in love, but I did that also. As would be revealed, falling in love with Miss Maxwell was like falling for a rainbow. Up and over in a blaze of color that lit my horizon, she became the bright expectancy in my world, as promising as the proverbial pot of gold at the end of it. May 1935, we married in Elkton, Kentucky, and soon afterward, in pursuit of richer opportunities elsewhere, we left behind the town that had been our home.

By the time our third son Hickman was born, we had moved again, from one southern town to another, having landed in Murray, Kentucky. The house we bought seemed to satisfy the home-shaped emptiness that, up to now, could have only been accomplished with a replica of her childhood home she lovingly called Hillbound.

That was 1944, and although the world was at war, our lives moved in a modest progression toward normal living. Gracie had birthed the last of our children. Her agenda overflowed with decorating her new surroundings. Beyond those responsibilities, she had set out to chase something yet untapped, jumping hurdles like an Olympian runner.

An odd silence that afternoon had surrounded Gracie. I'd noticed it the minute I sat down with the evening paper. "Gracie, what is it?"

"Nothing," she said with an unmistakable heaviness.

"Honey?" I persisted from behind headlines.

"I'm pregnant, Simon."

Casually, I'd taken a peek at her over the bent-down top corner of page one. "Hmm, don't believe I heard you right. Who is it?"

"I'm quite serious." She squirmed to the edge of the divan's seat cushion. "I am pregnant, Simon," Gracie said, making the news glisten. "And it is confirmed."

The look she had given me was dreadfully amusing as if she might be angling for a morsel from a forbidden box of chocolates, but the tone in her voice was shaky. I folded the newspaper and laid it aside.

"And how long have you known?" I tried to sound golden, assured this was not her finest hour. I could almost see her shutting the lid on her patented ambitions to resume teaching next fall.

"Just since this morning . . . for certain . . . which is why I haven't said anything. I thought maybe something else was happening. Not another baby . . . I am almost thirty-eight, Simon!" She swallowed hard, forcing a smile. "But the doctor's office called at 9:00," she said, her lower lip trembling. "A perfect surprise."

It was one of those times when a cigarette would have been a welcome utility. If I'd been a drinking man, a stiff drink might've been desirable as well. But I was not. "It'll be okay, Gracie. We'll be just fine. We will." I moved over to the divan and scooted up next to her, took her hand in mine. "Four boys. Has a nice ring to it, honey."

Under the circumstances, my attempt at chipper got me nowhere. Gracie didn't laugh, and without looking at me she had pulled her hand away.

A look back on Gracie sitting on the divan next to me, picking at a hangnail that simply didn't exist, was befuddling now, how time had tailed off since the afternoon she made her announcement. Miraculously, the little surprise was now Alexandra, asleep in our bedroom. It isn't as if I've set out to top Mount Everest, I told myself as I drove the car inside the garage and got out, taking care not to hit my Buick's door on the foundational rock wall supporting the house. I'm just a meticulous sort, I supposed, as I latched the double doors of the garage and walked into the basement's musty warmth.

A single whiff, sometimes oddly reminiscent of the moss-covered embankment in front of my childhood home, had its subtle way of reminding me of the inevitable losses faced on the farm, possibly the endless canopy of a star-spattered sky over Todd County, Kentucky's rich farmland, or my huge family that had put me as its eldest son. And here in this house, built into the side of a rolling hillside, I was given every opportunity for immediate challenges: a wife, three sons, and a baby girl.

"Guess it's a good thing I finished dabbling in worthless nonsense a long time ago," I mused aloud. "And if I had been content with mediocrity, providing for them would've required a lot less energy."

I stoked the coals in the furnace before starting up the stairs.

Gracie's voice was coming from the kitchen above. Her chattering was as colorful as the Crayola drawing crayons that sprawled themselves on the kitchen table in front of three-and-a-half-year-old Hickman. "Let's see, honey . . ." she was saying to him, ". . . if you can't make the nice doggie brown instead of green. We don't want a green doggie. Do we? Here . . . Oh! Simon!" Her squeal was sheer delight, spelling relief at the sight of me.

"I'll take over where dinner's concerned, Gracie. Maybe I'll rustle up some fried potatoes and ham. How does that sound?"

"Why don't you take the other two outside before—"

"I know, hon," I interjected, noticing outside the kitchen window it was quickly dropping in the western sky. "I know . . . before the sun's gone."

The fedora I typically removed before I was two steps inside remained atop my head. "Come on, Jeff Lee. You, too, Maxwell. Get the ball . . . and your coats, and let's go, boys."

"Me go, Daddy?"

I stepped aside as the two older boys barreled past. "Not this time, son. Maybe another time," I said, mussing young Hickman's dark hair as eight- and six-year-old Jeff Lee and Maxwell made a dash for their coats hanging by the back door. "Y'all behave, now. Your mother's gonna have a bird's eye view out that window."

"You should say may I go, honey," Gracie said, her head cocked in Hickman's direction. "May I—"

"I wonder . . . baby Alexandra might like it if you were here when she wakes up. After all, Hickman, you're a very fine big brother," I said with a final hair-tousle, leaving him to be tutored through a grammar lesson by his mother, our ever-present English teacher.

Chapter 3

ALEXANDRA

Mommy wore a big-brimmed hat and white gloves that went past her elbows. She had jet black hair and blue eyes that danced. Her walk was fast, and she talked fast, too.

"Alexandra, baby." She called to me, and I took off running.

"I am not a baby. Not, not! Not," I said aloud on the way.

"Alexandra Elizabeth, have you brushed your little teeth? Let's see, baby." She examined the few ill-placed stalactites and stalagmites inside my mouth, prying it open with gloved fingers, then turned to my oldest brother in desperation. "Jeff Lee, come here and help your baby sister brush her teeth, and hurry along. I don't want to be late for church."

"I am not a baby! I'm five . . . whole . . . years, Mommy."

Jeff Lee strode into the bathroom like he was king of the hill, and from the rack where six toothbrushes hung, he picked out mine and pointed it at me. "You're the baby. Get over here."

"Am not."

"Are, too," he said, squeezing toothpaste from the tube.

It was important how we presented ourselves, and for the six of us, that meant we were routinely polished and packaged just so. We arrived at church on Sunday mornings like a collection of nice dolls. But it took some doing for all of us except my daddy. He never had to be told to straighten his tie or stand up straight. For him, being polished was usual, but that didn't mean Mommy couldn't find a way to give him instructions.

"Simon, why don't you get the car started?" she said, speaking up so he wouldn't miss hearing her from where she stood outside the bathroom. Even so, she clippy-clopped in her high heels across the short distance to their bedroom. "Don't you think we should be going? I do. I think we should be leaving."

It was understood: what Mommy said was more than a suggestion. Daddy was being directed to fetch the car. He was out of the bedroom before she could give another order, rounding the corner dressed in a dark brown suit and starched white shirt. He walked as if he'd heard her, and he rattled the keys in his pocket to let her know.

"Maxwell, Hickman, go with your dad. And Alexandra, honey, you've dribbled water on your pretty little dress Beulah ironed," Mommy said.

"He did it," I said, looking up at Jeff Lee, looking even higher up at Daddy.

"I did not," Jeff Lee said. "She wouldn't stand st—"

"That's enough, son," Daddy said and kept on moving.

The five of us looked small next to him—like short trees beside a tall one—in the hallway next to the bathroom. Even Mommy looked small.

Her face had a smile, and her eyes did, too, as they followed him while he walked to the kitchen. A lot of people looked at him the way she did. He was "sir" to most people. But to me, he was my daddy with a capital D.

"Just get a rag, Jeff Lee, and get it off. Please hurry," Mommy said, and she walked away.

With her out of sight, Jeff Lee quit jerking on my mouth and tossed the toothbrush into the sink. "You're done. Go get in the car," he said, still acting like he was king of the hill.

It took only a second to reach the car and climb in next to Daddy. I was used to being there, feeling him close to me—natural-like—as if I were a duck under its mother's wing, his arm bumping my shoulder when he shifted the gears.

No one spoke on the way to church about the two new chairs Mommy purchased yesterday, and we all seemed to know not to say anything about the pretty table between them. Daddy had said plenty when the moving men carried them through the front door and set them next to the living room window. Today he kept strangely quiet about them. It was Sunday, and I guessed that made the difference.

After he'd finished with the car's gears, Daddy slipped his arm around to the back of me and laid it across my shoulders. It wasn't long before the carload with my family arrived at church.

———— • ————

The next morning it was just the two of us, Daddy and me, going to get Beulah in a place on the outskirts of town. Mommy wasn't along to fill up the car's front seat with her purse and other stuff. Even so, I cuddled as close to Daddy as I could—the way I always did on trips with him along narrow streets where shabby little houses packed themselves together, side by side like the sardines in squatty cans he and I ate from on Sunday nights.

Short front porches had a wooden rocker or two, and rickety-looking posts held up their tin roofs. That's where Beulah lived, in Shanty Town.

Daddy slowed the car as we got near and stopped out in front of her house. With the motor still running, he leaned his head through the open window and called out, "Beulah ready this morning?" His voice was bouncy, loud enough for the skinny man on the porch to hear.

Without looking up, the man pushed his knife across a stick he held fast in his hand. He paid no attention to us. Back and forth he went, whittling on the stick, rocking in his rocker.

A mangy old dog wandered across the porch to bark and hung back long enough to see if his tired growl would scare us. When it didn't, he moseyed back to his post, slumped down, and rested his head on a paw.

"Beulah . . . you ready?" The man looked down at the stick. "Mista Hagan's here," he said, calling out in the direction of the screen door that stood ajar.

Nothing happened.

He raised his head and turned it toward the door, "Wo-man?" he shouted, then nodded at Daddy. "Purdy day. Ain' it?"

Creases twitched in the corners of Daddy's eyes. "Yes, Matthew, we do have us a mighty nice day today," he said with a held-back smile.

A second passed.

Beulah appeared at the door in a bit of a tizzy and stopped to check the front of her dress, then jammed the last two buttons through buttonholes near her neck. She pushed open the screen door—chin in the air—and rushed over to our car, hopped into the backseat behind Daddy, and closed the door. Huffing and holding tightly with one hand to the handles of her floppy bag, she smiled, adjusting it on her bony knees. "Mornin,' Mista Hagan."

Beulah turned to me. "Hidy-do, Miss Zan'dra.

I was up on my knees in the seat of the car, turned around, watching her. "Your dress is pretty," I told her, and that's when she and I gave each other our special friends' look.

Daddy tipped his hat to Matthew, then spoke to Beulah as we pulled away from the curb.

"It's pretty, Beulah," I said again. "I like it because—"

"Best sit down, Sweet Pea, so you won't fall," Daddy said and made the car speed up, passing house after drab house until he braked to keep us from jostling as we bumped across the train tracks. Then we were on our way again. "It's a beautiful day, isn't it, Beulah?" He eyed the rearview mirror to catch her response.

"Aw, yessir. Shore-nuff . . . 'tis at that," she said. Her gaze seemed to be stuck somewhere outside the window, on the fluffy green trees or the tall telephone poles.

"Sweet Pea, you're gonna take good care of Beulah today. Aren't you?" Daddy winked at Beulah in the mirror.

Without budging my bottom off the car seat, I turned enough to see if she thought what he'd said was funny. She did. I heard her chuckling. But Beulah laughed at anything—throwing her head back, smiling really big with her gold tooth sticking way out in front of her lips. And when her chewing gum would nearly fall out of her mouth, her tongue would go after it. She'd keep on laughing anyway. It wasn't so odd for her mouth to be open; it was open most of the time, laughing her laugh, or talking her talk, or chewing her gum. Black, black eyelids would close over eyes that bulged like a stepped-on frog's, hiding for the moment the bloodshot, yellowed whites that circled big brown centers.

"Beulah," Daddy said as we passed the big hospital where I was born, and he started turning the car onto our street, "there's new furniture in the living room. It's going back to the store. Guess you should just work around it."

I didn't look back at her, and she didn't chuckle.

Daddy parked the car outside, next to the rock wall. He'd left one of the big garage doors standing open a little bit—enough to let us get inside. He didn't need to swing it wide, but he gave it a push anyway to keep us from getting bumped going past. Its bottom scraped on the concrete drive like always.

Mommy was waiting with a troubled look for Daddy when we got to the top of the stairs. "We're running a little bit late. Come here, honey," she said to me, ready to hurry off to her job at Murray State College the minute Beulah arrived. "Give Mommy a kiss. I need to get your father to his work." She turned to Beulah, putting in a smile between quick instructions about how to handle things around the house—and me.

So here we were: another Monday had rolled around where Beulah showed up and took over the house, getting lunches fixed long before the boys were herded off to school so Mommy wouldn't have to.

Mommy didn't seem to mind if I went back outside to catch bees in a Mason jar. "Fine, fine," she said on her way. "I'll be involved at the Wesley Foundation till 3:00."

I could say Wesley Foundation before I knew how to ask for milk. It was a very important name around our house, and getting to go there made Mommy hum. Beulah could handle me all by herself.

As long as I was cleaned up before Daddy came home from work, everybody smiled,. But Daddy coming home was a long time off.

I left through the back door and let it slam shut behind me. Beulah was looking at me out of the open kitchen window by the time I got to the edge of my yard. Wires and tin cans were stretched way up above me.

It was Maxwell who knew how to get the cans strung between ours and the Fosters' house. All the big boys could talk to each other through the wires Maxwell hooked to the cans. He acted like he knew a lot because of being eleven, but it was Jeff Lee that had taught me the tricks of bee-catching, being thirteen and all. Hickman didn't know nearly as much about yard play since he was only nine.

I was unscrewing the lid off the jar Beulah had given me when I saw Jeremy Foster coming across the driveway.

"Wanna watch me catch bees?" I hollered to him, and without waiting for an answer, I ran to the spot where bushes grew in a row between our yards. Bumblebees swarmed around them, darting and diving at the little white flowers. Jeremy couldn't see over the top. Neither could I, making me go 'round. Laddie-dog was close behind, wagging his tail, sniffing the ground.

Jeremy followed.

"You can't catch 'em, Jeremy. Maybe when you get to be five. Stand over there and just watch," I said, using the lid to snap one bee after another into the jar until there was an angry buzz coming from it. "They'll bite you. Get on back, now."

I snapped the jar lid shut before the bees could escape, but a big yellow one came after me from where I didn't know. I screamed and swatted. The Mason jar fell on the concrete driveway and broke into pieces.

Laddie-dog, and Jeremy, and I scattered as Beulah ran out of the house and came after me, waving her arms till she caught up and grabbed me by the hand. "Inside! Right now, Alexandra. Ain't gonna be no more bee-catchin' ta'day." Her long legs were fast, taking us across the yard. Mine were barely letting me keep up. "You is lucky you didn't get bit up! Move it, now," she said, and I moved it, all the way past the kitchen to a chair in the dining room before Beulah let go of my hand. "We'll sit a spell," she said over a deep breath, "a'fore I hav'ta go pick up them jar pieces." Her eyes were still wide and wet. "You done scared ol' Beulah half ta death."

Chapter 4

GRACIE

Running late, I raced up the basement stairs and through the kitchen, glanced at the clock above the window, wanting desperately to move back its hands by an hour. The heat of the day had me moist—that and having stayed at the Westley Foundation way longer than expected. Alexandra and Beulah were nowhere in sight.

In a matter of seconds, I was past the dining room, having kicked off my high heels along the way. I stopped abruptly in the hallway leading to two bedrooms and the bath. Plunked within the longest wall was the telephone cubby. I groped with sticky hands inside the recess for the telephone book. Having flipped through the M's to the number for Meyer's Furniture Store, I picked up the receiver.

A pair of Gainsborough chairs sat like staring eyeballs in the living room a short distance away. Between them was an elegant piecrust table. From where I stood, now tethered by the telephone wire to the cubby outside the bathroom, two Pembroke tables were hidden from my view. In Simon's opinion all had overstayed their welcome, but for the moment, all five new pieces of furniture were present.

I took a deep breath and began dialing.

If my purchasing them had not ruffled Simon's feathers, then certainly my lingering today at Murray State College would if it meant I failed to inform Mrs. Carnahan prior to the end of the business day that the furniture must be returned. My endeavors to launch a campus ministry for emphasizing study, prayer, and self-discipline among students was one thing, but buying furniture without Simon's consent was another.

I twirled the telephone cord as I waited.

"Meyer's Furniture . . . and how may I help you?" The gentleman's voice was startling.

"This is Mrs. Simon Hagan," I said, settling myself. "Gracie Hagan. May I speak with Mrs. Carnahan. She had—"

"Mommy!" Alexandra bounded through the hallway, headed for the bathroom.

"—Uhm, furniture delivered to my home on Saturday," I said to the man on the other end of the line, spinning around at the same time to shush my five-year-old daughter.

Alexandra's knees were muddied. Beulah was on her trail. I motioned the two of them on through, and Beulah shut the bathroom door behind them.

"—Thank you. I will hold on," I said over the roar of running bathwater.

A moment passed, followed by a melodic voice coming through the receiver: "Mrs. Margie Carnahan here."

"Yes. Yes, hello, Mrs. Carnahan. Lovely, lovely day, isn't it?" I quickly swallowed a sizable lump. "Yes, well, I have decided to return the chairs and tables. My husband is not quite ready to commit to purchase. But I do appreciate your help—"

"Oh, my dear! Dear Mrs. Hagan," the saleslady began. "Of course. Of course, and certainly, you may return the Gainsborough chairs . . . and the cherry table. The Pembroke tables as well. But may I tell you something?"

I switched the receiver to the other ear in time to hear: "These are a wonderful investment you will never regret." I sensed the warm smile sliding across her words. "Those pieces are ones you'll want to hand down to your children, and they to theirs. They will never go out of style, Mrs. Hagan. Their beauty is something to cherish . . . now and always will be."

My conversation with Mrs. Carnahan pushed on somewhere between reality and wishful thinking and ended on a high note. I felt myself float into the living room.

After strolling over to the window, I sat on one of the soft upholstered chairs next to it, resisting resentment. Inside my head, thoughts were churning.

Outside, the view dotted itself with attractive, well-kept homes. Those across the length of Elm Street sat on flat planes with shortened front yards. Others, including mine, sat atop a banked hillside. Every property had pruned shrubbery and recently mowed grass. Nothing about the neighborhood dubbed the Silk Stocking Street by enlightened circles resembled the tobacco fields and stables for Thoroughbreds of my youthful years. I surveyed the space around me, knowing my Kentucky home, Hillbound, would never leave the core of my heart.

Needing neither to replicate Hillbound nor desiring to coddle the resplendent memories of its finery, I wanted only the richness of its bygone beauty and the essence of the mold that had shaped me like a pot of clay into Gracie Mae Maxwell, imperfections and all.

I wriggled my back against the Gainsborough chair, sitting straighter, taller than before, and I closed my eyes. In a few quiet moments of reflection, the mental image of my brother Henry crept in as nagging evidence: his plight to keep our homestead was mine as well. Even with Father and the indefinable Francine gone, their influence had taken its toll.

Henry's return from war in the Pacific proved that looming aftermath had the power to hunt my brother down and crush him, but my life had taken a productive turn despite the excuse named Francine Delany whom Father had chosen to replace my mother. Henry, however, might always struggle with the lies she'd embedded at Hillbound. The fact that such a vicious woman could continue to show her face anywhere around Todd County was testament enough to the resiliency of evil.

Interrupted, I gasped as Alexandra emerged freshly scrubbed from the bathroom, dripping wet and naked. I quickly shook off the daze that had overtaken me and bit my lip with an effort to smile in defiance. It was not the new chairs, and not the new tables, and not some uppity binge that had immersed me in extravagance. It was letting the freedom within me draw on fresh resources of grace. Rising above unfortunate past occurrences was, and always would be, the next right step.

"Honey," I said, chasing after Alexandra, wrapping her in the towel Beulah handed me, "your pretty curls need a little more drying. And careful of the chairs, please."

Finished, I responded to Beulah's pleasant nod with a half-smile. "Let's have her wear the yellow pinafore dress. The new one from Sears 'n Roebuck," I said as Beulah led Alexandra away.

I smiled at Alexandra. "Daddy's going to be home soon. That one's his favorite!"

The reminder was a good one for both of us. Simon was a reasonable sort most of the time, and whether or not he understood, he would simply have to accept the full import of my need to be surrounded by beauty.

With little remaining in the way of heirlooms and not many of my mother's things to delight in, I admiringly ran my hand across the rectangular tabletop's radiant mahogany surface, savoring—

"Gracie?" Simon called out, and the back door shut with a menacing snap.

I jerked my hand away from the new Pembroke table as if I'd touched the hot burner on the stove, and he strode into the living room with a side glance at the errant furniture ensemble that was still in place.

"Hello, hon." He placed a perky kiss on my cheek. "The boys are on the neighbor's lawn. Scrimmaging, if the Fugates don't mind," he said, as Alexandra bounded from her bedroom, freshly dressed.

"Well! Well, and did my girls have a good day today . . . hum?" He lifted Alexandra high into the air and let her down with a playful twat on her leg, to which she let out a stream of giggles.

Beulah followed her, folding the bath towel. "Gots the chess pie fo ya, Mista Hagan," she said, and her announcement rolled out on a mirthful laugh. "Yore favorite."

Thank Heaven for small favors, I thought.

"Now that is good news, Beulah," Simon said. "You do make the best. Mind taking little Miss Alexandra out to the porch for a few minutes? Then I'll run you home. Hope you don't mind. Do you?"

"Aw naw, sir," Beulah said.

With her and Alexandra making a beeline for the next room, Simon and I exchanged cagey looks.

"Gracie?" he said, his head swiveled to a peculiar angle. "You did call about the furniture going back. Am I right?"

He loosened his tie, and with every reason to avoid his big brown eyes, I looked away.

"Remember, Simon, when we had a new baby on the way? . . . " having turned my back to the porch, I nodded in Alexandra's direction . . . "I knew then, you'd want my pursuits at Murray State to end. So I ended them." Facing him, bolder now, I whispered: "Well, she's five now, and the war's been over for five years. Times are different. Good, different. I need to get back to contributing. We live in a college town. I could be using my education—"

"The furniture, Gracie," Simon said and pulled a pack of cigarettes from his coat pocket. "Then we can talk about the college thing." His elegant hands moved as though they were conducting an invisible orchestra. "Is the furniture being picked up yet today, or tomorrow?"

Silence.

"Gracie?"

"Neither." Having spoken, I stood very still, waiting, convinced it had not crossed Simon's mind that when I wanted to be extremely independent, stubborn, and willful, I would be. "Just so happens, I've been thinking of filling out a job application at the college," I said. "My involvement in the Missionary Society's about as close as I'm ever again going to be to Sudan and the wonderful experience I had to teach the Sudanese children. Don't you see it? My teaching students here at Murray State would do two things: reward that deep part of me, yes, but also a job would pay for—"

"Ah! I thought I was beginning to see past the winding direction," Simon interjected. "Gracie, hon! Be reasonable. Where would you acquire these guarantees on such short notice?" He lit a cigarette, inhaled deeply, and let the smoke ease between tight lips. "I want you to have whatever makes you happy, but I don't want you to work. I want you to be here with the children. I think you can understand that."

"No, Simon, I cannot. I've prepared my whole life for this, and now I'm in a position to make a difference. There are ways to make it happen. Beulah's available to be here as much as I need her. She can take care of the house, and we can use the extra income. Teaching is where I belong. My energies with the students on the campus are purely volunteer, honey. Perhaps they've been leading up to a rewarding job. I believe I've made my decision."

"Gracie, listen to me. Let's give this more consideration. I know your heart's been set on launching this Wesley Foundation thing. But now you're adding a much bigger ambition."

Without taking his eyes off me, Simon removed his jacket and seemed to be mulling over what more to say. Except for the seriousness that covered his face, he looked outright spunky—his jacket hung from one shoulder with his index finger provided a hook for it.

"It's a grand vision—both," he began. "And I completely understand that. It's not as if I'm altogether blameless. It simply means selling my share of the tire business to Raymond was a gamble on my part. And certainly, investing in fluorspar to the tune of $7000 represents taking a big chance. Hopefully, it wasn't a foolish one. I believed it was the right decision . . . provided security for the future. Besides, owning the Goodyear tire stores was more up Raymond's alley than mine, anyway. Not that a supervisory position at Tappan has fulfilled any vision of mine, but it did bring us here. And that's a plus. Look at it though, hon: I'm arranging for rides home from work so you can have the car, and you're off furniture shopping. We're going to the poor house if we aren't careful."

Casually, I walked toward the porch, intent on shutting the door that should already have been shut. "I want to be able to buy a few things without repercussions and certainly not this complete objection to new furniture," I said, looking at him in earnest.

Alexandra beat me to the threshold. Golden-brown curls set off her brilliant yellow pinafore. Pure inquisitiveness spread on her upturned face. "Where is the poor house, Mommy?"

Simon took my sidelong glance in stride, batting slow eyelids over his soft brown eyes.

"Honey . . . " I squatted beside her and began retying Alexandra's sash. "Daddy's just talking silly. We're staying right here, and I'm going to get piano lessons for you one day . . . when you turn six or seven. Run along now. Maybe Beulah will fix you a little lemonade before she has to leave," I said. With a quick thought, I raised my eyebrows and patted her head. "Miss America plays the piano . . . so you must brush your teeth, and they'll be pretty like hers. She is quite tall. Someday you might be as tall as she."

Unable to force even a flicker of a smile as she and Beulah traipsed off to the kitchen, I stood up. "Now see, Simon . . . little ears hear everything."

He swallowed, chin jutting, and his Adam's apple bobbed beneath the loosened knot of his tie and crisp, white-collared shirt. "Don't go thinking we're going to compete with Fosters' luxuries and not with any of the other neighbors for that matter," he said in a steady tone, but do as you please, Gracie." He turned and was hightailing it through the dining room before I had a chance to speak. "You're going to do it anyway," he said.

I was still in earshot, well aware that once again I had frustrated the security he tried to provide, but inside the fall and winter months that ended the year, 1951, and the several that began the new one, I did it anyway.

Even so, it was not my teaching at Murray State that had Simon a little on edge. It was the $7000 fluorspar investment in Kentucky's mineral industry.

Chapter 5

SIMON

All by itself, the balmy day in early March was not quite the answer I needed. The interview with Mr. William Ramsey at 2:00 this afternoon could be.

Entering the first-floor lobby at the Tennessee Valley Authority job services building in downtown Muscle Shoals, Alabama, I was eager to introduce myself to the young lady at the reception desk. My application for a top-level management position at TVA preceded me.

I straightened my tie and flicked a speck off my coat lapel. The sensation in my stomach was a persistent reminder I was nervous. Nevertheless, the job as personnel manager for the soon-to-be constructed fossil plant at Gallatin, Tennessee was on my horizon. Lord willing, I'd make a favorable impression or know the reason why not.

Nothing but confidence registered on my face. "Simon Hagan's the name," I said. "I received a call from Mr. Ramsey's secretary to schedule this appointment." With one step back, I stood straight and smiled.

"Yes, sir. And he is expecting you. Please, take a seat, Mr. Hagan. I'll let him know you're here."

Only moments passed before the young lady led me into a modest office, windowed and well-lit. The man behind the desk was about fifty-five. I judged him not more than four years older than I—bald, round, and with a dimpled chin. I felt like a beanstalk by comparison and a folksy one at that.

His handshake was firm, his manner pleasant. "Be seated. Make yourself comfortable. Quite a solid background you have, Mr. Hagan. On paper, anyway."

"Well, sir, I've been plenty happy with the job at Tappan for close to twelve years. It's certainly provided a livelihood for a family of six. Before that, a younger brother and I shared ownership in two Goodyear tire stores. I've held good jobs, nothing to complain about . . . just hardly characterizes my energy and enterprise." I glanced at the fish swimming in the bowl on the credenza behind Mr. Ramsey. It was a quick distraction. "After nine years of the tire business, I had the opportunity to sell out to my brother and move on. But vulcanized rubber for automobile tires throughout the Depression years was a gainful commodity, so the business was good to me. Tappan's been satisfactory, but as my application says, I'm looking for something else. I believe personnel management's the answer."

Mr. Ramsey tapped his pack of cigarettes, encouraging a couple of Camels to slip from the opening, then held it for me to take one.

"Sure, thanks. You know," I said, leaning into the flame of his lighter, "I've been swimming in circles—a lot like your fish over there." Smoke eased from my nostrils and between my lips. "Being the personnel manager at the Gallatin Fossil Plant would have me . . . well . . . swimming upstream if you will. Yessir, an exceptional opportunity beats a safer alternative any day, even if it's a difficult course of action. This one has me excited."

Mr. Ramsey lit a cigarette of his own, pushed back in his chair as smoke curled in the air above his head. Without warning, his chair squeaked forward. A bland expression stayed in place on his face as he propped his elbows on the desk and balled his fists together. The cigarette remained fixed between two fingers. For a long minute, I was sure I'd overspoken.

"As you know, TVA's serving the nation as one of its fastest-growing electricity suppliers. We've experienced an outright demand for public electric power since 1933's . . . means we're providing triple-digit job opportunities, no question about it." The cigarette bobbed between Mr. Ramsey's lips as he spoke. "So you're right about TVA having an exceptional opportunity, Hagan, for someone with managerial skills. I've studied your background—backward and forward—done some investigating on my own and pretty much had my mind made up. I just needed to meet you in person." He stood, squashed his cigarette in the ashtray. "Congratulations!" His outstretched grasped mine above the desktop.

Both knees felt wobbly, but I was on my feet, uncertain how I'd gotten there.

"The Gallatin plant is set to break ground on May eleventh. We need upstream swimmers out there," he said with a chuckle. "I like your way of thinking, Mr. Hagan. Employees for those jobs will require interviews numbering in the hundreds . . . all of them during the next seven weeks. It's a job for a person of your caliber and credentials, and I am quite confident you're the man for it."

Following a slap on my back, he handed me a manilla folder. "Pay is spelled out, but essentially, it's the amount outlined in our employment bulletin," he said with an amiable head nod.

I could feel heat rush from the bottom of my spine to the back of my neck as our hands clasped again. "I'm prepared to give it my all," I said. "Much obliged, sir. I'll need two weeks to turn in my resignation at Tappan."

"And I'd certainly be disappointed if you didn't. Plan on starting March 23rd. 7:30 a. m. Now, sit back down if you would, Mr. Hagan, and we'll cover some items you'll need to know. Sign some papers."

I grinned, unintentionally having noticed the fish in the bowl was disturbing the water's surface and decided, in addition to air, they expected attention for services rendered. With the interview finished, Mr. Ramsey stood, and I did the same.

"I will be there on the 23rd," he said. "You'll need to drive east of Gallatin on Main Street, Highway 25 toward Castalian Springs. Turn south on North Street. Take the gravel angle back west at the Y and keep on it until you see a low, flat-roofed building." He paused, laughed: "My gosh, Hagan, I hope you'll be able to stand up in it. How tall are you anyway.?"

"Six foot four when I need to be. Six foot three most days."

"Lord only knows what you may need, Mr. Hagan," he said on a cheery note. "Now, one more thing on finding the place: if you get as far as the Cumberland River, you've gone too far. Glad to have you aboard. Further details are in the folder you have there, along with my telephone number in the event you've got questions."

With yet another handshake, I was on my way, elated. Next to the fishbowl on the credenza and the American flag beside it was an optimistic-looking photograph of the recently inaugurated President of the United States. Dwight Eisenhower had a smile. That made two of us.

Except for the growing gray cloud over the source of security I held for my family—one that stemmed from my $7000 investment in Kentucky's fluorspar-producing mines—I might have floated in a clear blue sky. But from all evidence, the Commonwealth's output of fluorspar was now at the lowest point since 1938. With it about to fly southward on the winds of chance, my investment had me on alert. Foreseeing an inevitable move to Gallatin, I could only pray this new job would provide all I'd need to make ends meet.

On the return trip home, I began guessing how Gracie would receive my news, and on the long stretch of roadway between Alabama and Kentucky, I couldn't help musing how I'd have to commute close to three hours from Murray every Sunday afternoon. I thought about living in a boarding house in Gallatin, staying the week to work, and returning late on Friday nights for the next five months. Recalling my boarding-house landlady and the crusty old Scotsman from my youthful years in Detroit brought a smile. Mrs. B and Doc Begbie hadn't seen the last of me, I told myself.

A few more miles up the road and I was back to thinking about Gracie's prized teaching career and how it was about to end—how our home on the hill in Murray would be rented to strangers.

————— • —————

"Why, Simon? Why?" she said, testing me after hearing the news. She looked earnestly through the living room window to the shaggy mimosa on the front lawn. "There are new opportunities right here in Murray all the time. Why can't we just wait for something to open up?"

"This is an opportunity at its finest. It has opened up, Gracie. This is not a cockamamie scheme. Neither is it reckless. Why can't you see that? Better days are coming. This is what I can do today; never mind what I can do tomorrow. And if it doesn't work out as well as expected, we can always move back. We can rent this place. It'll still be here if we decide to come back."

Anticipating we would one day return, Gracie reluctantly closed the cover on her fairytale. Magically, all the puzzle pieces would have to fit, but until they did, another family moved in to rent the house that she had come to love. It was the summer of 1953.

"Where will Beulah live in Tennessee," Alexandra asked, not knowing Beulah would not be moving with the rest of the family.

"She has folks of her own, honey. Beulah can't come with us," Gracie explained to our daughter. "Ask your father."

Alexandra seemed stunned. Beulah belonged in the middle of Alexandra's eight-year-old world, and I was the culprit, moving her far away, leaving a hole as big as if I'd uprooted a perfectly healthy rose bush in full bloom.

"Why, Daddy? Why?"

"Sweet Pea," I said, "things don't always stay like we think we want them to stay. Usually, though, there's a reason. Maybe we won't see it till later. There's a bright future for us in Tennessee." I rummaged my brain for answers. "We're mighty fortunate. God's planned lots of good for us, and you're going to like it there, baby. I promise. This story has a happy ending."

Like a crystal ball with a mysterious aura, my new job awaited in Tennessee, but for Alexandra, Beulah was her world, and no amount of reasoning was adequate to console her for the loss. Her three brothers would come with us, and Laddie-dog would come with us, but Beulah could not. Alexandra's pleading to substitute a brother, any brother, making it possible for Beulah to come along was trampled.

"Things are a'changin," Beulah said and stared out the kitchen window as she spoke, slowly wiping a towel across the counter on the August moving day.

The radio in the living room was tuned in; Eddie Fisher was singing as if he understood I needed a soothing ointment. Somewhat reassured by the words, I listened.

"I want you to know . . . That if things go wrong . . . And fate is unkind . . .

Look over your shoulder, I'm walking behind."

I would've preferred to think of the words as God's, filtering through the mesh on the radio box, but they were Mr. Fisher's. I had no choice but to make-do.

Chapter 6

ALEXANDRA

Nothing unusual existed about today. Daddy was sitting at the kitchen table in his place like he did most Saturday mornings, reading the newspaper, smoking a Camel, and rarely looking up. The limp edge of the *Gallatin Gazette* headline page had usefully flopped down just far enough for him to peer over it and let Mommy and me know he was distracted by the conversation going on between us.

Mommy was in a hurry, making last-minute preparations to leave for the day, running in and out of the room with increasing momentum. She stopped abruptly in front of the pile of dishes on the drainboard and looked in my direction.

"Oh, goodness! I haven't finished the tuna salad." She darted over to where I was standing. "Move over, honey. I need to get there—" She gave me a hip shove. "—so I can get this done."

With bare hands she plunged into the mixture of chopped pickles and boiled eggs, shooing me with her elbow to a spot she wanted me to occupy at the other end of the short counter.

"Why don't you take the trash out, Alexandra? Run along now. Hurry up, and do that for me, please. My new friend Mrs. Buxton's going to be here soon. You could watch for her and tell me when she pulls in the drive. Wouldn't that be fun? That would be fun."

She turned her attention to Daddy. "Simon, see to it the two of you are fed. And no 'Mrs. Nightingale' til I get back."

Daddy's position shifted from one side of his chair to the other. He rattled his newspaper, ensuring it would send a subtle message all its own, then took a sip of coffee, flicked his cigarette, and went back to reading.

Not thinking she really wanted or even expected answers, I moved out of Mommy's way and picked up the trashcan. Daddy uncrossed his legs without flinching a muscle and allowed me to get past him with my bulky armload. The tightly coiled spring slammed the kitchen door shut behind me.

I headed across the back yard with the insert from the trashcan and disappeared behind the garage long enough to empty it into a beat-up container, then put the lid back on and came around the far side of the garage.

The morning was a clear one, sunny and free for the taking, the way Saturdays often felt in the summertime. Most days I had no real plans, but this morning was different. Lots had changed in the last few weeks. It was unclear when the newness of our move to Tennessee was going to feel right, but for sure, it wasn't ever going to be the way it had been when we lived in Kentucky.

I had outgrown my sandbox long ago, but choosing on rare occasions to play in it or not, or asking Jeremy Foster to play hopscotch or not, had been my decisions. Jeremy, along with the babyish things I'd outgrown, had stayed in Murray. Without him, hopscotch was not fun, and jumping rope was not fun. No bumblebees flew in and out of honeysuckle bushes—there weren't any.

Except for Laddie-dog, and my parents, and my three older brothers, everybody I had known still lived in Kentucky. Nothing was the same as before. Beulah was not going to be around to cook our dinner or make the beds, and if what Daddy said was true, Mommy was going to be doing both.

Just thinking about life without Beulah made me stumble on a dirt clod. I regained my balance and continued walking along next to the garage.

My new neighborhood seemed like a photo album stuffed full of unknown people—seen, but not felt. Boys sped past on bicycles, and older girls roller-skated past on the sidewalk, looking my way as if I didn't exist, pretending they didn't know I was alive.

There was no getting around the truth our move had dumped us here, and I was stuck in a boring yard with a few scraggly trees. Except for wandering over to the trailer park on the other side of our driveway, there wasn't much for an eight-year-old girl to do.

My brothers weren't around this morning. Lately, they had been getting away with everything—taking off, going wherever they wanted, doing what they wanted—in full command of their days. One by one, they had ridden out of the garage on bikes, touting unmistakable smirks of one-upmanship on their faces and broadcasting loud rat-tat-tats of noise from the Rook playing cards they had fastened with clothespins to the spokes of their tires.

It crossed my mind to run and tell Mommy since we weren't supposed to even have playing cards, ever. But before I'd gone too far with the notion, it had occurred to me the likelihood of their revenge was not worth pushing my luck. Besides, Beulah had always told me never to tattle.

She had been more mommy than maid on days like this, taking care of me and the mountain of things that came up when no one else was around. But she wasn't here and never would be, and the first few days without her felt like getting to the bottom of a bowl of ice cream. Suddenly, the goodness was gone with nothing left but cold emptiness.

Everyone else was old enough to decide for themselves what they wanted to do, but I was neither old enough nor big enough for most things.

But no one had exactly said I couldn't go by myself to Dillingham's Grocery Store, and I wasn't about to risk asking permission. There was no point in mentioning it, so I'd kept the plan in my head, letting it churn there for days. Until today.

This morning was as bright-shining as the sun, and my idea beamed in happy rays right out through my head and across my August Saturday.

I knew every step of the way to Dillingham's Grocery Store. Mommy would be gone for hours, shopping in Nashville with Mrs. Buxton. Today was the perfect day to go.

———— • ————

I had almost gotten past the garage and was still hugging the trashcan when the sound of Mrs. Nightingale's voice drifted across the short yard that separated us. It was easy to hear her plain-talking to Mr. Nightingale, curtly telling him to go inside and put on a shirt since there was now a young lady living next door. I knew she was talking about me, and when Mrs. Nightingale noticed me standing there, she didn't say another word. I watched her half-naked husband vanish inside their trailer. She was close behind him.

There was no telling how long I would have to wait by myself for my mother's friend to show up in her car, so I plopped down on one of the few grassy mounds available and began the dutiful watch for Mrs. Buxton to come down the street. Laddie-dog meandered over to sniff the ground next to me. I sat there, considering the fact I had never seen my daddy without a shirt, wanting to believe Gallatin, Tennessee was going to be a fine place to live because that's what Daddy had promised. I was mulling over all that when Mrs. Nightingale's cheerful yell cut in.

"Yoo-hoo, yoo-hoo?" she called to me before stepping down to the last step that led from her trailer to the platform below.

In the couple of weeks since we had lived near her—and ever since the very first time I had seen her—Mrs. Nightingale had been friendly from a distance, as if she were one of my best-loved dolls that sat patiently on the shelf, waiting for me to take notice.

She yelled again, her smile bursting into giggles, her frisky arms waving wildly. I scrambled to my feet and ran in her direction, and Mrs. Nightingale stretched out her hands. "Come! Come here and let me see you this fine morning!"

I ran directly into the center of the pink-flowered apron she was wearing. Her wanting to be friends felt perfect. Big hugging arms dropped around me, the same way Beulah's always had.

"Going to the swimming pool today, are we?"

Neither Mrs. Nightingale nor Beulah asked questions the way as other grownups did, and it made answering them almost impossible. She and Beulah were a lot alike, although Beulah was black and skinny and tall.

But when Beulah squatted down and looked straight into my eyes, suddenly we were best friends of the very same size.

Oftentimes grownups made themselves my size no matter how big they were. But Mrs. Nightingale was really big, like a circus elephant. She wasn't able to squat, and making her eyes level with mine was not possible. She would never have been able to squat down. Even if she had, I don't think she could have gotten up.

"No ma'am," I said, knowing this was not an invitation for me to go swimming with her and that she was merely asking if I had plans for today, hoping to spend at least part of it with me so she wouldn't have to spend hers with Mr. Nightingale. "Not today. My daddy's looking after me because my mommy and Mrs. Buxton are going shopping. That's a lady from church. She's supposed to be here any minute to get Mommy."

"Oh, I see. All right then," she said, assuring me the explanation was a good one. "I know what we could do instead! What would you think if I taught you how to make potholders?"

The subject of swimming was dismissed. She had understood my disappointment. Given an opportunity of this type, Mrs. Nightingale might've squatted to sympathize, but she must have thought of the next best thing instead because she went into giggles over it.

"We'll have lemonade," she exclaimed, "and make potholders! What do you say?"

"Alexandra! Alexandra! Come here!" My mother's unwanted call hurled itself through the open window of our kitchen and cut short Mrs. Nightingale's rising excitement over the possibility of our making potholders.

"Hurry up, honey. I'm leaving soon. And bring in that trashcan before Mrs. Buxton arrives."

"I have to go, Mrs. Nightingale," I said. "Maybe I can come back later if Daddy will let me."

"Run on now," she said, "so your momma won't be put out with us."

Without giving much more than a nod, she gathered her wide skirt above her knees and pushed herself up the difficult step back onto the platform beside her trailer. Our conversation ended, and I headed home, running toward the back door that led to our kitchen.

———— • ————

Our house, too small for the six of us, was not that much different from the others that lined the street like rows of sugar cookies in a bakery window. Trees and brush grew at the back of the small plots, defining where I could and could not play. Way off in the far corner was the one-car garage sitting by itself. My daddy's car was parked there. Laddie-dog romped about, enjoying his freedom, and I ran swiftly to pick up the trashcan I'd dropped by the wayside.

I reached the kitchen door with the smell of tuna fish filtering out through the screen just as Mrs. Buxton's car came crunching down the gravel drive. Laddie-dog barked indifferently, the way I would have if I had been a dog.

Mommy stepped aside as I bounded through the door. A hint of unspoken thought crossed her face. I pictured a question mark from my old second-grade reader stamped down the middle of it.

"Mrs. Buxton just got here, Mommy! She's out there!"

I blurted the news in hopes it would satisfy her. She smiled but didn't say anything.

"Mrs. Nightingale is nice. Isn't she, Mommy?"

"Yes, honey. I suppose she's very nice." Her answer was flat, and her smile faded, "But I don't think you should be going over there. Not so much, anyway."

She turned to Daddy and continued: "Simon, Alexandra shouldn't go over to that trailer park again today. Are you listening? She's been there enough lately."

Having said that, she wound up her flurry of activities, delivered her last tidbit of instruction, and was eager to scoot.

"But Mommy, Mrs. Nightingale said she wants to—"

The toot-toot of Mrs. Buxton's car horn rudely broke off any further discussion of Mrs. Nightingale and the trailer park.

"Mrs. Buxton is waiting," Mommy said. "Go tell her I'll be right there, honey."

I had no chance to get to Mrs. Buxton before Mommy made her move. She jerked her purse from the countertop and was out the door, throwing a lazy wave to my daddy and me. I stood motionless in the corner, holding onto the trashcan. Daddy eyed the action with his newspaper in hand and refolded its pages. His half-smile said he was not getting involved.

I stayed put until Mommy was out of sight before restarting my day. Lunchtime was a long way off. It would be easy to go to Dillingham's and be back in plenty of time. Daddy wouldn't be making our tuna fish sandwiches until noon, and leaving him by himself while I spent my allowance on something I wanted was not asking for trouble. I went to my bedroom and rustled through a drawer until I came upon the dime I had buried under a pink undershirt.

———— • ————

The attic fan in the hallway moved in slow, boring circles, attempting to soothe the sticky summer day. It clicked an already familiar sound above me as I came out of my bedroom with the money in my pocket and traipsed back through the hallway to the kitchen.

It was close quarters with little more than enough space for a stove, refrigerator, and a few cabinets. Daddy's chair was angled beneath the end of the table, and his legs were crammed against the end of it. Both sides were folded down to make it smaller, but still, there wasn't much room to get past him. I needed to squeeze between the table and the Frigidaire to get to the back door. Daddy smiled to acknowledge my presence, crushed his cigarette in the ashtray, and went back to reading.

The window over the sink hung open, its glass panes swinging outward in a single wooden frame. Through it I could see the rounded silver tops of the trailers brightly gleaming in the morning sun. Some were parked across from our driveway. Mrs. Nightingale lived in the one closest to us. I knew she was expecting me to return and make potholders, and even though Daddy was not used to taking care of me all day or making decisions about such things, I didn't think he would have a reason to keep me from going over after lunch. Never mind what my mother had said.

I approached the small gap next to Daddy. His head was hidden behind the wide spread of the newspaper.

"Where're you going, Sweet Pea?"

I tried to come up with a better answer than *outside*, but when I opened my mouth, that's all that came out.

"Outside," I repeated a second time, a little louder.

Having him uncover my plan to go to the store without him might not be a good idea. That's where he might draw the line, put his paper down, and say, "You'd better stick around until your mother gets home," or "I'll need to go with you, Sweet Pea." I didn't want to hear either. He was probably never going to say, "You're Daddy's big girl now, and you can go to Dillingham's all by yourself," so I hoped he wouldn't ask me any more questions.

I wiggled my nose to avoid the drifting fumes from his smoky ashes and waited for a response, all the while studying the worn pattern of the linoleum floor, but nothing was said. He shuffled his feet restlessly underneath the table.

Holding my breath, I slipped past him and went outside. The screen door closed with a quick snap. Again I waited, but still no response.

I reached inside the pocket of my dress and fished for the dime. Feeling it safely between some rough threads, I quickly cut across our backyard, turned into the woods that bordered the neighborhood, and started toward the grocery store. In the distance, the gigantic smokestack from the shoe factory puffed tunnels of fluffy gray clouds over me. Cautiously, I continued through the underbrush until straight ahead in the clearing I could see the brick factory standing between me and Dillingham's. It loomed high in the sky above. Voices came from the huge open windows.

It was much too early to hear the afternoon whistle that would pierce the sky at three o'clock to announce the late shift, but as I recalled its shrill, deafening pitch that would burn in my ears, I covered them as I hurried past row after row of windows. The smell of leather and sweat hung in the air. I zigzagged past the workers' parked cars. Finally, the narrow street that ran in front of the factory was all that separated me from the grocery store.

Stopping to look both ways, I let a car pass, remembering my conversations with Daddy about crossing the street, cars, and the like: "Now that's a fine-looking car, Miss Alexandra," he had said the last time, using my proper name, prompting me to think the way an adult would think. "A brand new '53 Buick!" I had nodded my head in agreement, the way I thought he wanted me to, and he'd held my hand as we crossed the street.

He always reminded me to look both ways before crossing, but he wouldn't be doing that today. Proud that I was big enough to do it all by myself this time, I hesitated, focusing on the sign across the way. Another car passed.

DILLINGHAM'S GROCERY STORE was painted in bold red letters across the top of the building. Underneath were two big picture windows. Several cars filled the parking spaces in front of them, nosing in like nursing puppies. Trucks were angled in disarray down the slope by the side of the store.

Another car passed.

Nothing was coming. Again, I looked both ways and crossed the street.

Inside the grocery, people were milling about, minding their own business. I went unnoticed to the packages of Kool-Aid, and Daddy's voice was stuck in my head, warning me sugar was bad for my teeth. I'd heard it before. It meant Kool-Aid was off limits.

Not now and not then had that kept me from looking longingly at their delicious colors. They had flashed through my mind for days after I first saw them. Now they were stacked up on the shelf, comfortably within my reach. Irresistible red cherries and tangy oranges stared back at me from the pictures on the packages. Seeing them caused water to puddle under my tongue. I felt again for the dime with one hand and selected the bright red package with the other, then started down the short aisle stocked on both sides with cans and jars. Eagerly I passed them and went all the way to the back of the store where I had been with Daddy several times before.

Always in the past, he strode right up to the glass case where the cold meat was kept. From there Mr. Dillingham could see us. Daddy would have taken off his hat by now and loosely held it by the side of his leg. He would have started shaking hands with Mr. Dillingham with his free hand, and they would have stood there, smiling at each other over top of the case of cold meats.

Clutching the Kool-Aid, I looked at the ceiling, waiting for Mr. Dillingham to see me. It didn't seem right for me to holler at him or call out, "Mr. Dillingham," or use his first name the way my daddy would.

"Bert," he'd say, "how are your prices today?" Or he would say, "Give me a pound and a quarter of your ground beef." Then Mr. Dillingham would show it to Daddy on a piece of brown paper before wrapping it up. He'd slipped in a bone on our last visit, then winked at me, telling me to give it to Laddie-dog. It was probably because Mr. Dillingham respected my daddy. Never mind Daddy's complaints to my mommy about Bert's darned eggs being three cents apiece, he kept going back to Dillingham's Grocery Store.

I almost jumped at the sound of Mr. Dillingham's voice as he came from behind the meat counter. "And what can I do for you, young lady? Laddie-dog needs a bone, does he?" He wiped his hands on his stiff, white apron. His undivided attention awaited my answer as if he had all morning to discuss it.

"No sir, Mr. Dillingham. I want to get this Kool-Aid." I held up the colorful package for him to see. "I have a dime," I said and held out my hand to prove it. "See! It's mine. Honest. I earned it."

"Well, of course, you did, Alexandra. Okay. You bet! You bet!" Mr. Dillingham smiled at me.

Taking the money, he put the cherry Kool-Aid in a sack, folded down its top. Still smiling, he dangled it over the case and held it for me to take.

"Here you go, honey. Now you be careful crossing that street, you hear? Give my regards to your dad."

"Yes, sir," I said, turning to go. "Thank you, Mr. Dillingham."

In a matter of seconds, I was on my way, crossing the street quickly, running toward the shoe factory, then back again through the parking lot.

Safely in the cover of the woods, I told myself there was nothing to hide. I pulled up with all my strength to the perfect spot on the bottom limb of a maple tree and sat down, tore the top off the package, and began shoving down its deliciousness.

The taste of sweet, forbidden sugar and tart cherries melted in my mouth. Again and again, I turned the package upside down, smashing it against my lips and onto my tongue until there was not a speck left. Then, without wasting any time, I skidded down the tree and made my way back home before Daddy could notice I was gone.

I could see as soon as I got close to my house that the screen door was slightly ajar, not how I had left it earlier.

Inside, Daddy was standing at the sink, facing the window. He turned in my direction. Something about the way he studied me felt odd, and his eyes told me he was going to quiz me about where I'd been. I looked down at my shoes and began to walk, knowing he watched me cross the kitchen. Without a word, I started through the hallway to my bedroom.

In an instant his hand was heavy on my shoulder, dropping there like a bag of wet dirt. Its heat sent a tremor down my spine and through my body. Running was impossible. There was no place to go. The tiny corridor closed in around me. Trouble was certain.

"What have you been eating?" Daddy said, and his question was fiercer than the shoe factory's piercing whistle.

The sound made my shoulders shake. My knees wanted to buckle beneath me.

"Nothing." My answer dribbled out, weak and unconvincing. I paused, expecting something to happen in the hush that hung around us.

The fan circled and clicked overhead the way it always had, its laps swatting at hot air, broken only by Daddy's response.

"Go look in the mirror," he said, and I felt iciness drip from his words.

As if I'd opened the Frigidaire, the hallway turned coldish. Ever so slowly, I walked three steps to the bathroom at the end of it, scared silly, and went to the washbasin. I stiffened my arms to make them like stilts and pushed high enough to see myself in the chrome-rimmed mirror of the medicine cabinet. Looking back at me was my clown-like face.

My smeared red lips did not make either of us laugh. Nothing was funny.

Daddy stood behind me, a towering reflection, like a prehistoric monster in a storybook. His soft brown eyes had turned to burning balls that poked out at me through bushy brows.

"Go to your room," he said, handing down my guilty sentence in a breathy whisper.

Life flowed out of my legs like water draining from the tub after a bath. From the top of my head to the tip of my toes, I could feel myself tingling.

Even so, I minded him, and the door closed with a resounding smack of separation. Nothing remained but silence. I fell on my bed and sobbed, and after I was too weak to cry any more, I lay there, motionless. Except for the swaying leaves on a tree outside my window, nothing moved. I was hypnotized by the spell of their rhythmic wave, unable to take my swollen eyes off them.

Replaying what had happened, erasing it, telling Daddy the truth, making myself his Sweet Pea again was impossible. I couldn't change what I'd done, and I couldn't put the Kool-Aid back on the grocery store shelf, or fix what I had broken between my daddy and me. Fibbing was bad enough; trying to cover up that I'd eaten sugar was maybe worse.

What if he thought I'd stolen it? Maybe eating Kool-Aid was going to make me die. Confused thoughts spun uncontrollably like the loose ends of a film on a broken movie reel, flipping madly in every direction.

Maybe Daddy did not love me anymore.

Hours passed. The afternoon sun disappeared behind clouds. It wasn't until later in the day that it reappeared to show little bits of brightness. Shadows transformed the fuzzy outline of the tree into a glowing silhouette. And I lay there, rocklike, watching my leafy friend wave back at me as the afternoon passed into evening.

Chapter 7

A distant door slam and the dull scraping of a chair leg on the kitchen floor let me know Mommy and the boys were home. Their muffled sounds came from the other side of darkness that had slipped in and—except for the moon laying its light across my bedside table—had quietly taken over my room. Peanut butter between two pieces of bread and a glass of not-so-cold milk sat in the shadows, having appeared there during the night while I wrestled with fitful spells of sleep.

I propped myself on one elbow and listened through the dead stillness to Mommy tiptoeing past, saying something about us going to church tomorrow. Then came the thump . . . thump of Daddy's footsteps in their bedroom across the hall, proved the mess I'd made of things was causing him to clomp around.

"It'll do us all good to go," my mother said. "You might have been a little heavy-handed with Alexandra."

Daddy's clomping had stopped. "I merely sent her to her room," he said. "Maybe you'd better let it go, Gracie. She was not forthcoming. She should have told the truth."

I crammed the sandwich between my lips. Parts of it oozed distastefully past the crust. Gooey peanut butter stuck to the roof of my mouth.

Silence said they had shut the door to their bedroom, but then heavy thump . . . thumps said Daddy was pacing again, with the door still open. "Well, why wasn't she truthful? Can you tell me that?"

"Because she was afraid, I guess. She's been in her room for hours, Simon. And no dinner? Sometimes I wonder—

"—Don't brush aside the fact that she lied." His voice was distant now, muffled. "Your opinion of me doesn't seem to be very high, lately. And where were you?"

Silence.

"I'll tell you where. Gracie, you insist on going out, spending money we should be saving. This new job is tentative at best."

Silence.

"TVA's taken a risk hiring me, and I've taken a risk moving us here, doing a job I'm unaccustomed to. It's a big responsiblity, hon. I'm simply managing the best I can."

Silence. Nothing.

"Well, this is certainly different, I must say," Daddy said, and I pictured him giving Mommy the same look he had given me yesterday. "Are you just going to stand there, gawking at me? Speechless?"

"You tend to take things too seriously. That's all I'm going to say, Simon. What do you want me to say? I'm letting go of my home in Murray, my friends back there. One day at a time. My ministry at Murray State. All of it . . . gone. And here we are, living in this house next door to —" Mommy's voice had picked up, not sounding at all like she was going to stop talking like normal.

I freed the goo from the roof of my mouth with a gulp of milk and set the glass back on the nightstand.

"—To what, Gracie? What's so wrong with Alexandra going over to talk to Mrs. Nightingale, anyway? Besides—" Daddy's voice melted away, and outside my door, life went on without me.

I chomped hungrily until the sandwich was gone and then rolled over, wishing I could move back to Kentucky. Maybe tomorrow, I thought, Daddy will change his mind about me.

But for now, he did not want me for his Sweet Pea.

———— • ————

Later that night, I was dreaming of my home—the way it used to be in Murray when I was younger—*back*—*back*—where the concrete driveway that separated Jeremy Foster's house from mine leveled off in front of his garage. He and I pulled our wagons there in the afternoons, and Beulah watched from my kitchen window to make sure we stayed where we were supposed to. It was mostly her job to watch me, but she kept a lookout on both of us, the same way the maid at Jeremy's house did. If the two women got busy with their chores or they started talking to each other, it wasn't likely a beast was going to get me or Jeremy.

Already, however, one day had started awful. It did include a beast: Jeremy's sister. On most days, Pricilla tried to make Jeremy and me think we were in trouble for most everything. But this time it was worse. This morning—just because we'd made Jeremy's pet duck hunker down under his wagon so that it wouldn't get away, and we had taken the duck for a walk, and just because the duck didn't walk fast enough to keep up with the wagon—Jeremy's sister had screamed her head off about the blood, the dead duck, and how it couldn't breathe.

It was our first murder. I promised myself it was my last, but that's when Pre-cilla started telling us what to do whenever Beulah wasn't around.

Pre-cilla got away with acting as bossy as she wanted on that particular morning, and she kept it up—on into the afternoon. All the while, she wore a weasel-eye like the same sort some grown-ups wear.

Weasel-eyed people had a way of ruining playtime. Pulling wagons wasn't fun anymore, and none of the usual stuff was. Both wagons were upside down by the side of Jeremy's driveway, and by late afternoon we were looking for something to do. Playing doctor where the grapevines grew at the back of my house was my idea. Under the cover of huge leaves, we were hidden from the monster. Then *Pre*-cilla showed up as a nightmare between the wild vines, poking in her head through the big leaves, pushing them back as if they were a stubborn shower curtain.

"Jeremy! *Jeremy Foster*!" The look on her face was not nice. "I'm going to tell Mother on you!" Her breath was hot, blowing down on Jeremy and me. "You two had better *not ever* do this again! *Do you hear me?*" Both our heads were bobbing yes, our eyes bugging out. "I'll tell on both of you. I *will* tell! That's a *promise*! Humph!"

Playing doctor turned out to be a bad idea, given her huffiness that struck the same fear as a single weasel-eye from Beulah would have. But Beulah was busy with the laundry, and Mommy was off at her job. Even so, playtime was over. Jeremy pulled up his pants, and we crawled out from behind the grapevines and got to our feet.

I didn't get to wave good-bye to him. *Pre*-cilla shooed me off and dragged him away by the hand. I moped on over to the screened porch by the far side of my house and climbed onto the swing's wooden seat. Sometimes I had too many mommies.

I sat down and settled myself against the back of the swing. "Beulah didn't treat me that way. And *Daddy* wouldn't treat me that way, either," I told the swing's armrest in earnest, taking a second to practice a weasel-eye look of my own. Afterward, I began the necessary sways and sweeps to make the swing move back and forth. *Pre*-cilla had made it look easy—bending her legs at the knees so her feet went under the seat, then stretching them straight out in front as the swing climbed higher and higher—back and forth, back and forth. That's when she would start singing, so I did, not knowing the song's meaning. But it sounded pretty, and she would look all dreamy, singing about the stars, and why they shone, and why the ivy twined, and why the sky was blue. So, I did the same.

I copied her every move, pumping my legs, looking at the ceiling, gliding, trying my best to make the swing take off, wanting more than anything to be like the part of her that wasn't bossy, the part that could swing, and sing, and wear red lipstick.

It was not so easy, and I was getting dizzy. Besides, Beulah was calling.

"Yo'r daddy's home, Alexandra," she hollered.

At the mention of his name, I stopped singing and scooted myself to the front of the swing's seat. My feet couldn't begin to touch the floor, and it took a tall hop to get myself down fast enough. As soon as I could feel the floor under me, I ran past the open door and into the living room.

"Well, *there* you are, Sweet Pea," he said when he caught sight of me.

A bunch of pearly teeth flashed behind his big smile, and I flew into his open arms. "Alexandra! How's my big girl?" His words were warm and fuzzy ones, his mighty hands lifted me high into the air. Higher I went, higher than the porch swing ever could have taken me. But suddenly, I was awakened.

"Alexandra!" *Mommy's* voice was real. "Stretch your little wings and get up, honey," she sang out, waltzing blissfully over to my nightstand, and scooped up the leftover curled crusts of my peanut butter sandwich from the pillow. "You must have been having a happy dream."

Rain pelted the windowsill outside my bedroom. The morning had awakened gray and dreary. Tree limbs outlined the night before in a silvery glow were almost hidden now. Their leaves drooped helplessly in the steady downpour.

"Breakfast will be ready soon, honey. Church today."

Chapter 8

No indication said this Sunday would be any different from another. Mommy ignored the red sugar smears of Kool-Aid and the tear-soaked mess on my pillow, pretending it was all very normal. But nothing about it was, particularly not the soggy puddle surrounding my bottom.

Bed-wetting is for babies! I scolded myself at the very thought of it. That's when I remembered it was the man in my dream, dressed as a king. *He* had given me permission to potty.

So no, this was not a normal morning. Even so, Mommy was here, filling the room like she was the sunshine itself.

"Stretch those wings, big and high. Here, honey, let me help you get up and into the bathroom. I've laid out your pretty brown dress with the ladybugs on it."

Ugh.

"Let's wear that today. Now then, honey," she carried on, "go . . . hurry and finish in there. The boys may want to use it, too, before we leave for church."

Church.

It was already decided the boys, Jeff Lee, Maxwell, and Hickman—mostly called Jeff-Mac-Hick—all with the jumbled-up name, never

52

mind which boy it was—were going to eat breakfast. I was going to be taking a bath and putting on the ugly brown dress.

With the door to my room open, I could hear the unmistakable crackle and pop of bacon sizzling in the pan. The savory smell made it seem within an arm's reach, but I couldn't make either arm move in any direction. It was too soon to know if my eyelids would open totally.

"Mommy, do I *have to* go to church? I don't want to," I pleaded, inching toward the bathroom in yesterday's clothes.

Daddy was nowhere in sight.

"Of course! And I know you want to go! We'll get you all dressed up, and then the boys can take a turn in the bathroom. Let's hurry, though, honey. We need to scoot right along."

Taking turns belonged with other instructions: looking my best and treating others like I would want to be treated. *Church-talk.*

That required extra attention. Rules appeared to be originating at church, and today was probably not a good day to balk at them. I was in enough trouble, not wanting to get into more or encourage Daddy to use his belt on me. That was reserved for the boys when *they* misbehaved.

Hot water crept up around me and filled the tub as I sat there thinking of Daddy's belt, thinking of when he had fired a look of warning down the church pew at Jeff Lee a while back. I'd known Daddy would deal with him when we got back home because Jeff Lee kept on annoying Maxwell. Then he pushed Maxwell. *That did it.* Being the two oldest somehow made them push and shove each other every chance they got. Another day it would have made me smile, even laugh out loud, like it had when I'd told Papa Jeff about it. But now all I could think of was Daddy's belt and how it sounded, flipping past each loop: *slap-slap-slap.*

In the end, Jeff Lee hadn't even gotten a whipping. He'd been so clever, putting a pillow in his pants at his be-hind, I thought as I turned off the water.

Hoping to be as smart as Jeff Lee when I got to be a teenager, I finished my bath and got dressed, just in case—in the night—Daddy had been considering using his belt on me for lying about the Kool-Aid. Although he hadn't threatened me with it, this morning seemed like the perfect one for me to slip quickly past his bedroom.

———————— • ————————

The newspaper was loosely folded on the kitchen table. Daddy had been there and gone. Maxwell was pouring a glass of juice for himself. Rain bounced off the window panes over the sink. Someone had closed the sash and rolled a towel across the sill. Cracked eggs sat in a bowl next to the black iron skillet, waiting to be stirred into the drippings were the two last pieces of bacon that had started to shrivel and curl. A plate of eggs was staring at me.

"I don't want eggs, Mommy. I can't stand eggs. Do I have to eat them?"

"Yes, honey. Drink your juice, and bacon's going to be ready soon. You look so pretty. You're a princess in that dress. Brown is one of your best colors."

"I don't like brown."

"Don't you agree? Alexandra looks as pretty as a princess," she said to Maxwell.

"But I don't want to be a princess," I protested.

"You're going to meet more new friends . . . adding to the ones you've met these last few Sundays," she said, glossing over my unenlightened comment. "Now, when you've finished breakfast, run and brush your teeth. Be sure you use paste. I suspect Miss America brushes her teeth three times a day!"

"You could end up with teeth like Laddie-dog's. *Fangs!*" Maxwell barked over top a mouthful of his Kellogg's Sugar Smacks. Milk squirted and ran down his chin. "Then you wouldn't be *a princess* at all. No one would want you around," he added on a vicious note.

I didn't care what Miss America did with her teeth. I carried my egg, watching it slide from side to side on the plate, and walked to the table. Slowly, I sat down, ignoring Maxwell as best I could, and eyed the wet, white egg pieces that usually made me shiver at the sight. Without trying to pick them out, I ate as fast as lightning—then bolted. The door to Daddy's bedroom opened as I neared the bathroom, and I stopped breathing on the spot.

He took a step out and rested one hand on the knob. "Morning, Alexandra."

I couldn't tell if he sounded any different. He looked taller.

"I'm going to get the car," he said. "You and the boys come on out. We should be leaving soon. Otherwise, we'll be late. Turn off the light when you're finished in the bathroom."

"Yes, sir." I felt like a mouse in the corner.

Daddy walked past. For a split second I breathed the tangy smell he left behind.

"Hurry up, Alexandra," yelled Hickman from some other place in the house. "I have to get in there, and so does Jeff Lee. *So hurry up!*"

Brushing my teeth without dribbling spit on my dress was all-important, especially now, when I did not need to make anything worse than it already was, but Hickman pushed his way into the bathroom. He continued to boss me.

"Stop it, Hick-Hacky-man!" I tried to defend myself as best I could . . . name-calling with a mouthful of toothpaste.

Ordered about on all sides by everyone made being the baby of the family un-fun and not to be envied the way people liked to think.

"Alexandra, aren't you finished yet? Come on, *let's go*," Hickman said, intentionally bonking me, grabbing the toothpaste tube off the sink in front of me, leaving me to do the only thing I could do.

With toothpaste foaming, I stuck out my tongue—as far as it would go.

———— • ————

By the time I reached the yard's edge, Daddy's car was backed out of the garage. Its headlights were staring me in the eye, suggesting I shouldn't get inside and sit next to him, but I hurried. I slowed my steps as I got closer, unsure.

Daddy's hairy hands were wrapped around the steering wheel. His faraway look told me he was already somewhere else.

"Hurry along, honey," Mommy urged, holding the car door open. "Jump in."

She slid in next to me and began straightening the buttons on her blue dress. With them all neatly fixed in a row, she situated her patent leather purse at her lap, clutching its handle at her side, then took hold of the hat Daddy handed her over the top of my legs with her other hand. Times were when Daddy would've let me stroke his hat as if it were a kitten, but I didn't dare touch it today, and we all kept our hands to ourselves. I tried to shrink out of the way, certain I didn't belong here—and not at church either, where nobody did anything wrong. The ride started out quiet.

"We don't want to be late, Simon," Mommy sounded like she was dishing out more than a lazy thought. "You'll recall the names of the nice couple who greeted us so graciously last Sunday." I could hear the prompting in her round-about question. "Ray and Lucille Bledsoe. Lovely people. He owns the five-and-dime store on Main Street. You remember."

Daddy looked straight ahead in silence. His head nodded like the swish of a mule's tail.

I took a peek at my socks, having been reminded of the department store where Mommy had taken me to buy them. Neither sock had ruffles like the other girls' socks, and not only was I wearing the ugly brown lady-bug dress and ruffle-less socks, but I was filled to the brim with forbidden Kool-Aid sugar. My teeth could be rotting at this very moment. Everyone would know it. Plus, they'd know I lied to my daddy.

I felt cruddy.

"What difference does it make, Sweet Pea? You're the prettiest girl there," Daddy had said, sweeping away the suffering after my first day at Sunday school. "So what if your socks don't have ruffles?"

But today I didn't say anything about my socks. Neither did Daddy. He parked the car, and we all got out.

"We'll plan to meet you in the hallway when Sunday school lets out. Go and have fun," Mommy said. "And be yourself!"

'*Be myself?*' Halfheartedly, I walked toward the third graders' room and through the open door. A few people were seated in chairs arranged in a circle.

"You can sit right here," said the girl sitting a few seats away. She pointed to the one beside her.

"*Me?*"

"Of course, *you*! Who else would I be talking to?"

She popped up from her chair, her head bobbing—almost like a jack-in-the-box—her blonde ringlets jiggling.

"Your ladybug dress is cute," she said. "My name is Suzette. What's yours?"

"Alexandra. It's Alexandra Hagan. We moved here, well . . . not very long ago."

Suzette cocked her head to one side and looked at me as if she were thinking really hard. Her eyes got big. "*You could come to my house!* Would your mother let you? *Would she?*"

"Girls and boys," the teacher said. "Let's settle down. Class is beginning."

———— • ————

Sunday school ended, and the teacher scurried between incoming parents and rushing children. I lost Suzette somewhere in the middle of the hustle and bustle and found myself back with my parents, being frog-marched through the crowd to the grownups' church. Even then, I wanted to make a run for it so that I wouldn't have to sit between them, enduring the songs, having Jesus look directly at me from where he stood in the stained-glass window—knowing everything in that scary, peculiar way that Jesus knew *everything*.

I slumped down on the pew. And there he was: Jesus, wearing his white robe with a red curtain-like cloth draped over his shoulder, peering at me. He was near enough for me to see the details of a baby sheep resting itself on one of His arms. And Jesus held a long pole with a crook at the top in His other arm. More sheep were looking up at Him, and I guessed they were hoping to get some food as they walked along.

But today, Jesus was looking straight at me.

I scooted even further down behind the pew in front of me and sat as still as a dead mouse.

Daddy didn't blink but instead, stared straight ahead. Pastor Owen rose and smiled, and everyone got settled for the long hour ahead. My mother shot a warning glance down the row at my brothers in case they were about to consider embarrassing her.

Pastor Owen's eyes were as bright as the plastic buttons on my old teddy bear, and when he smiled, little sun-ripened mounds of redness raised under them, and crinkles darted out beside them. If I'd needed a cuddly toy, I'd have wanted the likeness of him stitched from my flannel PJ's.

Before long, from the front of the church, Pastor Owen began yelling, but no one acted like they believed he was mad. People stayed awake to hear what he had to say and moved their heads and shifted in their seats because he was telling good stories. Knowing from experience a pastor's stories aren't very interesting if you're eight years old, I had come prepared last Sunday with a couple of marshmallows to tide me over until lunch.

This Sunday, however, I hadn't brought a snack. Doing it last week had not been the best idea; doing it again would have been really stupid and not because marshmallows were hard to carry. Stuffing marshmallows into Mommy's black purse was easy. She didn't mind if I poked quietly through her purse during church.

The perfect chance to eat my marshmallows had arrived when everyone jumped up to sing. I had slipped my hand into Mommy's purse and located the morsels; my fingers worked their way around a cushy one like an ant crawling on its dinner. At the right moment, I'd pushed most of the marshmallow into my mouth. It was about that time I realized it was too large to eat in one bite. But it was too late to rethink and bite off only half and put the other half back.

Usually, the songs took *forever* to be over, but this one didn't. In a jiffy, Pastor Owen told us to take our seats, and I had to finish cramming all of the marshmallow into my mouth at once—quick-like and be done with it, and Pastor Owen's sermon began. He couldn't keep from looking directly at our family because we were seated like statues in front of him. Peering over the top of his wooden stand, I could see him, and that meant he could see me. The instant he noticed my mushroomed mouth, his normal smile got wider than his usual ones. He smiled first at me, then at my mother. Back and forth.

He continued talking to everyone while I tried to eat the marshmallow without choking. I could feel the white powder on my lips, and I worked hard to brush it away with the back of my hand. Mommy acted like everything was alright. An amused look passed between her and Pastor Owen. Jesus-filled windows patrolled the entire scene.

It was the very day when I first came to know Jesus had his eye on me.

That thought was terrifying enough, but now the hours without anything to eat from breakfast to lunch were almost unbearable. The worst part was having to sit still through another sermon that had no end. I hunkered down and settled in on daydreaming.

Finally, clanging cords came screeching out of the piano and jolted me from the memory of last week's marshmallow ordeal, and at long last, the painful wait for the morning to be over arrived. Noise bounced off the church walls as everyone sprang to their feet and began singing about the friend we have in Jesus.

I imagined what Jesus expected in a friend. It did not look like me. I tried to remember what Papa Jeff had said about the church, it being a place to learn what God had planned for us, but nothing came. I played it safe and kept my gaze straight ahead, cowering behind the pew until the song was finished and even then was not about to look across the aisle at Jesus in the window. He knew more about my mess-up with the Kool-Aid than anybody.

With the song ended, the congregation filed out the front doors of the church. Small groups of people clustered here and there, talking in their grownup ways, saying what a nice day it had turned out to be after such a hard rain in the night.

"Cat got your tongue?" The lady standing with my mommy plopped her hand on my head, talking to me.

As usual, I couldn't come up with an answer.

Without a response from me, she and Mommy turned toward each other and laughed impishly the way church women do when there is nothing to say. It was perfect timing that brought Suzette. I spotted her rushing up with her blonde ringlets bouncing all over her head. She was dragging her mother by the hand. They landed in the midst of us.

"Mama!" Suzette was completely out of breath. "*This* is Alexandra! She's going to be in third grade, too! Can she come to our house sometime? Can she? *Can* she?"

Chapter 9

Pot roast, potatoes, and carrots in the pressure cooker smelled delicious once we arrived back at home, hungry and ready to get out of church clothes. Sunday lunch with its beefy aroma was as welcome as the warm sunshine that had pushed its way up into the noonday sky by the time we left church. My brothers and I leaped out of the car and hit the ground running.

Daddy sauntered from the garage and across the yard and promptly took off his hat as he came through the kitchen door. He was the last one inside. Mommy left her high heels on the floor in front of the sink and moved quickly to lift up the dining table's side leaves. She pointed me toward the dishes with peach-colored flowers stacked nearby.

"Set the table, honey. And use those plates. Get the silverware out of the drawer and turn the knife's blade to the inside," she reminded me. "That's the correct way."

"I know that, Mommy. You don't have to keep telling me. I don't see any napkins."

"There." She glanced toward the cabinet and pursed her lips. "Well now, I don't know where they are . . . Simon," she called, "have you hidden the napkins?"

"Of course not," Daddy said as he rounded the corner and entered the kitchen, rolling up the sleeve on his white shirt. The dark yellow stone in his ring caught the sunlight as he patted the shirt's crisp fold to his forearm. "But I've taken the liberty to organize a few things around here," he said, "and they're in the second drawer down."

I waited for him to sit so that I wouldn't cross his path while I fetched the napkins, and within minutes the place was in a tizzy. Everyone bumped about, getting seated but quieted for Jeff Lee to take his turn saying the blessing. He thanked God for our food; then the noise picked up again.

Hickman took one look at the platter of food. "We had this last Sunday. Are we gonna have it ev-ve—ry Sunday?"

It was a brother-question. He was the first of the three to get out of line—one of them had to be. I didn't even look up. They all asked dumb questions.

"Yes, and it's delicious!" Mommy chimed in. "And your father makes some of the best pot roast there is. Didn't you hear Pastor Owen talking about gratitude? Hum-mm? Let's be grateful. What did anyone learn this morning about gratitude?"

I looked at Jeff Lee. He looked at Maxwell. Maxwell jabbed Hickman with an elbow.

"Okay, boys. That's enough," Daddy said and kept on eating his carrots.

On other Sundays, he told me carrots would make my eyes pretty and coaxed me to eat them, but not today, and nothing was said about gratitude. Instead, the two older boys began making plans to roust up a touch football game after lunch.

"—So I told Ralph and Eddie to meet us in the vacant lot. The earlier the better," Jeff Lee said to Maxwell. Both took a swig of milk. Neither wiped his mouth.

"I'm coming, too," Hickman said with a look in Daddy's direction, inviting back up.

"No. You're not, Hick-man." Maxwell jumped in, irritated. "You're too scrawny. And besides, you'd get hurt. Go find some girls and play dolls." He eyed Hickman as if his being two years older than Hickman earned him bossing rights.

"Let's not have any harsh words today, boys. It's Sunday," Mommy said, pouring iced tea into Daddy's glass, and the kitchen got really quiet except for the sound of Daddy's fork jabbing at his food.

I finished and took my plate to the sink. "Can I go see Mrs. Nightingale? I mean, may I?"

At the mention of Mrs. Nightingale's name, Mommy sighed deeply, then dabbed her napkin against her mouth.

"Yes, Alexandra." Daddy spoke up before she could respond. "Go ahead. I think that'll be fine."

I could tell by the look in Mommy's eyes, she wanted to object. "Simon . . . ," she muttered before dabbing her mouth some more with a wad of the napkin.

Nobody else looked like they cared one way or the other, so I went outside, into the early afternoon heat.

———— • ————

Mrs. Nightingale spotted me immediately and called out, motioning at me from her chair when she saw me coming.

"Yoo-hoo, you-hoo, there!"

The closer I got, the happier became her short smile. "Come here, child." Her teeth stuck way out—square, stubby, and far apart, with a pink, pointy piece of skin hanging straight down between the two front ones. "Come over here and see me!"

Other days her smile might've caused me to smile back at her, but today—except for meeting Suzette—I wasn't feeling much like smiling, and my feet kept slowing me down.

"Is anything wrong, Alexandra?" Mrs. Nightingale's smile started to die away as I eased closer to her chair, and before I reached her, I stopped walking altogether, silently begging her not to ask why I had not come back yesterday to make potholders.

I swallowed hard and shook my head.

"I thought you'd come back yesterday," she said and eyed me like I was a lost puppy.

After a minute she started in again, snapping the ends off from a handful of green beans while sagging skin dangled beneath her arms and flopped effortlessly from side to side beneath them. Not missing a bean, she pulled a string from the part that remained and tossed it in the bowl she held between her knees.

"Went to church this morning," I said, not wanting to show my face, hoping she would not know what had happened with the Kool-Aid after I left her yesterday.

We both got really quiet.

"That's nice." Her smile was back. "I always wanted a little girl. One just like you."

"Not a princess?"

"A princess?" Her mouth dropped open. "Heavens, no! What on earth would anyone want with a princess?"

I needed only a second to think. "Princesses are pretty," I told her.

"You're as pretty as can be, Alexandra!" she said, then began to squirm, trying to sit a different way in the chair, and even though most of the seat and back were covered by red oilcloth, its wide boards were plain to see. They jutted up behind her, arching high above her head as if she were wearing a strange crown. The rest of the chair was hidden by her sprawling body. "You eat green beans, don't you? I'm sure you must," she said.

"Yes, ma'am, a little."

She nodded delightedly, so much so she needed to swat at a clump of black hair that had slipped from her barrette. She brushed it from her eyes with the back of her hand and started in again, yanking beans from her lapful until all were broken and strung while I waited.

Another of her short smiles presented itself. She took a deep breath and set the bowl on the ground beside her chair. Plainly, she was ready to get up.

I was certain she was stuck in the chair.

Twice she tried to pull herself forward, away from the slanted back of the chair. Then, with both arms bent, she forced herself upward and brought her big body to the front of it.

I watched helplessly, uncertain of my own next move.

She held tightly to the ends of her apron's bottom, cuddling the beans to keep them from falling to the ground, then steadied herself. Suddenly, she stood with a mighty move. She sighed deeply and with slow steps hobbled to the end of her trailer and flung the end pieces and strings out of her clutched apron in the direction of the nearby garbage bin.

"There!" she said, then circled back to her chair. "You want to hand me that bowl, child."

It wasn't a question, more of an instruction, and it didn't need a long answer. I nodded and picked it up with both hands. "Here." I handed it over, glad for someone to talk to.

"Chuck!" Mrs. Nightingale yelled toward the trailer. "Come out'n get these beans."

Still holding the bowl of beans clutched up next to her big bosoms, she mopped some perspiration from her forehead with the crook in her arm and again called out to Mr. Nightingale.

After she tromped back and forth in the space below the two steps up to the trailer, trying to keep out of the mud, Mrs. Nightingale was about to call him a third time when he showed up in the doorway, struggling to get his shirt over his shoulder. From the looks of things, I knew he had not been to church. Whiskers prickled all over his chin.

He snatched the beans from Mrs. Nightingale and was gone without a word as quickly as he had come.

Mrs. Nightingale turned to me, her smile right in place. "This would be a good day to start the potholders. Any reason why not?"

I tried to think of how to answer. "No ma'am. Is it hard?"

"No, child. Not one bit hard. Not'n the least! Wanna try?"

My head bobbed to let her know I might get excited if I were given half a chance, and she turned again toward the trailer. "Chuck? Oh, Ch . . . uck?" she hollered in her husky voice. "Luv . . . ove! Get my basket by the rocker . . . Would ya? I'm gonna show Alexandra how to go about making potholders."

A moment passed before Mr. Nightingale reappeared with a basket, fidgeting with the bottom button on his shirt. He leaned out the trailer door and bent down, holding the wicker handle, huffing till she took it.

The whiff of his yeast-smelling breath reminded me of Beulah's homemade rolls, but nothing else about him did, and something made me think he would not think kindly of being bothered by any more interruptions. I made up my mind Mrs. Nightingale and I should be glad for whatever it was in the basket, and be done with him.

"Let's sit over here in the shade, want to? You sit there," she said and pointed to a lawn chair, then lifted a bench from under the picnic table for herself.

She plopped herself down in the center of it with her back to the table. But in a second she was back on her feet.

"Better yet, child, grab that cloth and spread it over this bench. Still feels a little damp. Sit there, and I'll fetch a dry chair. Lawsy mercy! We had us quite a rain last night."

I smiled, and she smiled, and finally, we both were situated on dry seats.

"Yes ma'am. We did." I smoothed my dress over my knees and watched as Mrs. Nightingale took colorful cotton bands from the basket, stretching each one tightly across the metal loom.

Looking pleased with the rows of bands, she sighed, then peeked at me to see if she had my full attention. "That's what you'll do first," she said. "Next . . . here. You'll pick a color, and I'll show you how to weave it in and out. Then I want to hear what else you've been doing . . . if you want to tell me."

With the loom in hand, I was about to pull a pink yarn from the basket when I heard the screen door to my house snap shut.

"Alexandra, honey," Mommy called to me from the short distance. "You need to come on home . . . I'm sure Mrs. Nightingale has things to do, and so do you. Come along now."

I scooted to the edge of the chair, a clumsy scoot—like the clumsy silence before Mommy spoke again.

"Hello, Mrs. Nightingale," she called out. "Lovely day, after all, isn't it?"

"I'll come back in the morning. I promise," I said in a whisper.

"It is indeed," answered Mrs. Nightingale. (Indeed. It was a freshly polished-up sort of word. One Mommy would approve, I thought, and Mrs. Nightingale sounded respectable saying it.) "And I do want you to come for tea some afternoon."

With Mrs. Nightingale's invitation drifting off behind me, I ran inside, through the back door to the kitchen. It slammed with its usual smack. "Mrs. Nightingale is really nice," I said, huffing.

Silence.

"Isn't she, Mommy?"

Right then I could tell, asking Mommy about Mrs. Nightingale was not making her happy. Mommy was tired of hearing about my new friend in the trailer park. A disappointed twinge worked its way into the empty place inside me, left there when we left Beulah behind.

"Honey, yes. Yes. I suppose she is . . . nice." Mommy's answer felt like something icy had spilled on me.

Mrs. Nightingale was not acceptable, but it was too late to change the truth: I liked her. Mommy did not.

Chapter 10

SIMON

Absolutely. Gracie was calling me.

With the heat of the day, the walls were closing in, as if Sunday afternoon hadn't been long enough.

I got up from my knees. "Lord God. What now?" I said under my breath before opening the door to leave our bedroom. Bad as I wanted to see what Gracie was up to, I had a hunch it would be nothing less than anything within her power. Half-hearted, I walked to the kitchen.

Gracie was rustling some pots and pans. The smell was unidentifiable.

"I need to talk to you, Simon. In private. After supper," she said. "You can certainly make time."

"What *is* that?"

"What?"

"That . . . smell?" I took the lid off the saucepan. Steam rolled through the air with a disgusting push. "I thought you'd let a dog in here and fed it a can of beans, honey. Guess it's only burning broccoli—"

It was as if I'd said nothing.

"We can go for a drive," she said. "See to it Jeff Lee knows he's not to leave the house, and he's to make sure the others don't."

I covered the pan and set it in the sink. "What's this about? Can't be anything we haven't already gone over, hon." I turned on the cold-water tap, trying to help her with doing a new task, one I knew full well she was not thrilled about, one she was not so good at it either. "I'm a little concerned about leaving them too long," I said. "This neighborhood—"

"That's my point, Simon." Her eyes were ablaze. "This neighborhood. We really must have a discussion and get some things straightened out. Plan on coming to bed early."

I wasn't inclined to think the worst, but there was no doubt about it: the sooner this affliction could end, the happier Gracie would be. Better still for her, moving back to her beloved home atop the hill in Murray would resolve everything. Every turn said I'd made a mistake moving us here and confirmed nothing but my bad judgment.

In a matter of minutes, all four children were filing into the small kitchen, seating themselves at the table.

"I sure do wish Beulah was here to make chicken and dumplings," Maxwell said, kicking off dinnertime with his critique of the meal I'd salvaged.

"Me too! What is this stuff, anyway," Hickman said.

If I guessed correctly, it was going to be a long night, beginning with supper. "Watch your mouth, son. This is hash. Corned-beef hash and . . . steamed broccoli. And your mother says there'll be peaches for dessert. That makes a fine Sunday night meal if you ask me."

Hickman rolled his eyes. "Oh, boy. Where's the chess pie Beulah used to make?" He didn't seem to know when to quit.

"That's enough," I said. "And you can plan on washing the dishes after dinner, Hickman. And Maxwell, you can dry them. Tomorrow night Jeff Lee and Alexandra will take a turn. Now, not another word. Your mother and I have things to discuss after we finish here."

Jeff Lee gave me a quick look out of the corner of his eye. He knew better than to let it last more than a second. I scooted my chair away from the table and got up. "I'll be in our room, Gracie."

"No peaches, honey," she asked.

"Thanks," I said. "Not a big appetite tonight." I hadn't had much of one, period. Not since the move from Kentucky, in fact, and even less since yesterday's encounter with Alexandra. But a lie was a lie. I told myself that Alexandra knew better. Or if she didn't, she should.

I went into the bedroom and shut the door, took off my shirt, and waited for Gracie, trying to picture myself as the strong father, the necessary leader, and Godly man she wanted. It's what I promised her, but the changes, new job, and everyone squeezed in close quarters with half the space we were accustomed to made life difficult. The boys seemed to have overnight become small, gangly men. With a little more togetherness than we were prepared to endure—living on one level instead of two—mine and Gracie's sweltering bedroom was bound to melt me tonight before tomorrow's intense work day had the chance.

———— • ————

"First of all, Simon," Gracie began after closing our bedroom door, "Alexandra cannot continue to go over to the trailer park. Apparently, she was over there most of the day on Saturday while I was away. Well, I've seen Mrs. Nightingale's husband. Frankly, he is despicable. There is no telling what that man might do, given half a chance. I've noticed the way he looks at Alexandra, and I'm worried. This is not where we need to be, Simon," she said as the tears began to flow. "We have little more than a postage-stamp yard for the children—"

"Hold on, Gracie," I said. "This was not some fly-by-night decision. I'm paying for the house in Kentucky in case we ever go back there and renting this one at the same time. All I've ever wanted is the best for us. This is the only house I could find. Truth is, we can barely afford this one on top of payments for the one in Murray."

"It's more than that," Gracie stammered. "Our children are exposed to an unsuitable environment. Just look at the influence Mrs. Nightingale is having on Alexandra. That woman is all our daughter talks about. I agreed to this move . . . temporarily."

"So, in your estimation," I blurted, "I've failed as father, provider, and guardian. What else, Gracie? We're not even three weeks into a move that was supposed to—"

"Supposed to what?" Gracie stood her ground. "Alleviate tension? I see nothing but tension, Simon."

I was not happy. I'm sure my face showed it. "We've been here less than three weeks, as I said. Three weeks! That's temporary, alright. Look at what's happened in that amount of time. I've started a demanding job, and there hasn't been a day that you haven't talked about going back to Murray. I desperately need your support, Gracie, not your antagonism. It leaks like a contentious drip. Is that what you want me to do? Sacrifice all I'm trying to do . . . for a house? A better house so we can eat in a dining room, enjoy the comforts of someone to cook and clean, and be with proper people?"

"Look, Simon, "she said, trying to remain calm. "I don't think I need to remind you what I have risen out of, and it had nothing to do with how big or how proud the house was. In the end it had everything to do with believing God had a plan for my life. On the surface, surroundings don't matter, but in truth we are who we associate with."

"What about the fact that I need to start planning for the future," I said, running my long fingers through a headful of graying hair. "College for four children. Does that count for anything?"

"Yes, but what actually happened with Alexandra and the Kool-Aid? She has a broken spirit, Simon. She won't go near you. Is she afraid of you?"

"Nonsense, Gracie. Alexandra lied to me. I sent her to her room. That's it. Are you going to start questioning how I discipline the children?"

"Lower your voice, honey," Gracie said, pulling Kleenex from the box next to the bed. "These are thin walls. She's eight. She adores you and looks up to you. What else can I say? It's up to you to make sure she's not reaching out to the wrong people for the wrong reasons. Moving here required us to abandon what it'd taken thirteen years to build. In essence, we're starting over."

Chapter 11

ALEXANDRA

Without even trying, I heard what Mommy and Daddy had said even though one of them had shut the door to their room. A band of light slipped from underneath it. I pictured thin walls Mommy had mentioned—flimsy, floppy like the paper dolls that fell when I wanted them to stand, and they would not. Maybe the walls were going to fall down.

Living in Tennessee was not feeling like a story with a happy ending. So far, Daddy had been wrong about that. Nothing was the same for any of us in our cramped little house. He walked around in it like a lion trapped in a cage. I could hear him now, across the hall, pacing their bedroom. Mommy didn't want to live in this house.

I closed my door, wanting to make what they said go away. I could put my pretend friends back in the box, but I couldn't make believe I hadn't heard Mommy and Daddy.

I moved the paper dolls off my bed and undressed. Outside my open window, a squirrel or something rustled in the bushes up next to the house. After climbing between the sheets, I listened for the squirrel, not caring what my brothers were doing. I only cared that Mommy was upset with Daddy, and Daddy was upset with me. Everything was quiet except for the hum of lowered voices across the hall.

"I think if we had stayed in Murray a little while longer, Simon, you'd have gotten a better position," Mommy said, her voice muffled.

I fought the urge to get out of bed. Laddie-dog had started to bark; the sheets were scratchy, but I lay still and stared at the ceiling instead, churning the events of the bad Kool-Aid day and my daddy's anger as if they were rocks in an ice-cream maker.

"Who knows what might have happened. This was an opportunity I had to take . . . " Daddy's words sounded far away.

After a while, it was completely dark outside. I could hear Mommy whimpering in the night. At first, I thought I was hearing Laddie-dog— that he was hurt—but it was Mommy telling Daddy she could not live here with so many unwelcome changes.

I poked at my pillow and rolled over. If only I hadn't gone to Dillingham's store . . . and lied, I told myself. This is all my fault.

When I next opened my eyes, it was daylight. Morning seemed to gloss over the events of the night. Bright sun came through my window, and birds sang on the tree limb nearby. Mommy had pulled the shade and opened wide the sash.

"Breakfast soon, honey. Stretch your wings and get out of bed," she said, talking to me over the commotion the boys had already started. "Let's start the week off with a good attitude." She stopped at the doorway and turned to me, "Be sure, honey . . . always pull the shades down. Now, everyone to the table."

I couldn't have guessed there was a bad attitude anywhere in the house or that one had been across the hall from me in the night.

The six of us sat at the table and ate what was put in front of us. Daddy gave us all a peck on the forehead and was out the door. The boys weren't far behind, and as usual, with plans up their sleeves.

Mommy carried the dirty plates to the sink and went to the living room. I finished my glass of milk and got up to leave. I could see her pick up the bowl her friends in Murray had given her as a going-away gift. I stayed back, watching her hold its dainty handles as if it were a gem-covered crown. Before returning it to the coffee table, she ran her fingers over the flowers that were painted inside. I knew it was called French porcelain because she told me so, but it looked like a bowl to me.

Nothing, maybe nothing, was going to console her for the loss of her friends or help her replace the lifestyle she had enjoyed.

"It's pretty, Mommy," I said and waited for her to see my smile. "Do you like Suzette?"

It was worth the push to know the answer. It took only a second to get one. "Of course, I do. Suzette and Mrs. Mullins seem delightful," she said and stroked the bowl one more time. "Yes, the Mullins are a lovely family . . . very gracious of them to invite us to their home. We'll go there Thursday . . . something to look forward to. Isn't it? And we will see them again at church next Sunday. It will be good to make those new friends." She gently placed the dish on the coffee table. "Nice for you to have a little friend your age, and maybe let's leave Mrs. Nightingale for those times when . . . let's just not go over there . . . not so much, anyway.

"Now then, honey, why don't you run on and read your book? School will be starting before we know it," she said, all cheery, "and you'll want to be on top of your reading. I can hardly believe you'll be a third-grader!"

"But Mommy, I told Mrs. Nightingale I could come over this morning. I promised. We are making potholders. I can make one for you!"

"All right, Alexandra, this once, but let's not make a habit of it. Don't make any more promises like that. We'll have to see. And you need to stay outside, honey. Don't go inside Mrs. Nightingale's."

———— • ————

Mrs. Nightingale was nowhere in sight. I bounded up the steps and knocked on the door to her trailer. Laddie-dog waited behind me, panting. Just as I was about to leave, she appeared.

"Child! Oh, my goodness! Let me get my wits about me, and I'll be right out. Don't go away. I'll be out in a jiffy! You just pick out a chair."

I considered which place would be a good one to sit, glad Mrs. Nightingale had not asked me to come inside. I parked myself and waited, then noticed Mommy was looking out the kitchen window. The curtain moved a little. She ducked away.

The door to Mrs. Nightingale's trailer slammed shut behind her and she came shuffling down the stairs.

"My husband is sleeping, child. I couldn't get to the loom, so we can't work on our goods today." She laughed and continued. "How about we just chat. I'm the motor-mouth, but I'll be Miss Zip-lip today so you can talk! How about that?'

We both thought that was funny. She laughed with a little pig snort. It was a perfect start to the afternoon.

"Mrs. Nightingale, does your daddy ever get mad at you," I asked, and she cocked her head. "I mean your husband."

"Of course, of course. And I get mad at him when he says I have to stay right here. I don't always like that. But I guess I don't have anywhere to go anyway. You have somebody mad at you, child?"

I hesitated. "Yes ma'am."

She waited for more information, and when I didn't offer any, she pursed her lips.

"It's just like a dog. Sometimes they growl for no reason. Laddie-dog growling at you?"

"No ma'am. It's my daddy. I-I fibbed to him," I told her, instantly going from giggles to the verge of tears. "He sent me to my room because I was bad. I don't think he likes me anymore because . . . well, lots of other things."

I didn't know how to say how bad I felt, so I left it at that. Mrs. Nightingale sat real still with her soulful eyes looking at me.

"I'm going to Suzette's house Thursday. She's my new friend at church. I like her. My mommy likes her, too," I said, trying not to cry, hoping it would help to talk as much as Mrs. Nightingale did.

"It's okay, child. We do the best we can. Some days the sun shines. Others it don't. I'm seeing the sunshine right now. You must have brought it," she said. "That must mean you're a sunshine child!" Then she smiled. "Your daddy loves you, Miss Sunshine. Don't you forget it."

"I like you, Mrs. Nightingale."

"And I like you," she said.

"I'd better go now."

"Okay. You run home. I understand."

———— • ————

Thursday at 1:05 p.m., Mommy and I were in the Mullins' neighborhood. At least Mommy thought we were.

"Can you read that sign, honey? We are running late," she said, stretching herself over the steering wheel. "Look at it, quickly. Does it say Hawthorne?"

"No ma'am. I think it says—" With effort, I sounded it out. "—Bill . . . ings . . . ly."

If I'd had a magic wand, I would have wished us to turn onto the street we needed. The next block, to our relief, had the welcome name on the sign. Mommy turned the car with a swift jerk.

"Oh, d-deuce!" she exclaimed as the vase of flowers we were taking to the Mullins—filled to the brim with water—dumped into my lap. Keeping an eye on the road, she scratched around inside her purse for a handkerchief and handed it to me, motioning for me to dab at the wetness. "Maybe it'll dry in a hurry," she said. "If not, we'll get you dried off at the Mullins. Can you put the roses back in the vase?"

I had them jammed back in by the time we pulled up to the front of the Mullins' house. Suzette's mother welcomed us. Being late and being wet hadn't made one bit of difference.

"Would you have some tea, Gracie? And, Alexandra, darling," Mrs. Mullins said, "how about some Kool-Aid, or maybe a glass of milk?"

"Milk, please," I said, and a cold chill ran down my back.

"Now then, let's go!" Suzette said once we had our snack. "I want to show you my favorite spot! It's out back! Com' on!"

Suzette and I carried our cookies and drinks outside and found a shady spot to sit and play Chinese checkers. Finally, with the afternoon about gone, we cleaned everything up and headed inside. Our mothers were still talking, but our entrance brought them to their feet.

"Well, this has been lovely," Mommy said to Suzette's mother. "I'm delighted we could get together."

They talked more as we all walked outside and down the sidewalk. Something was said about the flowers and the piano teacher who might be available when the time was right.

On the ride home, after a zillion questions about Suzette, Mommy was satisfied. She turned the car onto our street and slowed down as we passed house after house. "I'll look for her mother at church," she said.

But Suzette and Mrs. Mullins were not at Sunday school the next Sunday and not at church either. Jesus was, though—in the colored glass window just across the aisle—and back a little bit—from where I sat with my family. Being that close to Jesus might have had its rewards if I'd been good, but nothing had changed with my daddy.

I craned my neck to look at Jesus, spellbound by the brilliant morning sunlight that streamed through his robe, making it whiter than white. The blanket over his shoulder blazed red. I stared for as long as I could. When I turned away, I was certain he had not taken his eyes off me.

Following Pastor Owen having said his piece, everybody sang, and the grownups went to the altar to pray. That meant it wouldn't be long before we could leave unless my parents found lots of people to talk to—which they did. It was a chance for me to see for myself the altar that circled the organ at the front of the church. Unable to resist, I made my way down the aisle to have a look.

The wood railing was rubbed satiny smooth from all the people putting their hands on it, and I guessed it would take hundreds of Beulahs rubbing it with rags to make it any smoother. On the back side was a little trough where you could put money. A long velvety pillow with mashed-in buttons was next to the floor to keep a person's knees from being hurt. In the middle of the stage was a table with a white cloth. I could see it was a place for special prayers.

And God, I thought, probably listened up close at that spot—Jesus, too—but I was unsure how the two of them worked that out. All I knew for sure was this: I needed to talk to God, and I needed a setup like that. If I could make an altar, Jesus might listen to me, and Mommy had said she talked to Him about everything.

Before the afternoon was over, I decided to take matters into my own hands.

Chapter 12

ALEXANDRA

Going over to Mrs. Nightingale's on this Sunday afternoon was not as important as building my altar. I poked around the house to see what I could find, beginning with a white towel from the linen cabinet. I went into the bathroom and chose a large one.

The altar needed to be a box or something like a small table. I thought about Hickman's hamster cage, but it had a hamster with it. I thought about climbing the stairs to the attic but couldn't reach the string to pull down the trapdoor. I decided to go to the garage instead.

Underneath some paint cans was an old orange crate. I rousted it, swept off the spiders with a broom, then carried it to a spot inside my closet. Below the clothes rod where my dresses hung was a place safe from the boys. They wouldn't find it and mess it up or make fun of me.

The open space inside was quiet and hidden. With the door partly open I wouldn't be in total darkness. Mine was not exactly like the altar at church, but I laid the towel across it anyway and waited for the right time to talk to God and Jesus. They would be somewhere in the towel.

When that time came, I knelt and put two nickels side by side on my altar. The floor was cold and hard, but I stayed there anyway, praying.

"Dear God . . . Dear God and Jesus. Now I lay me down to sleep . . . I mean, here I am on my knees. My daddy—and I'm pretty sure you know who that is—Mr. Simon Hagan . . . Well, Jesus, I don't think my daddy knows I didn't plan to be bad. If you can use these two nickels to fix him being upset . . . I'll put them right here." I laid them on the towel and continued. "They may not be enough, but right now that's all I have till my next allowance."

I used the corner of the towel to wipe my eyes and keep stuff from dripping from my nose.

"Please, Mr. Jesus-God, I promise not to buy anymore Kool-Aid. I promise not to eat candy. I know it's bad for my teeth, so I'll try harder to be good. Amen for now."

But a few days passed, and I ruined everything. The morning I let it happen had started out as a plain ole day. Laddie-dog ran for the stick, and I waited in the shade of the tree for him to fetch it.

Except for Laddie-dog running and the conversation between my parents drifting outside through the open window, not much else was going on.

"Tied up," Daddy said, and I could see his shadow through the curtain, "her arms strung over her head. Raped. Bludgeoned. The newspaper indicated she's alive . . . didn't give much more information. No suspect yet."

It sounded to me like Mommy gasped.

I perked up, not knowing what any of it meant, and all the while Laddie-dog tugged on the stick that I wouldn't give him. There was something curious about the way Mommy and Daddy talked to each other, so I sat quietly, soaking up the seriousness, straining my ears so I could hear more of the story over Laddie-dog's loud breathing.

"It's hideous," Mommy said, "to think someone could do such a thing, right here in this quiet town! And that evil man is on the loose! We just can't be too careful . . . and I don't want to judge, but Alexandra should not go near that . . . She should never go inside the Nightingales' trailer. What's happened is just the type of awful thing one never knows—"

I could barely hear what Daddy said back to her, only a few words that didn't make sense. Then he raised his voice. "I should be home around six. Have Jeff Lee mow the front yard before I get home."

"Alright, Simon, but it's a hot one already. I have laundry to do all day," she said. "Supper's going to have to be . . . light." Her tone lacked the musical notes that used to accompany the description of her upcoming day at the Wesley Foundation.

Their talk ended, and Mommy's heels clacked across the floor. The very next moment she was at the back door calling me.

With Laddie-dog in the lead, we ran around the corner of the house and jumped the one step up to the concrete stoop. There was barely enough room for both of us. I pushed him away and went inside where Mommy stood beside the doorway.

Daddy gave her a kiss on the forehead, then turned to me. "You're keeping Laddie out of the street, aren't you? That's a big job," he said. "Stay out of trouble. I'll see you this evening."

Stay out of trouble. Daddy's words scraped like the sound of carrots being pushed on the grater. Getting into trouble had not crossed my mind. All I wanted was to outside and give Laddie-dog some water. Laddie-dog wanted to play with a stick instead. That wasn't trouble. Was it?

By the time I answered Daddy with my head nodding yes, he was gone. I turned my attention elsewhere. "Can I have something to eat?"

"May I, honey," Mommy said. "How about some oatmeal? You can still play outside. I just want to know where you are."

"I don't really want oatmeal. It's so hot . . . May I go over to see Mrs. Nightingale?"

"Humm. Not now, Alexandra. It's too early. There are lots of other things you could do. How about some orange juice?"

"Okay. Orange juice. Like what? I don't have anything to do, and the boys won't play with me."

"You're a smart girl. You can think up something, I'm sure. Stay in the yard, though. No trips to Dillingham's."

"Is there an evil man, Mommy?"

"What on earth are you talking about?"

"Is there an evil man?"

"Alexandra, I don't think you need to worry about such things. Now, drink this juice and maybe play with your paper dolls. Pick out one or two to take to Suzette's for when we go there tomorrow."

"Ugh! Paper dolls are boring," I said and headed to my room.

"Don't say boring, honey."

If she told me why not, I didn't hear, and copying what I heard or saw grownups do was, at times, enough to keep me from being . . . bored. Paper dolls were not.

Having a plan in mind, I went to my closet. If copying adults didn't work, my own inventions would, and my interest was fully sparked by the icky-sounding story of the evil man raking the girl. I tried to unscramble the bits and pieces of it, like another Nancy Drew mystery book. I pictured what it would be like if my arms were tied over my head and someone raked me. "A curious use of a rake," I said aloud.

With a reckless sweep, I removed the white towel from my altar, dismissing its meaning as though it never existed. Nickels fell and rolled across the floor.

I ignored the pang of regret that surfaced when the orange crate's worn label stared back at me from the spot where I had knelt to talk to God, but I stepped high upon the crate anyway and regained my balance. The thin slats creaked under my weight. I waited a minute to see what would happen. When nothing did, I raised up on tiptoes and tied one end of the towel to the clothes rod next to my dresses. It dangled there, limp and unexciting, so I pushed the dresses as far back as I could without falling off the crate, giving myself some space to hold my arms over my head and hang onto the towel. I hung there, expecting inspiration.

Nothing.

I let go of the towel and stood alone on the old, dirty orange crate that had been my altar. It was once more just a box with the faded face of a genie holding his armload of fruit. Everything felt wrong. I fought back tears. In the emptiness that followed, shame began to stir inside me.

For this, I had ended my connection to God.

I stepped down off the crate and picked up the nickels. Spreading the towel back over its splintery corners would not restore my place to talk with God. All that was left were the reminders of forbidden sugar, and the lie I had told my daddy, and the altar I had ruined.

Like a swarm of pesky flies, they would not go away. I took the towel to the laundry hamper and dropped it inside.

———— • ————

Mommy was in the backyard pinning Daddy's wet shirts on the clothesline when I went outside. Mrs. Nightingale was sitting in her yard in her wide chair, its back to a big tree.

"May I go over to see Mrs. Nightingale?" I hollered across in the direction of my friend, and Mommy looked up from the bag of clothespins.

It was a loud question. Mrs. Nightingale poked her head around the side of the chair.

"Of course, Alexandra," Mommy said, then turned toward the trailer park. "Oh, hello, Mrs. Nightingale . . . I think you're going to get a little visitor."

Mrs. Nightingale was all smiles. "Wonderful!" she sang out at the top of her lungs.

I was there before she could get up, seating myself next to her underneath the long, leafy arms of her huge tree.

"Why, hello, sunshine." She reached across and gave my hand a happy pat.

"I'm not really sun-shine," I said and dropped my chin on my chest.

"No? And what makes you say that?"

"Sunshine is nice," I told her.

"And?"

Wriggling to the edge of my chair, I looked over to see if Mommy was watching. Satisfied that she was busy with the laundry, I turned to Mrs. Nightingale. "Do you talk to God?"

"Sometimes I do. Yes, I do. How about you? You been talking to God?"

"I used to. Not anymore. I don't have my altar. So not now . . . except at bedtime when I say, 'Now I lay me down to sleep.'" I kicked at the dirt under my foot. "I need a grownup to talk to God about my daddy. Could you? Have him tell my daddy I'll try to stay out of trouble."

"Oh, sweetheart. I don't know for sure, but I don't think God does things like that. Why don't you talk to your daddy?"

"He's still mad at me. That's why . . . Have you heard about the evil man on the loose?

"Why, no, I haven't," Mrs. Nightingale said. "What evil man?"

I told her what I knew, ending with, "Yes! He raked her! Doesn't that sound really, really mean?"

"You-hoo! Alexandra! Come on home, honey. I need your help." Mommy was standing in the driveway, laundry basket in hand.

"I'm coming," I said and slowly scooted off the chair's edge. It was so hot outdoors that the back of my legs almost stuck to the chair.

An August sun was high in the sky. It beamed off the metal roof of the shoe factory in the distance and beat down on the yellowing grass. Mommy hung the last of the shirts on the line while I held the basket for her. Then I was free to go.

"Fix yourself a sandwich, honey. I'm going to pull a few weeds, and I'll be in."

It was even hotter in the kitchen, so I took my bologna sandwich out to the side of the house and sat cross-legged in the shade next to the water spigot. Laddie-dog came and sat beside me with his tongue hanging out. The drip of water in his bowl made both of us cooler.

Daddy was busy at work. The boys were busy complaining. Mommy was just plain busy. The sound of the mower in the front yard drowned out everything but my thoughts.

"Don't you think it's time we addressed some things," Mommy had said to Daddy. "I need some help. I'm at home with the children and cooking . . . laundry . . ."

Thinking back on their every word, I pulled the crust off the bread and dropped it for Laddie-dog.

"You know we can't afford someone like Beulah. Give it some time. We'll just have to do the best we can for now."

"Maybe one day a week . . . some help with the cleaning and cooking. I'm not used to this, Simon. I didn't expect it. School starts the week after next. I've applied to the high school. There are surely some substitute teaching jobs."

"Oh? And you would be home when the children get home?"

"Of course. You know as well as I do, Simon, I'm not leaving Alexandra here with that man around."

It wasn't clear to me if she was talking about Mr. Nightingale or the evil man.

I looked across the yard at my red wagon, upside down in the dirt. For now, it was okay there since Mrs. Nightingale and I were through making potholders. The wagon was of no use. I missed the days when it had been.

"Sunshine, take the ones you've made through the park," Mrs. Nightingale had said. "Take them in your wagon. See if old Mrs. Merkel doesn't need one or two more. She's probably already set fire to the others—" And Mrs. Nightingale had laughed out loud before she could finish saying it: "—the ones she bought the other day!"

When I laughed with her, she laughed even more as we sat and made potholder after potholder until all the yarns were used. Then she said she had figured out a way to get us some more.

Everything about me, from the potholders I made to Laddie-dog and our game of stick, pleasured her. Everything caused her to smile, from the stories I read with her to the piano recital dress I peeled from its storage box to model for her.

But piano recitals weren't happening since we'd moved to Tennessee. Even though Mommy said we'd start piano lessons again, the dress was useless and plain. I imagined safety-pinning rhinestones to the layers of netting so it would shimmer like it was diamond covered. And I imagined making it a dress a princess would wear.

Mrs. Nightingale hadn't seemed to care if it shimmered or not, but Mommy wanted a princess. She wanted her house in Murray with flowers on the wallpaper, crisp curtains at the windows, a dining room with cupboards to display her china, and a maid. Instead, she was stuck in our plain vanilla house.

I could have easily taken my Buster Brown shoe box and made a pretend house for my tiny toys, making it look a lot like our house, but I wasn't in the mood. There wasn't much point. A silly, pretend house was not needed to remind any of us of the beauty Mommy was missing—no screened porch, no fireplace, no hilly yard, no lily of the valley. Joy seemed lost in everyday rumples, like the ones in Beulah's apron after she made a mess of it, wadding it up when she dried her hands on its front side. I could still see her whisking the rumples away with slow, easy strokes from her bony hands, and when they were gone, she breathed a little easier.

"I can't do this without you, Gracie," Daddy had said, and I wondered if he needed to be able to breathe a little easier, too.

Chapter 13

September and the fuss over the first day of school had my brothers and me zipping around, giving orders to each other, clamoring to get into the bathroom, stuffing down breakfast.

"Breakfast is important to a good day, so I want you to take your time and eat it," Mommy said. "Then be sure you brush your teeth."

None of us were inclined to skip teeth-brushing since not brushing was sure to be a handy fact one or all of the other siblings could use for tattling. But this morning we all brushed without the usual glares back and forth over mouthfuls of frothy toothpaste. Hickman was the first out the door to the yard's edge to wait for the bus. I was right behind. Then Maxwell, followed by Jeff Lee who got there just in time before the driver left without him.

I was already looking for Suzette as the bus pulled to a stop in front of the school. Beginning the third grade was the second-best thing happening to me—Mrs. Nightingale was still the first-best.

Without yarn to make potholders, all Mrs. Nightingale and I could do was snap beans and talk about stories from my Nancy Drew books—or God, and she wasn't long on answers about God. Talking about the evil man was a subject she didn't have much to say about either.

Even when her husband wanted me to come inside their trailer to see something he wanted to show me, Jeff Lee had shown up out of nowhere to stop me. So summer's days had started to drag in the four weeks that had passed since our move from Kentucky to Tennessee.

"Alexandra! Alexandra!" Suzette ran toward me from the schoolyard, yelling as I stepped off the bus. Her familiar voice was the one I wanted to hear above the background of new people buzzing like bees in a Mason jar, but in the days to follow the newness faded quicker than leaves on the trees.

School took over and reshaped my days. The boys did homework in their room, and I did mine on the kitchen table. Without any of us around, Laddie-dog often strayed into the street; we had to start tying him up.

"We're going to find a new home for Laddie," Daddy said at suppertime when the first week of school was ending. "He's a nuisance. Cars have to stop and make him get out of the way. It's a shame he's got to be tied up all the time. The dog will be better off and happier on a farm where he can roam around."

My heart stopped, I thought, and a fork-full of fried Spam stuck in my throat. Gagging, I took a gulp of milk to force it down.

Everyone at the table continued eating, ignoring me. I couldn't look Daddy in the eye; instead, I spied his face through my glass of half-finished milk, crooked and bent, and his ears might have been upside down. Everywhere that my glass had twists, his face had them, too.

I set my glass back on the table and took my plate to the sink. Daddy was wrong. Laddie-dog would die without me.

I walked to my room, and in my head, a painful quiet was lasting forever. The daddy who had carried me on his shoulders through crowded parades and held my hand so nothing would hurt me, and shielded me from a big brother's teasing, and offered me endless measures of goodness in a single cone of cream at the old man's store on the way to Papa Jeff's—that daddy was gone.

In front of the bathroom mirror on that awful day, my lie changed everything. Like holding a twisted glass between us, Daddy hadn't looked the same since, and I couldn't fix the crooked picture of him in my head any more than I could put Humpty-Dumpty back together again.

Daddy didn't say anything about my lie or the Kool-Aid. I guessed he didn't want me to either. It was only Mrs. Nightingale who mentioned it from time to time.

"Sunshine," she'd said. "I would feel better if you and your daddy patched things up. He's probably really busy with his new job . . . and that's why he doesn't have time for much else. He's got a lot on his mind, I'll bet'ya."

"Yes ma'am. I know," I'd answered, and another walnut had dropped from the limb that hung over my chair.

"We aren't gonna be able to sit out here much longer. Those things'll get us," she said and waved her hands up at the huge tree above us.

I sat with my hands in my lap and said, "I know."

"Guess I should be ready for cold weather—hot as it's been! But what are we gonna do about our little get-togethers?"

"No, ma'am, we can't sit our here, and I sold all the potholders. I don't have any more people to sell them to," I said.

"Well, I'm so proud of you. When the chance comes, we'll get us some more yarns. You might wanna pick the colors yourself. But then again, they're cheaper if you get a whole, big bag of colors someone else has done picked. We'll just have to wait and see."

It didn't matter that no one had gotten around to buying more yarns. We had plenty to talk about without them. Mrs. Nightingale did, at least.

I didn't have an idea what we were going to do about our get-togethers, and when autumn brought a downpour of walnuts from the big tree, I didn't see much of her. Day after day her chair sat empty, and the walnuts bombarded it. She waved from the window, came outside, and stood on the trailer's platform long enough to give me a hug and see how I was doing in school, but the chill in the air sent her back inside, and I didn't dare go with her.

I picked up a stick on the way home, wishing Laddie-dog could be there to fetch it.

———— • ————

SIMON

Another November day was drawing to an end. Gracie's and my bedroom was darkened. Unnoticed, I slipped in and hesitated by the bed, then knelt and clasped my head in my hands.

"Lord God," I whispered, "where else can I turn but to You? It's time to make this move permanent—this town, this job. But I desperately need your wisdom and clear direction. It's been almost four months . . . time enough to feel it was a right move. I promised good would come out of it, a promise that very well may include selling the house in Murray. I hate it for Gracie . . . but selling it would enable us to move to a safer neighborhood. I can't continue the upkeep on two houses. Not indefinitely. Finances are killing me. I haven't put a red cent in the bank.

"I'm only a man. I want to do Your will, but it's hard to see Your plan. The transitions's been hard for us all . . . hard on Gracie and hard on the children. Is it ever gonna smooth out? We could've stayed in Murray, Lord, but I was so sure, and now I'm not. I need Your help to guide my family. This turmoil . . . I didn't expect it, and not this move into utter uncertainty. Was it a mistake? How can I have lost my way so soon? Was it pure selfishness? Me?"

The room was way too quiet, only the tick-tock of the Westclox on the bedside table. Shifting on my knees, I lifted my face, waiting for . . . what. I didn't know. Even to hear myself breathe was a relief.

"I thought this move was bringing us to a better place," I said aloud. "If it was selfish, I'll take full responsibility for having put us in harm's way . . . bringing us into this neighborhood. But I could never forgive myself if something happened—

As if I'd waited long enough or needed to push myself into immediate action as the protector, I got to my feet as a sliver of light vanished past the length of the bedroom door. "God in Heaven," I said, "I need to know the next right step. Stop me if I'm wrong. The decision's not mine alone; I'll talk with Gracie. Ultimately, Lord, it rests with You."

Chapter 14

ALEXANDRA

I did not still believe in Santa Claus even though I wanted to. A mere turn of the page on the calendar from November to December made me wish I could, and the unwanted telephone call for Daddy from Uncle Raymond made me want to go at least one more time to Papa Jeff's farm in Elkton. But he had died in the night. The news of his father's death hit Daddy hard.

We rode to Elkton in near silence and reached Papa Jeff's property. Our tires bump-bumped across cattleguards on the narrow dirt road. Nothing was discussed how the cows came and went or whether or not they would break a leg if they stepped into the spaces between the bars. The way my older brothers and I would have argued about it on normal trips to his farm was left unsaid. This trip was different. One brother didn't agitate the other, and sideways looks didn't rile them.

The closer we got to the house with the butterscotch stone pillars, the more I remembered our last visit when I had skipped along beside him, filled with suspense for what he had in store. His smile was an ancient one, wrinkled and a little bit tired, and his ruddy old pants and open-collar shirt were unlike anything Daddy would wear. Under his brimmed straw hat was a crop of wavy white hair with bushy eyebrows to match. They jutted out like wires, making his eyeballs look deep and scary—but he was not.

"There, baby," he'd said to me, pointing a feeble finger toward the milking barn off in the distance. "We'll go in there."

So I had run after him that day, past the hay barn that sat near the wooden gate and beyond to where the cows stood in rows. The animals chewed the hay, and their milk spurted into waiting containers with a rhythmic squirt and pump, squirt and pump.

"What's that on his titty, Papa Jeff?" I didn't think the question sounded right the minute I'd asked it.

"It's a milking machine, and she is a female cow, so she is a she," he said with a nice calmness. "This is a teat. Remember that. It's a teat and not what you said. Did you want to try some fresh milk?"

I had nodded in agreement and sipped the warm milk from a cup. It smelled odd and didn't taste nearly as good as the cold milk I drank from the refrigerator at home, so I handed the cup back to him, and we had kept on walking until we got to his truck. He let me sit close beside him as he drove to the stables where the horses slept and to the other side of the stables to a church nestled among tall pine trees.

"I helped build this church. It's a special place—a place where you learn the good that God has planned for you. You go to church, don't you, baby?"

"Yes, sir," I said, "but we had to leave early last Sunday before we spoke to Pastor Owen 'cause Jeff Lee did something he wasn't supposed to, and Daddy told him he was going to take a belt to him." I chattered as fast as I could, recounting the appalling specifics of Jeff Lee's big bad; then I took a deep breath and began again. "Jeff Lee ran home and got there before we did and put a pillow in his pants' bottom. And Daddy kept shaking his head when he saw it and didn't even spank him, Papa Jeff!"

Papa Jeff laughed out loud. It was okay to laugh. So on that day we had laughed together as we rode on down the bumpy road in his old, red truck.

"Your daddy's a good man. Does what's right. I like that story, honey. How's about I tell you one?"

"Yes, sir," I said in a little-girl voice, and he'd told me a long, long story about a boy and his boat.

But today Papas Jeff's house was washed out in the setting sun, and somber faces on tall, thin men came down the steps to greet my daddy. Our car pulled to a halt.

Daddy got out before the rest of us. Another car came and pulled in behind us.

I recognized Pastor Owen from our new church. We hadn't known him very long, but there he was. He walked over to my daddy and lifted his elfish arms up as high as he could so they could hug each other. It looked like Daddy might pick him up, the way he would a child, but instead, he reached for his hanky. When they backed away from each other, both had hankies. Tears were rolling down over their cheeks.

Uncles surrounded us; aunts and cousins were everywhere. Handshakes stretched into awkward hugs, and tears were quickly brushed away.

It was later in the day before I saw Papa Jeff. He looked as though he might at any moment break into his gentle smile as he lay there in the big, silky box. I knew, though, he was not about to move. His wrinkles were gone; his hands were folded across his chest. Everyone seemed pleased to see how peaceful he looked.

An endless line of cars with little flags rode away from the church after he was loaded into the long black car parked outside. I'd never seen so many people in one place, and we all motored slowly to the cemetery, first passing the courthouse in the town square as its bell gonged.

Daddy's car came to a stop close to a big, gray stone with HAGAN in raised letters. We eased out and walked to a tent raised over the stone.

The preacher talked, and I stood, stiff as a board under the tent, reading the name on a small marker beneath my patent leather shoes. Alan Geoffrey Hagan was the top line, then some numbers I couldn't read because they were covered in mud. I was about to squat so I could get a better look when Mommy cleared her throat and aimed her look directly at me. I knew I was doing something wrong, so I stayed stiff. Pastor Owen smiled at me, acknowledging my dilemma. Afterward, my mother wiped away some tears with a gloved finger, then hung on Daddy's arm as we walked back to the car.

The cemetery was kind of scary. I was glad to be leaving. No one said anything until Mommy broke the silence.

"Simon, could we ride out to Hillbound? It's been so long since we've seen Henry . . . simply say hello? It could be as quick as that. Since we're here and Henry—"

She stopped before completely choking on her words. Daddy gave her a sympathetic nod but said nothing. His personal grief seemed deep enough.

"We're so close. Let's stop by for a minute. I suspect Henry will be there."

———— • ————

Mommy was right. Someone was home at Hillbound, but nothing was mentioned about all of us piling inside to see if it was Uncle Henry. Only Mommy went.

She walked up to the house, stepping here and there on some broken pieces of flat rocks, trying not to fall.

Uncle Henry didn't answer the door at first, but then it opened. Mommy gave a ta-ta wave to us from the door and followed Uncle Henry inside.

The rest of us got out of the car. I sat on a tree stump, and the boys chased each other around. Daddy leaned on the fence, took a pack of cigarettes out of his pocket, and hit the end of it with his knuckle. He took one and lit it.

"Don't mess up your good clothes, boys. Just take it easy," he said, puffing curls of smoke into the cold-ish air.

He was lighting up another by the time Mommy came walking out. She and Uncle Henry stood at the gate and talked. We waited.

The boys must have been thinking up ways to irritate each other. Daddy gave them a don't-go-too-far-with-it look and slid into the car. With the door still open, he turned on the motor, then the heat and the radio. "Want to get inside where it's warm, Alexandra?"

I climbed in next to him in time to hear a man talking on the radio: "Detroit Lions in a knock-out win! Seventeen to sixteen over the Cleveland Browns!"

As far as I'd seen, it was Daddy's only smile all day. He flicked off the radio. It seemed like forever before we were all packed in and on the way home. Mommy was quiet.

As he drove down the lane, I thought back to being at Uncle Henry's last Thanksgiving when I had ridden out with Mommy to Hillbound. I remembered how freezing cold it was inside and how Uncle Henry had given my mother a hug, then led her through the hallway and into a large room. There wasn't much light, so I was close behind. I couldn't see very well where I was walking, but for sure I could see Uncle Henry's two little boys.

"You remember your cousins, Alexandra," Mommy said, "and they have a new baby sister named Madeleine!"

Richard and Sonny were playing with some empty thread spools on the floor in front of the open fire. Aunt Rose was sitting there too, holding the baby, and I went over to take a look. My cousins didn't pay any attention to their mother nursing their sister, but I sure did. Mommy kept trying to hide Aunt Rose because she didn't have any clothes on her top parts. They were the size of cantaloupes and about the same color.

Mommy suggested I might want to play someplace else.

Uncle Henry didn't say anything—not why the big room served as their whole house or why it had a bed against one wall and a mattress on the floor in the far corner.

Because Mommy kept after me, I wandered out into the great hall where we had come inside. It was spooky, cold, and dark. I started to explore it anyway. There were other rooms, but they were empty, and an upstairs, but I didn't dare go up. Instead, I had tried to open the tall door on the other side of the hallway from where everybody was. It started to fall toward me, and I could feel its weight pressing against my arms. It would have squashed me like a bug if Uncle Henry had not been right there to rescue me. I hadn't even needed to cry out. He just suddenly appeared out of nowhere.

"Let me help you, honey," he'd said, moving swiftly to catch the mass of wood.

I jumped to one side and hunkered down in fear while he wrestled with the door. Both his arms were spread wide around it like eagle's wings I'd seen in a picture, and he leaned it upright over the dark opening to the empty space.

Finished, he whisked his hands together to get rid of the dirt and gave my shoulder a squeeze. "That was a close one. Wasn't it, honey? It's all right, though. What d'ya say, let's go back in yonder," and he pointed the way.

I had followed him back into the warm room. Aunt Rose had quit nursing Madeleine. There wasn't anything else as interesting as that had been, so I sat quietly until Mommy said we should be going.

"Now, Henry," Mommy said, opening her purse, "I am concerned about that cough. Will you please take this and see a doctor?"

Uncle Henry frowned as she tried to give him some money.

"No, Gracie. Thanks all the same. It's just a nasty tickle. It'll give way here 'fore too long. Don't you worry."

"Well, take this anyway. It's not much, but I want you to have it. I insist. It's a gift for Madeleine. She is a beautiful child, Henry."

"Thank you," he said and followed up with a sad smile.

And then we left. It had been a long time since I'd seen Uncle Henry's smile. Today I'd not even seen him, and Mommy was in and out of his house without mentioning why we could not stay.

I laid my head on Daddy's shoulder, wondering aloud: "Daddy, does Uncle Henry still have Baby Madeleine?"

"Of course, he does. She's what, Gracie, about a year and a half. Why do you ask?"

Mommy was staring out the window. "It was once a glorious place, Alexandra. You would've loved the peacocks that strolled in the yard and the flowers that bloomed in the meadow. And when I was your age, honey, I had a room upstairs with a fireplace . . . a wonderful home." She pointed to the window at the end of the house as we drove past Hillbound.

The boys sighed in unison in the backseat and soon fell asleep.

"Simon, do you think Henry will succumb to the moral decay?" Mommy was lost in thought. Her question seemed to arch over my head like a ball I was too short to catch.

"Let's discuss it later, Gracie." Daddy lit a cigarette and rolled down the window just enough to let some smoke move out the crack at the top.

"What does see-come mean," I asked, needing some answers. "And why couldn't we see Madeleine?"

"Shhhh, Alexandra," Daddy said.

It was late and very dark when we pulled into the garage, back at home in Gallatin. The day had been a long one.

———— • ————

"Gracie, did you see the headlines? Looks like they got him," Daddy said across the supper table. "Humph! Wasn't that character next door, at least."

The newspaper didn't interest me. And the headlines didn't, so when Daddy spoke, I finished the last bite of my toast and made a face at Hickman; it included blackberry jam on my tongue. My youngest brother returned the face.

"That's enough, you two," Mommy said. "Eat your food and get ready for school. Got whom, Simon?"

Daddy looked up at her as if she had two heads and took another sip of coffee. He didn't answer.

"Uhm. Oh, oh. Yes, well, isn't it a nice day today? Simon, why don't we talk about this later? Now then, children, off. Off, if you're finished."

"That's wonderful. Let me see what it says about him. There couldn't be a better Christmas gift for this town," she said to Daddy as I trooped away. "We can all sleep better now!"

They weren't talking about Santa Claus. That much I knew. It must be the evil man. I'd almost forgotten him. Being reminded of the whole episode that had cost me my special talking-place with Jesus made me shudder. It didn't help that my winter coat was hanging over the spot in my closet where the orange crate had sat. I grabbed one of its wooly arms until the whole coat came with it and ran.

The school bus rolled up out front. Voices and laugher came from inside, louder than usual. No one was talking about homework or tests. With only two days remaining until Christmas break, the excitement had taken over. It was all about class parties, traveling to see grandparents, hope for snow, bikes and balls and games, and the other things on everybody's list. Roller skates were on mine.

With no guarantees, it was another wait-and-see kind of situation, but surely Daddy was still planning to take me to the store tonight. The pink glittery hairbrush I'd picked out at the five-and-dime for Suzette was waiting for my last payment on layaway. If all went according to plan, I would ride after supper with Daddy to get it. He would buy tins of Leo stick candy for all the aunts and uncles, then drop me off and wait while I went inside for the hairbrush.

I had forgotten we also needed to drop Mommy at church for Wednesday night's prayer meeting.

She mentioned it after school. "You'll need to take out the trash, Alexandra, and fold your clothes before I give you your allowance. Supper is early since we have a big itinerary. Your father's taking you with him while I go to my prayer meeting. When he gets in, we'll eat right away. So please set the table after you finish your other chores. How was school today?"

"It was fine. My teacher got some Christmas gifts from students. Do I get to take her something?"

"That's a lovely thought. Maybe you can ask your father to help you choose something."

"We're not really going shopping, Mommy. He said he would drop me off at the dime store and let me run in."

"Well, let me get you a dollar. You take an extra minute and get something you think Miss Perkins would like. Maybe a pretty handkerchief. That would make a wonderful gift!"

The thought of spending all that time in the car with Daddy had me wondering what we would talk about.

"Ready to go, Gracie? Button up, Alexandra," he said when the time came. "It's cold as rip out there. Ladies: in the car. Boys: behave while we're gone. We'll be back in an hour or so."

The church wasn't far away. Mommy hopped out, shut the car door, and waved to us as Daddy drove off.

"I'm going to find a parking place, hopefully in front of the store, and go in with you," he said. "You can help me find a little something for Bertha. She's been a big help for your mother. Then we'll swing by Dillingham's and get stick candy for your aunts and uncles. How does that sound?"

It sounded scary. Going past or even going close to Dillingham's wasn't something I wanted to do. Not now, not ever.

"It's okay, I guess. Are we going to see Aunt Millicent during Christmas . . . give her the candy?"

"Not this year. No, we're going to be at home, the six of us. It will be good to have our own traditions, at least for now. Who knows about next year? I'm mailing the candy in the morning, so everybody will have it in time for Christmas."

"I miss Papa Jeff," I said, looking out the window at the red lights strung across Main Street. "Do you think he's in Heaven?"

I knew better than to bring up Papa Jeff or Daddy's old home place. He hadn't said much about Papa Jeff lately. The mention of either seemed to make him sad. But I'd already done it.

"He's in Heaven, you bet. Your Papa Jeff's life is a story with a happy ending. That's one fact I do know."

Chapter 15

Mrs. Nightingale waved from her window for me to come up the steps to her trailer. She opened the door, motioning me inside. "I'd better not, Mrs. Nightingale. Is everything all right?"

"Sunshine, we're moving. In less than a month," she gasped aloud. "By the first of February. Are you sure you can't come inside for a minute? But I don't want to get you in trouble. Tell you what: I'll dig out my heavy coat. We'll go for a walk . . . a short one."

As we walked, I found out Mrs. Nightingale's move was not going to be to another trailer in the park next to me and not across town. She and Mr. Nightingale were going to move to Knoxville, miles and miles away.

When January twenty-ninth came, boxes were hauled out of her trailer and stacked on the picnic table while two men loaded a few chairs and other stuff onto their truck. Then they came for the table and chairs where Mrs. Nightingale and I had sat for hours.

"Step to one side," the mover said to me and flicked his cigarette toward my driveway. "Ralph, grab some of these boxes, and we'll wind up here."

It was too cold to wait outside her trailer any longer, and the school bus was due any minute. I went up the platform and stood at her door.

"Mrs. Nightingale," I called, "I really have to go."

She shuffled outside as quickly as she could to where I stood, her arms open wider than the door itself. She was too large for me to get mine around, but that didn't keep me from trying. Afterward, I climbed on the bus and sat by myself, thinking of all the times I'd played in her yard, romped with Laddie-dog, and chased his ball across the platform in front of her trailer.

The move to Knoxville would take her too far away from Gallatin for me to think I would ever visit her again.

In the weeks ahead, crocus popped out of the ground close to where her chair had sat.

———— • ————

The sweet smell of flowers floated past me on a soft breeze. Skipping from one side of the walkway to the other and past a row of bushes, I pranced toward the open door of the school, then stopped abruptly before crossing the threshold, halting as if someone had snatched me by the nape of my neck. A little voice inside reminded me there was no running or prancing in school. I knew that. Everyone knew that. Knowing it took me from my blissful daydream.

CAMDEN ELEMENTARY was etched in the concrete lintel over the double doors, defining the hallowed entrance. It had been there all along, but now it implied seriousness.

I slowed down and walked obediently toward the doorway in case God or Jesus might be watching. Pleasing them was every bit as important as pleasing Daddy.

"School means buckling down, Alexandra," Daddy had said.

"You were such an excellent little student in second grade, honey. The work is not that much more difficult in third. You can do it if you try harder," Mommy had said.

The more I thought of Mrs. Nightingale, the more I wondered how things would be if she still lived nearby. She wouldn't scold me if I could not satisfy everyone's expectations, and if she had been the one to see my report card, she would have laid it on her outdoor table and gone in and fixed us some lemonade.

But Mommy had frowned. "'Needs Improvement.' NI. That means you will have to do better, honey. Work harder. Do you understand, Alexandra Elizabeth?"

Work hard. Try harder—in one ear and out the other.

I pushed on up the one remaining step and avoided the gaping crevice that stared back at me, proud that I was not stepping on a crack because that would break my mother's back. I didn't want to do that. I wanted to please, but sometimes it was hard.

Unused books lay in the crook of my arm. Lately they hadn't held the attraction they once did, and I had not been studying them. School was all about expectations, and I was not measuring up. Pleasing everybody was bound to require redoubling my efforts, so the very least I could do was walk quietly and not run through the hallway. That much I could do.

Where Jesus was concerned, I wasn't sure what it was going to take. My altar attempt, wanting to please Him, had started out good but ended badly.

Sunlight streamed through the huge window above the wide staircase. Its brightness loomed over me like an enormous ball of fire, and the shiny waxed floor looked like a glistening lake on the cover of a magazine. After several steps, I reached the landing beneath the window and stopped. Other students pushed past me. Suzette ran on ahead, too, yelling at me to hurry up.

Whatever it was that Daddy had promised in Tennessee, I was still waiting for it. Except for weekends at home, he was gone to towns all over, doing his job.

I felt the dead end, unable to go up the next few steps to my third-grade classroom, and the last bell sounded before I made it up the half-flight of stairs and past the landing. I hoped the teacher would not notice I was late, but she saw me through the door's window panes. The door opened wide for me to enter while everyone turned to look at me.

I took a seat, determined to stop any more fuss over my predicament, then tucked my books beneath my desk, saving one: Geography for the Third Grader. I flipped it to page 84.

———— • ————

"We can start looking for a house somewhere over by the high school," Daddy said at the supper table.

The announcement seemed to me like it had come out of nowhere.

Mommy wasn't surprised. "Yes," she agreed, sounding enthusiastic. "We are officially Galla-tonians! This is a wonderful place to call home. You'll all graduate from Gallatin High and maybe go on to the University of Tennessee, maybe on to medical school. Who knows what's in store?"

"Now, now, simmer down, Gracie," Daddy said with a grin. "You'll have them being Mr. President and Dr. Hagan before we're finished with dinner."

I'd almost forgotten he could smile. He faced me, and after a pause, lifted his iced tea glass high in the air. "Here's to you," he said with a soft gaze that once went hand-in-hand with calling me Sweet Pea.

I hadn't seen the gaze or heard the name in a very long time. Everybody eyeballed me, wanting a reason to laugh.

No sooner had I decided smiles all around felt good when the boys began to complain, starting with Jeff Lee. "Well, I sure don't wanna be a dentist and have to look in people's mouth all day."

"Mouths, Jeff Lee," Mommy said.

"It's got to have a fireplace," she continued. "The new place has to have a fireplace, Simon."

It was June. A fireplace didn't sound right to me.

"Y'all can call me 'Dr. Hagan.' I'll be a brain surgeon," Maxwell said.

"Okay, okay, we have plenty of doctors at the table, thank you very much. And one order for a fireplace. How about we finish up here and go out for a root beer float . . . to celebrate?" Daddy had a big grin that beamed through his suggestion.

There was relief in the air that could've been like Beulah's rumple-free apron. Just as simple as that, everything was better with the rumples gone.

Daddy whistled a tune as we inched toward the front of a house he'd read about in the newspaper.

It was boxy with a brown, flat-ish roof and a round chimney. The house wasn't pretty to me; I didn't think Mommy thought so either. A shiny metal tank was propped up on wood stilts underneath the window. We stopped at the curb.

"This one has a fireplace, Gracie," he said with a proud air. "Given the inheritance from Dad, I believe we're in a position to buy it."

With the mention of Papa Jeff, I felt a splintery pang. Daddy looked like he'd felt it, too.

Mommy shot him a sour face before her head snapped away with not so much as a second look at the house.

"Simon," she said in a toned-down voice, "I will not live here, and that's that."

All I knew was this: the mood went downhill. Daddy had flubbed up. From where I was, sitting in the back of the car, I knew he deserved to be rescued. His whistling ended, and our car sprinted from the curb like a checkered flag had been waved. The next house had to be better. Decidedly, it must not border a trailer park.

It didn't.

"This does look nice. The boys could walk to the high school. And later, Alexandra, you too," Mommy said, turning toward me to see if that might've struck a chord.

I had managed to pass the third grade, but that's all. High school might not even happen, I thought. "Yes, ma'am. It looks nice."

The house was not in any way similar to our small one that sat next door to Mrs. Nightingale's trailer on Murphy Street. It was better, even without a fireplace, maybe because her old piano from Hillbound could fit inside.

Our search had been on a Saturday morning in July, and by August we were packing boxes. I watched on moving day as the orange crate was pitched to the trash heap. No one made a big deal about it. No one besides me knew I had once shared it with God. Putting the towel back on it had not restored the altar to a place where I could talk to Him. Shame resided there instead. That's when lies had started to look like truth.

———— • ————

In a matter of a few short years, not only had the fossil plant become Gallatin Steam Plant with three units in operation and number four set to open in August, but also Daddy's job had mushroomed. We'd moved to yet another house, one that Mommy had her heart set on, and the fallout from his decision to stay in Gallatin was a rumple of the past; but like the wind, something rocked the boat.

It was more than a ripple. By early spring of 1959, he was traveling a lot—to and from East Tennessee as Personnel Manager for Tennessee Valley Authority.

If what I was hearing in the undercurrent, we were moving again.

"That's right. Things don't stay the same," Daddy said. "And I'm turning over a new leaf. No more of this traveling and seeing so little of my family. We'll find us a home in Knoxville once I see my way clear."

Hickman's mouth formed an "O" in disbelief and stayed so until he caught his breath. "I'm gonna be a senior! Playing football! I'm not going anywhere!" My youngest brother pushed his chair away from the table. From down the hallway, the door to the room he shared with Jeff Lee and Maxwell slammed.

But Daddy's comment didn't completely seem to register with the rest of us. There was no question that it signaled a new beginning, and Mommy was covering up. Whatever was going on went beyond flipping a page in an imaginary book, and when our house in Murray sold to the family who had been renting it for the past six years, she had a long face that practically stretched to the floor. With no chance of ever going back, her house on the hill was about to be gone for good.

"Why, Simon, why? I don't understand," Mommy said. "Now that we're involved in the community, and I'm substitute teaching, why?"

"It's complicated, Gracie. It's complicated," Daddy said, and except for the comment about the small size of the dessert Mommy served him, the conversation was put on hold.

Chapter 16

SIMON

Gracie remained silent, so I poised myself to penetrate the murky waters. A continuing discussion on a move to Knoxville was inevitable. I closed the door to our bedroom.

"After Dad's death, his estate enabled us to move to better neighborhoods, hon," I said, "but we have two in college soon with two more not far behind. One thing's crystal clear: we simply don't have that kind of money . . . the kind it's going to take, anyway. Selling the house in Murray is the practical thing to do. We aren't ever going back there, Gracie. I'm sorry. It was a mistake—actually, I don't mean that. Moving wasn't the mistake. Counting on the investment in the fluorspar mines was, and you know as well as I do it was $7000 down the drain. It didn't come close to doing what it was supposed to. I was ill-advised. That's all . . . ill advised."

Needing her full attention, I waited while Gracie finished closing the curtains and sat down.

"My job here at Gallatin Steam Plant has provided a decent income. It's gotten us this far. Question my judgment if you will, but I believe there's a far better opportunity in Knoxville, and I believe we should go. Can you see that?"

"I don't see anything, Simon," she said. "I think I'm entitled to see the usefulness of another move. That's all."

"What? You're the one with all the belief in the unseen. How can I give you proof in advance? This is about trusting me." I paced across the floor, ran my palm overtop my head. If I hadn't quit smoking for the umpteenth time, I'd have lit up by now.

Gracie was on her feet. "My aspirations have been cut short in these last six years, Simon, while I trusted you," she said. "I've followed you here and, of course, I would, but I left behind something I haven't been able to replace, and—"

"And I haven't been able to earn enough . . . Is that what you were gonna say? Frankly, not much I do is ever enough. God knows I've tried! What more can I do to make you understand? I've been given this opportunity, and God's fingerprints are all over it. Why not take it? You make it seem like I'm full of harebrained schemes!"

There was no point in raising my voice. I waited in silence until I got a grip.

"Well, anyway, if you think everything I have ever aspired to has worked out, then you are sadly mistaken," I said. "You and the children are the best that I have in this world. Moves seem to be a ritual for me. When I left home, I was a kid, Gracie; and I left with a vision. I thought I had life by the tail. Tuberculosis showed me I didn't. I moved to Albuquerque to survive. I started over with another vision, and I believed with every ounce of my being I was destined to become a doctor. I was prepared to make sacrifices to get there. When the Depression hit, I saw the death of every vision I'd ever had to date.

"My dreams have been dashed at every turn in the road. An acting career looked like a consolation prize for a time; then came the smell of decay. Moral decay that tried to get its hooks in me. It gave me a very rude awakening, hon. I saw firsthand what the depths of depravity do to a person, and it made the entire experience almost unbearable . . . went against my grain. Everything about it . . . utterly contrary to everything in my upbringing."

I reached out for Gracie, took and held her shoulders, and gazed into her eyes. "But then I came back to my roots and found you. We've come a long way on this road, honey. I don't want to stop now and later have to acknowledge I pulled over in the ditch and waited for someone to come pick us up."

Taking a deep breath, I continued, stroke after powerful stroke like an oarsman maneuvering upstream. "I've got to claim this opportunity for you and for the sake of the children. Maybe I'm just scared; I'm not trying to be morbid . . . just trying to be sensible. Here's the thing: Alexandra's at that age. She doesn't need her mother out somewhere, working as she begins high school. She needs the strongest foundation I can provide. May I remind you how worried you were when that degenerate was on the loose a few years back . . . the man who assaulted the young girl? Until he was apprehended, you couldn't forget he was somewhere close by. Well, loonies are everywhere, Gracie, and it is up to me to make darned-well-sure I've done everything within my power to guard and protect what's mine." I pulled my oars from the water and breathed deeply, hoping Gracie was convinced.

"I know the concerns," she countered, "but how on earth can you make sure another move is more financially right than staying here?"

"I can't. How could I? For Pete's sake! I've made my share of mistakes . . . the fluorspar one, especially. It was financially driven. I corrected it . . . well, with what Dad left, I corrected it. That can account for one of the moves, but I wanted more for the children, for us. You make me feel like I'm failing to provide."

"I don't see the point of uprooting us with nothing more than what we have to go on. It would be our fifth home in six years," Gracie said.

"I've said it before, and I'll say it again: I can understand why you're questioning my judgment, Gracie." I paused to get my bearing. "Or are you questioning your ability to find connections . . . the right connections? Which is it? Or have you simply given up on my ability to lead us? And as for you wanting to teach, I'm hopeful you won't have to."

"Now there's an opinion that says I have little to offer, isn't it?"

"Gracie," I said, "you're as stubborn as all get out! I'm just saying I don't think you need to work. I believe better days are coming."

"You keep saying that!" Her jaw was set. "Hickman's in his senior year. A move would kill him."

"He's resilient. He'll adjust. We have to do that in life. Are you forgetting that you had to change your life at that age? You were even younger. And what about me? I left everything I'd ever known at eighteen, completely unaware what I'd find in a big city like Detroit . . . close to a million people after living in little ole Elkton. But if it's luxury you want—"

"Hardly! Not luxury, Simon, but definitely a certain standard. I had to rise . . . No, I had to climb, scraping to clear the pit where Francine tried to bury me. I cannot stand to look at that climb as some mandate for luxury! It was survival, no less than your fight for your own life, Simon, and don't ever forget that. The road Henry is traveling, he's traveling because he lost his will to survive."

"You're overreacting, Gracie, comparing Henry's life to ours or any one of our children's. What does that have to do with us?"

"How can you say that? He is my brother! I feel as though I left him there on the farm to shrivel and die."

"It was wartime, Gracie. Stop blaming yourself for what happened."

"Francine ruined him. That's the type of monster we need to fear the most—one that fills the soul with lies and makes them look as real as the nose on your face. Evil takes on many faces, and I know hers all too well. She tried very hard to make me her scapegoat," Gracie said. "She's a monster that went after Henry. He is lost, Simon, broken beyond repair. What Francine did to my family requires me to conquer lies. So no, I will not stop my climb. I believe I have a high calling. Because of it, I cannot . . . and will not . . . ignore the urgency I possess to use my abilities to glorify God. The future depends on us embracing truth and the decisions we make as a result of it."

"You didn't abandon Henry, hon. If you wanna know what abandonment is, look at what I did to Alan. Now there's a wasted life for you. He looked up to me as his big brother, and I failed him. But we have to move forward. Isn't that what we do? You and I need to stand together. We both lived through the Great Depression, and this, by comparison, is not the end of the world. You are a strong woman, Gracie. We both want the same thing for the children."

"I want something I can count on. That's all. Hickman might do fine, but Alexandra would be jumping from her tiny grade school to probably a very large high school. She's fragile . . . vulnerable, and the influences and people she and Hickman associate with are crucial."

"A small town has its advantages, but you have to admit . . . Gallatin's a lot like Elkton; potential is a bit limited. Knoxville's a new beginning, Gracie. I will prove my worth. I can, and I will." I felt my heart pounding wildly in my chest. "Dad would be proud to know I became a top-notch personnel manager," I said, wanting to hide the emotion that was about to take over. "It's gotta be a tough job, a big responsibility. Just think: I'll hire every person who'll build the TVA dams."

I was drained. Gracie was neither black nor white but some shade of in-between gray. "Honey, this story has a happy ending," I said and blew my nose on a handkerchief. "This move's going to make everything . . . good."

"I just want us to do the right thing, Simon." Gracie's voice was mellow. "I'm through arguing. Just know we're shaping their future." She tilted her head with an air I'd come to recognize. "And my piano goes. Alexandra needs to take lessons; the piano is going with us. Now then, I've said my piece."

PART TWO

Chapter 17

ALEXANDRA

Swiftly, smoothly, with precise rhythm, Daddy moved us to Knoxville, and fate showed its knack for shaping surprises.

Once more Mommy underscored the need for a house that had a fireplace. Being able to burn a rip-roaring fire behind a fancy screen with brass andirons was the number one requirement before she would enter. That alone ensured her a decent house.

The house had a fireplace. The time was summer of 1959, and next on the list was finding a church. Whether or not it would be Papa Jeff's type of church, a place where I would learn the good that God planned, remained to be seen. Mommy's old piano found its new home: crammed in the garage along with the other items she wouldn't give up; and we began our new journey, hanging on to things that supposedly mattered so we would not be separated from beauty. It was a tough puzzle—most of the pieces were about the same color.

I was not too young to recognize that Beulah could never have made the moves from Murray plus various places in Gallatin, and now to Knoxville. She would have been lost in the shuffle. I was unsure if I wasn't, too.

As far as I knew, Mommy hadn't touched the French porcelain bowl, and there had been no talk of the Wesley Foundation, but she still wanted a princess. And Daddy apparently still wanted a perfect Sweet Pea. I was not either. What God wanted was a whole other subject.

———— • ————

"You have the longest eyelashes I've ever seen."

The noisy auditorium did not begin to quash his way-too-loud comment. Everyone around was obliged to hear it, but not a person alive could have doubted it was directed at me. Coming from the row behind me, his voice was noticeably deliberate. I could feel his breath by the side of my face.

Eyelashes were eyelashes like knuckles or knees, and never before had any of them been an attraction. For a second, my mind raced to come up with a response to the guy's random observation. I sat in dead silence, pretending not to hear him, savoring the flattery, then toyed with my lap full of books. I wrestled with what to say and how to say it, then chose to ignore him.

It was the first day of school, and I was a freshman. My brother was a senior, and our school was new to both of us. Already "Hux" was acting out the role of an upperclassman and had started to exercise his latest edge over me. It allowed him a certain advantage at every turn, even to the point of warning me within an inch of my life if I told anyone his real name was Hickman.

Plain Hux was off somewhere else in the building in a classroom of his own. It wasn't that our move in August had turned out to be unbearably traumatic after all or that he had a chip on his shoulder. But it did mean leaving behind his hard-earned position on the football team at Gallatin High and more objectionably, losing his friends. In particular, he resented having to break off his tight relationship with Connie Sloan.

For me, most of it was dubbed insignificant. Even forfeiting my cat in the move had been treated by everyone but me as no big deal. But Fluffy knew something was up with all the boxes, clanging, and confusion. She'd made it through that part. However, when we were packed, loaded and on our way across the mountains, Fluffy didn't fare so well. Her fatal mistake was jumping over the backseat into the boys' territory. Without so much as a word, Jeff Lee simply rolled down the window and pitched my cat out. That was the end of Fluffy.

With days like that, by comparison, today was going to be nothing. I had no choice in such matters. Hux was the one and only person I knew in the hundreds of strangers that filled Ridgewood High School.

I sat in the auditorium in the middle of bustling people. Everyone was settling into seats close to those they already knew, laughing and carrying on the way old friends do when they haven't seen each other since the close of school at the beginning of summer vacation. Inwardly, I recoiled. The newness that had surrounded me throughout the day, and the overwhelming crush of everyone I didn't know, and didn't know how to get to know, had not ceased since I set foot into the building.

Not another morning could ever match the morning I had just lived through, nor could another one ever be singled out as the first day of my high school years. This one held that singular distinction. It had begun hot and muggy. My curly hair had responded unfavorably to the humidity, and I'd beefed about it all the way to the breakfast table.

"It's not fair! I can't stand this mop. It's ridiculous. Why did I have to have this hair? It's ugly! It's awful!"

"Sit down, Alexandra. Eat your eggs before they get cold," Daddy said. "This should be an exciting day for you."

"Maybe if I'd been born with a different head of hair!"

"Sit down and eat."

Sit down and eat. It was his answer for everything, but at least this time the neighborhood where he'd bought a house was a respectable one; and in the short time we'd had to meet kids our age, Hux had succeeded in becoming friends with all of them. Attracting a crowd of buddies and pretty girls came easily for him, and his efforts certainly weren't hindered by his ability to drive the family car any time he chose. It was only after Jeff Lee and Maxwell left for college that Hux no longer had to jockey our five-year-old '54 Buick between him, them, and my mom. That tension, all by itself, had been enough to keep our house in an uproar. It lasted barely a week before Jeff Lee and Maxwell were off to campuses in different towns. With them gone, it wasn't hard for Hux to persuade Mommy to let him borrow the car.

"I'm gonna take a few of the guys to get burgers. I'll be back around three. Is there gas in it?"

"I've hardly driven it Hickma—. Humph! It's going to be unusual, son, calling you Hux," Mom told him, "But if that's what you prefer, we'll see about it. Now go! Go! You should be fine. But do be careful. Have a nice time."

She was a pushover, keen on him finding places to meet new people, and she expected me to be out doing the same.

"Now, Alexandra. You go, too. Ride your bicycle down the block, honey. Meet new people! See if you can find someone your age," she said like a coach from the sideline. "I'm speaking with someone today about piano lessons for you."

"I don't want them, Mom."

In my view, fourteen-year-olds were not going to be riding around in ninety-five-degree temperatures, hoping to meet me. They were more likely at the swimming pool or movies. But I rode through our neighborhood anyway, just to get out of the house, easing into those early mornings before the humidity got so bad. The earlier it was the more bearable, as close to crisp as any late August days were going to be.

That had transpired in the short span of time before the start of school, but now only hours had passed since Hux and I walked to the intersection of Bates Road and Hanover Drive where several kids had gathered to wait for the bus. Hux had walked faster than I possibly could, on purpose, just so he wouldn't be associated with his tag-along sister. I trailed him like a pull toy behind a toddler, never letting it be known we were related.

We got there as the yellow dome of the bus was rising over the top of the hill on Bates Road. We could see it long before it reached us, and in a matter of minutes it pulled up with its brakes noisily objecting. The double doors opened as the chassis ambled to a stop, and we piled on. I sat next to another girl in the first empty seat. Hux filed past me without acknowledging I existed, then parked himself at the rear of the bus and settled himself for the bumpy ride to school.

Everyone split the second the bus doors opened in front of Ridgewood High. Hux was lost in the mass that headed inside the main building. Instructions were lodged in my brain; I knew where to go. Freshman orientation was taking place in the huge auditorium. It would begin promptly at 8:30 a.m. The entrance was supposed to be recognizable by three sets of double doors.

Kids had already begun to fill row after row of seats when I got there, and teachers with arms folded high across their bosoms barked instructions about choosing alternating seats. It was all about discipline, trying to make us operate like well-oiled machines, but it wasn't happening. The intoxicating buzz of disorder had filled the hallways all morning, and that had not changed as the day continued.

———— • ————

Returning to the auditorium for study hall later in the afternoon, I discovered everything was upside down and picking up speed as it went. My small-town Gallatin-girl identity watched in wonderment. A brush of mascara and some Peggy Sue pink lipstick would have to suffice. Tomorrow, for sure, I would return ready to conquer this big town of Knoxville and Ridgewood High School.

I sat quietly and sorted through papers and books, trying to unpack events of the day while continuing to guard my composure after the guy behind me pitched his "longest eyelashes" comment. It still reverberated in my ears, along with the echo of locker doors slamming and horns blowing for classes to change. I resolved to fit seamlessly into the thrill of it all. Maybe, just maybe, I could go unnoticed as a new girl on campus.

"You're new here, aren't you?" Mr. Who Knows was not letting up.

His ability to destroy my concentration was annoying. Between his nudge and his question, I could feel my spine rattle. He didn't hesitate to take another stab, so now I was compelled to answer. Turning around to talk to him shouldn't take so much nerve, but it did. I prepared a nonchalant look to face him and was instantly met by an infectious smile that curled on his face.

No doubt he anticipated some interaction. Flustered and disarmed, I couldn't keep myself from a smile, meager as it was.

"I'm Ted. Ted Torrens," he said. "And who might you be?"

Thumping his pencil as if it were a drumstick on top of his books, tapping his hand in rhythm to an imaginary beat as if his drum roll might prompt my answer, he waited.

"Alexandra Hagan."

It was a thud at the bottom of a bucket. I recognized that. After a short pause I turned again to show off my communication skills.

"Hi."

Giving me barely long enough time to straighten back around in my seat, he started in again.

"Alexandra. Alexandra Hagan," he said out loud, repeating my name like an important announcement. "I'll bet your folks call you Alex."

"No. Alexandra," I said with my back to him.

"Oh, okay, I got it!"

He tried to sound huffy, feigning his astonishment, but I knew he was restraining laughter, decidedly amused by the challenge I presented. He struck me as melodramatic. I supposed he was also reeling in anguish to demonstrate how my gruffness had undone him, but he waited and said nothing more until study hall was about to be over. Seconds before the horn sounded, he piped up with a feisty little ultimatum.

"So, Alex," he began, tapping my shoulder, "I desperately need to talk to you. Don't try to disappear."

Desperately needed to talk to me. I let that roll around in my head a few times. Sounded interesting. Very interesting. What a flirt! The more I repeated it to myself, the better it sounded, but he didn't need to know that.

The loud horn blared and the auditorium went crazy. I eyed him as he waited for me at the end of the row, doling out coolness as I approached. By then the crowd had poured into the aisles, so we were forced to untangle ourselves from each other as we made our way toward the central hallway. All the while he fired his arsenal of questions, and I responded with my one-word answers. Somewhere between the study hall and the walk to my next classroom his babbling began to loosen me—on the inside.

"I saw you the minute you walked into the building. That's when I said to myself: 'Ted, ole boy, you're going to get to know that girl. The sooner the better.' And now look at you! You're trying to make it really hard for me. Aren't you?"

He let me fumble with that one while we continued fighting the masses.

"Hey, Lannie," he said, now walking backward, trying to flag down a friend passing in the corridor, "you think your basement can hold another pretty girl Saturday night?"

Lannie Sutherland had a winsome smile. Every aspect of his appearance was stylish and impeccable. He stopped to consider the question, bracing himself with the cane that supported his weight. Then he shifted his position to get completely balanced before flashing a mischievous wink in my direction.

"Yeah, okay. Where is one?"

Being teased was nothing unusual. Three older brothers made it the routine, and I was an easy target. Ted stepped forward defensively, grinning.

"Hey, watch out! Lan, you don't yet know who you're talking to."

It was understood both were joking, but there was a tinge of protectiveness coming from Ted; I liked it.

"This is Alexandra, but she'd prefer to be called Alex."

He gave me a side glance to see if I objected to his changing my name. I was too busy to object, trying not to stare at Lannie's cane or have it appear like I had never seen anyone under eighty years old using one.

"This is Lannie-my-man-Sutherland, and his house is the place to be this Saturday," he said as we began walking again. Lannie limped along spryly, keeping up with us.

"My next class is right here, room twenty-two," I said.

The three of us approached the door to my English class and blended into the nearby group forming outside it. With Lannie there, the talk immediately turned to the upcoming party at his house, and he took over as ringleader.

"Guys, Ted here is trying to lure the new girl to my house Saturday night," he said.

"Woooo-we! Not Ted and this young thing. Nah! Ted wouldn't do something like that," said one of them.

Lannie piped up, "'Young thing!' Speak your name and let everyone decide if you should be seen at my party with the likes of Ted."

A girl who was standing by—quiet until now—intervened to deliver me from the playful torment. "You'll learn to ignore him; believe me. He acts sinister, but he's harmless," she reassured me. "Plan to come to the party. It'll be fun, regardless of him."

"You're a tough cookie, Gorham," Lannie replied, then brandished his cane and brought it down playfully on the toe of her shoe. "Can't argue with justice."

Everyone burst into laughter, and the joking didn't stop until the sound of the horn signaled the halls should be emptied for the beginning of class. We dispersed in all directions. Ted waved to me, more of a salute than an ordinary wave, and without taking his eyes off me, walked away. Lannie punched him with his elbow to keep him from stumbling over his own feet, and I turned to go into Miss Freeman's classroom. My would-be defender was right behind me.

"Hi, my name is Alexandra Hagan. Uhmm, I mean, Alex," I said to her.

"Hi, I'm Kathryn Gorham. Kit. Everybody shortens my name, too. We rode the same bus, you know. I saw you get on this morning. Hope you'll plan on the party. It's the first event Lannie's been part of for a really long time," she said, lowering her voice and taking the seat next to mine. "He was in a terrible motorcycle accident a while back. Anyway, come to the party. It'll be fun."

"Well, I think I could. Maybe. We moved here a couple of weeks ago from Gallatin. I haven't met many people. Just Ted . . . and Lannie. Ted sits behind me in study hall. He seems pretty nice."

"They're big buddies, ya know," Kit said, "and have been since we were in grammar school. Lannie barely made it. I mean he came close to dying in the crash." The final horn blasted, and with it she quickly added, "But, yes, they're pretty cool guys."

———— • ————

Within a few days of meeting new friends, it was easy spending time together in the hallways, classrooms, and cafeteria, especially with Kit. We were already in the habit of talking forever on the phone. She told me about Ted, because I was very interested in any and all details I could extract. Having known him throughout the early grades, she told me he'd had back surgery as a nine-year-old, and that limited him in sports. It made perfect sense now. He was older than the rest of us because he'd spent a year out of school, recuperating.

"Gosh! He and Lannie have both had serious deals," I said. "Lannie's motorcycle wreck sounds awful."

"Lucky for both, they missed being paralyzed," Kit said.

Not bothering to knock and providing for herself a partly opened door to my bedroom, Mom poked her head through. "Time to hang up, honey. There'll be plenty of time for friends tomorrow. Maybe practice some piano," she said.

"See ya tomorrow, Kit. I've gotta go."

I hung up the phone and sat a moment, thinking about Ted and what Kit had said; tomorrow night would be the first football game of the season. I could hardly wait to see him on the playing field, however limited he may be.

After messing around with the twisted phone cord, getting it just so, I headed out of room to look for my mother and found her in the garage.

Daddy walked past with a rake in hand. "Hello, there, Alexandra. Wanna help me?" He glanced over his shoulder with a hopeful eye in my direction.

"How am I supposed to rake whatever and also practice piano when I haven't even had a lesson in six years?"

"Play some chords," she said, and Daddy stood there, looking as if I'd kicked him. "Your fingers should get nimble before you meet with Mrs. Kirkland on Saturday, Alexandra."

"I don't really want lessons, Mom. Hate to tell you that . . . again."

"You will once you begin. Now go on. And hold your hands like you're holding a baby chicken, Alexandra."

"Oh, brother!" I said, hands on my hips.

Daddy brushed by me like he might side with Mom, then started around to the outside of the garage. "Never mind," he said on his way past the door. "I'm going for a walk."

Chapter 18

SIMON

The evening was far from cool but had offered a break from the blistering heat and sweltering humidity. I liked being outside, so I took off, walking down the driveway. At the mailbox, I turned up our street whistling "Catch a Falling Star," with an apologetic nod to Perry Como for butchering his song.

Barely unpacked and eager as I was to have my family living with me in Knoxville, I felt various degrees of adjustment as Jeff Lee and Maxwell left for college. The remaining four of us were finding a routine, settling in for another weekend at our most recent address.

The move had changed everything except the demanding work at TVA. No longer was I traveling 175 miles to spend a day and a half in Gallatin settling crises on the home front or following up the weekend with a commute back to a cheap boarding house. Newly altered circumstances made it worth the lonely stretch of isolation that had punctuated the last six months. Everything considered, it wasn't tuberculosis, and it wasn't a loss of life. Sometimes it took only a reminder of how far I'd come and how many times I should thank my lucky stars—or Providence. Father would much prefer me to give God the credit—not sheer luck.

My heart reacted at the thought of my father, Geoffrey Hagan . . . Geoffrey Newton Hagan . . . with his gently commanding manner. Funny in a way, I thought, how his passing from life to death had polished and refined the patina of the legacy he'd handed down and caused it to glow like a beacon in the darkness.

Deep down I begged to know if I'd given him the honor due, and I walked along, past neighboring split-level and ranch style residences with sprawling lawns, grass struggling in the September heat, thankful I'd stayed in a boarding house for the last time. The separation had reshaped more than our housing situation. I couldn't help but sense it.

"Gracie's gotten the upper hand; Alexandra's growing up, too fast . . and the older boys are off to college." I was muttering aloud. I sensed that as well, strolling the hilly street in our new neighborhood.

So, what did I expect? Some means of putting everything on hold while I put my ducks in a row in another new town? And what's this with Alexandra? She's now Alex, with a little attitude, doing a disappearing act in her room every night, on the phone for hours on end. I don't understand a lot about raising a daughter. Must be the case: boys are easier to raise than daughters.

"Shoo! Get on home, buddy," I said to the dog that caught sight of me and sprinted in my direction, yapping, running circles in the street next to a neighbor's driveway. "Shoo!"

A stray animal? Heaven forbid! I could only hope Alexandra wouldn't adopt the mongrel if it were. Quick to judge . . . am I? Evaluating people . . . circumstances? Judging? But it's my job; and if I'm gonna hold the personnel manager's position, then I'd better be darned good at it.

I lit up the cigarette I wasn't supposed to be smoking and blew into the air. Who better than Gracie to fill the gap in my absence? And I did want her to have whatever would make her happiest. This home. But giving Alexandra her own phone and a bedroom with her own bath?

I should've put my foot down. Did it have to be decided in the same instant that had me making multiple decisions on multiple levels at work? Something's not aligning here quite the way it should.

I wiped sweat off my brow and inhaled again the smoke from my Camel. Half a block from home, I turned and headed back.

Lord God, I feel as if it's only an ounce of prevention existing between me and this great big world out here. An ounce isn't going to cover it. Alexandra has no idea how much I love her. Am I just lacking skills to convey it? Am I? I want to protect my little girl from—no, I must protect her from—what? Everything. Yep . . . that's right . . . just about everything.

I hiked up the slope of the hill that was our driveway and walked into the garage.

The piano was sitting alone, as was the rake where I'd left it. I turned off the light, clicked the switch to bring down the overhead door, and went inside through the laundry room.

Chapter 19

ALEXANDRA

By Friday, I had persuaded my dad to let me join the kids meeting at Lannie's house on Saturday night. It looked like it was going to take longer to convince Mom I was not interested in taking piano lessons.

Dressed out in monstrous shoulder pads and Ridgewood High School colors, players hustled onto the field for the kickoff. Ted ran down the field toward what looked like less than a speck of a ball at the end of it, and the thunderous roll of the drums drew us to our feet. Cheering fans awaited the outcome of his kick; then Ted returned to the bench, making a quick effort to spot me in the bleachers where I said I'd be sitting. Kit stood next to me, nudging me with her elbow to confirm the unrivaled impressiveness we had just witnessed.

Kit was getting a huge charge out of the chemistry between Ted and me. I could feel it all the way up in the stands. It was far more than my imagination. If this was a preview of what was to come, my Friday night promised to be a long one filled with a big bunch of teasing from Kit. She was coming home with me after the game for a sleepover.

My mom was absolutely thrilled with the possibility of me getting socially involved. From the moment Kit entered our house, Mom's questions for her were continuous. Dad offered Kit a chair at the big hexagonal table with a lazy Susan in the middle that had been Papa Jeff's. I thought Kit and I were going to have the kitchen to ourselves, but not so. The four of us ate pound cake and sipped hot chocolate, and Mom's questions kept coming while I guarded any hint of my attraction to the guy named Ted. If any worries existed over this phase of letting go of me, Mom dismissed them all.

Daddy, on the other hand, seemed to be sharpening his senses. He listened closely when Ted's name was mentioned. With elbows on the table, he hovered like a mother baboon over her infant.

Kit and Mom did most of the talking. When everyone had finally finished the after-game snack, Kit and I headed off to my room. The next morning at breakfast, Mom started in with round two. Kit was a good sport with a complexity that puzzled me, especially the mysterious way she hesitated over everything she ate, but she managed to make her plate look reasonably empty. When it was time to take Kit home, Daddy volunteered.

Driving the new '59 Buick he'd purchased only this week, he drove like a proud chauffeur with Kit and me in the back seat still chattering nonstop.

After leaving Kit at her front door, we said our goodbyes and headed back home. As we were pulling into the garage, Daddy brought up the party I was planning to attend tonight.

"You're fourteen years old, Alexandra," he reminded me. "That's mighty young in my book. I'll be glad to drive you to the place and wait with the other parents."

"Nobody else's parents are coming! I am in high school, Daddy! I'll meet up with some kids to listen to records and stuff," I said to him as we passed through the laundry room. "And you can't come inside, for Pete's sake. You can drop me off. I'll meet you outside when the party's over."

"I'll plan on picking you up at ten sharp," he countered. "Right where I drop you off."

Mom looked up from her cup of coffee, about to be sandwiched in the debate.

"But the party's not over till midnight! Mom," I said, appealing to her in my rabid-dog voice. "Tell him . . . Mom?"

"We can agree on eleven o'clock, Simon, until we know a little more about these people. That will be lovely," she said.

Her eagerness for me to become involved showed as brightly as a neon sign, but Daddy seemed to be repressing a growl. Nothing changed his disposition in the hours before driving me to the party.

He vanished into the bedroom, and I didn't give it another thought.

Chapter 20

Daddy was hesitant as the evening approached. He looked at me once and partly smiled during our ride to Lannie's house. It was awkward, nearly as weird as him saying it was a nice night like I couldn't see for myself what kind of night it was. But then he drove up Lannie's driveway and stopped the car, cleared his throat, and said some even weirder stuff:

"I know you don't think I know a thing, but it was just yesterday I held you in my arms. I knew then you were a precious jewel."

All I could think was: Then why did I get a scratched suitcase from the Army Surplus Store for my fourteenth birthday? It translated to unworthiness. I was so disappointed I could still taste the tears.

I just looked at him and half-smiled back, rummaging through my purse to find a mirror. He got out and opened my door while I sat there.

Bewildered he would do such a thing, I glared at him, hoping no one saw him treating me like a child. How unwanted it was to have him acting as if I were a twelve-year-old when I was so mature and so not in need of him. I looked around to make sure there were no witnesses to the scene, and without a backward glance, I hopped out of the car, went up and knocked on Lannie's front door.

The party was alive and jumping when I entered. Ted spotted me before I reached the bottom step to the basement and, without wasting any time, crossed the room. The stereo was blurting "Mack the Knife," and Bobby Darren was giving his song every possible ounce of gusto. Ted tugged at my elbow to pull me into the loud arena of pumping music. Kids were flinging their arms and gyrated to the beat of the stereo sound. The latest releases of 1959 records were stacked high beside the equipment.

"I was afraid you weren't going to show," Ted said, his words pressing in close to my ear so I wouldn't miss them. His cologne smelled like the clove-studded oranges that hung in my aunt's hallway at Christmas. "I really am glad you did."

I hadn't stood this close to him before, and I sensed we were making a spectacle. I adjusted my position, trying to appear poised.

"Thanks for the invitation. I really believed my dad was going to come in with me," I said, and my comment made both of us laugh.

The record was ending. Ted used the chance to snag a couple of his friends to introduce me. We joked and chatted with Wesley Turner and Stephanie Dukes until the next record dropped onto the turntable. Ted hollered at everyone else, making sure they all looked our way.

"Hey guys, meet Alex! This is Alex Hagan!"

The sudden applause flustered me. I could feel my vulnerable side showing. I was pretty sure my blushing delighted Ted.

Boogieing along, he led me through to the center of the jammed dance floor and turned to take my hand so we could do the bop to "Party Doll."

"You made a hit! I sure am glad you came," he yelled over the music. "So how does that feel?"

"I'm glad, too. It feels good. This is the best party!"

"I can't hear you," he said, forcing me to repeat what I'd said, standing on my tiptoes so I could say it in his ear.

"I'm really glad I'm here . . . with you," I said.

Dance after fast dance, we were still at it, bumped on every side and hanging in there through countless songs without a break. His offer to grab a Coca-Cola made it easy for us get away to a less crowded spot. Then he steered me to an old church pew along the farthest wall. Friendly greetings followed us. We sat there, sipping icy bottles of soda that he'd taken from a galvanized tub.

"What do you think?" he said, trying to make himself heard over the ruckus.

"You have lots of friends. They're really neat. I'm glad you asked me to come."

"We've hung out together since we were kids. In fact, most everyone in this room has. Lannie's motorcycle accident made us even closer. He almost died," he said as the record played out.

"Kit told me that too. Maybe you'll tell me more about it sometime."

"Later," he said, removing the soda bottle from my hand. Then he set it on the floor and dragged me until I was on my feet. "I'll tell you all about it, but not now. You want to dance. Don't you?"

"Well, yes. Of course, I do," I said, posing no objection since he had already maneuvered me through the crowd again and was holding me close.

"Dream Lover" dropped onto the turntable. Someone was making selections that were noticeably quieter. The tempo suggested romance, and Bobby Darren's song began shifting the mood, slowing the pace, suggesting "love, oh so true." I found myself wanting to be in Ted's arms, enfolded in magical charms being sung about from the turntable.

The song ended, gently winding down, and everyone clapped, but Ted playfully refused to release my hand, indicating we would be staying on the dance floor for the next song. Smiles and affirming gestures brushed by us. Ted was eating it up.

When the music began again, it was Paul Anka singing, "Put Your Head on My Shoulder." I made every effort not to do that, even though I sensed Ted's shoulder was waiting. Nearly every person was up dancing. Bodies squeezed closer together, and dance steps were reduced to intermittent side shuffles.

Daddy would have killed me if he thought I'd put my head on Ted's shoulder. Well, maybe not kill me, but he sure as heck would have had something to say about it. With his being so hesitant and moody about bringing me here tonight, who knew what he was envisioning. If he saw me in Ted's arms, feeling the way I was feeling, he would not be happy. It was evident my growing up had not provided the missing link. I was still not his Sweet Pea.

Rocking back and forth, secure next to Ted's six-foot-two frame, I was melting faster than chocolate in the sunshine. The melody intoxicated me with the words speaking softly of falling in love, and we danced ever so slowly. Ted held me nonstop as one record followed another. Finally, everyone was ready for a break—a chance to take a deep, deep breath and talk. Kit motioned us toward her.

"Well, now, aren't you two quite the item?" she said teasingly, then let the question drop without waiting for an answer. "Alex," she continued in a less taunting voice, "have you met Sara Stokes? She lives on Westmoreland in Windsor Hills."

Everyone was talking at once. Kit's quiet voice didn't help matters. My response would've been drowned out if I'd spoken. I shook my head no, and despite the racket, enough emphasis was placed on Windsor Hills to make the name easy to hear. I knew the area. It didn't require a full name to be said. I recognized it as the prestigious country club that sat in the middle of old wealth.

Windsor Hills Country Club. My family had certainly not joined, only driven past to satisfy my mother's longing.

"I merely want to see it, Simon," she'd said. "No harm in that, is there?"

Daddy had shrugged in response. Any harm was not going to be discussed right now. He knew, and I knew—we all knew—we were going to see Windsor Hills Country Club.

Riding by late on a Sunday afternoon, we had passed through the neighboring properties of Windsor Hills, where houses backed up to the golf course. The drive was enough to confirm we could not qualify, not even close. Money was an issue, and I knew it. With Jeff Lee and Maxwell in college and Hux going next year, Daddy was doing all he could to buy a house at all. Possibly for Mom, it was not going to be enough.

"It might be a good idea to join the club, Simon," she had said with conviction, choosing her words carefully in an attempt to soften him with her slipped-in suggestion.

It didn't strike me that he was considering membership. His apathy had visibly disappointed Mom but had not dampened her spirit. Not much could. To her, it didn't seem pointless to wave in front of him the newspaper's debutantes, but her efforts had fallen limp. He was not easily influenced by society, and the demure young princesses—presented in the prime of loveliness to their awaiting world of well-to-do young princes—prin-ciety did not change his mind. The privileged few did not impress him, but that didn't rule out Mom's desire to be associated with the right people. So the pursuit continued.

"Maybe we can do that next year," she'd persisted as he kept driving.

He was doing what had to be done, and that meant finding us a home. In no way would we be able to live in such a posh neighborhood. Therefore, except for his agreeing to drive the car past the beautifully manicured grounds of the golf course, he ignored the one-sided discussion. His hand signaled for her to pause, an unspoken shush, for he was trying intently to concentrate on navigating the tree-lined streets of Windsor Hills.

I sat in the back seat with my window rolled down and looked at the passing scenery. The distinctive smell of chlorine was in the breeze, blowing at me as the car picked up speed. Behind the tall fence was the swimming pool where the sound of laughter and splashing water beckoned. I was probably not going to be participating there. And what about this debutante talk? What a joke! My dad's provisions were far too inadequate for such a way of living, and I was beginning to see it. Mom's expectations, as strong as the air in my face, were rubbing off.

I had concluded on that day we probably belonged miles away in a very different neighborhood, possibly on Nelson Street where Mrs.

Nightingale and her husband had moved when they left Gallatin. Oddly enough, after all these years, we were again living in the same town as them. We had driven past their house on Nelson Street on a different day, all part of a weekend allotted to seeing various areas before my parents made their final buying decision. Houses on Nelson Street were much smaller, and yards were shorter, and the pressure to be well-heeled was nonexistent. The comparison had me picturing myself at the bottom of the social heap. Mrs. Nightingale's neighborhood was not being considered—not any more than Windsor Hills, but for altogether different reasons. Mom would not allow the embarrassment of living on a street such as Nelson Street. Still, she was interested to see where Mrs. Nightingale lived. With her matter-of-fact observation, she commented on the Nightingales' ability to escape living in a trailer park. I was certain she believed not escaping would exceed a fate more appalling than death.

Going past Mrs. Nightingale's house that Saturday might allow me to run in and say hello to her. That's all. Then we could be on our way. That was the plan. It had been five years since we'd seen one another. I wondered if she would even remember me.

Without warning, Daddy made a sharp left, and we were quite unprepared to find her standing by the mailbox as our car turned onto Nelson Street. Her large silhouette was an easy one to recognize, even from a distance. Mom began fidgeting, perhaps wishing we could turn the car the opposite way, but it was too late. It would have been rude to bypass her, so we stopped, exchanging niceties for a while, pretending we had planned the meeting. Dad waited patiently. After a bit, he turned off the engine and lit a cigarette.

Miles that had stretched between me and Mrs. Nightingale were immediately inconsequential. Without a doubt she was flabbergasted and chatted nervously, unable to stop tugging at her house dress. Tamping her disheveled hair, she rattled on with pride for having taught me to make potholders, commenting on how she had missed me and how ill Chuck had been. At the mention of Mrs. Nightingale's husband, I checked Mom's reaction and hoped I was alone in noticing how irreverently she cringed at the sound of his name. More than once, Mrs. Nightingale said how much she appreciated the Christmas and birthday cards.

My correspondence had been erratic, and I was sure she was not at the mailbox to find anything other than bills.

It would be a couple of years, I told her, before I would be learning to drive, but I suggested we could visit when that did happen. Afterward, our conversation seemed to wind down. Dad took that as a cue to start up the car. Shortly thereafter the three of us were off, continuing down Nelson Street.

It had been an odd coincidence to run into Mrs. Nightingale, but from that meeting on Nelson Street to this day, I wanted to believe my mom had taken a new interest in her. They had talked on the phone. That much I knew.

Nothing, though, had landed us any closer to Windsor Hills. Mom had not referred to it again, at least not in my presence, but decidedly she would have wanted me to meet the perky blonde in Lannie Sutherland's basement. Amid the crowd of Ridgehighers who were continuing the ruckus, the affluent-looking Sara Stokes was making her way toward me. In her understated way, she had Windsor Hills written all over her.

I abandoned further reflections about Mrs. Nightingale, the odd run-in with her, and the chance of renewing our closeness. The present moment hinted at being far more interesting.

Chapter 21

"Hi, you must be Sara Stokes," I said. It was all I could manage above the loud voices and surge of people reaching for platefuls of brownies and chocolate chip cookies someone had put on the bar. A marvelous frenzy filled the air, and the introduction to Sara was lost as the music restarted. The record began playing "Smoke Gets in Your Eyes," and without explaining anything or asking for permission, Ted took my hand and deliberately moved us to the dance floor. With the Platters' low, melodic voices singing in the background about hearts on fire and Ted's voice dittoing the words in my ear, I didn't need an expert to know at least two hearts were on fire. If what they were singing was accurate, smoke in our eyes was inevitable.

After several dance steps, he tugged at my arms and raised them to his shoulders.

"There, doesn't that feel a lot better? I like having you this close to me," he said, looking straight into my eyes. "You do have the most beautiful eyes, you know."

I glanced self-consciously from one side of the room to the other to see if Sara or anyone else had noticed Ted's tenderness. "You're embarrassing me," I said. "But thanks."

"You're easily embarrassed. That means I can take advantage of you."

"Oh? Not really," I said, but it felt right to be held as if I were a baby, rocked in my mother's arms. The fact that he was fifteen and I was fourteen, that I had known him for only six days, didn't seem to bother either of us. Fledgling as it was, I told myself I was growing up and okayed the sensation despite knowing Daddy would have a cow if he saw me wrapped up like property belonging to Ted.

"Yes, really," he confirmed, and effortlessly his arms slipped from my waist, enfolding me as the record crooned the words and drizzled them over us, and we shut out the rest of the world.

The lights had lowered significantly, and our secluded corner of the room was dim. I had never been kissed—really kissed. Somehow, I knew this was the last time I would ever think the thought. I anticipated the inevitable touch of his lips, and it was as if we had both been waiting an eternity. Ted leaned in closer and his mouth pressed against mine, entirely awakening my senses with a kiss, cautious at first, then pressing in more. It continued, sensationally and in detail, every second of it making me weaker than the one before. The feeling remained until the music ended.

Neither of us had noticed the odd silence that surrounded us.

The next moment was broken by a spontaneous burst as catcalls erupted everywhere with whistles and clapping. Even so, something very quiet was defining the night. Unfazed by their hilarity, Ted's body still snuggled all over me, cuddling me as his treasure.

I didn't resist. I was Ted's girl.

———— • ————

In addition to what was happening with Ted, my relationship with Kit was blossoming, undeterred by the way she kept other people at a distance. I had the impression she was concealing a wound of some kind, even though she said all the right words and produced smiles with perfectly aligned teeth that only braces could have engineered. She clung to an unseen perimeter like a skittish feral cat measuring a safe distance for itself. Compared to the uncomplicated friendship Suzette Mullins and I continued to nurture through letters and phone calls across the miles, I had come upon something mysterious in Kit.

Regardless of what was going on, we were drawn together as good friends, and that led to more sleepovers after Friday night home football games. Sock hops in the gym lasted until midnight. Dad was emphatic about picking us up promptly at eleven whenever we planned to spend the night at my house. That made us opt to go to Kit's instead.

Tonight though, she was coming to mine. I anticipated Dad would have on his perfectly knotted necktie and long-sleeve white shirt.

"Dinner's ready, y'all. Here, Simon, take these potatoes before I drop them, and feel free to loosen your tie, honey," Mom said to him. "Alexandra, you sit next to your father."

"Kit, you sit next to me." She turned undivided attention on her. "I've been so looking forward to talking to you."

I glanced at the bowl of plump Idahos, picturing lumps in them as they circled around on the table's lazy Susan.

"This was my father's table, built on his farm with cherry trees off his place." Daddy's comment to Kit brought an admiring smile from her, which made him continue. "You'll never see another one like it."

A plate of fried chicken stopped in front of Kit. Instantly she declined. I knew we were in trouble. Mom's fried chicken was going to be her best bet, but it went past her, and I warned myself not to be embarrassed if Kit had a problem eating the rest of the offerings.

She was not expecting the conveyor on the lazy Susan to move again, but it did, turning, then stopping in front of her with the big spoon from the potatoes left precariously overhanging the bowl. The spoon hit the glass of milk and accidentally tipped it into the middle of her dinner plate.

Mom jumped up from the table and casually swabbed at it, smiling a Pollyanna smile as she tackled the mess. At first, she used the skirt of her dress, then a rag that had probably mopped the floor. Distractions such as a little spilled milk were unimportant. Once it was cleaned up and everyone had resumed eating, Mom continued, giving the impression nothing was amiss. Without skipping a beat, she started in again, interrogating Kit with questions that sounded like innocent dialogue.

"What do you know about this young man, Ted Torrens? He must be a nice person. I suspect he's very nice," she said, directing all conversation to Kit. "How long have you known him?"

Kit tucked a silky strand of dark hair behind one ear and methodically prepared her answers. She held up well under my mom's probe, employing all available resources, producing appropriate words to fill in the blank, enduring the banter. Her long artistic fingers gracefully held the fork she used to poke at the mound of food on her plate, pushing parts from one side to the other to avoid eating.

My dad's comparison of her appetite to that of a bird gave Kit little choice but to eat some—squirming—selectively nibbling every bite as if each one had wormy bits in it. He treated her kindly in the event a sudden move or a too-loud voice might frighten her away, pouring out tenderness I had forgotten. Although he was not saying so, his behavior spoke approval, and they bantered jovial exchanges.

Mom kept firing a volley of questions, accompanied by her own answers for her neglected questions. Kit appeared to be undaunted by the nonstop harangue that lasted the entire length of the meal. Nothing Kit said hinted at the evidence she withheld—evidence Ted and I were already way too involved—and the evening went off without a hitch.

Chapter 22

Ted and I had totally flipped over each other. We had been going steady for five months, since the beginning of summer after our freshman year. Now, deep into our sophomore year, I was definitely Ted's property. To prove it, I had his onyx ring, one his parents had given him. Pink angora wrapped the back of its band so I could keep it on my finger. But tonight, it was dangling from a chain around my neck. Daddy did not approve, and he didn't mind saying so.

Ted was constantly near me. That had not let up. He was due at my house at seven o'clock, and usually he was right on time. Dad sat in his favorite floral Gainsborough chair in the living room beside the big window. From there, he had a useful vantage point, including when Ted's car came up the hill. Daddy was calling out to me before it was parked on the slope in front of the garage, hoping I was ready to leave. It was fairly clear he didn't want to entertain Ted for long, although he was accustomed to his presence.

The doorbell rang. After a bit of time lapsed, I heard Daddy opening the door.

"Come in, Ted," he said. "Alexandra will be ready momentarily. You're welcome to have the others come inside. They don't have to wait in the car."

"Thanks, Mr. Hagan, but they'll be okay. How are you?"

Ted sounded confident, given that he was standing face to face with the one who had the authority to reconsider letting his only daughter go out with the crew that had rolled onto his turf.

Even if Daddy hadn't been suspicious before, he was now. I'd overheard his conversation with Mom last week. His defenses were up. Something had put him on alert.

"She's too young to be getting this serious. You mark my words, Gracie," he'd said to my mom as they talked in the kitchen. "You mark my words . . ." And he had closed the door so they could have privacy, muffling the remainder of their discussion about me.

Ted and my dad hadn't stopped talking. I was almost ready.

"I'm fine, Ted, doing well," Dad said. "Wish that darned weather would give us a break. We need rain."

"Yes, sir, that would be nice."

In a matter of seconds, I met them in the living room, skirted past my dad, and uttered a subdued word of good-bye; a noticeable chill went with it. Things weren't right between us, and the hostility earlier in the evening had taken it to a new level.

Suppertime had been hurried. I'd had little patience to dispense, moored to my parents at the dinner table when Ted would be here in less than an hour. It was just the three of us now that Hux had begun his freshman year at the University of Tennessee. Jeff Lee was in dental school, and Maxwell was in law school.

"Put your napkin in your lap, honey. Sit up straight," Mom said to me. "And watch your posture. You don't want curvature of the spine. Do you?"

I took another bite of meat and stared lackadaisically at my plate, then picked at the green beans. My thoughts drifted. Without warning, my mother's stiff fingers raked down my backbone. I shot straight up in the air. Green beans went everywhere.

"Much better, now. Isn't it, honey," she asked.

Somewhere between the scattered beans and a mouthful of meat, the silence was broken. Both parents seemed bent on stirring things up.

"Looks like a bird crapped over your eyes," Daddy said to me, then nonchalantly resumed eating his dinner as if he'd spoken a sweet blessing.

"Simon!" said my mother in astonishment.

"Well, look at them. I don't think Cleopatra herself wore that much makeup. Did she?"

I shoved my chair back and got up to leave, tossing my napkin on the table. "I need to go," I said. Tears burned against the backs of my eyelids. Angrily I held them back as I turned toward the door to leave.

"Aren't you going to help your mother with the dishes?" Daddy blurted his question, perfectly okay with having belittled me.

"I have to get ready," I said, coldly. "Besides," I proclaimed over my shoulder with a degree of arrogance that did not go unnoticed, "I'm getting out of here."

"Watch that tone with me, young lady!"

Mom braced herself as I brushed past. A word formed on her lips, but it dropped with the first syllable. I knew she wanted to intervene, fix it, repaint the scene to match the flowers on one of her china teacups. My dad simply turned away; he seemed stunned, stuck to his chair, his fork in midair.

Mom jumped up and walked rapidly behind me. By the time she reached my bedroom door, I had shut and locked it. She was not going to side with me, and I knew it. I didn't see any point to my reopening it when she knocked.

I dove in my makeup drawer with both hands, slinging lipsticks, creams, combs, and wands across the top of my dresser, then snarled at the surly face in the mirror and finished the process of getting my hair backcombed into a bouffant before taking another look.

Ted was my ticket out of the house, and he couldn't have arrived a bit too soon. Reluctant, dreading to bump into my dad, I was in high gear and motoring when I reached the foyer.

"Hi, Ted, I'm ready," I said. "Let's go."

Ted offered a respectful nod. "Good night, Mr. Hagan."

"Don't stay out too late. Be in by midnight, honey," called my mom from down the hallway.

Ted followed closely as I marched toward the waiting car. The October sky had darkened earlier than usual this evening, and I was ready to take it on.

"Hi, Wesley. Hi, Donna. Let's get out of here, y'all," I said, climbing into the front seat.

Ted closed my car door and went to the other side, jumped in, and closed his door as he backed down the steep driveway. Wesley gave me a patronizing smile.

"You can call me Wes, darlin.' We've got to stop at the package store. I won't have any trouble gettin' a six-pack. Head over to North Shore, Turk," he said to Ted. "Take a sharp right at the next light."

I gritted my teeth. Wes got away with calling me *darling* because Ted treated it as fun. If it had been anyone else, Ted would have been fuming. I didn't want the possessiveness he exhibited; a fine line lay between ownership and protectiveness. It was all part of being his girl. That's what I believed; and having to tolerate Wes and his cocky football-star attitude was part of the scenario. I accepted it. He was Ted's friend.

———— • ————

The party at Lannie's house was underway when we arrived. Blaring music from the stereo had Ray Charles singing "What'd I Say" at the top of his lungs. Lannie's family room was hyped; everyone inside was dancing. Greetings were lost in the hullabaloo as we pushed ourselves through the crowd to the patio out back. A handful of the guys and girls had started to congregate undeterred by the evening's cool crispness. Laughter and cigarette smoke came from the far end of the walkway where beer was freely circulating.

Football weekends with away games were typically good ones to count on for a party at Lannie's house. His parents were Ole Miss grads and keen on going to all the pregame festivities, leaving town on Friday, heading south to Oxford. Lannie was in charge of taking care of the happenings at home.

The night was perfect, the sky a canopy of stars winking devilishly at anyone who chose to notice. A distinct smell of burning leaves wafted across from a nearby field. The night had hardly begun, but I wanted to be close to Ted as it ticked away. The episode at the dinner table was still raw in my gut. Thoughts of it were sickening. I took a deep breath. Being out from under my dad's heavy hand was a relief.

Having Ted near made everything easier to forget. His arm draped my shoulder, gentle and reassuring. It belonged there, and we floated privately in a world of our own without really knowing how long the intimate moments lasted. Flames pulsated from tiki lights at the corners of the patio. The entire perimeter was aglow.

He brushed the dark brown waves away from my cheek. "You okay, baby? What's going on in that pretty head of yours?"

"Just stuff at home," I said. "Not a big deal. Am I being a drag?"

"Listen, you know you can tell me. You can be whatever, and whoever, you want around me." His kiss reached my lips before I could say anything, and I wanted it that way.

Ted didn't need to know about stuff at home.

From our remote point on the patio, we could hear our favorite song beginning, luring us like a siren song. Its message had all the implications of us being seduced by a sea of love, and something about tonight felt very different. For all we knew, everyone else had vanished, and Ted and I were alone—two warm bodies holding each other close. Too close. The next thing I knew we could not be stopped. Neither of us tried.

"Let's go inside," he said.

Chapter 23

Fresh air, filtering in through the partially opened doors in Lannie's basement helped curb Ted's and my passion.

The room inside had heated up, and the air was getting stale. Fewer and fewer people were coming and going. Some were paired off and focusing on each other. Except for Lannie, there was not much action. He popped in to check on things and discovered trouble. Right there in the middle of the romance-filled room, he sounded a verbal alarm.

"Somebody's already spilled soda pop or something on the rug. Dang it! Quick! Give me a hand, would ya?" Lannie was shouting.

One could suppose the mess was serious enough to ruin the ambiance several love songs had created, but Ted and I were oblivious to anything beyond ourselves. In the darkened room, Lannie could somehow see the problem that had to be addressed immediately. Even so, I didn't feel his panic, and neither did Ted. The way we were dancing afforded little prospect of prying us apart anyway. We heard his question but didn't react. Everyone else passed off the request, too.

Ted's arms wrapped around me, and the closer we got to each other the more intense his body heat. We edged toward the darkest area of the room, aroused, emotions overtaking us. I hadn't considered in the passing months where the long kisses were leading or what consequences might result.

"Hey, Turk! Help roll this thing up." Lannie's urgency registered with Ted. "Let's get it out of here! My mom will have a fit if she sees it soaked with beer, or soda, or whatever this is!"

Reluctantly, Ted let go of me so that he could help Lannie. They began wrestling the oversized rug. Wes joined them. The rest of us began moving to the patio.

"It will take a wee second, and then you can get back to it, darlin'," Wes said to me with an interesting inflection I didn't like.

I hesitated, wanting to tell him so, then reconsidered. Cooling off outside was probably a better idea. Whatever his innuendo meant, I felt covered in slime. Getting outside helped. Joining the others eased the awful sensation.

The moon's amber glow covered the autumn sky, and I mellowed beneath it. Without Ted, a familiar awkwardness crept in, carrying with it the instant disconnect of a plug yanked from an outlet.

I told myself it was silly to hang onto Ted the way I did, but Hux's absence had intensified my insecurity even more. An older brother's shoulder to lean on and his influence as a senior had dribbled down, helping me adjust through the early days of our move. As exasperating as he was, I couldn't stop remembering how it had been when Hux was around, right after we moved to Knoxville.

"Have you met Hux Hagan? He's really cool," a girl in the restroom had said, and the other's response was, "Oh, yes! He sits next to me in physics. He's a doll!"

My being related had the potential to elevate me higher than anything I could possibly merit on my own. With such a pedigree I could rise above the nothingness that attached itself to me.

"Hux is my brother," I said. I knew I couldn't possibly mess that up.

His trying to distance himself from me in the halls at Ridgewood High didn't disguise our affiliation. Hux and I lived at the same address with the same parents; we had the same last name, and in a kooky way he provided comfort as real as a cashmere sweater in a brisk wind.

I had done nothing to earn the status of Hux's sister. I didn't do anything to become the detestable, cheap, imitation Cleopatra-slut that Daddy had insinuated either.

It didn't matter, I told myself. I belonged with Ted now anyway.

I was about to step back inside where the room was filling with friends when Ted appeared, drinking a Coca-Cola.

"Have one," he said, handing me a dripping-wet bottle.

Taking the cold drink made no sense, and trying to prevent it from tipping while I pulled my cardigan closer and remove the iciness was even more impossible.

"Aren't you about finished with the rug? It's way too cold to stay out here," I said.

"Well," he said, smiling, "we're finished. What do ya think? Time to go back in?"

"Yeah, let's. I'm freezing, and this thing is an iceberg."

"Want to dance," he asked, pulling me close in an all too familiar embrace.

"Nothing I'd rather do. But people are watching, don't forget," I said.

It was a flirtatious warning. Ted ignored it. He adored me, and he let everyone know. We were in love and eagerly acted on it; so when he drew me even closer, it was okay. The evening was still young, but already we were wrapped in feelings usually saved for later in the night.

"Let me get rid of this," I said and twisted out of his arms.

The mantel was full of empty bottles. I put mine there with the rest of them, but before I could fully turn back toward him, he was there. His body was against mine as we slipped into the shadows.

Wes didn't let such an opportunity go without moving in. "Hey, Turk!" he called to Ted, "You'd better get on with it."

I pulled back and looked inquisitively at Ted.

Wes gave a chug-a-lug to a beer and waited for Ted to react. It was Wes's style alright. Ted bristled.

"Wes, my man, shove off," Ted said. "And you can quit calling her darlin' right about now. Got it?"

Ted was sufficiently annoyed, enough to confront Wes. I could see it and feel it, but he continued to hold me, intentionally cutting Wes off.

"You're dragging your ass, Turk," Wes said and turned to go.

It was a comment too crude to glide past. He had Ted's full attention. Coming through too many beers, Wes's parting shot had hit its mark. Abruptly, Ted let go of me and went over to Wes. With their backs to me, I couldn't understand what Ted said, but I knew Wes was not reacting favorably. Even so, he threw back his head with a cavalier laugh.

Ted enjoyed covering me with his protection. I knew that. It probably wasn't a close call, just an idiotic drama. Still, I couldn't help wondering if Wes issued a mandate or a threat of some sort, maybe a requirement to be fulfilled, or a box to be checked as a member of their clique. His suggestive ultimatum made me feel cheap. It was possible he and others saw the slut my dad had seen. The 'Ted's girl' label seemed to be validating it.

Ted regained his composure as he started back in my direction, then paused at the stereo equipment. He interrupted the record that was playing. With something in mind, he sorted through the ones that had not already dropped on the turntable. Our song was a private thing, and in a matter of seconds, its melodic first notes started again. And then came the lyrics. He lowered the volume. As he reached me, the words from "To the Sea" began.

I held no question in my mind that Ted and I both wanted to drift off in a sea of love, and the song didn't have to outline the details. It was a moment that belonged to us, and it had flowered without either of us trying.

Ted elevated me, valued me. I was Alex, just Alex. That was enough—not a princess needing to be polished like the silver service that sat on my mother's buffet, nor a circus act waiting to be brought out by my dad and shown off when perfection was reached.

The potential for the unforeseen at the next turn was concealed. I was not watching for it, nor did I know it held a point of no return. The mild conflict in my head over what I was doing watched as helplessly as an unsuspecting bystander while the combustion caught me off guard. Whatever it was went unchallenged, and neither Ted nor I wanted to stop what we had started. No rational decision had been made in advance, and suddenly it was too late to change course. I could not change my mind. Ignited by the feeling of something very out of control, I let it pick up momentum.

There was a long pause. Silence came between us.

"Wait, Ted, I can't.

"Alex, I love you. You are the only person I'll ever love."

His seductive whisper tickled like a soft feather inside my ear. In a steady, easy move we slipped unnoticed past the others slow dancing near us to a bedroom down the hall. Ted closed and locked the door behind us. And in the darkness, innocence was lost before he reopened it.

———— • ————

The next morning arrived like most others. I crawled from under the covers, went to the kitchen, and sank in the closest chair possible. Lightning had not struck me dead. Thank you, Jesus.

"Tell me you're not going out tonight, are you?" said my mother. "Put your napkin in your lap, honey, and please, sit up straight. I don't want you to go out tonight. Are you babysitting?"

"No," I stated in a perfectly flat answer.

"What, then? Are you staying in? I hope so, honey. Don't you have homework?"

"I have a date with Ted."

"Again, honey? You need to go out with some other people. Let's stay in tonight. You have school tomorrow."

"We're going steady, Mom. I don't want to go out with other people," I said with some degree of finality, squeezing in responses between spoonfuls of cereal.

"Well, exactly what does that mean, honey? Sit up straight," she repeated for the umpteenth time.

I could hear the car pulling into the garage. *Daddy*! I jumped at the chance to leave before he came inside, turning the bowl up to gulp the last of the milk at the bottom. Then I heard him rustling between the car and the entrance to the laundry room. I swallowed as fast as I could and stood up to make my getaway. "I have to get ready for church if I'm going." Hastily, I plopped the empty bowl on the table.

"Of course, you're going. And now, sit down and read a slice of life," Mom said, her assertiveness kicking into action as she pushed a small plastic replica of a loaf of bread in my direction.

Slice of Life was lettered on the side, and individual cardboard cutouts to resemble slices of bread were stacked inside. They were aged and worn from use, each one having a Bible verse on both sides.

"Oh, Mom, this is so dumb," I said, trying to bolt before my dad got inside.

Too late. Through the door he came, wagging a box of Krispy Kreme doughnuts he'd no doubt bought the day before and stashed in the garage to ensure they would not be eaten until now. He set them on the kitchen table and with one hand turned the lazy Susan. It creaked in objection as if it, along with every other person and piece of matter, should challenge him. When it stopped turning, the doughnuts glared back at me.

"Have a doughnut, Alexandra," he said, trying to look straight into my eyes. I avoided his gaze in case he would recognize I had, just last night, justified his assessment of me.

"Well, go ahead, honey, and read a verse for today," Mom said.

Randomly I selected a card from the container and crumpled back in my chair, disgusted at having to comply with the insensitivity of both of them. Glibly I read it, jammed it back into its container, and straightened up to leave, moving as fast as I could toward the pocket door that—with any luck—would separate me from them. I slid it shut and glared at the distasteful chandelier that hung from the family room ceiling. It impressed me in this way: uglier than usual.

Without question, uglier than usual. I reached up to swat at its wooden yoke the way I would if I were throwing my basketball at a hoop. The glass chimneys rattled like they always did with the routine abuse, and the metal shades shifted to their accustomed crooked position.

"Stupid-looking thing," I said to myself. "Why would anyone want a light fixture that looks like it belongs across a pair of oxen?"

———— • ————

Fifteen years old, I'd lost my virginity as of last night, and my parents were eating Krispy Kreme doughnuts in the kitchen while I braced myself for church. Thoughts on what my next move would be, along with reflections on what had gone on with Ted were still churning in my head as I put the finishing touches on my churchy appearance, detached and borderline ashamed.

Not wholly ashamed, though. Part of me wanted to justify my actions, but I was getting nowhere with it. Guilt was not diminishing. It pointed instead to rebellion, doing what I did last night to get back at my dad with a newly sprouted arrogance, acting out something I had planned for weeks. But I had not planned it, and it was not defiance, I told myself. It simply happened.

In the aftermath, I wanted to disregard God, fight Him the way I was fighting my dad, but there wasn't a way. Nothing battle-worthy appeared; only a nagging question remained: What if God was in on this, reducing me to this worthless heap? It refused to stop hammering, and deep down I agreed with Daddy: I was a Cleopatra-slut. Even though I hardly considered him a real person, he was my dad, and God was on my heels.

Chapter 24

Even before last night I felt slightly flawed, but today—if a flaw the size of a mountain could be called *a flaw*, a body without its head and a heart that dangled *a flaw*—I was *that* flaw. The whole inside of me slumped under the weight.

The clock on my nightstand reminded me time was running out. An outfit for church had to be chosen in a hurry. I didn't dare pick up the phone and call Kit, or even consider getting into a conversation with her about Ted. Not now, anyway. She was going to hear about it soon enough. So I decided to give her a quick buzz to see if it was okay to come over after church.

"Hey, Kit," I said when I heard her voice on the other end of the receiver. "You doing anything later?" Her plans to be home all day was the perfect answer. "Yeah, thanks! Okay, great! Around 12:15 or so. You aren't going to believe this one. I'll tell you later. See you then."

I hung up the phone and stood for a second, then went to the hallway.

"Mommy!" I yelled through her closed door, making certain she wouldn't have to open it, ensuring we wouldn't come face to face. "Y'all can drop me off at Kit's after church. We're going over her notes for the math quiz on Monday."

That should buy me some time. I strode back to my room.

———— • ————

Sitting on the edge of her bed, gawking at the sophisticated decor as though it was my first time seeing it, I wondered if Kit had been deposited in this distant point in her home so she wouldn't be a part of whatever went on upstairs. French posters depicting colorful caricatures and high-stepping ladies in black silk stockings plastered the walls of the suite on the lower level that belonged solely to her. The reproduced Toulouse-Lautrec art collection was expertly framed and hung in perfect tandem with custom furnishings that filled her room. It was evident in the spacious two rooms and bath that were secluded in the otherwise unfinished basement, she had it all.

Her parents were rarely there when I visited, and today was no exception. Kit explained that her dad traveled a lot, and she left it at that. Only three or four times during my entire freshman year had I ever seen him; a couple of months ago at the beginning of our sophomore year, I had seen him once. Mr. Gorham was a stout man with glassy eyes and a fake smile that made me feel cold and a little bit antsy.

Mrs. Gorham insisted I call her Jackie. That didn't feel comfortable either, but since she almost never came around when I was there, it was not hard to keep from calling her anything. When she did show up, she dashed about, preoccupied, flitting like a rabbit in tiger country with little to say to me or Kit.

I was glad we had the house to ourselves. I expected to tell Kit what had happened between Ted and me.

"There you are!" Kit spoke frantically. I guessed she had been searching everywhere and finally found me. Startled, I jumped to my feet. My math book fell to the floor, bounced and tumbled underneath the bedskirt. I bent down to pick it up and saw the arm of a doll lying beside it.

"Gosh! You've been hiding your doll from me!" I laughed, razzing her.

Kit didn't laugh. "Give it to me," she said. "I thought you'd be starved by now. Come on. Let's go upstairs."

It was obvious I'd uncovered more than a doll. With a hasty pluck, she took it from my hand and forced a grim smile to gloss over the panic she'd not been quick enough to mask.

I batted an eyelid, suspicious.

"Come on, Alex. Let's get something to eat," she insisted. "I want to hear some juicy details about last night. There's math, too. Don't forget."

"Juicy details," I said, following closely behind her as she went up the stairs, "are in the eyes of the beholder. Shakespeare."

"You're nuts. Stop the baloney and start at the beginning. I know you did something. Don't tell me you and Ted went all the way. Just don't."

"We did."

"Are you crazy? I mean really, what exactly did you do?"

"Kit, I dunno! I mean, I'm scared. What if I get pregnant?"

"Take it easy," she said as if rescuing me from a bad dream. "Grab that pan, would you? We can rustle up some food and sit over there."

She pointed to the bay window with a banquette outfitted with a row of neatly arranged pillows and indicated I should sit. Something more than the posh seating piqued my curiosity, and not for the first time: it was mealtime and there was no one here but Kit.

"Grab something from the fridge first," she said.

She scurried around the kitchen, snatched two hot dogs to boil in a pan of water as easy as clockwork, timing them with a buzzer on the fancy cooktop, then forked them on a plate and waited for the pile of green beans to cook.

Maybe I am spoiled, I thought. I don't know a thing about cooking. And when it's time to eat, we eat together. Oh, well, the Gorhams and the Hagans are different.

I went to the fridge. There was always potato salad or pimento cheese in Tupperware bowls, but Kit didn't ever touch either of them.

"They're fattening," she said, "but help yourself. You're so skinny."

We had often run this drill. I made my selection of pimento cheese. Once her beans were cooked, we sat. She squirted a dollop of mustard onto the hotdogs and promptly dug in with a fork before any of it had cooled.

"Don't you ever eat with your folks?" I pulled crust from the bread and laid it on the side of my plate, waiting for her answer.

Kit shrugged and offered some excuses for why they didn't eat as a family, then quickly finished and left the room while I rooted around in the fridge for more to eat. I could hear her, gagging in the bathroom down the hall.

"I need to lose five pounds," she said, mumbling her vague explanation as she returned. "Want some more pimento cheese?"

On the face of it, her unsupervised homelife was appealing and uncomplicated, and no one was pressing us. Compared to the complexity of do's and don'ts and sit-up-straights and smile-and-look-pretties at my house, hers was a simple question to answer.

"No. No, thanks. I'm fine," I answered and turned off my inquisitive push.

"So, let's hear it," she said, looking at me with birddog eyes.

I could have misinterpreted her directive. It wasn't flippant. But she knew I was dying to talk about Ted, so I sat down and began at the beginning. She listened intently. Our laughter diminished, and I waited for advice, knowing Kit would have it. Then more secrets passed between us, and I felt the level of trust that deepened as the afternoon stretched out before us.

"The doll belonged to my sister," Kit said from out of nowhere. "Melody died when she was four. It was my fault. She was playing in the backyard."

Kit's head began to droop as she recalled events. I wanted to make believe it was a sick joke, but I knew Kit wasn't joking.

"Melody drowned in the little pool my dad had just filled with water." She stopped talking and gazed straight at me, triggering unstoppable tears. "It was my fault," she said. "I was swinging on the rope swing. It hung from a big, old tree beside the house. We moved away from there after everything got so bad. I was six."

"That wasn't your fault! It was an accident, Kit. An accident!

"I was supposed to be watching out for her," she sobbed, "but I went inside to get the doll."

———— • ————

It was getting late, and we hadn't touched a math book; we had, however, bared our souls. I had heard Kit's story, and she'd heard mine. She knew the details of what had gone on at Lannie's house, all of it, but she hadn't said anything negative about the incident with Ted. If she judged me, I hadn't spotted it. But neither could I detect any measure of approval. Whatever happened, she was there for me, and the others in our clique didn't have to know that Ted and I had gone too far.

I couldn't see him going around blabbing about it to his friends, either. It definitely wasn't going to be widespread knowledge, so no harm was done. Our group of friends would be the same. Nothing would change, and whoever was supposed to have the next party would get the word out. As simple as that, we would all show up.

Chapter 25

Ted had his driver's license; he'd turned sixteen in September, way ahead of the rest of us. Put that with his dad's Olds' Cutlass, and he was number one with our gang of friends. As many as could fit piled into his car. I was crunched in so close to him that he could barely turn the steering wheel. We anticipated it would be just the two of us by ourselves at the end of the night. Ever since what had gone on just a couple of months ago, that's the way we wanted it. Once in awhile it was different.

"No one is up for a party this Saturday," I said to Kit on the phone. "Ted and I are going to the movies. "West Side Story." You wanna double?"

"Alex," she began, and I could tell by her tone that she had more than my name on the tip of her tongue. "Never mind . . ."

Something was brewing that didn't get finished. Instead of badgering her to tell me, I changed the subject. "What should I get Ted for Christmas? Any ideas?"

"That's your department. We're not even doing Christmas this year. At least not like in the past," Kit said.

"Is that what you started to tell me? Why no Christmas?"

"No, it has nothing to do with Christmas. But my folks are going out of town before the holidays or somewhere around then. So I'll think of something."

"That's not right. Kit. You're kidding."

"Let's talk later. I need to run. Double-date Saturday, sure. Then come sleepover afterward."

We hung up.

Being on our own in Kit's home where no one cared what we did would always make overnighting at her place an easy choice. We enjoyed total freedom there even though she seemed more comfortable with my folks than hers, especially her dad. We could stay up all night and sleep all morning on Sunday if we chose, come and go through the back door downstairs and never see another human. No one interfered. We puffed cigarettes long into the night. By morning, when we dragged ourselves out of bed, a thick haze of smoke hung close to the ceiling. No one objected until I returned home. My clothes reeked of fumes.

"Honey, I think it's time you stopped spending Saturday nights at Kit's house. I'm just not sure it's the best choice. You miss church, and then you're worn out for the rest of the day," Mom said. "Plan to have her here if you want to, but no more Saturday nights there for a while."

"You're not smoking, I hope," Daddy said as I rounded the corner on the way to my room.

His suspicions were randomly couched in the profound disapproval that I hated. Restrictions and structure may have looked loving from his perspective, but from the outside where I stood, they looked like rejection. Once again, I had ruined everything, strayed too far, and princess-hood didn't feel as royal as others liked to think it was.

"It's my friends. Some of them smoke," I said, certain he perceived my smug half-truth.

For a moment I monitored his disappointment, longing for his approval. My indifference toward him reflected in the sadness of his eyes.

He looked away, muttering to himself. Still, I heard what he said: "Lord God, where have I failed?"

———— • ————

With the holidays rapidly approaching, anticipations were magical and beginning to rise. My personal tradition of traveling on a Greyhound bus back to Gallatin to spend several days with Suzette Mullins and her folks loomed as the best part of Christmas. Routinely spending several days at Suzette's house easily kept alive the friendship we'd begun years earlier.

Kit, on the other hand, hadn't said what her Christmas plans were, but I knew they weren't going to be the usual. Her grandmother had passed away late last winter, ending the tradition she had known. It seemed automatic to want to include her in mine.

My parents encouraged me to invite Kit to join us on our family trip to Aunt Emma's house in Kentucky, going on December 25th to spend Christmastime with my mother's family. It meant a long day, starting early, opening gifts at home before loading the car. After that, we'd travel forever to Aunt Emma's house on the outskirts of Elkton. Kit agreed to come along.

Without a doubt, Kit was going to be shocked at how people lived in rural Kentucky. Thankfully, where we were headed, indoor plumbing had been installed since last year after Aunt Emma and Uncle Rodney struck oil on their property. Other than that, nothing had changed the lifestyle they lived. Overnight, bushels of money flowed in, but Aunt Emma and Uncle Rodney were the same people I had always known. There was no question Aunt Emma would be delighted to have my friend stay the night at her home with the rest of us.

I was sure Kit had never heard a rooster crowing at sunrise or seen peacocks spreading their feathers in spectacular fans of intense blues or picked fresh eggs from under a hen. Her artistic sensibilities would probably go nuts. Already I could see it in my mind. This year Christmas was going to be the best one ever.

The only piece of the holiday unaccounted for was Ted, but for sure we would spend Christmas Eve together, alone. After that, for the few days without him, I would just have to survive.

———— • ————

Wee hours of the morning ushered in a crisp cold day, precisely what you'd expect in the few days before Christmas in east Tennessee. Along with talk of snow coming our way came visions of flurries that would sift a shimmering blanket across our lawn and give us a white Christmas. That put excitement in the air.

Daddy and I sat on the floor of the living room plowing through the tangled mess of tree lights that lay in a nearby heap. Without any warning, he stood up and left the room. I continued to tug impatiently on the wires, hoping by some miracle they would unravel themselves.

I couldn't decide if I'd made any progress on them by the time he returned with a scrawny tree. It had two boards nailed to it, forming an X across the bottom of its trunk. He flopped it down between the Gainsborough chairs that flanked the picture window, then stepped away. It was an ordinary tree, but he smiled, indicating the tree deserved our admiration.

I stared first at it and then at him, unable to cover my disapproval or the fact that I was not impressed with his efforts. It was nowhere near as pretty as the enormous flocked tree that graced the living room at the Mullins' home. Suzette's dad had put their tree up just before I had to end my visit with them, and Mrs. Mullins had beautifully decorated it even though Christmas was still a week away. The smell of fresh pine was matched only by the savory aroma of pastries baking in the oven and fudge boiling on the stove. In the middle of all the preparation, the anticipation of Christmas was reaching its height at Suzette's house when I returned to Knoxville to spend Christmas with my own family.

It would be summer before Suzette and I would see each other for another extended visit, and here I was with my dad, begrudging his ugly tree, fighting this task he had saved until I returned from Gallatin.

I hadn't said anything yet, but he knew I was ready to complain when in walked my mom with an armload of magnolia leaves, evergreen sprigs, and holly—no doubt planning to make a wreath for the front door in the midst of the chaos already going on in the living room. She was oblivious to Daddy's rising exasperation.

"Gracie, please don't bring another thing in here until these lights are on the tree," he said, deliberately maintaining a quiet exterior.

He turned to me: "Alexandra, I want these cords straightened out across the floor. Then I can put on one strand at a time," he said, directing me every inch of the way on how to deal with the lights. I eyed the familiar, poor excuse for a tree skirt—green plaid, skinny, ugly; I took and laid the wooly, old thing aside.

Mom paid no attention. She breezed merrily across the room, carrying her mounds of branches in the unstoppable manner that typified her. At the far end of the room, she stationed herself at the dining table against the backdrop of scenic wallpaper and unloaded her fresh greenery, a handful of artificial fruit, and some red berries on wispy stems tied with a wad of crumpled red ribbon. The entire time she talked to herself about how glad she was to reuse the cluster of artificial grapes.

A plastic orange fell out of the mix. It dropped to the floor, bounced across the carpet, and came to a stop in front of my dad. Briefly, he looked up from his position on bent knees and exhaled a huff. Without a word, he tossed the orange into a pile of ornaments that she'd dumped on the sofa.

A brave twinkle shone in Mom's eyes. She shrugged her shoulders with a hint of delight as if she were a mischievous little girl challenging the opposition. I, however, failed to find the humor. The sooner I could finish and leave, the better it would suit me.

The telephone rang. Mom reluctantly left the room to answer it, preferring to remain in the hub of activity. The sound of her voice came from the next room, low and muffled. Then she called out to my dad with a panic that underscored her tone. "Simon! Simon, you need to come here. Right now, honey."

He pushed himself up from the floor, knees popping and stepped over my sprawling legs as he crossed the room, bypassing tins of Leo stick candy that were stacked off to the side waiting to be wrapped for aunts, uncles, and cousins. He picked up speed as he rounded the corner.

I could hear my parents' urgency as they spoke to each other in the den. Some moments elapsed; when he returned to the living room, his face was troubled and ashen, his tall figure—typically so straight—was bent.

"Leave these, Sweet Pea," he said absentmindedly, pointing to the lights, his hands shaking. "I'll finish when I get back," he added, then disappeared down the hallway to their bedroom.

My mother was at his heels.

I scrambled to get out from under the tree lights, realizing I had not been Sweet Pea in a very long time.

"Mom," I protested hysterically, calling after her, "what is going on?"

"Just wait, honey! Let me help your father."

They came rushing back into the room; he opened the door to the hall coat closet, wrestled on his overcoat, and slammed his hat on his head as if it were a lid on a boiling kettle. Then he was gone. I heard the garage door lifting and the car starting up, and afterward, there was silence. I turned to my mother, totally confused.

"Simon has to go talk to a young mother," she said, stopping to calm herself. "Her husband was killed at one of the dams this morning. It's tragic. Your father has to go to her home and tell her that her husband had a horrible accident . . . part of his job, honey. Your father needs our prayers."

She left the room, and I sat back down on the arm of the sofa. It is Christmas, isn't it, I asked myself, and thoughts raged in my head as tangled as the lights that lay on the living room floor. My father dealt with some tough situations, I guessed. This one was plain to see. It, and the rest of them, gave plenty of reasons for why the vitality was slowly seeping from him. Too, I felt him silently giving up on me, slowly releasing his hand of protection. But the part of him that had not budged—the one that was quietly influencing me—had not let go. I kept my distance, noticing the respect he garnered from others while he pressed on, reckoning with his other responsibilities.

Chapter 26

Christmas morning, with the car loaded and suitcases and tins of Leo stick candy in the trunk, we were off down the road to Elkton. It was later than anyone had originally intended, but not much had gone according to plan, including Kit. Her parents had booked reservations at a ski resort and couldn't fathom why she would even *think* of traveling to Kentucky with us. They'd insisted she go with them.

After the tragedy that had taken place, it was just as well she wasn't coming along. I couldn't trivialize or brush off the event of a couple of days ago. Neither could I pretend nothing had happened to Daddy. If Kit had come along with us, the effect of the terrible news he was stuck having to deliver to a young mom about her husband's accident would have been glossed over.

My mother tried to infuse a supportive attitude into all that was taking place, but in truth, she was failing. The Christmas spirit had fizzled just after the last package was opened before we left home, and now we rode along in silence heedless of the fact it was Christmas Day. It appeared the trip was going to be a long one. Aunt Emma's house was hours away.

Hux and Maxwell sat dutifully in the backseat. I could hear them breathing. I could hear everyone breathing despite even with the extra space in our car. Kit could have easily occupied Jeff Lee's vacant seat since he was gone—married and living with his bride—but I didn't need a friend on this trip. I was sick to my stomach. I needed to be quiet and sit next to my daddy and try to relive the exceptional moment when he had called me Sweet Pea.

Daddy sat rigidly in the driver's seat, both hands on the steering wheel. He could trigger a smile as quick as a wink, but I had not seen one today, other than a half-hearted attempt when he opened the gift Mom had wrapped in last year's crimped paper. Instead, he sat tall with his shoulders straight, buttoned up in his usual white, starched, long-sleeve shirt and perfectly knotted necktie. There was no denying the anguish he must have gone through, telling the woman her husband would not be coming home, ever. It was hard not to see his need, and harder still to realize I didn't have any words to make it better. I wasn't sure there were any words to be said or any he would want to hear. He just kept doing what needed doing, which for now was driving the car with the same intensity he did almost everything, maintaining a distant look with a gaze that never left the road.

At least he isn't smoking in this cooped-up car, I said to myself. I hadn't seen a cigarette pressed between his fingers in weeks. Mom told me he had given it up, hoping it would influence me not ever to start such a bad habit. I had not been persuaded by his effort. Smoking was cool. Revealing that I did it behind their backs would have spoiled everything.

I must have dropped off to sleep, encouraged by the drone of the engine and the hush that continued unbroken, and I didn't come to life till our car turned off the main road onto the rutty lane that led to my aunt's house. Loose gravel churned underneath the tires and jarred me awake. I was still licking my lips and trying to get some moisture moving in my mouth when we came to a halt in front of the deep porch that wrapped the two sides of Aunt Emma's house. It was lit up and welcoming, and through the large windows, I could see relatives filling her home.

Uncle Henry sat on the porch, giving little if any notice to the chill, smoking a cigarette. For whatever reason, we hadn't seen Mom's older brother last Christmas, but he continued to sit—parked like a statue—as if the strong smell of pumping oil was sufficient to greet us.

We were the only ones who had traveled any distance. The rest of the relatives lived close by, and Uncle Henry and his family had only to travel from Hillbound a few miles down the road. His children weren't people I'd seen recently, but I recognized the three of them. Sonny looked grown-up; Richard was scrawnier than I remembered. Madeleine was next to him, hanging on to the leg of his baggy pants. They had seen us pull up but chose to stay together, clinging to a post that supported the roof. I guessed they were daring each other to go near us, but not one of them moved.

Richard was the closest cousin to my age, maybe four years younger. He was about eleven, and Madeleine wasn't much more than eight or nine.

Uncle Henry got out of his chair, steadied himself, and walked slowly across the porch. I could hear him instructing them to go on inside, out of the cold. All the while he waved somberly to Mom. It looks as though he was using all the energy he had to get himself to stand.

Mom reached for her purse on the floorboard. After grabbing it, she couldn't crawl out of the car fast enough. Outside, she began trekking toward Uncle Henry who stayed at the top of the steps, unable to keep his balance without leaning against the siding.

Before Daddy and my brothers could get the trunk unloaded, Richard showed up again, peering at us from the porch. "A'nt Emma's in the kit'chin' whip'in' cream for pies," he announced and disappeared again into the house.

We didn't dare laugh at his twang. Mom had given us reasons why we should be especially kind to Uncle Henry's family, apart from the fact he was her brother: "They're less fortunate than we, and they've had overwhelming sickness. I want you to mind your manners, and don't say anything about anything," she had said.

Nothing was mentioned regarding exactly what it was that had taken its toll on Uncle Henry, but something had. Stooped over and pitiful, there was no hiding the melancholy that gripped him. I was sorry for him without really knowing why.

He scarcely participated when the family gathered for the holiday feast and didn't seem to be attracted to the center table, laden with platters of country ham, turkey, and every morsel anyone might have considered a favorite. He took little notice of the numerous pies, and coconut cake, and boiled custard. He bowed his head (I checked) for the blessing for God's provision and for God's bounty. When the prayer for the season and for the families that were gathered on this auspicious occasion went on and on, I joined the others of my generation who, by our restlessness, forced an end to the offering of gratitude.

Uncle Henry remained respectfully quiet through it all.

Afterward, Aunt Emma removed her apron, and we dove for the food like pigs at a trough, loading our plates and scurrying to find a seat because the huge dining table with its pressed linen cloth was for the older folks. The rest of us could choose a smaller table that had been converted to provide a place, or we could sit on any chair with a plate on our lap and precariously balance it on our knees.

Uncle Henry chose the most remote chair in the parlor. He seemed content to go unnoticed, neither bothered nor amused by the presence of the rest of us. I bounced from my chair to the floor, inserting a bite of food from time to time, engaged in mindless antics to make Richard and Madeleine giggle, but I couldn't help being curious about Uncle Henry.

When the meal was over, all the relatives gathered in the parlor where gifts were piled underneath the decorated tree and stacked partway up the wall. Aunt Emma and Aunt Millicent had a gift for every person, even if it was a tube of toothpaste. Not one of the forty-some people was without a package, complete with bow and attached name tag.

The adults stayed in the doorway, sipping their coffee, taking in the scene, but Uncle Henry sat in his chair, watching listlessly, his head lowered, his hands shaking as colorful wrappings flew and fell beside him.

The image stuck with me, even as the gathering wound down. "Mom," I said as we began the trip back home the next day, "is Uncle Henry going to die?"

Hux thumped me on the back of my head. I thought my question was a reasonable one. Apparently, he didn't, but I wanted to know.

"No, honey, he's simply not feeling well. Maybe you could ask the Lord to help him."

"Okay, I will," I said, and I tried not to notice the ache I was feeling. A hunch said Uncle Henry and I might unintentionally be on the same disastrous path. I quickly dismissed it, but lodged in my conscience in a dark shade of gray was the picture of my relationship with Ted. Whatever my path, I vowed its consequences would never catch up with me the way Uncle Henry's seemed to have caught up with him.

Chapter 27

By the time Christmas break ended and I returned to class, Ted's and my little secret, as far I as could tell, had worked its way through the entire sophomore class and kept on going. Our crossing that carnal threshold had marked me solely as his possession. Rules had been broken, major ones and they were out there for everyone to see. Ted and I were in love, but that didn't seem to authenticate anything. Inwardly I longed to be good, longed to be free, longed to be rid of the claustrophobia that made me a captive specimen in a Petri dish.

Teachers eyed me with their well-informed glints, whispering as I passed in the corridor. Wishing circumstances were different didn't change anything.

During the wintry months that followed, bare trees and frozen ground, and the zip of frigid air in my face confirmed I was stuck in a flowerless season.

Mid-semester Ds and Fs on my report card accurately reflected my lack of motivation and placed my self-image as low as it could go. The small voice of hope I'd tucked somewhere between guilty feelings and denial would've sugarcoated and returned me to innocence and made the ugliness go away, but the seediness of bad-girl mistakes stifled it. Inner conflict had me by the throat, right where it intended: isolated and filthy.

School could not have mattered less. Saturdays took forever to arrive. Becoming Sweet Pea in my daddy's arms once more was not possible. Aside from the temporary closeness I'd felt during Christmas, our aloof standoff continued. Defeat and shame fed like maggots, chewing away at my insides.

Kneeling the way I had knelt in Gallatin's little church, bending my eight-year-old knees on the crimson velvet cushion on Sunday nights was a nice relic in the attic of my mind. I could almost feel the cushy softness that had crushed beneath me as I steadied my elbows on the wooden rail and bowed my head. Clasping my hands, I'd felt Jesus peering down at me from the window. Something about the rescue had seemed real.

If it was a father I'd needed to fill the emptiness, the void didn't last long. Ted showed up. Overnight our bond became bondage. Requiring him was fine until I couldn't breathe, and the irksome reality of dependency choked me. Worse was the fear my parents' God might take hold and mess up my life. I wanted to be connected, but I wanted to fly. I wanted to find the Jesus that would take me in His arms like one of His sheep.

In a single weak moment, moving toward inner peace became as simple as a walk down the aisle at the First Baptist Church on Hill Street. It was not the church I usually attended, but something had drawn me there on an unguarded night. When the preacher summoned all sinners to come forward, I figured he was speaking to me. I went without knowing I would.

If it released my burden, it didn't take long to return; if I had been cleaned up by a walk to the front of the church, then apparently there was another reason I still felt dirty.

It was more than immorality, more being a naughty-girl and not pleasing my parents, more than not measuring up. I was lost and confused, and so very similar to Uncle Henry. Thinking of him convinced me that I was on the same disastrous path as he had been. Or, if not the same, then a similar one. Walking down the aisle to the front of First Baptist Church was not going to erase it. Breaking up with Ted might.

———— • ————

Friction and its scraping background noise exceeded the restlessness that arrived before a change. It was bound to come between Ted and me. It arose quickly. Words flew, heated and emotional. Everything escalated. In the next moment, there was no turning back.

Ending it was what I'd thought I wanted. But then I didn't. With my security blanket gone, I was cold even though it was April.

Sobs coming from the bathroom caught Mom's ears that night, and she begged from the other side of the locked door for me to let her help. Frantically, she called out the way she might if my anguish were a pain she recognized, but I refused to let her in.

"Please, honey," she persisted. "Let me in. I can help. Please, open the door."

She carried no possibility of helping, but her voice was peculiarly peppered. I ignored her anyway, and like Ted upon whom I had built my security, both were cut loose.

Given time, I unlocked the door and stepped out into the shaky awareness of a brand-new day. I found springtime had, on every shrub and tree, officially painted fresh snippets of color to oust the grays of winter; but balmy nights with starry skies wouldn't let me forget my deep involvement with Ted was over.

Chapter 28

SIMON

Alexandra had me concerned.

I glanced in the rearview mirror at her sulking in the back seat, then steered the family's '59 gray Buick out of the parking lot at the Holiday Inn in Cincinnati and headed north toward Detroit. Having stayed the night in a bed that wasn't my own, I discovered my lower back was in a knot. At least the sun wasn't shining in my eyes, thanks to an overcast day.

She hadn't spoken more than twelve words the entire first leg of our journey. With 250 more miles to Detroit, I was beginning to wonder how important it was to drag her and Gracie along on what might very well be my own desire to see, after 32 years, the haunts where I spent eight years of my young adulthood. As fascinating as the Ford Motor Company and police work had been for me in the 1920s, a return trip to see those places could prove I was a selfish so-and-so.

I huffed my breath onto the lens of my glasses, then handed them over to Gracie. "Could I get you to clean them off if you have a Kleenex, hon? I need clear vision; they seem smeared."

Until now, it hadn't crossed my mind to second guess my bright idea to take Gracie and Alexandra on a road trip. A little change of scenery before the summer got too hot was only part of my vacation plan. The rest of it included Toronto and Niagara Falls, but nothing coming from Alexandra indicated she was enjoying the sights, and not anything else had made her smile.

Gracie had shown enough interest for both of them, but hers could easily be piqued by a snail on a leaf.

Leaving the city limits, I entertained myself momentarily with the remembrance of having arrived by train at the Cincinnati station in October 1920. "Eighteen years old . . . just a couple years older than you are, honey," I said to Alexandra.

A grunt was her less-than-enthusiastic response. I left it at that for as long as it seemed reasonable and drove in silence.

"Want the radio on," I asked, eventually. "Anything but that Presley fella."

"Maybe not. You could read a book," Gracie said, twisting her black curls at the nape of her neck.

"Better not. I'm driving," I said in a feeble attempt to earn a chuckle from someone—any-one.

"No, Mom, I'd get car sick," Alexandra countered. "Who are all these old people, anyway?"

"Honey! Be nice. These people are Virginia and Charlie Mallory. Apparently, wonderful people and they're eager to meet you and see Simon after such a long time. Also—"

"And you, Gracie. Let's not forget you. Virginia could hardly contain herself on the phone. It's gonna be an interesting visit. And then Mrs. B and Doc Begbie. You'll meet the two of them tomorrow. We'll settle in at the motel. At some point, we'll drive by a few places in downtown Detroit—"

"What? Get back in the car, again? After riding all day?"

"How about you driving, Alexandra? With your driving test next month, it'd be good practice for you, and—"

"On the highway, Simon? Or in Detroit? Simon, no," Gracie was shooting me her dagger-eyes gaze, head cocked.

"I actually meant in the parking lot of the motel," I said. "Lots of space."

"What a blast." Alexandra's contempt could've fogged my rearview mirror. "How long do we have to stay at the Mallory's?"

I didn't appreciate her arrogant air. "Maybe you should know a bit about them," I said. "They were the first people to befriend me when I moved to Michigan. Virginia worked at the Ford Motor Company with me, in the factory where Model Ts were made. She and her husband took me under their wing and gave me a home away from home, but I lived in a boarding house a couple of blocks away. Charlie was pastor at New Life Baptist Church. Always trying to influence me, in a good way, you know."

Alexandra pulled a face, rolled her eyes. At least, I'd struck a chord.

"They had two daughters. I married one of them several years later."

Gracie squirmed. "Simon, honey, a little . . . abrupt, don't you think?"

Feeling the need to cover for me, Gracie turned around in the front seat of the car as completely as she could to the back seat. "Alexandra," she said, "it's a sad chapter, honey. Your father and young Miss Mallory were married for a brief time before an accident took her life. I'm sure it's—"

I passed a slow-moving car and glanced once more in the rearview mirror. Alexandra's head was turned toward me, her mouth already forming the inevitable first word.

"What? You were married?"

"Yes, and there's more," I said. "Our infant daughter named Nellie Virginia died when a train collided with the bus she and her mother were riding. In my wallet, I have a small photograph of the child if you'd like to have a look; maybe at supper would be an opportune time. They're buried in Highland Park near Charlie Mallory's church . . . or what used to be his church," I said, hoping to be respectful but brief, opening a door if need be. "He and Virginia moved but still live somewhere in the area. We'll see. And then, Doc Begbie and his wife—"

"I know. The woman had the boarding house, and he's a quirky guy that lived there and came from Scotland. Why weren't you on the bus?" Alexandra's voice lacked the edge it carried just minutes just prior.

"That's a good question, honey. I've asked the same one myself a number of times, only not about the bus 'cause I wouldn't have ever been traveling on it anyway. I was recuperating from tuberculosis, working, attending classes. Generally speaking, I was in the process of establishing a home for them. They were in route to that home when the accident happened.

"But to answer your question, as best I can, I believe it's called Providence. And that's not something I can argue with . . . can't even say I always understand why God does things the way He does. But it was your mother, she's the one He intended for me to spend my life. I taught her the Charleston, and we twirled through a three-year courtship before I married her in front of the fireplace at your Aunt Millicent's home." I stopped, took a couple of seconds to let what I'd said sink in.

Nothing.

I hadn't wanted to trivialize the moments that had surely taken Alexandra by surprise; and I wasn't prepared for, nor had I considered the possibility Gracie might demonstrate a chameleon-like ability to adapt when necessary. She was speechless. The entire inside of the car was quiet.

"Maybe your mother liked seeing herself next to me, all duded up in my felt fedora and gray flannel trousers. She looked quite stunning herself as she held my arm and allowed me to teach her the Charleston." I glanced in the rearview mirror, then focused back again to the wide stretch of highway in front of me.

Alexandra seemed absorbed in the view outside the car window.

"Lots to think about, Alexandra," I said, and the Buick's engine hummed. "Y'all holler when you need to stop."

——— • ———

ALEXANDRA

The night spent in another motel with a restaurant attached had Daddy bringing out the picture of a baby—his. The thought was so weird.

Mom managed to make the entire conversation normal and happy, and on an upbeat note, we finished our spaghetti and ate apple pie. She had a way of making it seem like Daddy's having had a wife and a baby was just one of those things that happen, and you move on.

She probably wouldn't have been so happy—or moved on—if I'd been the one having the baby, I thought.

We were somewhere near Detroit, and after breakfast the next day, the three of us piled back into the car again. Daddy drove us the few blocks away to 73 Pasadena Street in Highland Park. It was a quiet neighborhood and old.

He was commenting all along the way on how huge the trees had become. "So, this is it," he said and pulled the car up next to the curb. "This is Mrs. B's boarding house. Still here with the same feel of a temporary port in the storm."

He trotted up the sidewalk and continued up the steps. Mom and I were behind. She was sidestepping the cracks in the walkway and giving her dark curls one last tinkering; I was trying to fathom what the feel of a temporary port in a storm felt like.

The front door opened. Daddy's hand was in midair, preparing to knock. A young woman stood on the threshold smiling. "You must be the Hagans. Please, come inside. The Begbies are thrilled to have you! I'm Maureen, their caretaker. You and I spoke on the phone, Mr. Hagan."

A squeal came from the room to the right, near where we entered. Maureen shut the door. "Mrs. B can hardly contain herself."

Daddy laughed aloud, the color in his face noticeably changing to a rosy blush, and Maureen led us into the dim room. The curtains were pulled shut; a floor lamp in the corner was on, its shade turned to the corner. Maureen directed us to sit on the various overstuffed chairs, but the plump little lady whom I assumed was Mrs. B was having none of it.

"I'm giving you a hug if it's my last, Simon Hagan," she bellowed, and Daddy met her at the archway to the room with a gentle embrace, after which she turned to Mom and me. "Gracie and Alexandra! My, my. Prettier than I could've imagined . . . the both of you! And Alexandra! After three big brothers, you came along. The baby. Bet you don't like that. Do you?"

She didn't let me answer, just smiled with a sunken-in smile. I immediately took a liking to her.

"I'll not be shaking your hand," said the man, seated, smoking a pipe. "Not much that I've got left works anymore if you know what I mean. Most of it didn't work that well anyway."

"Doc Begbie! Sir, don't get up—"

"Laddie! Didn't plan to. Come over here. Let me take a good look at ye. Guess I won't be call'n ye such, seein' how you're an old man!" He roared and tamped his pipe.

"You son of a gun," Daddy said to him. "It's great to see you. And I have my wife, Gracie, and daughter, Alexandra. Both want to meet you, Doc."

"Got yourself a good man here," he said in a gravelly voice. "Glad to meet ye. Whar ye living now?"

"We're in Knoxville, Tennessee," Daddy said. "I'm the personnel manager for an electrical company. You've got bits of that nice Scottish accent still hangin' on."

"And what do ye call the one hanging on ye?"

"Southern, I guess," Daddy said with an embarrassed nod.

"He's with TVA—Tennessee Valley Authority, Dr. Begbie," Mom said and took a seat next to him.

Mrs. Begbie was bent over and wrinkled with a pointy nose. She walked painstakingly to a chair and plopped down. "Please, have a seat, Alexandra," she said.

I made myself comfortable, looking at the faded paper and aging pictures that covered the walls.

"Mrs. B was kind enough to take me in when I was not more than a wee lad," Dad said with a wink at her.

Doc Begbie returned a sly smile and waved his pipe over his head. It caused the whole place to smell like mint. "Mrs. B's not nearly as crotchety as she used to be," he said, his head jerking in laughter, but the rest of him hardly moved.

He looked every bit of eighty like Daddy had said he must be—heavyset, with a big white mustache and white bushy eyebrows peeking out overtop his glasses.

"We had some memorable times in this room . . . still have the scarf from Scotland. Remember the green plaid one you gave me at Christmas? I wore it for years. We use it nowadays to wrap the base of our Christmas tree. It's a keepsake alright."

Both Begbies were eyeing me. I smiled. Mom smiled.

"Same time you gave me the mint julep pipe tobacco. Aye. That and a whole lot more. Best year of my life, having your father around here with me and the Mrs." He glanced past me to my daddy. "Hard times, too."

"Unjust . . . your cop friend dying for no good reason," Mrs. B said, jutting her chin.

"Aye. Killed is what he was! Murder plain as day. And that fella who done it never was brought to justice." Dr. Begbie shook his head. "If you'd been around longer, Simon, he would've been thrown in the clinker . . . feel sure of it. Darn shame tuberculosis had to whisk you right out o' here. But he'll get his reward, pitch-forking around in Hades . . . be my guess."

"Lieutenant Dugan. Yessirree. He was a corrupt one, alright."

Dr. Begbie pointed a gnarled index finger. "That's the guy. Roast him; be my advice."

"You had a lot of worthwhile advice, sir. I'm still appreciative."

"Your father here, had some losses, he did. Aye. What'er their names? That preacher-man, Catholic fella . . . ? Married us."

"Charlie Mallory. His wife is Virginia. They used to live over on Manchester just a few blocks from here. Between you and them and Mrs. B, my time here in Michigan at the factory, policing, all of it . . . you were a remarkable influence on me."

"I can vouch for that." Mom moved to the edge of her chair. Her eyes shown clear blue, even in the dim light. "Simon has spoken so highly of you through the years. I'm happy to meet you and finally be sitting in the place he called home."

"Maureen has the room upstairs that was yours, Simon," Mrs. Begbie said. "What if I have her bring in some coffee for us?"

"No, no thank you. We'd better be going," Daddy said, rising to his feet. "The restaurant's not too far from here, and we're meeting the Mallory's for a bite. Maybe we'll take a spin around the neighborhood so I can show Gracie and Alexandra where they lived on Manchester Street.

"Aye. They'd be getting up in years. Not as bad as me and the Mrs., a'course. I have to say, laddie—and I guess I'll always think of you as such—I hope this daughter of yours understands there's an undeniable supreme dispenser of our destinies. Our paths didn't cross by accident. Just wanted you to know I'm grateful they did."

Daddy walked over and stood next to Dr. Begbie's chair, laid a hand on his shoulder. "That's a mighty powerful sendoff, Doc. I never really paid much attention to my heritage until I lost my father a while back. You and Mrs. B have certainly been a tremendous part of a fine heritage handed down to me. I hope I can do the same."

"We're here and gone," Doc Begbie said, looking directly at me. Best go deep, lassie, way deep where yer roots can sink yer soul into nourishment that'll carry ye forward. And I'll tell ye what that means: follow in your father's footsteps."

"Yes, sir," I said and stood up. In a word, I was scrambling, perhaps to know what to say to him, moreover, to know who I was. Corny as his words sounded, Dr. Begbie's warmth had me by the throat. I swallowed hard. "I'm glad I came to meet you, and you, Mrs. Begbie," I said, turning to her. "The scarf—it kinda has your faces on it now. And Daddy makes sure it's around the bottom of our Christmas tree every year. I never knew—"

"Aye. She's a nifty one, that girl."

Dr. Begbie had interrupted me. Otherwise, I was about to cry.

We finished the visit with hugs and a few moist eyes and were off through the entry with waves and goodbyes, down the steps and sidewalk.

The visit had been as close as I'd come in a very long time to kneeling on a crimson velvet cushion. Jesus was somehow nearby, and again, something about the rescue seemed real.

"Do you think I could drive, Daddy," I asked as we approached the car. "Over past the Mallory's house, and to visit them, and around to some of those other old places?"

"Simon?" Mom had already gripped the chrome door handle on the door to the front passenger's seat. She was giving him her eye.

Daddy paused for a quick moment, considering, gazing at me by the side of the car.

"I'll help you into the backseat, Gracie," he said, "then I'm gonna sit up front next to her."

He fished inside his pocket and produced a tiny snapped leather case: "Alexandra, the keys. Not downtown Detroit, not Lake Erie, not Toronto, but around here . . . why not? I believe you can do anything you set your mind to."

Chapter 29

Passing from fifteen to sixteen years old in the month that followed the road trip up north was surpassed only by my earning a driver's license on my birthday. Close to two years had gone by since the day I promised myself I would travel, on my own, back over to Mrs. Nightingales. We hadn't seen each other, but we had talked several times on the phone.

She and Mom chatted occasionally, following the brush we'd had in front of her house when we first moved to Knoxville. It was hard to think we had allowed so much time to pass, busying ourselves completely with our friends, and Mrs. Nightingale didn't fit the description of those who belonged in Mom's circle of friends. She was still the uneducated, overweight, under-polished woman who was married to the uncouth man in the trailer.

Now at least, they lived in a house. Her home was barely fifteen miles from us, on the other side of town. She might as well have lived a hundred miles away, because a multitude of excuses presented themselves, giving us reasons why we couldn't just get in the car and go see her. We simply had not, until today.

"It will be lovely to see Mrs. Nightingale again," Mom said with a cheery note.

I nodded affirmatively, trying to guess why Mrs. Nightingale's given name was never used. For some unknown reason, using it must have been improper.

This was not a good time to bring it up. My newly acquired driving skills were making Mom anxious, so I paid attention to the road and drove on, past the zoo and fairgrounds, and continued through neighborhoods that became less and less impressive the closer we came to the industrial section of town.

Moving south on Nelson Street gave little indication anyone, anywhere, was alive. A handful of kids played, but that was about all. I could feel apprehension the minute we arrived at Mrs. Nightingales. Mom might have been having second thoughts about inviting her to lunch. She had been under no obligation to extend the invitation, but I'd wanted to see her. It was as uncomplicated as that. Mom hadn't commented on the lack of previous visits, and the subject hadn't come up.

I parked the car and inched myself out. Only a couple of adults strode here and there, one on the sidewalk and one in a nearby yard, but neither spoke. People went unnoticed as far as I could tell, and more likely than not, Mrs. Nightingale coped as best she could.

I walked up to her house, knocked on the door, and stepped back. There was a little wait before it opened, and when it did, her immenseness filled the space between us.

She was smiling, but loneliness showed in the depths of her eyes, and heavy droops of skin puffed below them. I was convinced she probably went out of the house infrequently. She couldn't have fit behind the steering wheel, and the inability to drive wasn't a new predicament. If anything, she was bigger now than when I had known her in Gallatin.

"You are beautiful, child," she said, same as she did from the first day she saw me, despite the hint of maturity I'd acquired in the interval since we left Gallatin. "Beautiful! And honestly! Are you driving us? I can't believe you are already driving! I've always wished I could drive, but Chuck said it wasn't necessary," she babbled, locking the door behind herself.

I guided her down the sidewalk to the passenger side of the car, leading her every step of the way, recognizing her dependency on me. Obesity has summed up her life. She walked out of her house, but from what I could tell, she was a prisoner there, released on a short rope to roam about for a time and return to captivity.

We reached the curb, and I opened the car door, helping her ease inside. She dropped on the front seat with a mighty flop, then strained to pull her dress out of the way so I could shut the door.

Immediately, I recognized we had a problem. The weight of her body had tilted the side of the car and thrust the wide-opened door downward. It had sunk like a battleship into the muddied grassy area next to the curb. Desperately, I tried to move the door, but it wouldn't budge. I stood there, stricken, having no idea what to do.

From the backseat, Mom looked helplessly at me without offering a solution. Mrs. Nightingale smiled her familiar cautious smile and revealed her little square teeth—yellowed with age—then gradually rolled herself over to the middle of the car.

As tactfully as I could, I wrestled with the door, jerking and lifting until it dislodged. Once it was extracted, I gave it a victorious shove. Mrs. Nightingale looked ecstatic. She rolled herself back into an upright position against the armrest. I returned to the driver's seat, shifted gears, and the car lunged forward.

On the outside, everyone had smiling faces; inside it hurt me to see Mrs. Nightingale in such a state. Perhaps she was accustomed to dealing with awkwardness, I thought. Maybe being stuck in the mud was merely one more example. What if experience had taught her to shrug off humiliations so she could make it through a day?

Lunch at the restaurant brought another. Somewhere, aside from the too-small booth and the too brusque server, Mrs. Nightingale took a bite of hamburger, swallowed hard, and said, "Yep, that no-account husband of mine found himself another woman and just took off with her."

The comment touched off a hidden alarm in Mom. I could see it strike. She was uncomfortable, and the gong simply wouldn't quit. She fidgeted with the lettuce on her chicken salad sandwich in between pats on Mrs. Nightingale's hand to console her, and for whatever reason, the I-cannot-condone-mediocrity attitude faded from Mom's manner.

Toward the end of lunch, I couldn't resist telling Mrs. Nightingale my long-lived relationship with Ted had recently ended, also about the upcoming weekend church retreat that was only a couple of weeks off and how I had forced a commitment from him back in April before we broke up.

She got a kick out of hearing how much pressure I had put on him to attend. "My goodness, child," she said, "you've turned into quite a talker!"

"Ted's going to the retreat, and I'm going, but it's not like we're going," I said, trying to make the fact sound acceptable to me, and Mrs. Nightingale and I chuckled about it over our hamburgers.

Mom offered a modest smile, apparently unable to finish her sandwich and unspoken relief reigned once we arrived back at Mrs. Nightingales.

———— • ————

A few days went by, and a handwritten note arrived from Mrs. Nightingale. It was glowing with kind affirmations and had worked in several ways of saying thank you. Because she and I kept in contact after that, I could picture her shuffling down her sidewalk to the mailbox, checking on whether one of my *Thinking of You* cards had found its way inside.

Thursday afternoon two weeks later, a phone call came to my house. It was for Mom with the message Mrs. Nightingale had been found by a neighbor. The news was worse than terrible. According to the caller, the odor from Mrs. Nightingale's home had raised extreme suspicion. The police were forced to break down her door and discovered she had died, alone, several days earlier.

I sensed Mom was about to be sick. I thought I might be, as well. It was impossible to understand—more difficult than putting my arms around her had been when I learned she was moving away from our neighboring homes in Gallatin.

Thoughts of Mrs. Nightingale showing me how to make potholders, encouraging me with her smiles to believe in myself, telling me not to worry when I'd lied about the Kool-Aid—those thoughts and all she had done for me flashed in my memory. She had stood on the sideline of a tough, transitional, growing-up year and loved me the way she would have loved the child she never had.

I left the room wondering if, in her forty-one years on this earth, she'd suffered more from loneliness than from her heart attack and if expediency might have resuscitated her. I wondered, too, if it was remotely possible she'd called out for help but was just too fat for any of us to hear.

It took no time to acknowledge the sad truth Mrs. Nightingale had been trapped by her enormous size in her own tiny world. I couldn't stop asking myself how much different than she was I? Obesity was merely another form of bondage wielding the same damning power as lies. It had her convinced she was nothing apart from the house that held her.

I didn't know who had decided she could claim so little. With no debate, she was gone; she had missed out on life.

It was hard at first to know if I would be well enough to go on Friday to the church retreat, but when the time came, I went.

Ted was there. It wasn't long before we were back in the groove.

———— • ————

The late July weekend church retreat was a mistake. Ted was as out of place in attendance as a person could be, and reasoning didn't make it exceedingly clear to me, either, why I had gone. It brought more of the same introspection that had landed me at a crossroad, wanting to start over, hashing out what it was about Ted and me that just didn't fit.

The kisses were disgusting, and the implications for us forging ahead were pure nausea. I could not make heads or tails of it, but neither could I make it go away. I couldn't look it straight in the eye, but it was impossible to look elsewhere. The arguments with myself continued the entire weekend.

I wanted to be free: free of the guilt, free of my dependency on Ted. Restarting on a fresh canvas seemed like a great idea.

No one could tell me where the road would lead as we moved through summer, but the day dawned when Kit's parents decided Kit should be sent away. She would be leaving for Gainesville, Georgia, very soon, whisked off to Brenau Academy to ensure her place among the ranks of those who attended private schools. Our junior year would begin in the fall at Ridgewood High without her, and like a butterfly with a broken wing, I couldn't fly no matter how many times I was pitched into the air.

Circumstances left me to consider something bigger than myself and exactly what might be the embedded hope that remained before anyone else tried to have a claim on me.

I waited, needing space to gain strength and mend, but the winds blew, and I was carried with them.

Chapter 30

Summer was practically over. The end of August in Knoxville was more than hot, and the humidity made my hair go nuts. That didn't bother me, not tonight.

The bright lights of the Ferris wheel spun 'round and round in a never-ending circle of electrified brilliance against the black and starless night. Finally, my upcoming date with Brian Fessler before my junior year began promised a fresh start.

Brian parked his car in the back lot of the designated property, and we walked to the edge of the fairgrounds on Knoxville's east side. The smell of restless animals pacing about in their cages filled the air. Chaos was in full swing, and the fun-loving rowdiness anyone would expect at a carnival was fully underway when we arrived.

Tempting attractions lured passersby to gamble hidden cash and perhaps win some useless trinket. Irresistible rides beckoned, and unsavory men shoved tickets at their would-be targets, entreating all of us to pay up and take a turn. The organ grinder played while his monkey did a balancing act from his shoulder to his head, adding to the menagerie that stirred the midway. Above it all, you could hear the harsh shout, "Come one, come all!" The scene was energized, twisting, and churning to the reckless rhythm of carnival music.

My second date with him was off to a perfect start. He reached out for my hand, and we strolled past sideshows of every description. I took pleasure in being next to a senior from Crider. It felt good to be free—something that had nothing to do with Brian and everything to do with being released from the same predicament of the pent-up creatures we had just passed. The freedom lifted me as though I were a helium-filled balloon, rising high above the tent tops, rising above the stench of caged animals and bondage. I was breathing again. I had escaped, and I was on top.

People of every description milled about, brushing past us, bumping into each other, spilling popcorn. From the other side of the midway, you could hear the solid gong of a bell, proving someone was powerful enough to hit the goal and no doubt impressing all who were present. Every booth competed for our attention, and I found myself distracted by everything from the ordinary to the grotesque.

"Come on, fella! Win a teddy bear for the little lady. Step right up! Step! Right! Up! Win it now! Right before your very eyes," implored a zealous barker, grabbing the perfect interlude to leap into our path. "Hey, fella, last chance! You can win it for the little lady," he persisted over the competing backdrop of similar propositions coming from every booth.

Clowns stood nearby, holding colorful balloons and armloads of sugary options, rocking this way and that in perpetual motion to mimic enthusiasm for their offerings. One holding cotton candy forced his way forward and nodded to Brian to let him know he would assist him with the tough decision: cotton candy or no cotton candy.

"Hey," Brian said, "you want some?"

"That would be great! Thanks," I answered, my mouth already watering.

Brian took the puffy pink cloud and handed over some money to the clown who was ogling me and the dress I was wearing. Then, with an off-handed comment about our "baby on the way," he disappeared into the stream of people.

Brian looked at me, embarrassed, and held the huge glob in front of me, waiting until I pinched off bite-size pieces that melted in my mouth like Kool-Aid. I let the unconscionable reminder of the episode years earlier with Daddy perish, and I laughed hysterically, making fun of how Brian dodged the oversized bites I pushed at him. My blithe freedom was sinking in, but Brian had changed somehow, and I was pretty sure I knew why.

My mom had tried to talk me out of wearing the stupid dress. It was Kit's, but we often wore each other's clothes. This one had landed a negative reaction from Mom who was eager to change my mind about wearing it.

"I wish you would wear your own clothes, honey," she had said. "You look better in your own things. Kit is going to be leaving anyway. I want you to plan to take her clothes back to her. Why don't you put that back and wear something else?"

It was considerably bigger than a question. It was a directive. She was right about the necessity to return Kit's clothes, but I was determined to wear the quirky dress. Overlapping and held in place by three big buttons in the back, hanging loosely like a maternity frock, the look was uncommon, particularly for a sixteen-year-old. That odd style was Mom's problem with it, but that uniqueness is what I liked.

Brian was too polite to mention what he might be thinking, but when references to his little lady pointed to him, implying he had fathered my child, he became quiet. He shook off the first couple of comments, and the buoyancy of the crowd kept everything laughable. But when it morphed into something uncomfortable, he couldn't look at me and blanched under the bombardment of titles such as your sweetie. The last straw came with the baby-on-the-way remark. From there, the evening went downhill.

I was glad to return to the car. Brian opened the door on the passenger's side and let me slink inside. Holding a Cupid doll he'd won at the rifle-firing booth in one hand and a Coke in the other, I plunked myself down on the front seat and slid across without a free hand to arrange my dress. A button tore off under the tension of my weight pulling on it.

"Oh, gosh," I said as Brian hopped in on the driver's side.

"What's wrong?" He directed his question straight ahead, not eager to see what had happened.

"Well, I've torn a button off my dress. Can you hold this for me?" I handed him my Coke and laid the Cupid doll on the dash.

The lot where he had parked the car was poorly lit, but with light coming from the midway, I could scoot forward and see to retrieve the button behind me. The second button popped off with the twist of my body, leaving the single top button to hold my dress together.

Brian grimaced. I could see it even in the darkness. He squirmed to straighten himself in the seat, both hands on the steering wheel.

"What do you think? It's getting a little late," he said. "What if we make it an early evening? I've got to work tomorrow anyway."

"That's fine," I said, and he backed out into the street and headed on.

Small talk was awkward; silence was more awkward. A blur of lights flashed through the car windows as we passed building after building in the commercial area of town. It seemed to take forever before we arrived in the quiet neighborhood where I lived. As Brian's car crept up my driveway, we could see the open garage and my dad tinkering inside. He stopped and moved quickly when he saw the headlights coming. The garage light promptly went out, and the overhead door began making its automatic descent while my cat scurried out to avoid being hit.

Brian parked, turned off the engine, and hastily scrambled from the car. In the brief amount of time it took him to circle to the back of it, I began trying to position myself to get out gracefully. What an idiot I am! I was deep in thought. Now what? Is he going to stand there while I look for the other button?

With the car door open, he extended his hand. "Why don't you let me take the doll?"

"Okay, but I have to find the other button," I said while he stood patiently holding the door so it wouldn't close and push me back inside. (I was certain he didn't want me back inside his car.) "Yes, here it is!" I tossed it in my purse along with the other one and got out.

"Hi, Carmel-kitty," I said, picking up my pet, nuzzling her tummy, grateful for her as a distraction until we could make our way to the front porch.

Brian politely walked in front of me, unsure of what my dress might be doing behind me. The porch light was on, and I knew my dad had purposely left it that way. The dilemma couldn't be mistaken. Brian had not kissed me on our first date, and he was not going to now. He held out the Cupid doll for me. I put my cat down, and Brian went for the door handle.

"It's been fun. I'll bet you can get your dress fixed," he stated with a nervous laugh, then stepped backward off the porch.

"Yes, sure, probably," I agreed, swatting at the bugs swarming the light fixture. "Good night, and thanks."

I shooed the cat inside and closed the door.

The evening had been a flop. None of it would have happened if I had been with Ted. Already, I was conceding; it would have been much easier to be myself with Ted.

———— • ————

The TV was on in the family room when I stuck my head past the door. Daddy was heading for his chosen seat on the sofa directly across from it, a bowl of vanilla ice cream in hand.

"Where's Mom," I asked nonchalantly and zoomed past him on my way to the kitchen, hungry and wanting to unwind, feeling as if I had reached the shore after a long swim. It was not unusual at the end of a date.

Without answering, he immediately leaped off the sofa. The bowl of ice cream hit the table with a sturdy smack, and he lunged toward me.

"What the Sam Hill have you been doing?"

His voice was more than cross. It was lionlike and heated, enough to melt his ice cream from across the room.

"What is this?" He wagged his finger savagely at the loose flap of my dress that a single button precariously held in place.

I knew exactly what had caught his eye. My spit-hissing belligerence was instantaneous. "What do you mean?"

He acted in an instant, intent on seeing the back of my dress, the hot moisture of his breath on my face. His eyes were aflame.

"This is what I mean!" he said between gritted teeth, fanning the unattached flap as if it were a burning rag.

"I don't know what you're talking about!" I screamed back at him, and the volume increased with every word, packing a fierceness that exploded in every inch of the room.

"The heck you don't!" And he yelled louder as well. The outcry continued. "I won't have any daughter of mine acting like some—"

"Some what?!" I screamed again, through erupting sobs I could not force back.

"Simon! What is it?" Mom came racing down the hallway in a frenzy. Her high-pitched demand for an explanation couldn't begin to mask her eagerness to find out if what she was hearing was real.

"Your daughter!" I spat the words with as much arrogance as I could before he could say it, the awful thunder having reached its height.

His hand struck me squarely on the jaw; then it dropped limp at his side. He stepped back, astonished—the way he might if he'd misfired a bullet from a gun he didn't know was loaded.

A mere second passed. "I hate you! I hate you!" I shrieked.

The reverberations rocked the room, and there was no control after that. Yelling was not enough. With all the force I could muster, I kicked him, and my entire being released its fury. Urine trickled down my legs, warm and unexpected.

I ran from the room, down the hallway to my bedroom, slammed, and locked the door. I threw myself on the bed, knowing the scattered pieces of Sweet Pea would never, ever, fit back together again.

———— • ————

How much time passed, I couldn't tell. Where was I, anyway? Hell, maybe? Then I heard a recognizable sound outside my locked door. Steady, soft knocks startled me.

Mom's desperate voice called to me in hushed whispers to let her in. The knocks grew louder. I had no intention of answering. The blowup over the stupid dress I'd worn to the carnival was enough to shut down the last fragment of connection to my daddy. No amount of her Pollyanna-ing could change that.

I knew what she would say if I let her in: "You need to tell your father you're sorry."

My response would be: "Sorry for what? Sorry that I peed on the floor? Sorry for hating him?"

Then she would try to redeem him: "Alexandra, he loves you so much."

And I would think: Oh, that is interesting. And what clues stand out to make that halfway believable?

The dialogue inside my head refused to end, and partway into the night, after the raps on the door had stopped, I lay waiting, wanting hope to appear and somehow change the color of darkness. I knew if I had never been born, Daddy would be glad. I detested where I was, curled up with my musty blanket and my thumb to suck while he stayed on the sidelines.

His fallen one. Not who he anticipated, not perfectly obedient, not perfectly stable on his wobbly pedestal. I should have been someone else, but I wasn't. *Sorry*. Why? For not liking that he falsely accused me, casting me off as a whore! Wasn't that what he had chosen to think? Wasn't that his own past creeping forward to judge me? He'd said it himself—all that garbage I'd heard through the years about his big acting career in Albuquerque. He was the actor. He was the one with a plan. Exactly what would he expect me to do now? Join the sideshow back at the carnival with all the other lewd acts? Okay, but I would not be his marionette . . .

And my spit-hissing continued.

All the damage that could happen had already happened, and a sickening smell hung in the air. Somewhere, death had parked itself, either under my bed or behind the plump chair against the far wall, or possibly beside me. Daddy's plan had died, and my mind tried to forget that I was the cause. I buried my head between my pillows and let my broken spirit console itself.

The monotonous hum of the air-conditioner unit finally went silent. In the moonlight, I recognized the wild vine growing up and over it, snarling out of control and rebelliously scratching on my window. I watched the weird shadow that its leafy strands cast across my rumpled bedsheets. Under the prickly vine, a flower grew. I knew it for a fact, but my eyes grew weary waiting for it to show itself.

Who cares anyway? I've seen that flower countless times before. When the sun rises in the morning, maybe then its face will be pressed in my direction, and everything normal will resume, I reasoned. Although the household had been rocked, and the foundation had moved beneath us, no one will acknowledge they noticed anything. I will drink orange juice, put my napkin in my lap, and stare into space, and Daddy will probably be nowhere in sight as another Saturday rolls around.

Loves me so much? Not true. Mom was so wrong! Even if he once had, his love was as obscured as the silly flower—hidden and easily overlooked, waiting for the sunlight to awaken it.

I rolled back over and kicked off the sheets.

What if there could be a way to earn his love?

No! I told myself with a deep conviction. It's not possible. It's not there, I said, inventing a deeper conviction.

After a time, I tugged at the sheet and covered myself again; and from the void inside me came a remnant of consolation: A day had not existed when my father wasn't waiting for me to return.

I threw off the sheet again. But I can't change, and I don't care.

Before my eyelids could close, Mom's knocks started afresh. As usual, I let them go unanswered. It was all I could do to roll over and cling to the wet, limp bag that had been my pillow. Exhausted, too worn out to battle any longer, I stopped fighting the sheets.

The air conditioner kicked on. Above its noise, scarcely within reach of my hearing, I was sure I heard a whimper like the voice of a saddened soul calling out to me.

"And I thought you would call me, 'My Father.'"

Lifting my head, I turned to listen. All I could hear was the steady whirr of the air conditioner.

Chapter 31

It wasn't Brian Fessler who cruised the local drive-in Tasty Freeze. It was Howard Murdock, and there I was, scrunched close to him in his 1957 turquoise Chevy convertible—didn't matter it was four years old. The top was down. The September night was mild.

Howard's arm draped out over the side of his car door. Single-handedly, calm, and collected, he steered with the other. Even though in my heart of hearts I knew only hoodlums had cars with loud mufflers, he was someone to be with. I wanted everyone to watch as we rolled into a parking slot. If Ted was there, I especially wanted him to take notice. Being noticed was the whole point of the chrome detailing and white sidewall tires. No one else's car even came close to attracting such attention.

We talked, waiting for one of the servers zipping back and forth on roller skates to spot us. I took off my headscarf and checked the mirror to make sure the wind had not disturbed my hair-sprayed, back-combed flip.

Howard was unusual. Nothing could accurately sum up his persona. He was just plain weird, even before weird was defined in the dictionary. I had to be desperate to be going out with him, but stuff with Ted had spiraled out of control. And for sure there would not be any more dates with Brian Fessler.

I was desperate. I hated the dirty connotations. Why not, I thought, a scarlet letter stamped on my forehead?

Breaking away from the reputation that labeled me was next to impossible. I was Ted's party doll. Howard Murdock ignored that about me. He treated me with respect and dating him afforded me some relief. The payoff was having to live through his incessant talking. It's what he did best, especially describing in detail what he had on his mind. Often it included telling how rose petals would be strewn all over our bed when we eventually married. He would articulate his passion, take a deep, deep breath, then exhale loudly through the wide space between his two front teeth. It somehow enabled him to sort out whatever he envisioned, along with the intenseness it was causing.

Daddy did not approve of Howard, and he wasn't alone. Kit questioned some of what he said and did, and I could tell from her letters coming from Brenau, she had concluded he was bona fide wacky.

It was hard, having the only real friends I could talk to living in faraway places. But in a matter of weeks, Kit would be back home for the summer. The good news was she would not be returning to Brenau but would instead be staying for our senior year. The bad news was her father had moved out of the house. Mrs. Gorham had divorced him, simple as that. Kit would be coming home to some drastic changes.

While I couldn't put a finger on why the departure of Kit's father was a relief, perhaps it had something to do with his come-hither eyes.

Suzette, on the other hand, was in Gallatin, and nothing would change that. The times we saw each other were no more than twice a year, but our friendship weathered the separations. We could easily pick up where we left off. I could only imagine what she might think of Howard Murdock.

From day one, he had pushed his way into our home, grabbing and pumping Daddy's hand wildly before Daddy had half a chance to extend it. Howard kept it up much longer than any reasonable handshake until Daddy's glare advised him to let go.

"Well, how in the world are ya, Mr. Hagan?" he'd yell in a grating voice, treating my dad as if he were deaf or in a distant field; then he'd force a huge smile and allow it to spread dramatically across his super-sized teeth. Enough drama and obnoxiousness abounded to bring out the defenses in the most normal person. Howard awaited the answer, looking up at my dad with the earnestness of a panting dog.

"I'm fine, Howard," said my dad, cranking down his tone as smoothly as if he were churning homemade ice cream. "Have a seat."

I suspected he would rather have said, "Cut the crap, Jerk. You're not fooling me."

I was relieved he didn't go that far, but he loathed Howard. After a few months, so did I. Howard and I had an ugly falling out; it ended everything between us.

With the breakup came a weak moment, and Ted was back to pick up where we'd left off. I had no backbone to resist. It was easier not to.

"Alex, I don't ever want us to be apart. Promise me," Ted said. "I love you. It makes me crazy when we're apart. Promise me, Baby, it won't ever come to that."

———— • ————

Dad was comfortable: Ted was coming around as before; Howard Murdock was not. Slipping back into the relationship was like slipping into an old house slipper, and Kit's arrival back at home simply put a cozy shoe on the other foot.

But by the end of October during our senior year, the comfort level with Ted bottomed out again.

"Y'all make me sick to my stomach," Kit said. "Why don't you just give it up, Alex? For Pete's sake. Take a break . . . like for ten years or something. You guys are on different tracks. Why ruin your senior year?"

"I know. I know all that! What's wrong with me anyway?"

"You don't want to be trapped. Ted wants to hold you. That sums it up. You'll have to decide, Alex."

"It's more than that," I said. "I want us, but it's all too complicated. You know what I'm talking about. Ted doesn't own me. It's like he requires me, or I owe him my soul, or something weird. I am not his property, Kit. Oh, I don't know what I'm talking about, but for sure, I'm not what I want to be. And I really, really hate the feeling."

Chapter 32

With our senior year half over, my options were swiftly running out. Something had to give. I could not keep body and soul together with my insides rotting. Ted and I were thick and talk of eloping dominated our conversations. Marrying would fix everything.

Kit told me I was insane.

Secretly, Ted and I made our plans anyway. Classes would break for a long weekend, and we would go to Ringgold, Georgia, and after that—nothing was decided. It didn't matter. I would be Ted's wife. God would recognize I was a decent girl after all.

God would be happy. Daddy would not.

I reminded myself I could never model what my dad wanted anyway. No matter how much I'd grown up or the many years that had passed since the day I ate the Kool-Aid and lied to him, it was still my daddy I wanted to please, but it wasn't possible. I'd quit trying. I think he had done the same.

Facing any more separations with Ted required too much courage. I couldn't do it.

The agenda for the weekend was taking shape. We would leave close to 9:30 on Saturday morning, travel to Ringgold, meet with the justice of the peace, make a beeline for the chapel, be married by midafternoon, return, and tell our parents the news. Quick and easy. Maybe his parents would let us stay the night at their house. Maybe not.

Then the unthinkable happened: someone unearthed our plans and ratted us out—to my mom. Just like that, the elopement fell dead in the water. I recognized how altogether Howard- Murdock-like the whole incident was. He had to be the culprit.

Nothing I could do.

———— • ————

Our plans were foiled, but Ted and I finished out our senior year; I began in the summer at the University of Tennessee. Feeling much the same way I had as a third-grader: lost, failing, and overwhelmed by something much, much bigger than myself.

To a degree, I'd already guessed I couldn't survive at UT, let alone graduate. Halfway through the summer semester, I was convinced. Be that as it may, I dragged myself through to its end.

American flags were going up all over our neighborhood, and the one at our house waved from its bracket on the front porch. Fourth of July capers were well underway. Kit would be joining my family to participate. Ted would not.

I was single once again; my house, however, would be full without him. Most folks were close enough to be family, but one newcomer was on the list.

"Let's be happy!" Of course, Mom was flaunting her favorite memo. She enjoyed nothing more than getting everyone together, and today was a perfect day for it.

"It's going to be so very nice. I've laid the badminton game out back on the table, and Maxwell, I want you to put the net up."

"Aw, Mom, no one's going to play badminton," grumbled my middle brother. Given his status as a recent law school graduate, one would expect more reverence, but he was adamant. "I've put that thing up every single time people come, and nobody plays! Nobody," he said, disgusted by such an illogical suggestion.

"Don't mess up your madras shorts, Maxie," I quipped, "while you're putting up the net."

That warranted a huff. He opened the sliding-glass patio door and paused. "You do know Ben's bringing his girlfriend, and she is super sharp, a Chi Omega. You know that. Right?" he said, cross-examining me. "And he wants to make a good impression on her. So, shape up."

Mom smiled at the mention of Ben Campbell's name. He'd been part of our family, seemingly forever, due mostly to Maxwell's encouragement. Orphaned as a young boy, Ben had made his own way, and the inclusion of him in our gatherings for the last four or five years was expected and fun for us all. He had a winsome personality, impressive accomplishments, and classic good looks.

While Maxwell and Ben were bound by the brotherhood of their fraternity, Mom and Maxwell shared a special rapport regarding achievement: climbing, putting your best foot forward, looking the part, walking the walk, talking the talk. Both were shaped out of a big chunk of stubbornness. Both were unflappable.

"Maxwell, do as I say. I want the badminton set put up. It's a beautiful day and not too hot either," she said.

With the door gaping open, heat poured into the room, and outside it couldn't have been more humid, insuring rain at any second. Ignoring that, Mom planned on the day turning out perfect, despite the typical morning shower that would leave it warm and sweltering. With her way of persisting, to question her was pointless. She'd be right, and everyone else wrong, and she'd put a twinkle in her already sparkling eyes and laugh her gleeful laugh.

The phone rang, and I answered.

Kit was on other end, crying. She wouldn't be coming after all. She explained she would talk to me later, then—*click*. It didn't sound good. Something was very wrong, but chaos would be plentiful at my home, and her situation might just take it over the top. Even so, her canceling didn't help my concern about why she was so upset.

Disappointed, I wandered into the kitchen and began slicing watermelon.

Dad was there, feverishly rattling pots and pans, fixing whatever we were preparing to feed the masses. He was in charge of the food, but Mom had been doling out instructions since early morning. Anticipation filled the air.

Jeff Lee and Melissa arrived late to no one's surprise. With their son in tow, his wife joined me in the kitchen, offloaded the child to my dad and began helping me with the watermelon.

Twisted red, white, and blue garlands of crepe paper dangled from the trees. The glider on the patio had a recent coat of paint, and the freshly mowed grass couldn't have looked any better.

As more guests started to arrive, a mild panic seized my mom. "Oh, dear! I'm just not ready yet," she announced. "Would somebody please help me? Get the grape juice out."

Kitchen duties were not a skill she cared about; however, where people were involved, she excelled. Everything had to be out of the ordinary so guests would receive a large dose of hospitality. She made every effort to ensure everyone was acquainted with everyone else, made them comfortable, and gave them something to eat.

In the middle of the festivities, the first and only grandchild who (on a normal day would attract all the attention) went practically unnoticed as he took his first steps around the coffee table.

From the crowded front hall came the grind of the front door opening, followed by additional chattering voices. One unfamiliar one debuted, melodic and birdlike, chiming in above those of my family members.

"Deanna! Please come in. I've heard so much about you," Maxwell said with the gusto of a politician. "Come in, come in."

I peeked around the corner watching her make a grand entrance: the beautiful swan with porcelain skin and wavy blonde hair. Wiping watermelon off my hands, I observed from afar.

Maxwell turned to Ben, who gave no indication he wanted to let go of the girl on his arm. "Ben! Gimme the handshake," Maxwell said.

Reluctantly, Ben pried himself from Deanna's grip. "Max, ole boy, so good to see you," he said, and the brothers clasped their free arms, pumping their fraternity handshake. "Thanks for having us," he decanted with a Charleston drawl, then repositioned himself for the introduction of the splendid jewel who had accompanied him.

"I want you to meet the Hagans. This is Maxwell, of course," Ben said with a degree of formality. "Maxwell: Deanna Cunningham."

My brother stepped back, displaying his favorable appraisal of Ben's girl. A gregarious smile spread across his face. "Well, hey, Deanna! I hear you're a Chi O," he said. "That's great! Wonderful! Where in the world did you pick up this character, huh?" He gestured toward his frat brother.

Ben blushed, his broad grin attesting to an obvious fondness for the young woman next to him. From as far away as the kitchen, I could clearly see it.

It would've been difficult to miss Deanna's aristocratic pose as she stood next to Mom's antique sugar chest in the foyer. "Well, Maxwell—" Her answer dripped off strawberry-red lips. "—honestly, I think he found me!"

I could hear her patrician voice with an equal measure of personality to match Maxwell's. It exuded wealth and sorority. Regally, she stood like a statuette, draped as the center of attention. Her hand was lying on the sloppily layered stack of yesterday's mail. She awaited the rest of the introductions.

A prize if ever I've seen one, I thought as my dad entered the room. His gaze fell on the beautiful blonde. He interrupted his intended destination, so he didn't miss the coquettish smile she seemed to have reserved just for him.

Ben was beaming. "Mr. Hagan, this is Deanna Cunningham," he said. "And Deanna, I want you to meet Mr. Hagan."

"Well . . . Ben," said my dad, and a long pause hung in the air . . . "you've certainly picked a beauty!"

Daddy set his tray of grape juice down so he wouldn't drop it and didn't take his eyes off her. He was kaput as a drifting boat that had run aground.

I was next in line to meet Deanna. My throat tightened. I wondered if Daddy would ever notice me again.

—————— • ——————

It was hours before the last good-byes were said. Dad walked thoughtfully back into the kitchen where my mom and I were loading the dishwasher.

"Whew!" she said. "I think everyone enjoyed themselves. Don't you, Simon?"

"That Deanna is delightful. A natural beauty, isn't she? I don't think she had on a stick of makeup. Do you agree, Gracie? Looks like an angel," he said. "Yessiree! Exactly like an angel."

Mom bent over to pick up a fork she'd dropped. "What are we going to do with this leftover pork? Answer me that, Simon," she said, turning her attention to the scraps on the platter.

And just like that, the conversation had switched from gorgeous Deanna Cunningham to the pig we had eaten for dinner, making it seem no possible solution existed for dealing with the excess meat. My mom's efforts were clearly devoted to the task of cleaning up the kitchen.

My dad's mind continued to be stuck on Deanna. "That Deanna! I'll have to hand it to Ben; he would do well to catch her! I'll use it for sandwiches, hon; wrap it up," he said, "It'll be good in my lunch."

Accolades for Ben's lovely girlfriend, so natural, so this, so that, reverberated in my ears. I swallowed hard and said nothing, mentally closing my eyelids with the bird crap on them.

Deanna was gorgeous. And, yes, she had arrived in our lives and taken over my daddy's heart. Her chariot rolled down our driveway, and the scene closed on a starry night with the aura of an elegant dream. Out of my jealousy, I asked my own question: Who exactly was that perfect princess?

I finished putting the final touches on straightening the family room and brought in cushions from the glider. Heading down the long hallway and into my bedroom, his words echoed off the walls. I closed the door behind me and turned the lock.

For Dad, Deanna was the new and freshly-placed jewel. He would have traded me in an instant.

For me, she was a complete realization that I was not worthy. The revelation may as well have been a cancerous lump on my breast, appearing out of nowhere, threatening, invasive, and promising to keep me awake at night with a desire for wholeness.

After a long phone conversation the next day, and a half-hour passed, the doorbell rang. It was Ted.

Chapter 33

Going through sorority rush in September solidified how unsuitable I was for campus life. Besides, Dad had no money for me to live in a dormitory. I'd begun to think I didn't really want to be on the same planet with anyone anyway.

Kit had pledged a sorority, a good one, but from what I could gather, her home life was a mess. I hadn't been to her house or seen her mother since Kit moved into the Tri Delta house. Neither had I seen her dad in years—not since the divorce. The relationship between Kit and him was tense. Kit was going to therapy.

"I can't sleep at night, and I certainly can't move back home," she said on Wednesday over coffee. "A lot of stuff . . . garbage. Counseling with Dr. Frazer helps sometimes, other times not. I'm not sure I want to go back."

"Back to the counselor or back in time? How can I help? You know I will," I said.

She looked at me and then away. "My dad used to come into my bedroom, Alex. I was six. I know because I was in first grade. He'd check my panties to see if I had wet them."

I covered my mouth, masking shock.

"Yeah, right. I was six years old. Not likely I'd be wetting my pants. You get the picture. Dr. Farley is digging into all that. Well, last night I had a nightmare."

Kit looked strangely apprehensive, hurting.

"Why don't you come home with me tonight? It could help to get away from campus."

"I might, but tell me what you think about this dream. Will you?" She waited for my nod. "Melody . . . you know, my little sister that drowned . . . Melody was thirsty," she began. "In the dream, she was very thirsty, very needy, very frail. For some reason I put her in a plastic bag, just to confine her so she wouldn't go near the water. I don't think I knew *what* water." Kit's brows were furrowed, her gaze steely. "When I remembered her, it was too late. Melody lay there with wide, piercing eyes, dead. Dead, Alex. And I woke up, screaming at my dad."

I slowly inhaled, hoping it wasn't obvious to Kit that overwhelming concern had knocked the breath out of me. "I am so sorry," I said, "I think you've got to tell your counselor."

I thought Kit was finished telling the saga, but she wasn't.

"Melody lay still and cold with those wide black eyes." Kit focused into the distance as if an image floated in her vision—one she could not erase.

"Oh, gosh, Kit. Promise me you'll tell Dr. Farley."

"Will you come with me?" Kit lit a cigarette.

Hesitating, I waited for her to look at me. "I can't go, Kit. Otherwise, of course, I would."

"You can. I'm sure of it. If you don't go, I won't," she said. "I can't see Dr. Farley alone."

THREE DAYS LATER

It was a sunny Tuesday morning. The doctor's office was pleasant enough: beige walls, beige carpet, low-level lighting, and upholstered chairs in varying shades of avocado green.

Dr. Farley indicated where Kit should be seated, and I sat beside her, feeling unsure of myself. Holding the ashtray was a feeble attempt at usefulness. Kit pulled an opened pack of Kools from her purse and lit a cigarette.

"What about your sister? We're talking about her today. Tell me about your sister," Dr. Farley said to Kit.

"She died when she was four. Melody. My sister's name was Melody Elaine." Kit's hands were shaking as she brought the cigarette to her lips.

"Yes, and tell me a little bit more about that."

"She drowned in the kiddy pool my dad bought for us. It was my fault. I was six."

"And how was it your fault, Kit?" Dr. Farley was attentive but expressionless.

"I went into the house to get it . . . Melody's doll . . . but I couldn't find it." Kit took a long draw on her cigarette and slowly released the smoke. She gazed at nothing for a moment. "It was on Melody's bed that morning, but when I went to her room later . . . after her nap, it wasn't anywhere in sight. When I finally found the doll, it was inside her closet. I grabbed it and hurried back outside . . . because I was supposed to be watching Melody while my dad filled the pool."

"I see," said Dr. Farley. "Take your time. And why did you go inside to get a doll if your dad asked you to watch Melody?"

Kit looked vacantly at Dr. Farley and continued. "He told me to. My dad told me to go inside and look for my sister's doll. When I got back outside with it, the pool was already filled with water, and Melody was—"

Kit's long pause made the room grow strangely quiet. "Here, Kit. Take a sip of water." The doctor handed her a cup and a box of tissues. "I know how hard this must be, but I think it's important to keep going. Do you want to continue?"

I felt sorry for Kit.

"Yes. I had a strange dream, a disturbing one," Kit said, holding the pack of cigarettes on her lap.

And the nightmare unfolded as Dr. Farley concentrated on chunks of the events. Kit lit another cigarette. I lit one as well.

"The doll, Kit . . . ," said Dr. Farley, what was it made of?"

"What do you mean?"

"Was it plastic, rubber, one Melody would take to the bathtub with her?"

"No, it was cloth."

"Would Melody have taken a cloth doll with her into the pool to play with it?"

"No . . . no," Kit stammered. "It was a Raggedy Ann. What are you asking?"

"Just clarifying. Your dad sent you after a doll that Melody couldn't—or wouldn't—have played with inside the pool. And while you were gone, she drowned."

Silence.

I extended the small ceramic tray to catch Kit's cigarette ashes before they dropped.

"Yes," she said, softly, after a few moments.

Dr. Farley wrote something in her notebook, raised her head, and presented a kind smile in Kit's direction. "I think we need to call the police."

———— • ————

No one had questioned Melody's death. It appeared to be nothing more than a terrible freak accident. Murder could look like that. A grim cover-up, a dad's dark secret concealed year after year while Kit shouldered an unbelievable burden. No autopsy. Accidental drownings just happened.

Later that same Tuesday, Kit recounted for me, she'd gone to her dad's apartment. Everything had come to a head. She confronted him, told him she was going to the police, that she knew what he had done and why he'd done it. From her own experience, she would testify, knowing he was capable of the unspeakable.

"He listened to my version," Kit said to me. "He hung on my every word. I told him I suspected he'd had me search for the doll while he held Melody underwater."

On Friday, in broad daylight, Mr. Gorham somehow lost control of his car and skidded in front of an oncoming semi-tractor trailer. He died instantly. The road was neither slippery nor curvy, not even dangerous. A pity, people said—just one of those horrible accidents.

In the days following his funeral, oddly, it was Kit's existence, not the end of Mr. Gorham's that seemed cordoned off like a crime scene. She'd look at me with empty eyes and expressed raw feelings, but when all was said and done, neither of us was equipped to soothe her shattered condition. Our relationship hobbled along in awkward attempts to find our common ground.

I would have been well-advised to focus on my studies, but like idiots, Ted and I laid out of class, skipping entire days away from campus so we could be together. By Christmas, we were officially engaged. To nobody's amazement, I flunked out before the end of my sophomore year.

Spring semester came and went without me. Kit finished hers, and it wasn't the issues involving her dad that had begun to distance us, rather that everything seemed to black out. She went to France to study art.

I didn't quite know how to interpret her parting words of advice, but I knew they were meant to be taken seriously. "Let go of Ted, Alex. You'll get over it. Cut him loose," she said. "Write me."

It wasn't that simple, given my attraction to Ted. Being with him was all I knew.

On the other hand, I felt continually pulled in another direction, wanting something different—wanting authenticity. Whatever was responsible refused to release me. The end of the line had come.

It was a hard snip, but I did it. I let Ted go.

Chapter 34

Possibly my dad had been there all along, hovering in the kitchen while I stared at my bowl of cereal.

"Work's going well for you, I hope," he said. "You're working a lot these days."

It was one of those funny verbalizations that asked and answered a question at the same time. I wanted to speak, but what I wanted to say had nothing to do with my job.

Antsy and a bit out of step after flunking out of UT, I'd gotten a job as a clerk at Bundy's Drugstore and created a little world of my own. My undirected plans were playing out as impotent background music, and although something was supposed to be happening, it wasn't.

His question might just as well have been directed to the air around me, but I answered anyway, with a cool drop of sarcasm. "Ever think I'd be such a grand success? I know how proud you are of me." My irrelevance said it all, and I intended to pin-prick any balloons he might be holding. The potential for our relationship had duly slipped away, and like the clay to the potter, from the inside, I screamed, *Why? Why have you made me?*

"What's it going to take, Alexandra? What exactly is it going to take to make you wake up? You have unlimited potential," he said. "Why don't you try and use it?"

"I had to wait, Dad, remember? Wait till way after the semester began to even get books. It's a little hard to make it at a university without textbooks."

"It took all I had to pay your tuition. Keep that in mind," he said. "Holding off a couple of weeks helped alleviate some of the financial strain. I don't recall it was way after the semester began," he gently quipped as he finished preparing his lunch for the workday ahead. "Seems like all I've done isn't enough for you, Alexandra."

His comment slid like an unwanted truth, down into my conscience, and I watched him pull out well-hidden Vienna Fingers from an upper cabinet.

He took two cookies from the package, methodically put them into his lunchbox next to a plain bologna sandwich and his red tartan plaid coffee thermos, then latched it shut. "Have a good day, Sweet Pea," he said and left the room, mumbling to himself, "Lord God, show me—"

I stood at the sink with my mouth hanging open.

———— • ————

Sweet Pea? Perhaps my dad's calling me Sweet Pea had been a mere slip of the tongue, but something inside me begged the beautiful sound of it never to go away.

Whatever affection my dad reserved for me had long ago become invisible, easily lost in the gray haze that settled over our relationship. Unimagined small misunderstandings mushroomed into unresolved differences, foreshadowing turbulence as real as a tornado sky. They had forced the winds of independence to whisk me through most of my teen years, biting and snipping.

No ifs, ands, or buts about it: I frustrated my dad; my mom frustrated him, too. He tried pressing her down in one arena, and while he could contain her some of the time, I would spring up in another place. He tried sprinting to subdue me, but Mom shot out somewhere else. We stayed slightly under his skin, like scabies, unseen but so very pursuant, as relentless as a constant and ever-present itch. She had a way of manipulating situations for what she expected to accomplish. We both did. Hers was a balancing act to secure rewarding opportunities for her children. Rising was part of her personal survival. Ensuring we all climbed to the heights was her reward; but my dad went to work, returned at night, cooked, and retreated, then closed out another day behind the newspaper, and I went on loving nameless illusions that could not love me back.

I never heard him say his dreams were lost—neither had he said they cheated him; he wouldn't. But I was pretty sure one had eluded him: the relationship with me—the one I couldn't reach out and take, the missed one that left me empty.

Part of me fought orphanhood; part of me fought everything else. Perhaps I should have been wandering a Paris street—like Kit.

She'd been gone for three weeks. I was beginning to wonder. Then her letter came. It sat propped against the lamp on the sugar chest in the foyer so I wouldn't overlook it when I came home from working my shift at Bundy's Drugstore.

Ripping it open as I went, I flew to my bedroom, made myself comfy on the slipper chair, and started reading.

Mom stuck her head around the corner. "How is she? Come to the kitchen; I want to hear."

"Fine, fine. Just a minute. Let me finish. I'll be in there," I said, waving her off.

The Paris scene, Kit wrote, was totally idyllic with the lovely Sacre-Coeur on the hill. The flat she was living in was adequate—nothing special—probably safe—in the heart of an artist colony, Montmartre—and oh, so near Paris. She shared it with a guy from a rural area who experimented with LSD. She was ecstatic, being in places Toulouse-Lautrec frequented. On and on she went. It sounded delightful, impressive, except for the LSD.

LSD? Really?

Reading between the lines, I could see her courage to patch up the hole that had been drilled in her heart. I felt her search for something she didn't name and wondered if we were similar people—many of us in the same boat allowing fake happiness to alter our destiny.

On an average day, I crossed paths with a number of people but had no understanding of what was going on in their lives. It didn't seem illogical to imagine all of us were covering something; and in the manifold cover-ups was a Mrs. Nightingale who went unnoticed, perhaps a Kit Gorham running, an Uncle Henry turning to alcohol, and an Alex Hagan who, deep down, wanted to believe God had not given up on her.

Kit's letter slipped from my hand and fell to the floor.

Surely she's too smart to get into drugs. Isn't she?

Kit hadn't expressed whether or not she despised her dad for what he had done or for drenching her in lies, but I did; I loathed him. She, however, just packed her bags and left the country. She'd tucked that pesky strand of silky, dark hair behind her ear and told me to cut Ted loose.

I retrieved the letter, folded, and put it back into the envelope. "Hmmm," I said aloud, "I could probably handle living in Paris—

"No . . . maybe think again, Miss Hoity-toity Hagan," I said. "You'll stay put, despising the guilt no innocent person like Kit should have to live with."

Neither, I thought, should I.

I didn't know how to fix emptiness or anything else that was broken; maybe God did. If His love was real, really real, I just might start thinking of cooperating with it.

"Mom! Kit's loving Paris," I yelled from my end of the house. "She's living with some guy for a roomie and will send a painting of the Sacre-Coeur! What's for dinner?"

PART THREE

Chapter 35

Working at Bundy's Drugstore since February would have spelled boredom were it not for the sheer reward in offering life-altering assistance at the cosmetic counter. Given the predicament in which I found myself—living at home with my parents at nineteen—I concentrated on an intense need for optimism, helping person after person with buying decisions from makeup to tweezers. Not until April did the pharmacist switch me from cosmetics to the drug counter. I thought of the move as a crowning promotion. However, on day one of the enhanced job description, I recognized it might take Lois Swank some time to warm up to sharing her territory. The area was, and for years had been Lois's domain.

She was stout, maybe 50, and sported a dyed black bob. Her eyes were gray and beady. Early on, Mr. Bundy had introduced us, but Lois had busily kept her distance during those three months until I was unavoidable. She brushed by me, stopped, and backed up with a fact-finding eye. "You're young for this sort of job," she said. "How old are you anyway?"

I smiled as if she's said something endearing. "I'm nineteen, Miss Lois."

"Don't call me Miss Lois, makes me feel old. Lois is fine." She gave me a once over, and as short as she was, it took some doing. Her eyes made the full climb; she craned her neck before coming to a conclusion: "You are too dressed, you know, for a drugstore clerk. A tall one at that."

I'd dropped my smile. Even so, I didn't remind her I was an assistant, and I didn't call attention to her incessant humming "Everybody Loves Somebody." It had been less bothersome when we were distanced at opposite ends of the store, but just shy of ten minutes into my new role, her humming was cringeworthy. The stars were not exactly aligning.

"Yes, ma'am. I'm five-ten. You must like Dean Martin's song," I said, blandly.

"Don't you?" She examined me overtop boxy horn-rimmed glasses. "You need to know I don't particularly care for ma'am either . . . also this: I was married for a month; then my husband was killed in a car accident. I just happen to think of my Lewis when I hear Dean Martin singing."

"Oh! That's terrible;" I said, "uh . . . not that you think of him . . . Mr. Lewis." I took a needed breath. "I meant because of your husband dying and all."

"Yes, the love of my life. Well, Alex, I've work to do. You should find something to do; you'll always find plenty of stock to open and place. Let's leave it at that for now," she said and took off, purposefully striding past me.

———— • ————

In the days that followed, her humming and my clothing were less of an issue: I had toned down my attire a couple of notches; she spiffed hers up one or two and only sang a line of her favorite song every now and then, but the day Steve Lovelace walked into the drugstore and seated himself at the soda fountain, Lois's song took on a whole new meaning.

She saw me gawking at the guy across the row of Pepto-Bismol and Tums and watched me freeze in my tracks. It was at that moment Lois and I became as silly as girlfriends, speculating who and what this guy was all about.

He sat down at the soda fountain for a cup of coffee, nothing that was going to take very long.

"He's a lineman!" Lois nudged me eagerly. "Works for the phone company," Lois said in a hushed tone before he'd even laid his yellow hardhat on the floor.

She and I watched from afar while he draped one leg off the side of the barstool and adjusted the tool belt strapped low on his hips.

"I daresay he's the best-looking guy I have ever seen!" It wasn't above a whisper, and I didn't care.

Lois nodded her affirmation, and we hadn't budged when he got up to leave. Our staring was not something he could've missed. He smiled.

Lois wouldn't leave it alone. Mr. Bundy had to ask her to stop humming "Everybody Loves Somebody."

The following day when the lunch crowd began congregating and the soda fountain filled with a steady flow of guys, the handsome lineman with a low-slung tool belt wasn't among them.

Lois didn't sing; humming was banned. People came and went.

About the time the place started thinning out, in walked the lineman with a smile. He looked straight toward the back of the drugstore where I was standing—unable to breathe or feel my toes. Even blind, one could see sparks fly.

Lois's fast thinking concocted a plan that sent her hustling over to where he was. She swooped in behind the soda fountain as if it were her job to take his food order, then motioned for me to assist.

Neither of us belonged, but there we were. At the sound of him introducing himself, Lois bunted my ankle with her pointy-toed shoe.

"Lovelace? I went to high school with Rhonda Lovelace," I said. "Hi, Steve. I'm Alex Hagan." Lois had vanished. "Are you by any chance related . . . to Rhonda?"

"Don't think so. My relatives are all in the Carolinas. I guess not. I'm co-oping at UT. Engineering."

Questions and chitchat lasted for a few minutes until his hamburger arrived; then I had to get back to work. "I'll probably be back, same place, same time tomorrow, Alex Hagan. See you then, maybe," he said.

In less than a week we were on our first date. Early May, June, then July was gone, and Steve and I had fallen for each other in those few short months. When he asked me in August to travel to his home in North Carolina, I took it as an indication he was serious about me. Staying the weekend in a countrified setting against a landscape of rolling hills and fenced horses, getting to know his parents—all of it pointed toward our deepening relationship.

"Don't you think Alex is mighty special, Mother? I do," he said, tying the apron strings at the back of my waist. She smiled to confirm his opinion as I dried the last of the dinner dishes.

What-ifs were never out of mind, and later in the day, from the spot Steve had told me was the most magnificent place in all the world, we looked out over the distant Carolina valleys and tree-covered mountains to the glow on the horizon. From behind me, I could feel him coming close. His arms folded around me, covering my shoulders as if he were a gentle, warm wrap.

In the balmy evening breeze, I was spellbound. When I turned to face him, we kissed. I wanted the moment to last forever.

It was not for me to say the mountaintop experience would further supercharge my heart, but in our hike back down the slopes, I knew it had. With my past behind me and new love overflowing within me, my mundane job at the drugstore could be whatever it wanted.

———— • ————

Working overtime on Friday night wasn't so bad. Steve didn't object to sitting at the soda fountain. The wait wouldn't be a long one.

With half an hour to go before I was off duty, I caught sight of Howard Murdock coming through the front door of the drugstore. Weird Howard, offbeat Howard, disgusting Howard.

By the stride he took—heading past the shelves of merchandise like a robot toward the soda fountain—I knew he wasn't bringing a prescription to be filled.

He saw me and nodded matter-of-factly, sizing up my every move with his air of arrogance. After a sinister smile, he smirked in a weird show of recognition and stuck a toothpick in his mouth, then sat down with his back to the counter.

Even though I had good reason to feel uncomfortable, I was busy and didn't have the remotest thought of displeasing Mr. Bundy, especially since he was letting me take off work early.

Engaging Howard Murdock in conversation was the last thing on my mind.

Moments went by, and my old boyfriend slid off the fountain stool and began walking, creeping smoothly like an alligator beneath a swampy surface, over to Steve. As gregarious as Howard was, it was no surprise the two of them started talking. Howard appeared to be doing all the talking. That wasn't unusual, rather that they had anything to talk about since, as far as I knew, they had never met. Howard gawked at me a time or two, perhaps determining my location so he could continue uninterrupted with his new acquaintance.

I was not at all entertained by his skit. Steve didn't appear to be either. I told myself there was nothing worthwhile about trying to untangle their expressions and bagged the last of the prescriptions, letting the cordial exchange between my customer and me end. Howard must have noticed the closure because he was out the door without so much as a wave. That suited me fine.

Steve walked over to me and was noticeably abrupt. It was unlike him, so I passed it off as his eagerness to go to dinner and still make the movies on time. But when we got into the car, he was quiet. I tried to remember if he had ever before failed to open the door for me. Tonight he had.

"Let's go to the drive-in," he said, and I whipped my head toward him so fast it hurt. If he was trying to be funny, he gave no indication.

We had never gone to a drive-in movie. I hardly knew what to say. I was unsure if he expected an answer. It took five minutes to get there, and all the way he was holding back anger. I felt it lurking in the awkward stillness.

He parked the car, hopped out, and headed for the concession stand, returning shortly with two hot dogs and two Cokes. In a brisk move, he situated the speaker on the window's edge and turned up the volume on the speaker. Then he turned on me. At first, I couldn't fathom the unwarranted passion, but for his next move, he tried to unbutton my blouse. I was shocked and hurt.

There was no need to stop him. One squirmy protest from me, and he quit.

"Well, now, according to your friend Howard, this should be right up your alley," he said.

In the dead heat of August, the night went stone cold, and everything was lost: the journey we had taken to the top of the world, the visit at his home, our stroll to the equine barn, his teaching me how to use a curry comb on his American Quarter Horse, the feeling of pride as I watched him proudly show it in the arena later that day. Lying awake at his home that night after his mother made sure I had everything I needed, I'd listened to the trucks on the road in the distance as they came up the hill beside his house, reflecting on the joy of being in a wholesome relationship. I'd fallen asleep in a world of dreams, awakening after a few hours to the morning's mystique that arrived in a breathtaking mist over the lush green mountains.

The memory fogged over in my brain as I sat next to Steve on the ride to my house, and the backdrop of a sensational Carolina setting where I believed he would love me unconditionally fell to pieces. I was wrong to believe anyone could.

Weird Howard was above nothing. It had taken approximately twelve minutes to reveal to Steve just how damaged I was. Although I'd begun to attend a remote little church west of town and permit God's love to overtake me in unmistakable ways, consequences of my past were following me. A record stood against me. There was no place to hide and no reason to.

The phone didn't ring in the days to come and not in the weeks that dragged on.

———— • ————

Work was work, and Lois's empathetic glances were just that. Her pats on my back served to have me know she cared.

I could completely acknowledge being doused with Steve's rejection. I bled all over with gaping wounds. Seared by the injustice of a beautiful romance gone seriously wrong, my burns would not cool. The smoldering proof was this: it made no difference that I wanted authenticity or that I might have started to cooperate with the fact God was the real deal. My past would never be erased, and I couldn't scrape it off with a stick the way you would scrape off stepped-in dog poop.

After heading home, I landed clumsily on one of the Gainsborough chairs by the front window in the living room on a September evening, only to become aware I had just taken Dad's favorite place.

"Keep your seat," he said as he entered the living room. "You look a little tired . . . long day at the drugstore, I'll bet. Sit, honey. I've got something I need to do before dinner anyway."

I heard him shut the door to his bedroom. It had to mean one of two things: he was back there changing his clothes or praying.

I sat motionless, gazing at the photo of Papa Jeff with his arms around his prize-winning New Hampshire sheep. Part of me wished for something to strike me from above; most of me simply hoped for a new life.

Chapter 36

SIMON

The bedroom draperies were open. I walked to the window and peered out, watching an autumn leaf drift lazily to the ground. Half thinking—half praying, I loosened my necktie, cross-examining my motive for not sitting down with Alexandra. It's plenty obvious: she's needy, but I'm certainly not the one she runs to; I don't think Gracie is either.

"Every attempt to talk to her lately is met with resistance," I muttered aloud and rolled up my shirtsleeves, trying to name the moody state Alexandra had adopted during the last few weeks, trying to keep from feeling like a failure as a parent.

I closed the drapery partway, allowing a stream of September's fading light to cross the bed. I knelt beside it and closed my eyes. "Lord God, I still believe in miracles. Why else would I bow my head?" I petitioned. "Alexandra needs to know how deep Your love goes. Her brokenness bothers me. Her anger does too. Anger doesn't come outta nowhere. I've had to face some truths through the years . . . no one except You is adequate to quiet anger. So, I'm just gonna have to turn her over to You, Lord. And I ask that You'd enable her to see .

. . someday . . . what You did to give her real life . . . far beyond the worthless one without You. And if it's me—if I've been in the way of her seeing You—forgive me. That about covers it, Lord. That's my prayer. Amen."

After pushing myself up off boney knees, I went to the closet and began gathering items I needed to take to the dry cleaners on my way to work tomorrow.

———— • ————

ALEXANDRA

Papa Jeff's photo stared back at me from Mom's mahogany pie crust table in the living room. I remembered the last time I saw him alive and lucid, and I began recalling the story he told me as we rode in his old truck down the rocky road in Todd County, Kentucky.

Bit by bit, story pieces came back, starting with a boy who'd made a boat for himself, and I could almost see Papa Jeff stretching out his shaking hand as if he were holding the boy's small boat, steering the truck with the other hand.

"That boy loved his boat. And why? 'Cause he'd given his best efforts to crafting it perfectly, that's why. And when it was finished, Alexandra, the boy treasured his creation because it belonged to him," said my grandfather, emphasizing certain words.

I had paid close attention, knowing what ownership was. Even as a youngster, I'd been able to understand the boy's love for his boat.

I could almost feel Papa Jeff winking at me yet today, from the sweet snapshot. For whatever the reason, his story resided within me.

Papa Jeff had continued as we rode along together, so many years ago: "The day came for him to try sailing it in the brook near his home," he had said. "The boy came up to the water's edge, trembling with anticipation as he released his prized possession into the water. The boat bobbed happily as ripples tipped it this way and that." Papa Jeff had swayed to the left, then to the right, before he began again. "The boat moved along exactly as the boy envisioned. But suddenly, without warning"—and Papa Jeff's bushy eyebrows had gone into a tizzy—"a strong wind began to churn the waters, carrying the boat away. Panic-stricken, he ran along the edge of the muddy bank, reaching out desperately to his boat being tossed in the rushing current. Faster and faster he ran, in the direction his boat was being swept. But soon it was out of his sight. Gone, Alexandra. There was nothing he could do."

I had looked in dismay at Papa Jeff, thinking it was the end of his story. But he had taken a deep breath. There was more.

"Days went by, weeks, maybe months, and one day the boy was walking along the streets of his town. He wasn't noticing anything in particular when—in the window of a pawnshop—a boat caught his eye. At first, the boy was amazed at how much it looked like his own. Then he realized it was his own! And he rushed inside to tell the shopkeeper the truth of its ownership. 'That boat belongs to me!'"

Papa Jeff's chest had puffed up, and his voice had become husky and ferocious. As a kid, I was eating it up.

Just now, I scooted closer to Mom's table and picked up the photo frame to get a better look at Papa Jeff's face. I had to smile at his gentle countenance and the loving way he wrapped his arm around two sheep pictured with him. After a moment, I remembered what he said as he continued his story:

"He made that boat, Alexandra, with his own hands," Papa Jeff had said. "Carved it, shaped it . . . Do you see that, baby? It's like he breathed breath into his boat that day when he set it forth on its own . . . when he turned its sails to the wind." Papa Jeff had scrunched his eyebrows. "But the shopkeeper was not impressed," my grandfather had said, shaking his head.

"'I paid cash for that boat, boy. I own the thing! Now get lost,'" the shopkeeper said, shouting at him. And Papa Jeff had been puffed up again, portraying the disgusting scene for me—all the while, his hands still on the steering wheel as he drove down the rocky road. "'If you want the boat, boy, come back with the money to buy it!' "

"Oh, no," I said, but Papa Jeff had shushed me with a wave of his hand.

"But the boy didn't have the money required to buy back his boat," said Papa Jeff, continuing, "but, Alexandra, . . . he did have a baseball mitt and bat, and he had *his bike*—the bike his dad had given him for his twelfth birthday. It had a broken chain, but it was there, parked in the shed, waiting to be repaired."

I had, at the time, felt something well up inside me.

"Now, Alexandra," Papa Jeff said, "that boy could've sold his bike and sold his mitt. Then he would've had enough to return to the pawnshop and buy his boat."

I paused to think about what Papa Jeff had said during that truck ride and how it had made me consider my own bike: aquamarine blue with its chrome basket fastened to the handlebars—parked in our garage and ready for an immediate ride. Giving it up for any reason would kill me, especially for something that was mine to begin with. I remembered my eyes watering and how I had batted them feverishly. I'd told myself this was only a story while Papa Jeff went on with it.

"The boy took all he had and returned to the pawnbroker and paid the price to buy back the boat that was already his. Every requirement was met, finished. His treasure was returned to him, and he left the pawnshop with it cradled in his arms."

I had imagined the boy holding the boat the way I would a homeless kitten. "That's a nice story. I like it. It had a happy ending," I'd said, wiping tears.

"And so does yours, Alexandra, because you're that treasure. God made you and me for His own. We drift, though. So then, He sent Jesus to pay the price to buy us back." That means you belong to Him. Always have 'cause He made you."

I set the photo of my grandfather back on the table and after all those years turned the story over in my head again, fully recognizing that winds had pulled me to the far side, leaving me lost in the same way the little boat was lost, adrift on the waters, picked up by the current.

'Jesus paid a price' was not a thought I'd pondered as a kid, but circumstances were different now. With no relationship to fence me in, no demands, no agendas, no school, no Kit—just ordinary me with my no-pressure job—I was adrift on my crippling choices, needing someone to rescue me from the pawnshop window.

"Hungry?"

I jumped like I'd been shot. Dad breezed by me, heading for the kitchen.

"I'll be right there," I said, "to put the salad together."

———— • ————

As I chopped tomatoes, Dad turned savory pork chops in the skillet.

"You ever miss Papa Jeff?" I glanced at him, feeling like I'd asked a stupid question—one with an obvious answer, and I wished I had kept my mouth shut; it was too late to rethink it.

"He was a tremendous source of strength. I could only hope to be half the father Geoffrey Hagan was to me," Dad said, tenderheartedly. "Why do you ask?"

"Oh . . . I was thinking of him earlier. You look like him," I said, realizing just how true the statement was. "Did he ever tell you a story about—"

"You two! All long in the face!" Mom beamed into the kitchen like a ray of sunshine. "Let's be happy! Tell me about your day, Alexandra."

"You're just in time to sit, Gracie," Dad said with a twinkle in his eye. "So, sit."

Bypassing him, she went straight to the refrigerator.

"Happy, happy, happy," I mocked her with a little bit of wonder at the joy that always seemed to prevail when she was present. "Fine, Mom. It was great."

"Oh?" She poured freshly brewed tea over ice in the glasses and waited for more information. "Oh?"

"Mr. Bundy's giving me a raise," I said, nonchalantly, taking pork chops to the table.

"That is wonderful! Isn't a raise what you've been hoping for? And what do you hear from Kit?"

No, it wasn't a raise at all. Living in darkness like a rotting mass of self-deception—searching for a life worth living—that hardly called for a raise. So, no, I was hoping for something beyond a raise.

I wasn't seeing any evidence Kit was on top of the world, either, but Paris was a whole lot closer to it than I was. "She's trying new things. Pottery . . . Oh, Mom, I don't really know what all. She's fine. Her world and mine are pretty different anymore."

My mother was on only the fourth or fifth question in her typical series of twenty, and I began getting nervous. I kept my head down and ate quickly, answering follow-up queries as smugly as possible. Daddy remained quiet. I glanced at him once or twice and caught him looking quizzical. When we finished eating, it was a relief. I wanted to be alone.

"Any dessert? If not, I think I'll run out and get a Dairy Queen," I said and put my plate in the dishwasher. "Good dinner, Dad. I won't be long, y'all."

One more gulp of tea and I was gone.

———— • ————

Inside the DQ, I ordered a chocolate-dipped cone of vanilla ice cream and took a seat in a secluded corner.

I wanted to be by myself to savor more than the ice cream, more than the memory of a childhood ride in Papa Jeff's truck. After all this time, his boat story had untidied me, and I wanted him to be across the table—his bushy white brows dancing playfully above peaceful, fatherly eyes—across the table from me, listening to my heart speak.

I wanted him to hear how very much like the little boat I was, bobbing aimlessly in the mocking ripples of a fast-moving current of my own choosing, merrily singing, catch me if you can. My grandfather would, no doubt, see personal strong winds had landed me in a pawnshop of lies and cunningly tried to convince me I was fine.

"Yeah, I'm a real treasure," I muttered, realizing ice cream was oozing onto my hand from beneath its chocolate-coated tower.

I gave it a circular lick around the rim and got the situation under control, but tears started to drip onto my napkin. I licked again—hard, and the chocolate tower toppled—splat—onto the table. Much like my cone-of-cream episode when I was a kid and my folks had been on the road to Papa Jeff's, I'd splatted my ice cream in the dirt outside an old man's store.

It was no coincidence, I thought, my traipsing to the DQ with a hankering for vanilla ice cream as if it were a similar subconscious longing to be Sweet Pea, covered with my daddy's anointing, traveling to Kentucky to see my papa. A mere cone of cream—so small, so insignificant, but it had endeared me—a means to reach me with my daddy's love.

From the feel of it now, I'd fallen headlong into an attractive form of disillusionment—*splat*, as it were—separated from my foundation. The distance between had masqueraded as the good life, leaving me right where it dropped me: nowhere.

I wiped up the ice cream with too few napkins and lingered a few more moments.

Neither could it be a coincidence, I decided, my having parked earlier on a chair in front of Papa Jeff's photo after another dead-end day—after my father, too, had ended his own routine workday of small sacrifices. He'd kept me going, providing all he could, cooking meals, working, coping, struggling, hovering, hoping.

Unnoticed, I walked to the trash receptacle, pushed my mess inside and watched the lid swing back into place. Leaving the DQ, I slipped outside into the September night feeling the significance of a silly cone of cream. From out of my childhood, my father's words to describe ice cream had resurfaced to remind me of his intentional kindness.

I walked to my car with a clear decision in mind. I wanted to be my father's child.

Chapter 37

GRACIE

It was seldom Alexandra and I spent time chatting on the back-porch glider and even more unusual for the weather on a November Sunday afternoon to be cooperating so beautifully.

"This might be our last hurrah out here. Probably we should take in the cushions after this, Alexandra, but for now, let's just enjoy the moment. Your countenance is radiant, honey . . . skin's like peaches 'n cream."

It tickled me to see my daughter happy.

"Thanks, Mom. As I was saying . . . about the kids at Wells Foundation . . . they're a handful; I really like helping, though."

"That's what I mean, and it shows in your face. You have so much going for you," I said. "I'm delighted you're going back to UT in the spring, and Jack's a nice young man." I cleared my throat. "He hasn't been married . . . you're sure?"

Alexandra gave me a sidelong glance. "No, not married, Mom. He loves those kids, and we must've had twenty out on the church lawn last Friday. They have so little. Guess God kind of pricked me to volunteer when I heard about the need. Who could've thought I'd meet

Jack Ridley at Wells Foundation . . . holding a cue stick across a pool table?"

I had to laugh aloud. Alexandra and I both did, but I suspected a scar was there, beneath the surface. "You ever think about Steve, honey? Or should we not talk about him? I just don't want you to be hurt. Y'all seemed—"

"No, not at all." Alexandra pushed against the glider, moving us gently back and forth; her arms stretched in the air above her head. "Steve Lovelace, no, nothing there. I'd just as soon skip it, Mom. It's been weeks . . . past two months. I'm over him; I've moved on. Jack's crazy about me, and I'm in love."

"I believe it. He's a wonderful fellow, and y'all seem to enjoy going to his church," I said. "It's amazing to think Thanksgiving's upon us. I wish we could all go to Elkton. It would help me immensely to see Henry; according to Millicent, he's just not doing well." I wanted to smile, but somehow I'd let the troubling subject of my brother barge in. Fighting tears, I looked out to the leafless trees lining the back of the property. "Henry's reeling from his loss of dignity. How else to say it? The ruin of my family's farm . . . Hillbound in its glory was already slipping through his fingers by the time he returned from the war. Rumors . . . a lot of rumors. And he just hasn't found the power source to get him on his feet. We all need the Lord."

That said, I looked at my daughter. My heart was overflowing: "You have a new outlook on life: plans for going back to school, the underprivileged children. I think I can imagine the joy of working with them is the same as my joy in teaching Sudanese children and the Negro children who lived near Hillbound. Sharecroppers like Moe Lee worked on our place—

"I've gone on too long, honey, but I just want you to know I'm happy for you. I think God's got His hand on your life. The way you treated your father yesterday was indicative of a changing heart, and our hearts are continuously being changed when God's in it." I paused, and being the immutable teacher, I shared an example of my own: "When

Mrs. Nightingale died . . . alone the way she did . . . God changed me in a new way. I don't ever want to hurt someone by my biases, not ever. I'm sure your father appreciated your loving-kindness when he got the news of Doc Begbie's death."

"Uhmm, yeah, Mom. God does. Thanks," Alexandra said and smiled. "Didn't you name Jeff Lee because of knowing Moe Lee? He must've been pretty special."

"He was! Moe Lee was my earliest friend. Yes, special, indeed. Hillbound was never the same after he and his family were gone. But as you know, Jeff Lee's your grandfather's namesake, as well as Moe Lee's. Both, wonderful men; your father had big shoes to fill after Papa Jeff passed, and he's done just that."

"How about Miss Francine—"

"Oh, honey, let's talk about your friends . . . your job before we have to go inside. Why don't we?"

Alexandra chuckled. "My friends are scattered, going after their pursuits, Mom, and my job's just a simple, no pressure one. I show up for it, in a pretty bland environment except for Lois Swank."

We were both sipping coffee when Simon stuck his head out the patio door. "Alexandra, the phone's for you, honey," he said. He covered the receiver with his hand and whispered, "I think it's Steve."

"You're kidding." Having mouthed the words, Alexandra stepped inside and took the phone, motioning for me to stay put.

"Hello? Oh, hi, Steve . . . I'm fine, really fine," I heard her say. "And how are things with you . . . Well, that's terrific, just terrific. I'm glad the job's working out . . . Saturday night?"

I watched her twirl the phone cord and roll her eyes.

"No, I'm sorry," she said into the receiver. "Actually, I've met someone, Steve; I'm very happy, and that's where I am . . . No, you don't need to regret anything. We've gone different directions, you and I, and it didn't happen without God's hand on it. I wish you the best."

I watched Alexandra smiling, confident.

". . . Sure, you too. Thanks. Bye, Steve."

"Well, good for you, honey," I said, bringing coffee cups inside. "I'm glad to witness a few theatrics of the past didn't have the power to dictate your future."

She gave me a triumphant look. "Mom," she said, "where Steve Lovelace and I were concerned, my past pretty much bulldozed any plans for our future. Who knows why he reconsidered his decision to ditch me? And now, I've simply made decisions of my own. At least, in those few months with Steve, I gained a clear understanding of the kind of person I want to spend the rest of my life with."

Chapter 38

ALEXANDRA

July 6, 1963, at my house was more than heated up, more than a summer day in Knoxville, Tennessee. Wedding festivities were overriding my every thought.

Suzette was due in town tomorrow morning.

Kit would arrive later on in the day and planned to stay a few days after the wedding before returning to Paris. Hard as it was to believe it had been a year, I could barely wait for Wednesday. Resuming our friendship where it left off sounded simple, but Kit's letters had been fewer and her news less and less appealing.

My parents, brothers, and sisters-in-law, old high school buddies, Lois Swank—everybody was caught up in the soon-to-be event when Ted showed up. It was Tuesday, five days before my wedding. He'd driven in from St. Louis and wanted to take a ride and talk.

Take a ride and talk! It was so illogical it made me dizzy.

I reacted with a laugh. It had to be a joke. Still, I agreed to go along, wanting to know what was on his mind. I wondered if he really did think I'd come back to him; maybe it was all about his seeing me just one more time. It didn't enter my head that being with him was a little dangerous, considering my history of caving in.

He came by the house, and we drove off with my mom holding back the words she obviously wanted to speak.

"Please reconsider, baby. You can still back out," Ted said, beginning his appeal as we rolled to a stop in an old, secluded parking place. He looked across at me; his arm lobbed itself over the back of the car seat.

"You cannot be serious," I gasped, dismayed by my boomerang boyfriend who couldn't have fully understood the changes in me or that I was no longer waiting to be plucked from a pawnshop window.

Ted had to be alien, I thought, not to know altering us was impossible, and we certainly weren't going to go back in time. "You're kidding me," I said, suddenly feeling nothing about the moment fit— like when Daddy had pulled my first tooth with a string tied to the doorknob. I had remained still while he wrapped the tooth with a thin string and stretched it across to the opened door on the other side of the room. I'd stood still, trusting Daddy, and he slammed the door shut; my tooth flew out of my mouth on the end of the string. When the bleeding stopped, I had tried to put the tooth back, but it didn't fit; it felt like it had never even belonged in the first place.

Ted did not fit anymore either.

"No, Ted. I'm sorry you came all this way," I said, seeing how difficult it was for him to accept that I'd not weakened.

With nothing left to say, he drove me back to my home, having underestimated God's power to reclaim me for Himself.

I closed the car door behind me, knowing I'd jabbed someone who once held a piece of my heart and left him sitting there with a look of abandonment. The emotions we'd shared had crossed paths for the last time. Even for a happy bride so close to her wedding day, the finality felt brusque.

The end had not occurred in that moment with a sudden slam of the door. False custody had gone beyond my relationship with Ted to the lies that tried to clamp me like a vise and jam its hinges forever.

Chapter 39

"Where are you, Mom?" I murmured, disgruntled.

Silence.

I stood outside the patio door for a moment, listening, and quickly redirected my thoughts to the array of urgent to-dos. Every minute counted with many tasks to cross off my list.

I needed her. Rushing back inside the house, I yelled for her, but she wasn't there either—not in the kitchen, not in the bedroom. Confused, I called out again and waited.

Silence.

Gazing around the quiet house, frustration turned to worry. Knowing my mother wasn't inside, I turned again to the backyard, loping past the sliding glass door, nearly tripping over its metal track, calling as I went.

At first, nothing. But then I spotted her, sitting up close to the house, nestled behind the bushes, trying to hide from me. Odd as it was, it didn't seem that far outside her flair for the unexpected, but I was not even mildly amused at her antics.

"What on earth are you doing? Some man has left a box of—"

I stopped. She'd been crying. I couldn't recall if I had ever seen her cry.

Mom looked down at her lap and fidgeted with some rocks off to the side that were lodged in the dirt. "I'm okay," she said apologetically. "I'm just . . . I was just praying you'll be happy. Help me up."

I held back a limb so she could come out from under the bushes without a scratch, and we hustled inside.

Mom and I had not spoken much about her prayer habits or changes in her life like the one she'd mentioned about Mrs. Nightingale's death and a bias that had been peeled away, but I'd noticed an urgency to apply to me what she had learned throughout her own life—a panic to fix me, possibly, so I would avoid regrets of which I was unaware. However, while I was searching for answers to who I was, she and I were apart. We'd spoken different languages, and I couldn't begin to understand hers. It was hard to read her Pollyanna face—always intact. My years with her had come and gone so quickly.

I recalled the times I'd heard her knocking on my locked bedroom door, begging me to let her in—

For a moment I thought I was dreaming. Someone was knocking.

"Anybody home? Hello, where are you?"

We both instantly recognized Suzette Mullins' voice. With my help, my mother had already scrambled to her feet. She quickly wiped away tears. A smile broke through her emotions, leaving me no choice but to match her enthusiasm for my dearest childhood friend who had arrived to be with me as my wedding day approached.

Hugging and squealing together, Suzette and I danced a jig as if we were giddy little third graders again, taking us back to the first morning we'd met, her bobbing ringlets bouncing into my life.

"It's really here! Can you believe it?" Suzette gushed as she held me tight; and when Kit arrived on schedule, she hadn't changed that much except she was exceptionally thin.

I had no hunch Kit had betrayed me.

——— • ———

Thursday, Friday, and finally Saturday arrived.

The ride to the church was half an hour away. With Saturday's slower traffic it could hopefully take less. Kit was driving, and in the backseat with my wedding dress resting in a gigantic mound across her lap sat Suzette, barely able to peer out over the satin and lace.

An earlier drizzle had turned the July day into a muggy steam bath, and the afternoon temperature kept climbing. The morning had been pure hysteria, but once we climbed inside the car, the three of us began to settle down.

"Alex, remember when Howard Murdock told your parents you were going to elope with Ted?" Kit piped up with the off-the-wall question out of nowhere, cutting into the brief silence. "I still remember how you despised him for doing it. Do you?"

"Of course, I do," I answered, and a shiver went down my spine. Even the fleeting memory of weird Howard felt toxic. "How could I forget such a thing?"

Kit was going to provide idle chatter, I supposed, to help ease my jitters. But Howard? Surely a friend as close as a sister was not going to badger me about him on my wedding day. Was she? "Okay, yes, and I was plenty mad. Maybe he deserves a big thank you now, considering. Except that he is such a creep on so many levels," I said, not wanting to rehash the past—not the one Kit had mentioned, not the more recent one with Steve Lovelace. Neither did I want to talk about Howard's overall disgusting personality. I was not able to add anything more to her question. "No contest. It worked out for the best. Thank goodness, I didn't elope with Ted. There. Satisfied?"

Suddenly, the frightening possibility of Howard showing up at the church crossed my mind. For the next mile or so, I assured myself the man I was marrying loved me unconditionally; no matter whom I had met and fallen in love with, and no matter how much he professed to love me, the potential for a backfire with Howard in the picture would continue to exist. The damage would be done.

I was almost afraid to ask. "Don't tell me you ran into Howard," I said. "For Pete's sake, Kit. Did you run into Howard?"

She looked at me for a second, glanced the road, back and forth while Suzette stayed quiet in the backseat. I couldn't imagine what required so much courage.

"Kit? Why are you bringing him up now? What's going on?"

"I was the one, Alex," she blurted. "I told your mother about your plans to elope, not Howard."

Nothing was going to top that revelation. In the few remaining miles, every inch of the way was a blur. My dad was waiting when Kit dropped Suzette and me off at the entrance to the fellowship hall. Kit jumped out of the car, gave me a big hug.

"I love you," we said simultaneously.

We knew it was genuine; we knew it was deep. We both had our pasts, and we both had moved on. Soon I would be Mrs. Jackson Ridley, and nothing about my past would make one iota of a difference. Suzette sat still until Kit got back inside the car and finished parking so they could wrestle my dress from the backseat.

I turned around in time to see my dad as he walked up the sidewalk.

It wasn't the best idea for him to be in hot sun in his tux, but he was determined to be the one to usher me inside. Tense, a little bit pale, but ever-so handsome, I could see his white hair glistening in the sun.

"There's still time to back out. You have all of an hour if you want to," he said jovially, offering the same unconscionable, last-minute enticement I'd recently heard from Ted. Both were mistaken to suggest I had even a flicker of hesitation about the person who was waiting to marry me.

Dad's hands were shaking as he held them out to help me up the curb, but he smiled. "Careful there, Sweet Pea."

He had smiled for the entire fairytale until Mom and I had started spending money, but only once had that look of his, reserved for incredulous situations, come over his face. Even with most of the fight in him gone, he'd questioned: "Would one of you—either one—please, tell me how in this world a pair of gloves can cost twenty dollars? I don't care if they are extra-long and extra white," he had said, trying to appear undone.

Today, though, he stood unscathed, unbroken, unbeaten. In another forty-five minutes he would walk me down the aisle. My new journey would begin with a twenty-seven-year-old, handsome, sandy-haired Jackson Edward Ridley.

Chapter 40

SEVEN YEARS LATER

Yes, years had flown past. It seemed Jack and I had merely flipped a few pages in the book of our lives.

The clip-clop of carriage-horse footsteps echoed a friendly rhythm. Williamsburg, Virginia was a quaint place with an assortment of restored village shops and proud merchants and townspeople, portraying life as it was when the town's cobblestone streets clamored with activity. Plantation tours, the militia's artillery salute, dining at the Wild Boar Inn, and soaking up eighteenth-century tradition proved a fascinating and restorative few days away from the routine for Jack and me.

The time spent on the road traveling back to my parents' home in Knoxville was a scenic drive through the mountains. Redbud trees laced a mint-colored backdrop of spring bursting out all over the mountaintops, and rhododendrons tucked themselves in the panorama wherever possible.

Jack drove up the driveway and stopped the car on the very same slope where various other ones had done the same in seasons past. The aging Buick sedan that Jeff Lee had given our dad one Christmas was parked on the hill in front of the garage. My brother's surprise gift, complete with a huge red bow and a ribbon tied from the front fender to the back fender, had unfurled across the top and down over the hood to show Jeff Lee's unexpected token of gratitude. It caught Dad totally unaware. You'd have thought he was a king, wearing a priceless crown.

That seemed decades ago. With my marriage and two young children, time had slipped by quickly, eroding the hard edges of my heart. The ride through the mountains reminded me of the reason.

I was glad for the undisturbed silence as we rode through the stretch of scenery, enabling me to recall the Bible verses from the forty-third chapter of Isaiah: "I will go before you and level the mountains. I will break in pieces the doors of bronze and cut through the bars of iron. I will give you the treasures of darkness and riches hidden in secret places so you may know that it is I, the Lord, the God Israel, who calls you by your name."

Called me by my name. That was great news—better than great. God's unmerited love had reclaimed me from the pawnbroker—not with a loud shout but deeply, down where truth spoke. As His treasure, I'd been bought with a price, and the lies that had manifested insecurity lost the power to own me.

But my parents were still my parents, and I was anticipating a long overdue talk with them. I still had not been reconciled, truly reconciled, with my father.

Their yard was lovely in May, exhibiting bright pink azaleas in full bloom and impatiens intermittently dotting the space below the boxwood shrubbery. Both the louvered front door and the wrought-iron chair, sitting beside it in the same way it had since we moved there in 1959, displayed their recent coat of custom-mixed Belle Meade green paint. Other than that, the house was the same.

The kids ran out to greet us, making us feel we had been gone for months rather than the extended weekend we had extracted from everybody's busy schedules. Ginger's blonde curls danced in loose pigtails, and replicas of my dad's brown eyes twinkled behind her batting lashes. Kent tried to outrun her to get to our outstretched arms.

Mom and Dad appeared on the porch with chatter and greetings, looking somewhat weary from the responsibility of taking care of our two munchkins, but both wore welcoming smiles. Dad's colorful necktie was trailing across his shoulder in the mild wind that pressed against his stride, and his hair was a bit tousled; still, he managed his usual impeccable appearance.

Energy filled the house as we brought in luggage and shopping bags.

"I'm so glad you took a little vacation," Mom said. "You look rested. Tell me about it. What did you see?"

So we launched the conversation that accompanied our coming home from a happy jaunt, and lots of questions cropped up pertaining to how the kids behaved—or didn't—and whether the dog posed a problem or not. And on it went into the afternoon until we took a break.

I relaxed outdoors on the glider, listening to Kent tell me his twist on time spent with grandparents before he was off again to romp with Duchess. I lay back on the cushion, basking in the sun-drenched joy that replaced what I had known here in my youth.

Not intending to, I couldn't help reflecting on the news coming from my mother's old home several years back—how it carried far greater repercussions than the heart-wrenching news coming through the same telephone receiver regarding Mrs. Nightingale's death. The repeating saga of a waste of a human life had cruelly unfolded on that awful day.

Madeleine—a pretty fourteen-year-old with beautiful blonde hair and a complexion like Mom's proverbial peaches an' cream—was dead. Uncle Henry's only daughter . . . gone. I'd seen my cousin a mere handful of times since she'd been that nursing infant in the freezing-cold house where my mother grew up.

I recalled Richard and Sonny playfully tormenting her in the same way as my older brothers. I sat thinking back on how I'd felt that day, knowing my agony couldn't begin to equal Uncle Henry's. He worshiped Madeleine.

At the time, it had been inconceivable any such tragedy could happen. Nevertheless, it had. Madeleine swallowed a bottle of her father's pills because a guy in her Sunday school class brushed her off, teased, and bullied her.

From that remote house in the country, he had not been able to get her to the hospital fast enough. She'd died in the car with Uncle Henry desperately trying to make it in time.

"Henry! No! Lord, say it's not so!" Mom had slumped lifelessly on the glider after speaking with her brother.

In my mind's eye, I could still see the receiver dangling from the stretched-out cord in her hand.

Although I was certain Henry and the loss of his daughter and the welfare of his remaining two children were a continual source of concern for Mom, nothing less than vibrancy prevailed at the Hagan household today. She hadn't mentioned Madeleine.

Life had its way of moving on, and I could attest; belonging to the Heavenly Father had put mine on higher ground. I was different. Even so, cracks remained in the relationship with my father—words needed to be said between us before it was too late.

"Won't you have a Co-cola and some pie?" chirped my mother, sliding open the patio door with a loaded silver tray and a handful of napkins.

I jumped up to help her.

"Here, honey," she said. "Have some pie. What did you think of Carter's Grove? I went there once. Wasn't the woodwork stunning? Williamsburg is a wonderful place. "

My window of opportunity to talk with my parents—especially Dad—was narrowing. Jack, the kids, and I would only be there for a night as we planned to leave the next morning. Getting my mom and dad's undivided attention might be impossible between chit-chat and children's laughter. With kids running in and out, the dog barking, and the TV blaring, it didn't seem like anyone was going to be still long enough to talk.

Mom finished futzing with refreshments and disappeared, and I went back inside to check on Ginger's whereabouts. She sat with her granddaddy, examining the leather key strap we'd bought for him at a tannery in Williamsburg. He was unusually attentive to her every word, protectively holding his hand in front of his eyeglasses to make sure her animated arm gestures did not accidentally knock them askew.

I stepped back outside to gather my thoughts in the event the chance came to have an adult conversation. Mom was still out of sight. Kent and Jack were tossing a football in the side yard, both deeply involved in their favorite pastime.

It occurred to me perhaps my timing was off, but I refused to believe it. Visualizing the perfect setting that could be possible later tonight, I continued my walk to the side yard and let myself hope. If not tonight, then tomorrow. In the morning it will be better, I told myself. We can sit there with an extra cup of coffee after breakfast. I could tell the kids to help their dad load the car.

Walking to the corner of the house, I paused to stare in awe at how huge the blue spruce had grown, remembering the day we'd planted it several feet from the kitchen door. The yard surrounding the house had been little more than a grassy plot over a red-clay wasteland when we moved here fifteen years ago. Now, the evergreens provided a towering curtain behind flowering bushes and annuals that bordered the backyard. A bird bath burrowed itself in the shade of the fluffy landscape.

Mom had made this barren property a paradise. Strolling through it now, I brimmed with admiration. Her determination and tenacity were evident here and in everything she did. The faith she possessed for the changing tides of living came from deep inside, and the belief in God's Word had given her power, developed her in the same way she had developed this beautiful landscape. In the space of time I'd lived here,

I had been as stubborn as the clay under my shoes. She'd tried to make me grow.

I quieted my footsteps. From somewhere I heard the faint voice of a cat. There was no mistaking the pitiful cry. I stooped down to find its exact location underneath a broad hemlock. Lifting the lowest branch, I could see the motionless animal could not get up. It saw me, and its mouth opened to cry, but no voice came with it.

There, in the red earth, maggots crawled in and out of the lower half of its injured body. I gasped, scarcely able to breathe. It was obvious the cat, although still alive, was slowly, pitifully being decimated.

My whole insides went berserk. Ever so gently, I laid the tree limb back into position, pulled myself up, and stumbled to the house, thinking I could somehow save the injured creature.

I returned to the spot seconds later with a bowl of water, only to find I was too late. Its head lay limp in the dirt, its mouth wide open in death, and I was stuck under the tree, holding up the branch, expecting something extraordinary to recreate a better ending.

"Come on, hon. Let's go before the kids come," said Jack, who had followed me, listening to my babbling explanation.

"It has a collar. We've got to call the owner," I said to him.

"No, honey. Let's go."

He bent down and picked up the dish of water. I lowered the tree branch.

Later that night the cry of the cat, its eyes begging to be saved from the agony, would not go away, and in my subconscious mind it haunted my sleep. How could you be alive when half of you is eaten away, crawling with—

"Stop it!" Scolding myself, I tried to squelch the similarity between the characteristics of soft-bodied, legless maggots and cruel, merciless lies. Both had the power to consume a living being.

I threw off the bed covers. It was impossible to sleep.

———— • ————

Morning broke with sunshine pouring in the windows, and the house awakened with a flurry of activity.

"We hate to see you leave so soon," mourned Mom, buzzing here and there in the kitchen, placing glasses full of orange juice on various sections of Papa Jeff's big cherrywood table. "Why don't y'all stay another day?"

"Oh, no chance, Mother Hagan. I've taken off all the vacation days I can. I am afraid the law firm would frown on my not being back at work," Jack told her. "We should head home when we've finished eating. We have a long drive ahead."

Breakfast was not on my mind. I had planned, rehearsed, and was counting on a serious discussion taking place before Jack, the children, and I returned to our home in Indiana. Uneasiness mounted inside me. Morbid thoughts of the cat still lingered. The children ate their Captain Kangaroo cereal and, in exaggerated bites, finished their toast.

"I'm done," said Kent.

"Me too," said Ginger. "Are we excused, Daddy?" She looked at Kent.

"You're excused," he said.

Soon Jack, too, had finished and was eager to make an exit and start the business of loading the car.

I desperately needed to talk, to say certain words, but they wouldn't come. A lump formed in my throat. Trying to make it leave, I swallowed a sip of coffee. The cup shook on the way to my mouth.

"Dad," I began with a tone that sounded like a high note on an out-of-tune piano.

"Are you planning to get your hair cut when you get back to Indiana," Mom asked. "I think it looks nice, but I liked it when you wore it a little shorter. Have some more grits, honey. They'll go to waste."

Dad pushed his chair back, signaling he was leaving, and the opportune moment vanished into thin air. I stayed seated, bewildered, and a little bit annoyed I had been so inadequate for something so important.

The miles that had separated me from my parents after Jack and I married were enough to limit family visits. Dad was in his mid-seventies now, and while the gap that existed between us had not widened, there remained something as real as a snowdrift. It forced us to stop, dead in our tracks—no way around it, over it, or through it was ever negotiated. The iced-over window of reconciliation I had waited for, prayed for, was obviously not going to be opened today. I focused entirely on removing the dishes from the table.

"Oh, don't do that, Alexandra. You go get yourself ready," Mom said. "Now go on. I can do these later."

Ginger came bounding into the room with her Humpty-Dumpty doll tucked under her arm, its legs wagging crazily.

"Did you brush those pretty teeth?" my mother said to her. "Let me see, honey. You don't want to drive all the way home with dirty teeth. Do you?"

Ginger looked over at me to confirm the answer was, "No, ma'am," and then she was gone as quickly as she had come.

Finally, everything sat in readiness for the trip back to Indiana. With the last good-byes said, I brought up the rear, hugging my mother as she leaned against the lamppost at the end of the sidewalk. She was already waving another good-bye to the kids in the backseat, wagging her hand up and down the way a four-year-old would.

Dad lingered on the slope of the hill by the car door, then moved deliberately between it and the car seat, holding the door open for me.

I slowed my steps to absorb the moment. His slender form still straight as an arrow, his clean-shaven face and perfectly knotted necktie, his handsome, haunting smile—all sealed themselves like a tin of freshly baked macaroons into my consciousness, and the whirlwind that had rushed me was suddenly inappropriate.

I approached him with halting steps. "*My Father*," I said, and a keen awareness welled in my heart: it was not the effusion of words

I'd rehearsed, rather the two I'd spoken to acknowledge the honor due him.

Where once the chrome-rimmed mirror reflected my disobedient, Kool-Aid-encrusted mouth, my loving, forgiving father instead smiled back at me. He reached out with open arms to embrace me. It was quick—typical—but his soft fixation was not. His eyes, so much like my own, were gently piercing. Tears oozed in the corners and then dripped over his cheeks like melting snow over a sun-warmed embankment.

Chapter 41

Happily married with grammar school kids, I had every reason never to look back on bad choices—until Kit came to Indiana for a visit. It had been ages since I'd seen her.

She'd exhausted her artistic pursuits in France, married, and when it didn't work out, she'd come back to the States. A special someone was in her life, but with all her accomplishments, her eyes didn't sparkle until she spoke of my father.

"Your dad was the kindest person to me," she said. "I loved going to your house because of him."

"He has dementia. It's rapidly progressing," I said and swallowed hard, knowing the memory of her own father.

Our conversation made me wonder if she had traveled each foreign port alone, longing for a father, and if that emptiness followed her everywhere. From our earliest meeting in the hallway as freshmen at Ridgewood High, Kit and I had few secrets between us. So much had sealed our relationship, but nothing more than knowing she'd risked stepping up to stop my marriage to Ted, changing the path of my life and what might have been.

"So, does Jack know about Ted?"

"What?"

"Does Jack know about Ted?"

"Well," I began, and a little ping sounded in my head, "I didn't see a need to discuss what went on with Ted. Jack even said something to that effect: 'The past is past.'"

"He should know. If you don't tell him, I'm going to."

"No, you're not." I could feel panic gripping me. The power was hers to expose what had been safely hidden in the dark. "Why bring it up now?

"You need to tell him," she insisted.

"Okay, fine! When the time is right." I agreed, knowing that fragment of my past was not a trampled souvenir to be restored, rather a ticking bomb with potential to destroy.

"Tell him tonight, before I leave."

I glared at her with a what-right-have-you look, but in the day remaining for us to visit, we covered the highlights, topics I'd missed out on when I moved ahead with my own life. Kit was right, and I knew I would not sleep that night unless I found out where I stood. Jack was going to hear the whole truth.

I went to the closet and found him changing his clothes.

"Jack," I said to his backside, "remember when you asked me to marry you, and I said, 'You don't know me?'"

We'd been married long enough for him to see it coming. He put his leg back into his pants, regaining his balance, then turned around and waited for me to begin. With more than a little nervousness, I did.

Having finished the account of all I needed to say, I stepped back, anticipating an explosion of shattering rejection.

"Alex, nothing you've ever done," Jack said, taking me in his arms, "or will ever do, could make me stop loving you. Can you understand that? You have my unconditional love. It's like God's love: we didn't do anything to earn it, and we can't do anything to make Him stop. Now, can I finish changing these clothes?"

Without really knowing it, Kit had done it again, intervened in a crossroads kind of way, and the saga of undisclosed facts about me which, if revealed, could threaten to undo me no longer existed. That person—that Alexandra—was no more.

Late the next afternoon Kit departed. I wondered when or if I would see her again.

Chapter 42

Daddy died the year following our meeting on the slope of the driveway. It was no small miracle our relationship was restored. Our past was healed. He had given everything he had in the best way he knew how. In acknowledging the Heavenly Father as the One whose ultimate sacrifice was sufficient—everything required to give me a life worth living—my true relationship with both enabled me to call them 'My Father.'

———— • ————

It had been only weeks earlier that the family had gathered. My brothers with their families, including "adopted" Ben Campbell—with his princess Deanna—all packed into the house. It was the same crew that came every Christmas, reminiscent of times when we'd sat at the dinner table, and hysteria and craziness abounded. Riotous laughter had filled every niche.

At this meal, however, no one retold the unbelievable story that never failed to be the favored joke on Dad: the one of my blind date—only date—with Tom Nutt. Dad had introduced him as Tom Balls, and as horrified as my mother was with every retelling, laughter always brought down the house. But that tale did not make its way into the table talk tonight. The evening was far too serious, discussing what needed to be done to take care of my father.

"Someone had better check on him," Mom said, passing the bowl of mashed potatoes, looking inquisitively off toward their bedroom.

Dementia had turned him into a person we knew part of the time. Sometimes he was someone we didn't know: the young Simon Hagan from his own past, making comments to us as if we were the people he had known in Albuquerque or Detroit. We somehow became participants with him in his youthful years.

Maxwell left the table and headed down the hallway toward the bedroom where earlier, Mom had tucked Dad in. When my brother returned, he told us what he'd found: Dad was kneeling beside the bed. For the moment, it was Daddy, lucid, his head bowed, talking to the Lord.

Maxwell checked his composure and glanced at his wife as he told us. Annie wasn't fooled by his smothered emotions and laid a reassuring hand on his wrist.

"He said he was praying about what we should do with him," Maxwell said. Without looking up again, he focused on the potatoes on his plate.

———— • ————

I had stayed beside my father that night, in the guest room, taking my turn to stop his late-night attempts to get up and wander. Sometimes having someone nearby soothed him. Other nights, it didn't. Tonight it wasn't working.

"Why don't we go for a walk, Daddy," I said, hoping to wear him down, and we walked toward the living room.

He gave me a glassy-eyed stare. "Tell me your name. I don't mess with strangers."

"It's Alexandra. You're my father. I'm your daughter."

"Yes, of course. And what is your name?"

"Here, Daddy, let's sit here," I said, pointing him to the Gainsborough chairs by the front window. "You sit right here, and I'll sit over there."

He comfortably settled himself. "Where did you get these things?"

"The chairs? Mom bought them, maybe forty-five years ago."

"I don't like them. Never did."

"Why don't you tell me about your family," I said, giving him full control.

"I'd like to go see my mother, Miss," he said. "Will you take me?"

"Would tomorrow be too late? It's past ten o'clock."

"It'll wait. I need to see the boys, though."

"You mean Jeff Lee, and Maxwell, and Hux?"

"My sons. Are they here?"

"Yes, Maxwell is. Jeff Lee will be back tomorrow. Hux probably will." I paused, watching as he started to rise. "What about your daughter, Dad?" I knew I was taking a risk.

Without needing a second to think, he answered: "Oh, she ran off with a truck driver. And you can call me Simon."

I had to laugh as I helped him out of the chair.

"What's funny?"

"Your story," I said. "It's funny."

"It has a happy ending," he said and turned to look at the Gainsborough chair. "This is a good chair. Where'd you get it?"

With no answer, I led him back to the guest bedroom. All night long, he scraped the wall by his bed with his fingertips, calling out as if he was trying to save his mother.

The next morning one of my brothers relieved me so I could sleep. The next night it was Maxwell's turn to keep Daddy at bay.

"He's trying to rescue his mother," I told Maxwell, "and you'll just have to go along with it—be part of it; otherwise you'll upset him."

"I'm afraid I can't stay up all night with him," Maxwell said with his attorney-infused voice. "I have a trial tomorrow."

I gave him a look. "You have one tonight, too."

———— • ————

Daddy had quickly worsened after many long nights, and when the end came, we were all there. Pneumonia took its toll. It was more than his frail body could overcome.

His personal belongings could have been sorted through, but Mom wanted to leave them intact. In the week that followed, she was comfortable with my brothers and me returning to our own homes.

Jack, the kids, and I headed back north. Jack's job awaited him; Kent and Ginger's school was in session. My college classes at Purdue had not let out for any reason, not even with a winter storm on the way.

We arrived home and unloaded, closely listening to the forecast of what was going to hit mid-northern Indiana sometime after midnight. I picked up the phone and called my neighbor.

"Hi, Emily. We're back, safe and sound, but the weather doesn't sound nice at all. Just in case, can I count on you tomorrow morning if the kids' school is closed?"

From the other end of the line came a perky affirmative response. Emily was all in.

"Okay, great, Emily. Thanks a million. I'd need to leave here by eight. Stay tuned, and we'll see what the weather brings. Good night."

Physically and mentally exhausted, I set the alarm for six and dropped into bed. Before I knew it, the next day was in full swing.

Chapter 43

The Indiana morning was heavy, a wet blur making it look like the inside of a slightly shaken snow globe. A sliver of sunshine caused the melting icicles to make their way down the creaking gutter beside my blue LeSabre, dripping onto the splash-block underneath. Snow had stopped falling sometime after midnight, and a steady wind had drifted it against the fence bordering the creek running behind our house.

The thin sheet of ice crackled under the weight of my boots as I plodded, carefully making my way across with my armload of books to my car. I pressed the thumb button, giving the door a quick jerk. The icy film broke with a wicked cackle, and after hopping inside, my car engine started with a slight delay; I turned on the defroster, then went back to the house.

The old wooden doors to the garage hung open, allowing just enough space to slip inside the small area. When it was built more than a century earlier, a carriage would have rolled inside. I hurried across the dirt floor and went inside the house to gather some incidentals while the car warmed up.

With no reason for them to get out of bed after the radio announcement of school closings, the kids were upstairs sleeping, but Purdue University was not going to close with less than a few tons of snow on the ground. Today promised to be just another day on campus with a normal day of classes.

Emily came through the back door of the kitchen. I heard her stomping snow from her boots; the door closed behind her. She was already talking, and I could detect from two rooms away her words were coming through smiling lips.

Ralph and Emily Hendricks lived across the meadow that bloomed in the summertime with an abundance of flowers. Only Emily could have cultivated and brought forth such an explosion of splendor.

"It's a mess out there, a real mess, but oh, so pretty, and the trees are so beautiful with the snow, and I truly love tromping it with my boots because it reminds me of St. Louis when I used to run and play as a small girl," she said as she came into view, huffing.

Her single run-on sentence had come to a halt only to allow her to take a big breath. Then her exuberance continued, greeting me like a fountain bubbling up and over the sides of some invisible source, bouncing down into happy splashes below: "I love it. Don't you?"

"Hi, Emily! Yes, it is beautiful when you don't have to drive in it. You are so sweet to do this. I really appreciate it, even more than you know. What would I do without you?"

"Oh, stop worrying. Go! Go. I've brought my book, and I'll have lots to do," she said, rubbing her hands back and forth against themselves. "Gloves certainly don't work well in this weather. They don't keep your fingers warm, and my mother knitted me the warmest mittens, and I simply loved pulling those on my—"

"Emily, I'm so sorry. I'd really better scoot. Do you mind? I'm very anxious about the road conditions, and I don't know how long it's going to take me," I explained. "The kids are still in bed. They rolled over to tell me good-bye and were gone again. Will you be okay?"

"Of course. Go, go. Be careful, dear. I hate driving on these roads. In fact, Ralph won't even let me, and I recently—"

Her words kept coming as I shouted a final good-bye and rushed out to the warming car. The ice on the windshield was reduced to a slushy mush my wipers swished away. I gave the back window a few quick strokes with a scraper and the passenger side a perfunctory swat so I could see out, then hastened to the other side of the car, piled in, and cautiously backed down the long driveway, the house fading in the distance.

I recalled the first afternoon Jack had driven me by our remarkable piece of history. Set away from the road against the backdrop of towering woodlands, the house had beckoned to me to come live in it; I was smitten. He knew the look on my face.

"Abraham Lincoln was President when this place was built! That's old," Jack had said. "Finished in 1834. Really old."

"'The name Piercestead,'" I read, feeding Jack the details from the realtor's brochure, "'was given by the pioneer who unearthed stones from his land to form the foundation for this two-story mansion built in the middle of his sixty acres.'" I had looked across the car at Jack to see if the full import of history was getting through. "Oh, Jack! Can we, can we?" I was squealing like a stuck pig.

Three generations of Pierces, a cholera epidemic, the Civil War, and close to a century would have seen this land before twenty acres of it, along with the home, sold to a new family. Now it and a mere three acres were ours.

Our decision to buy the relic had been instantaneous despite the arduous task required to restore it. Even that could not destroy the unearthly charm within its walls; it was nothing less than living inside a ghost story, and our first night spent there stood vividly in my memory as a restless one.

Noises from the deep woods awakened me. In the wee morning hours, I had wrestled with the here-and-now of the commitment we'd made, but with so many quaint offerings from each nook and cranny, every room became a mysterious treasure from the past.

I couldn't have guessed how, in the springtime to come, flowers—daffodils, jonquils, and narcissus nurtured by the hundreds—would line the roadway and fill the yard. I had gathered lavish armloads of buttery spectacles and held their faces that looked up at me, wanting to remind myself of old Mrs. Phillips's daffodils back in Murray, Kentucky when I had picked only a fraction of the abundance such as this from her yard to take to my first-grade teacher. It moved me to tears, knowing I had neither planted not watered these and yet they were mine.

The thought warmed me even now as I pulled off my gloves and braced for the trip to Purdue and the wintry harshness that lay ahead, heading off on the southern route. It would be, by far, the quickest way.

No one was on the winding, gravel road, and mine were their own lone tracks. If another vehicle had been close, the two of us could have barely passed. Thankfully, it was absolutely untraveled.

Jack had apparently taken the other way, headed northbound on Gleason, gone the back-county roads across to the main thoroughfare. I settled in for the drive to campus and tried to relax knuckles that were turning white on the steering wheel.

It was a picturesque wonderland on this January morning with virgin snow covering the road and everything else in sight across the Indiana farmlands. Unharvested cornstalks jutted up on both sides of the road. Ice concealed their husks, making them a sea of stalagmites as far as my vision could take me. Wind that lasted through the night had swirled mounds of driven snow against the underbrush and tree trunks. Nothing but the sound of rocks chortling under my tires broke the silence as I drove across the bleached, pristine blanket.

To my right, the barren fields contrasted strangely with the dense forest on my left, and straight ahead the familiar deep ruts were obscured. I swerved sharply, negotiating the hairpin curve to the east and abruptly back south again with a cluster of trees laying silhouettes against the deep snowdrifts to guide me. Frosted marshmallow-like icing coated the tops of their branches. On the underside, they were bare and black, mimicking tracery in a Gothic window, their lines extending outward in every direction.

Distracted by the beauty, I rounded the last sharp turn, not suspecting the wall of a purest white avalanche that had stacked itself on the road, swallowing it completely. The powdery force stood defiantly in my path, reaching straight up to the sky, a frozen barrier I could not surmount. For a split second, I weighed my chances of forcing my way through. Maybe I could step aggressively on the accelerator, I thought, and blast my way through; reasoning stopped me. I pictured my LeSabre stuck—a barrage of white sno-cone taking my life.

In the impenetrable silence, I prayed for the view in front of me to be a mirage, for the snow miraculously to disappear, but it remained: tall, cold, daunting. I turned on my wipers, making them beat as fast as they could. Slowly, carefully, I rolled toward the wall, creeping up on it, stalking it like a snowplow ready to pounce. Scaling it was impossible. Going through it was, too, and nothing positive was going to come of my being stuck somewhere in the middle.

I sat, looking at the frozen mound, conceding. With no way to turn the car around, I put it in reverse and inch by inch guided it backward, tentatively rolling along the tracks that had brought me here, acknowledging all the way the similarity to the frozen wall that had existed between me and my father, thankful that in time, it had melted.

Chapter 44

TWENTY-THREE YEARS LATER

Mom was sitting up at a bit of an angle, and her face turned slowly toward us as we walked into her hospital room. Hux reached her bedside first.

"How are you doing today, Mom? You're looking chipper," my brother said, bending over to kiss her forehead.

"Oh, fine, I guess. And, how are you? So nice of you to come all this way."

Her characteristic effervescence was mild but undeniable. It rose for the occasion. Hux and I and our spouses had made the trip to Knoxville to visit.

"And, Alexandra, how are you?" Her color was softer than usual, but she brightened to individually greet us."

"I brought you these flowers from my yard. They looked pretty when I picked them," I said, realizing I shouldn't have expected them to look fresh after a ride in a hot car. I was ashamed of how lacking in beauty the handful of limp stems was to express what I desired. "They look a little sickly now. I'll put them over here." I leaned over the bed to kiss her cheek, then went to the window ledge and began arranging the pitiful tulips in a paper cup.

"Thank you. They're quite lovely, honey," she said, looking at what I had intended, possessing still the wonderful ability to see things as she wanted them to be.

Jack moved to the bedside to greet her, and she began a fresh batch of questions.

"Did you drive everyone, Jack? How is your work? Not overdoing it, I hope," she inquired, then abruptly shifted from him to Hux's wife. "Laura, you're looking well in your pretty blue top. Matches your eyes." Mom gave her an affectionate gaze, and Laura stepped forward for a hug.

"Hey, Mother Hagan. It's good to see you," Laura said.

Mom looked comfortable, so the others of us settled ourselves in chairs and began filling the afternoon with recollections of our experiences together. Nurses flitted in and out, suspiciously lingering to catch the full import of some of the more comical tales.

"Remember that one supper when your baked chicken slid off the platter and onto the floor?" Hux had come up with yet another hilarious episode in the Hagan kitchen.

She couldn't escape being laughed at whenever anyone joked about her chicken specialty. Today—in that regard—it was no different. The levity was good. We all knew her time was limited.

"You picked it up and tried to pass it off as if nothing had gone wrong. A little parsley here, a little parsley there," I said, "and then it went straight to the table with no discussion—no confession either!"

The truth had come out, in the end, distributed amongst our friends and family. Given the slightest opportunity, shortcomings were told and retold. No bona fide Hagan would let one of the clan forget an embarrassment. And Gracie Hagan was the first to laugh at herself.

"Twenty seconds rule, right? You managed to make it look like it was supposed to," Hux said.

"Nobody—" and one of us just went ahead and said it: "—would eat your chicken floor-en- tine after that!"

And we all laughed as a way of keeping back tears. The positive spin Mom had placed on living had run its course. We all knew the music was slowing. Her doctor met us in the hallway outside her room.

"She's having difficulty breathing. That's the nature of congestive heart failure. She doesn't have long. Two days at best. After all, she's ninety-one. Better start saying your good-byes—however you want to handle that," he said with the matter-of-factness of a weather forecaster.

We returned to her room. A meal had been rolled in on a cart, and a tray of food was staring at up her. She ate a couple of bites and pushed it aside.

"You want me to rub your back, Mommy? I would be happy to," I said in a feeble attempt to offer some comfort, to be close to her, and connect to her.

She gave a weak affirmation, and Hux lowered the bed. We rolled her over. Maneuvering her took some effort. Her skin was loose and soft, and I could feel the frail bones in her back, sinking under the contours of my hands. I couldn't recall if I'd ever seen her bare back, and for a delicate moment, I sensed we both were conscious of the intimate tenderness passing between us.

"That's probably enough, honey," she said after one or two brief rubs. "Thank you. That was nice."

I helped return her to a reclining position. Our conversation had become quieter. The laughter was finished. A hush moved about like the flutter of angels' wings around us. The sun crossed over the top of the building and was setting on the distant horizon, causing a rosy glow in the room.

"We don't want to tire you, Mommy," Hux said finally. "We should be going."

Something was on her mind. I could tell.

"Y'all," she said, raising herself up on her elbow, sounding confident, strangely rehearsed, looking straight at us as though she had been called to address a Fortune 500 company. "I just want you to know I did not have a child out of wedlock."

Silence fell across the room. The quiet couldn't have been any quieter. No one said anything. Caught off guard—speechless—and trying to fathom what on earth she had said, Hux and I looked at each other, unsure if the jokes were continuing.

"I did not have a child out of wedlock," she said again with even more conviction. "I just want you to know that." And having spoken her revelation, she took a laborious, deep breath and added, "I just want everyone to believe in Christ, and to glorify Him, and to obey Him. Now go, and I love you."

Nothing was left to say that had not been said. Long hugs began.

"Go," she said again, lucid and with all the certitude that had made her triumphant, using the last shred of her energy to ensure we heard her story, firsthand.

———— • ————

Hundreds of tombstones dotted the landscape. With friends huddled close, my family settled into chairs near one with Simon Newton Hagan inscribed below its arch. A tent provided shade from the sun as the pastor spoke for those gathered to honor Gracie Maxwell Hagan expressing admiration for the woman whose life had touched theirs. Then we all stood as friends and loved ones filed past, giving hugs and kind words.

I dropped the flower I'd been holding and watched it fall on top of my mother's casket. I watched as it was being lowered, thinking of the promised destination prepared by the Heavenly Father for my mother at the end of her life's journey: "You have not come to something that can be touched. You have come to Mount Zion and to the city of the living God and to Jesus, receiving a kingdom that cannot be shaken," the Bible said in the twelfth chapter of Hebrews.

The void within me was filling with that truth as Jack and I and the kids made the return trip to her home. Silvery ribbons of light rimmed armloads of clouds that floated in soft blue skies, and redbud trees burst forth in Mom's favorite shade of intense pink. An abundance of mountain laurels bloomed everywhere. Her love for beauty, crowned by all of nature, lavishly repeated itself at every curve in the road as if an artist's brushstroke had painted it for such a time as this.

———— • ————

Many years had passed since I'd married and moved from this Knoxville home. It was odd to think of walking through one last time before its Hagan personality was forever dismantled.

"I'll start in the bedroom and empty the closet and chest of drawers," I said to Jeff Lee. "That's what daughters do. When are y'all heading home?"

"I've postponed seeing patients till next week, but Melissa and I," he said, referring to his wife, "will go back later tonight and come back in the morning to get a fresh start. I think we should have all the personal stuff out of the house by Friday when the realtor comes to take a look. By the way, any old coins you come across are mine."

"Yeah, right," I said as I pulled out bras and panties from the bottom drawer of Dad's old chest. "Oh, my gosh. Here's her diary. How about that!"

"Read it, and pass it on," Jeff Lee said. "I'm sure it will be something everyone wants to see. I'll be excavating in the garage. If I haven't been seen in an hour, send someone looking for me."

I paid little to no attention to my brother. The diary was already speaking to me—also a little bank book along with papers and cards—layers of them. I forced myself off bended knees and went looking for a box to put them in, knowing full well this stack of history would be better to read when I had the time and lots of it.

With box in hand, I piled it fully. The diary lay on top.

Chapter 45

In my bedroom, by the light coming from the table lamp beside my old bed, I sat against two pillows and began reading Mom's diary— the youthful account of Gracie Mae Maxwell during the time period following her mother's death.

The first noticeable entry was written on a torn page. Only a few undisturbed words remained. Mom had obviously torn other pages from the worn diary. Secrets, once hidden within, were now lost forever, and traces of a person named Marcus surfaced on some remaining tattered pages. Others had been ripped too close to the binding to see a remnant of her writing, but one had this:

Sister will surely let me stay with her when my next school term ends. I simply cannot stay here. How can I stay here?

I squirmed, feeling the anguish smoldering on a shred of evidence and not having ever heard of a guy named Marcus. No date was discernible until this:

AUGUST 31, 1923

I have to survive leaving my home and all that I've come to know on the farm. For my own sake and for Henry's. Together we can hold onto Hillbound, no matter what. If what Marcus says is true, then I am greater than any or all of my failures. If God is the—my— Potter, then He is able to mold and remold me as I submit to His wisdom and skill. If God, as the Master Artist, is able to take the dark thread of my life, my wounds, my scars, and the mess that's been made and blend them into a beautiful vessel, then I, a common earthenware jug, can contain the priceless treasure of His plan for my life.

Tears streamed down my cheeks, but I continued reading the pages, gently flipping them so they wouldn't disintegrate between my fingers, and it had to have been her tears, falling onto the open diary, leaving crinkly circles—a lot of them—on its pages. I had little doubt she had wept bitterly.

I kept going.

May 30, 1924

Were it not for the daffodils, I might never know spring has arrived. Surely Moe Lee is seeing the same moon this night, and God will shape his life as He is shaping mine.

"I do not consider that I have made it my own. But this one thing I do: forgetting what lies behind and straining forward to what lies ahead, I press on toward the goal for the prize of the upward call of God in Christ Jesus." Philippians 3:13–14

My term at Crescent is passed. The winter is gone. Hope abounds within me.

Unfortunately, Mom could not go home from the girls' school. That much I knew. I devoured the account of the years, ebbing away as she lived far from Hillbound where her youth came to an abrupt halt. Intermittently, she'd stayed at Aunt Millicent and Uncle Jim's place on South Main Street in Elkton. But that, I thought, was because of her stepmother, Miss Francine.

I read on.

May 31, 1924
A lie so big, so accomplished, so cunning, and nothing less than the material of murder mysteries I have read. A lie devised to keep me from my home, to send me to Marcus's for Christmas so that Miss Francine could carry out her scheme. A lie to keep me from going to my sisters or being near Henry or my home or my friends. A lie to indicate I've been away a year for the distinct purpose of hiding shame—having a baby—Marcus's baby! Absurd!

I couldn't read another word. I looked across to the very door where Mom had knocked on it, begging me to open on those horrific occasions when I thought my world would end. She had understood—more than I could have imagined.

Chapter 46

I wanted to return to see it again for myself. When I did, I found the old home in Murray, sitting humbly as an aging replica tucked back on the hillside. The neighborhood remained somewhat the way it had been in my childhood, recognizable at least. Whatever my father had relinquished so my mother could have the home she yearned for, as it turned out, had lost its luster. With all that had transpired over the years, if I'd been that house, I would have felt humiliated to see me coming.

Probably the sacrifice had been more than Daddy could afford, and probably it was all he'd had at the time. He did what he had to do, allowing Mommy to do what she was inspired to do. That had included loving and dressing the home on the Silk Stocking Street with the enthusiasm of a seven-year-old playing house.

The rock wall where I'd hunted for Easter eggs when I was not much bigger than a toddler struggled to hold back the terraced yard, bulging like an old man's belly. An enormous maple tree, a senseless projectile in the yard, flourished where once I rolled and tumbled with Laddie-dog. It looked out of place and unrelated to any landscape. The new facade was equally misplaced. Fluted balusters that had once flanked the brick porch were gone, as were the lacy evergreen trees that provided symmetry and balance.

I approached the front door and knocked, as reticent as Mom's soft knocks on my locked bedroom door that had gone unanswered in my growing-up, questioning years. It was then my daddy's voice came back, passing through the decades.

He could still have been inspecting the untrimmed tree, almost as if he were standing there. "Looks like bagworms. Darned things! Looks like bagworms on these trees, Gracie," he had said, his watchful eye upon their branches as my mother anxiously awaited the verdict.

She would have examined every possibility if it were in her power to do so, and the sooner the better. Neglect had to be attended before it was magnified, and she refused to sit on the sidelines. It went without saying her children shouldn't either—everyone on top of the heap, everything acting right, looking right, smelling right.

I knocked again, and the door opened before I was ready to relinquish the memories from fifty years past. A friendly person on the other side expectantly greeted me.

"You're Mrs. Ridley, of course," she said with a welcoming smile. "Please, do come inside. I'm Edna Brown. It must be strange to come back here."

"It really does feel odd. I've been looking forward to today for the last couple of weeks. Thank you for letting me come and bring my camera!"

I could not hold back my eagerness to get my hands on this morsel of my past. I would have preferred the woman who now owned my Kentucky childhood home to go away, and let me absorb it—let me listen to the sounds that resonated within these walls and hear the personalities that had shaped me and wrapped nurturing arms over me as I took my first steps. I wanted her to let me reach back and touch a place in my personal history, but she kept up with me everywhere I went, exuberantly telling me how this or that must have changed. Of course, it had changed!

She respectfully listened to the excerpts I painted from my assortment of mental pictures of how it had looked when I lived here.

She smiled, too, as I told her what had transpired on this very spot, beginning with the living room fireplace, how my dad had lectured my mother, emphasizing the hazards of a fire.

"Calmly my mother removed the wrought-iron screen," I told the current owner, "and said, 'Simon, just put another log on the fire, please.'"

"'You're going to burn the house down if you aren't careful,'" Daddy had replied. After the fire that burned my doctor's house to the ground, even I could sense his concerns for the dangers of fireplaces.

"'Well I don't care,'" came my mom's insistence. "'I want a fire.'"

She hadn't known I cared. The threat of its destruction was vividly imprinted on the reels of my six-year-old mind. I had to agree with my daddy and in my mind declared, "But Mommy, I don't like fires!"

Edna Brown chuckled, and the tour continued to the kitchen where Beulah had cleaned my small shoes in the sink. The spilled white polish was long gone, but I could almost see it on the countertop. When we reached the porch, the swing was there, and I could hear myself singing "Tell Me Why."

It was unrealistic to even think I'd find the cabbage-rose wallpaper in my old bedroom or be able to relive the cool sensation of iced limeade on my inflamed throat as my daddy lingered to hold the cup for me. The covering on the wall was gone, but across the room was the closet that led to my brothers' space upstairs. Its door was standing ajar, offering an invitation to peek inside.

"May I? My brothers used to sleep up there. It was off-limits to me. They were always traipsing in and out of my room to get up there," I said, but it was hardly worth explaining to the polite Edna Brown. She could not have fully understood the magnitude of my brothers' intrusion.

Cowboys, swinging lassos on untamed horses, still raced across the now-faded wallpaper in the tiny closet, lanyards remained strung around their necks, and leather chaps still guarded their legs. Turning the corner, I anticipated a staircase that would lead me to the attic.

Instead, I discovered rough two-by-fours nailed to a slanting wall. With enough headroom to ascend the crude little steps, I climbed to the topmost board and groped through the opening. It was like ducking into a Boy Scout tent.

The window where the wire-and-tin-can telephone system had once been rigged to Jeremy Foster's house next door was offering some daylight. I could see the wooden frame that had held a bed. Maxwell had carved his name on the side of its support board next to the floor. Never having been up here before today, I marveled at the lack of space—that it had sufficed as a room for the three of them. It was worth taking a picture, so I did and then climbed back down.

Grapevines no longer draped over arbors in the backyard or provided the lush backdrop for curious young minds to play doctor, but the charm that remained let me retrieve for myself a simple, lasting majesty.

"Here, I forgot, Ms. Brown. These are for you," I said, digging into my purse. "You might enjoy some photos of this place in the forties."

With a thank-you and good-bye, my car rolled away from the house and on down Elm Street past old Mrs. Phillips's house. It took only a split second to remember her intolerance. The vision of her running down the sidewalk in her ragged robe, arms waving high above her head, shouting for me to stop my calculated thievery of her precious daffodils flashed in my head. She would have been dead long ago, and no daffodils lined her walkway now. Even so, I nodded to establish that taking even one of them wouldn't cross my mind, and I thought about the wonder of it all: homely, jagged rocks had replaced buttery flower-faces, and weeds grew like little monuments to insensitivity.

Daddy had moved us away, to higher ground. The waters weren't rising; he just had nothing dry left to stand on. He did for us what a loving father does for his children: he adjusted without compromising and tried to hold on, keeping sight of what mattered most. For him it meant taking us to a new town where he could put his feet on something solid. For all of us, it meant leaving a part of ourselves behind.

———— • ————

Back through the streets I went, over the train tracks toward the place we'd called Shanty Town. Instinctively, it was familiar, its poverty imbued with the flavor of an existence on the fringe, its subsistence reduced and tottering. Decades had drastically changed the surrounding, but that didn't dampen my plans which were set on the slightest chance of finding Beulah's house. It would be worth the effort if—in my wildest dreams—she showed up to defy unlikeliness.

Ignoring my parched throat, I resisted the urge to drive through McDonald's for a Coke. Daylight was running out; the sun had begun to shrink in the sky, and I was not going to miss the prospect of finding her before leaving Murray. Instead, I pressed on, craning my neck, inspecting the decaying houses. There, huddled together, they clothed themselves in inexpressible sadness with sagging porches and splintering boards overdue for paint. Too long they'd stayed on these dilapidated streets.

It was impossible to be positive which little dwelling was Beulah's. My remembrance was sketchy and floated vaguely in and out—until my car turned onto Water Street. Then I knew it. My daddy had pulled up to this very place before, stopped while I sat in the car seat beside him.

In all the years since my family left Murray, Kentucky, not once had it occurred to me Beulah's tears were pointless as they streamed down her cheeks the day she boxed up the last of our dishes. She'd lifted it from the countertop to the floor, and my daddy told me to hop into the car if I wanted to go with him to take her home.

"You gonna be a big girl and helps yo' mamma unpack all dis stuff," she had said to me.

It could have gone either way, a question or a strong suggestion. My daddy came to the rescue.

"Want to go with me, Sweet Pea? I'm going to run Beulah home," he'd said again. "Let's go, if you want to."

Of course, I wanted to go. It was Beulah.

Without any discussion, she slid in the back seat of the Buick that day. Daddy and I got into the front, and silence fell with the same finality as the curtain on my puppet stage. Good-byes on the side of the street at her house felt strange. The uncharitable gap widened as we pulled away from the somber rows of underlit dwellings.

Moving day and miles would separate us completely by this time the next day, but I had not known that. Before we'd even crossed the hills between Murray and Gallatin, I had longed to be filled again with expressions that were hers alone and experience the head-rolled-back laughter that would expose her gleaming gold tooth. Her absence gouged my eight-year-old heart and left it to suffer.

Today, in returning to this place where I'd said good-bye to Beulah, I longed to have her see me as a grown woman. My childish stubbornness she had managed, but never would she have been able to understand how the tender connection she saw between me and my daddy was lost in the move to the next town. It wasn't the Kool-Aid I ate, or even the lie that I told, but rather the swiftly moving current of my own independence.

I didn't know if it was in recalling my stand-alone attitude or the sight of her house that shook me, or the old woman who sat on her porch, rocking and staring.

Emerging from my car, I wiped away tears and inched forward. Wild horses could not have dragged me from the scene.

The woman stopped, gingerly pressed her hands on her knees, letting me know she might get up, then reconsidered and started rocking again. I took another step. Sticks on the ground cracked under my feet.

"Excuse me, ma'am. Excuse me. Are you . . . are you Beulah Jones, ma'am?"

Several seconds of silence passed and lapsed into an eternity. Endless moments of time went by while the woman chomped her jaws, churning the way people do when they have no teeth. Engrossed in thought, she opened her mouth, and her answer rolled out like a lazy tune on a hot summer's night.

"She lived nex' do.' She died las' year."

The sound of her disappointing words slid down the back of my neck as slowly as honey down a tree trunk, sticking mercilessly to every crease in my sensibilities.

"Matthew—he's done gone now too," she continued, taking a slow, easy breath, then sighed and kept on rocking as if our brief conversation had, for no good reason, disrupted her Saturday routine.

From the look on her face, I had to have said something, but I didn't know what. I started walking across her yard, looking over the hedge to the shack on the other side. The place appeared to be empty. A window pane had shattered, and an old rusted ironing board and a wicker chair leaned against the side of the house. In the stale breeze, I could almost smell the distinctive aroma of starch and steam, rising from her hot ironing board as she pressed my little dresses; and I embraced Beulah's presence in the rustling sprigs of fragrant lavender still living in her yard.

On seeing me, she would surely have taken a minute or two; then pushed herself up from her chair to see if her eyes were playing tricks. Recognizing the eight-year-old child she had nurtured as her own, she would have flung widespread arms to greet me. "Lawsy, child! I jes knowed I'd see you again. I jes knowed it!"

———— • ————

I was glad I'd gone by myself on that trip to Murray, but my son and daughter had shown some interest in seeing where their grandparents grew up. Kent and Ginger agreed to come along to Todd County.

I led us along the same curvy corridor my daddy had taken my family, through the treelined backroads of rural Kentucky before we came to Elkton. Mile after mile, I traveled to the place where Daddy and Mom's life began, the trip reminding me of similar ones I'd endured as a child. I found myself wishing for that old man's store that had emerged as an oasis in the desert, and a cone of cream—Daddy's signature blessing—given along this trail of rustic bygones to soothe our parched throats as we journeyed.

"Let me get a cone of cream for each of these youngsters," he had said, overflowing with pride for his family. "And one for my wife. I'll take vanilla, please. Thank you, sir, and you keep the change."

By now it would be a ramshackle structure where Daddy had ordered ice cream for us, if anything at all still remained. I drove slowly, straining my eyes, appealing to my son and daughter to look for any remote possibilities, not knowing for certain where Daddy's car had rolled beneath the tin canopy next to the gas pump or where the six of us had piled out of it to stretch our legs.

Ginger noticed a gnarled piece of ribbed tin that lay in rampant weeds, so we stopped. On closer inspection, I could see the faint footprint of a crumbled concrete foundation embedded in overgrown grass, suggesting this could be the spot—but no deserted gas pump and no rusted sign with *Little Miss Sunbeam*.

I pulled the car back onto the country road, telling them about the days when my dad's Buick, packed with three people across the front seat, three people in the seat behind, ambled along at thirty miles an hour with my mother providing inventive means to keep the boys and me stimulated.

"Who can read the next sign?" she'd say. "Sound it out. What does SL sound like? Hissing, like a snake? Noooooo! What would that be? That would be SE. Wouldn't it?"

And the teacher in her kept up the harangue until someone from the backseat objected or otherwise disrupted the litany. It was usually Jeff Lee.

"Are we almost there? I'm tired of this," he'd gripe.

"Jeff Lee cut the cheese, Dad. It's bad back here," Hux would complain. "Let me out."

Daddy, pokerfaced, looking straight ahead, maintained his composure.

"Now, Jeff-Mac-Hux," Mom had said, inadvertently packaging their names. "I won't have bathroom talk. It's simply plebeian. So that's enough." And her running together my brothers' names would crack us up with laughter and mockery, causing her to refer to them differently on the next round. "You boys behave, or I'll have your father stop the car."

"Little did she know, y'all," I said, "soon afterward the car *did* have to be stopped on a fateful journey. It included a pitiful attempt to salvage Grandmother's Mouton coat after I'd gotten carsick and thrown up on it! Much later, after it hung in the closet for years, my cat pulled it down and delivered kittens on it. Grandmother tried to hide her dismay, or maybe by then, her hysteria over the coat was forever gone. The coat went into the trash."

Both of my grown children seemed to be enjoying my recollections of their grandmother.

Locating Hillbound, where Mom had lived as a child, presented an adventure Ginger and Kent, and I eagerly welcomed the rare moments. An old photo of the home had resurfaced, and Mom had shown it to me on occasions, but now it was missing. The house too was gone, its image altogether lost, much like her brother Henry who had grown up in its shadow and cowered in the face of its mistress.

Henry had passed away, leaving the Maxwell legacy to his sons, Richard and Sonny. The hundreds of acres of rich farmland, so prosperous during my mother's early years, were sold after Henry died. The house was torn down, and none of my family—as far as I knew— had ever returned to her old home place, until now.

Chapter 47

The short, rutted yard came to an abrupt halt next to the miniature house on the edge of the vast lands of Hillbound that once had been my grandfather Maxwell's.

Kent, Ginger, and I stepped from the car and started walking, unannounced, toward the door. It opened before we could get there, and a rough-looking guy struck a protective pose on its threshold. For a second, I pictured him in a coonskin cap, pulling out a rifle, taking aim at us, but my mind was fooling with me. It was Uncle Henry's boy, now grown into a man.

"Richard, it's Alexandra. Your favorite cousin," I said, trying for laughter as the three of us walked through his yard. It was grassless with uneven rocks defining the place where we should have parked. It ended under a tree. Richard's beat-up old truck was parked in the shade of it, and from the looks of everything, it was rare for him to have anyone coming to his house.

"Naw, I haven't forgotten you. You look like your mother. Come on in," he said with the hospitality of someone expecting overdue guests.

"This is Ginger, my daughter, and Kent, my son," I said, following him inside. "Can you believe that?"

"Yeah, I can. Kent's about as old as you were, last time I saw you. Ginger's pretty. Here—sit here," he added, indicating she should take the chair he had unmistakably occupied for some time.

"Kent, you sit there." Richard nodded toward the bed, then settled himself on the side of it and patted a place on the mattress for me to sit.

Immediately he jumped up. His small TV was on, and an announcer was covering a ball game. "Let me turn this thing off so we can talk. There's the poinsettia you sent me, Alexandra," he said, pointing to a pot on the window ledge where the flower from last Christmas sat. Its three parched red leaves were still clinging to a dried-up stem. "I water it every week."

A limp and aging blanket covered the doorway to the rest of the house. On the wall, a small framed picture of a young girl, holding a bouquet of pink and white roses, hung beside ragged curtains.

"Is this Madeleine, Richard," I asked, moving to take a closer look. I could feel him flinch at the mention of his deceased sister.

"No," he said, fending off my invasion, "but that's me when I was playing ball. I was going to the state championship, you know. I could play ball back then."

I did know. My mother spent years agonizing over Richard's life that began to fall apart about the time of Madeleine's death, and for as long as I could remember, she didn't stop. He'd been a senior in high school when Madeleine took her life.

"That's what I've heard. So why didn't you continue?" I coaxed him, hoping he would tell me his story.

"Oh, you know what they all say about me around here: I'm just poor white trash," he said, acknowledging the branding stamped on him. "That's what folks call me."

I regretted having opened the old wound that never went away. It sounded as if he had totally consented to the life-defining summary of some bullying folk.

He reached in under his bed.

Automatically, I guessed it: a weapon. What else? The stigma he wore deeply implanted in his soul, the stigma of his sister's suicide, and a drunk for a father, the lost family estate—this was his destiny. But no weapon appeared. With both hands, he lifted an oil painting from under the bed and set it upright against the bare mattress. He blew off the dust of a number of years and unveiled his treasure.

"I think this might be worth something. What do you think?"

Successfully, he had diverted our attention from himself, and we all breathed a little easier. Before I could give an opinion, still mulling over my answer, he filled in the gap.

"What brings you to these parts?"

My children and I looked at each other for reassurance our visit could be adequately justified, and Richard slipped across the very small room to empty an overstuffed ashtray. Next to it sat a picture of my mother.

"Oh, that's okay, Richard. I quit smoking thirty years ago. Doesn't bother me," I said, trying to put him at ease. "We just wanted to see Hillbound. The last time I was there was when Madelei—"

I stopped without finishing her name. I couldn't help recalling Richard's baby sister at her mother's breast some forty-odd years before.

"The house is gone, you know," Richard said. "This place here is all that's left. Me and the dad-gummed peacocks."

He seemed comfortably detached from the pain of his past and appeared to have accepted the loss of the stately manor and his birthright, living instead in the rundown place that had once belonged to the hired hand. Like an unwanted stepchild, it sat in submission on the far corner of the Maxwell's land.

"I know the house is gone," I said, then instantly realized I must have sounded snappish. "But where exactly was it? Or I mean, approximately where? My mother would be so tickled to think I'm intent on seeing her home, and where she grew up and having her grandchildren come see it. Maybe we could go to the small cemetery where the black folks are buried. You know, or do you? My mom taught them to read and write."

"Tombstones . . . all of 'em broken. And weeds are all over the place. But I'll clean it up. You can come back and see it. Check into this painting," he said. "Would you? I think it might be worth something."

I wondered as we stood to leave if it had come from his father, Henry. Perhaps it had hung over a fireplace in my mother's home. But I'd asked enough questions, and Richard was finished with the topic, holding the door open.

"You could be right," I said. "Let me do some research on it."

Peacocks came from the back of the house but kept their distance as we made our way toward the car. The shrill sound, reminiscent of a trapped animal, accompanied them.

"Those crazy peacocks have quite a history here, Richard. Mom used to talk about rushing them as a little girl."

Something inside me tried to think he might one day leave this place, move toward something more promising, and put behind him the disgrace that had held onto him. I didn't dare ask.

"I ain't gonna miss them if I ever leave," he said. "Darn things. Keep me awake all night. And there's other things been hanging 'round a long time. Wouldn't miss them neither."

It could easily be humiliation he's referring to, I thought. More than his share of it.

"You take after your mother. She's the only one that cared about me," he said. "I'd probably hold onto that picture of your mamma if I ever left here, and her letters. That's about it. I still have her letters," he said, running his sentences together, then pointed off in the distance, adding, "The old place was down over yonder if you wanna go."

"You were nice to send flowers to her funeral, Richard," I said as we hugged.

With our farewells said, Kent, Ginger, and I moved toward my car, then started down the roadway, waving as we went. Richard stationed himself against his truck and returned a wave.

Inside the car, the three of us looked at each other. Kent started the engine.

"Well . . . " I began as we left, "y'all didn't have much to say. What'd you think?"

"He's had a hard life," Kent said, driving toward what once was Hillbound. "What happened to him anyway?"

———— • ————

Kent was accurate in his evaluation of Richard. A lot about him didn't show up in the brief visit we had: a hard life, indeed, bequeathed to him by his father but having begun with his grandfather and mine.

"One man's folly in the form of a malignant seed of immorality," I said. "That's where it started. At least, it certainly seems the seed planted in Robert Maxwell by his compromise has yielded its fruit. Your great-grandfather's actions came with consequences, and they've been passed down from one generation to the next."

"Didn't Richard get in trouble of some kind," Ginger asked. "Grandmother wanted me to pray for him."

"Yes, but she didn't like to talk about it. It started with a threat Richard spoke in a fit of anger. He told a man he would kill anyone who called him poor white trash. The fallout from that landed him in prison," I said. "It was a legacy of defeat that held him there. It's almost as if he was branded like an ordinary cow as if a curse had been burned into his flesh. Sad, isn't it? All that's remaining of his inheritance is the little house he's living in. And that was the caretaker's house on the edge of Hillbound's estate."

"It looks rather woefully out across the fields to what might have been," Ginger said as we viewed the beautiful farmland.

We were quiet for a bit. I couldn't help thinking my mother must have recognized the good soil in which she'd been planted, and I was glad to absorb what I'd come back here to feel: the awakenings of my own heritage. We drove past the fields and navigated the hairpin turns in the road that led us there. I wanted to jump from the car and smell the tobacco on the land Robert Maxwell had owned, and touch the ground, and see the mature trees Mom would have seen as saplings in her yard.

A hay barn, nearly hidden, sat near the road under massive tree limbs, its usefulness long since exhausted. The land surrounding us merged with tobacco stalks in the distance as far as we could see, then melted into the horizon. A solitary railroad track traversed the landscape, most of it was lost from view by the abundance of crops.

"Your grandmother was watered, so to speak, by an inner strength provided by her Savior. She rose out of the weeds that tried to choke it."

"I've never seen more beautiful land," Ginger said, peering out the car window.

"Stop here," I said, and Kent pulled over. "Most of all, I just wanted to stand where the house she had loved stood. I think we're here," I said, soaking up the pastoral Kentucky sight. "And over there—the cemetery must be there. I'd give anything to go over, but we'd be trespassing. But look at the tracks, y'all. I remember from my mother's accounting that somewhere probably along this same track a bunch of boys dared one of their buddies, on a cold and frosty morning, to stick his tongue on the rail. Mom hadn't recalled his name but told me the boy lost part of his tongue because of it. She was so disgusted. 'Wasn't that the meanest thing? I think it was,' your grandmother said."

"She was a piece of work. I can just hear her telling that story," Kent said.

"We can probably head on back if y'all are ready to go, and I'll drive," I said.

I turned the car around to take us back the way we'd come. As we approached Richard's place, Ginger made the comment that Richard's truck was no longer parked under the tree. Only peacocks, screaming at the wind, were there as we drove past his little house, and it grew smaller and smaller until it disappeared in my rearview mirror. When we got to the bend in the road, I turned left.

Our last stop on the way out of town was Glenwood Cemetery. Someone had placed an Eden rose on Madeleine's grave.

———— • ————

It was late when we walked in the door. Jack had gone to bed. Three weary travelers were spent. "Hope y'all sleep well," I said, "and I really am glad you went with me. I might have backed down at Richard's house, seeing him—at first. You know what I mean. Anyway, it was a special day."

"Good night, Mom. It was a cool trip," Ginger said.

"Really cool," dittoed Kent.

I stumbled in the dark bedroom and bent down to move the box that jutted out from my closet. Stimulated by the events of the day, I decided to poke through one more layer of Mom's history. I took the box to the kitchen and ceremoniously placed it on Papa Jeff's old table, then sat down with a glass of milk and a handful of graham crackers. The creak from the lazy Susan made me smile, and I tried to think of why.

Day after tomorrow I had scheduled myself to return to Gallatin, Tennessee, to the church where the seed that Papa Jeff had planted in my heart took root.

I recalled him saying, "You'll learn the good that God has planned for you." I smiled again, knowing Papa Jeff's influence, too, had been passed down through generations. I gave the lazy Susan a little twist—an accolade for Papa Jeff—and the turn made the box of memorabilia topple.

"So much for one layer of history," I said to myself as I scooped up mounds of cards, photos, and a small book.

BANK of MURRAY was embossed across its front cover. I opened it and with growing interest, looking at the entry. *Alexandra Elizabeth Hagan* along with a two-dollar deposit was written in blue ink. Stamped in red was the date: *November 2, 1945.*

Decades had passed since Daddy had trekked to the bank to open that savings account for me. No more than a few pennies for interest were added to his investment, but the sincere desire of a father for his child was more evident than any bankroll. Circumstances got in the way, many of them, but I knew the desire of his heart.

I turned the empty pages, knowing it had taken forever for me to see him as the shepherd with his sheep, picking them up in his arms and carrying them, willingly sacrificing for them. I had not recognized who he was until I recognized God. At times I didn't care. I had stood helplessly at the wall of misconceptions, successfully built to persist between us as we went from broken to unfixable. Until I was ready to remove it, my father was on one side; I was on the other, laughing to hide my longing, running to keep ahead of my need for a Savior, kicking to show my independence. All along, it was forgiveness I couldn't put my hands on. I needed it but didn't know how to find it.

No one but The Heavenly Father could buy me from the pawnbroker. He alone could provide more than I could provide for myself: sufficient payment to buy me back and reunite me with my Maker.

Two dollars in the little bank book was more than I would ever need to affirm my earthly father had begun a good work in me, sacrificed all he had to cover me with his love.

My parents aspired to be the people God created them to be, to live on unseen resources, believing God would do in their lives all He promised He would do. By the model of their lives, they passed on the power of their faith. It kept me watching them from afar, and when I did slip from unbelief to belief, it was because of their influence, the foundation of it laid within the walls of the little church in Gallatin.

———— • ————

I wasn't sure if I would be able to see everything today, and I wasn't sure if I could go at all to my former house by the trailer park. So instead, I drove first to the church, parked, and crossed the street. Walking down the sidewalk, remembering how decades ago my long friendship with Suzette Mullins began right here on a bright Sunday morning. Reentering the church, I walked down the same aisle where a tall, genteel man and a voguish black-headed woman—with marshmallows in her purse—marched their four children to a place squarely in front of Pastor Owen's lectern and sat them down with a few words of warning.

No mistaking the Hagan family—new in town—sitting down front.

The organ looked the same as it had when Mom and Dad brought me here as a youngster, expecting me to listen respectfully while voices bellowed hymns including words such as "bringing in the sheaves."

Today though, sunshine rippled the colors of stained glass across the aisle to the torturous wooden pew where we customarily sat as a family. No living human was made to endure them, decidedly not my three brothers. They could not, and would not, sit still under any circumstance.

"Mommy, make Jeff Lee stop . . ." Quickly I had tried tattling so I could say it all before her firm finger darted to the front of her pursed lips. I hoped to speak my mind before her blue eyes could look at me from the side of her head, letting me know one of them might pop out and bounce in my lap if I continued to speak.

In the glass windowpanes, the robed man was there, unchanged by decades passed. He leaned on His staff with its crook at the top; and standing in the midst of His flock, and closely holding one rescued sheep close against His breast, His eyes shone with the same expression that had long ago captured my curiosity as an eight-year-old.

I started back up the aisle and felt the pierce of His relentless gaze follow me, grateful I'd never been able to free myself from it. "I know who you are," I said aloud, in case He might be listening.

THE END

About the Author

Annette Valentine's Southern roots account for her purposeful, historical fiction writing and the imaginative works found in her two preceding books of the *My Father* trilogy. Both novels, *Eastbound From Flagstaff* and *Down to the Potter's House*, are acclaimed as eloquent sagas masterfully portraying the resilience of the human spirit.

Author photo by Erin McCaffrey

Annette holds a degree from Purdue University and owned an interior design business that showcased her award-winning career as a professional designer. She and her husband happily reside near Nashville, Tennessee, in historic Franklin.

To learn more about the author and her work, visit www.annetteHvalentine.com

Printed in the USA
CPSIA information can be obtained
at www.ICGtesting.com
JSHW022210140824
68134JS00018B/963